BRAM STOKER

DRACULA

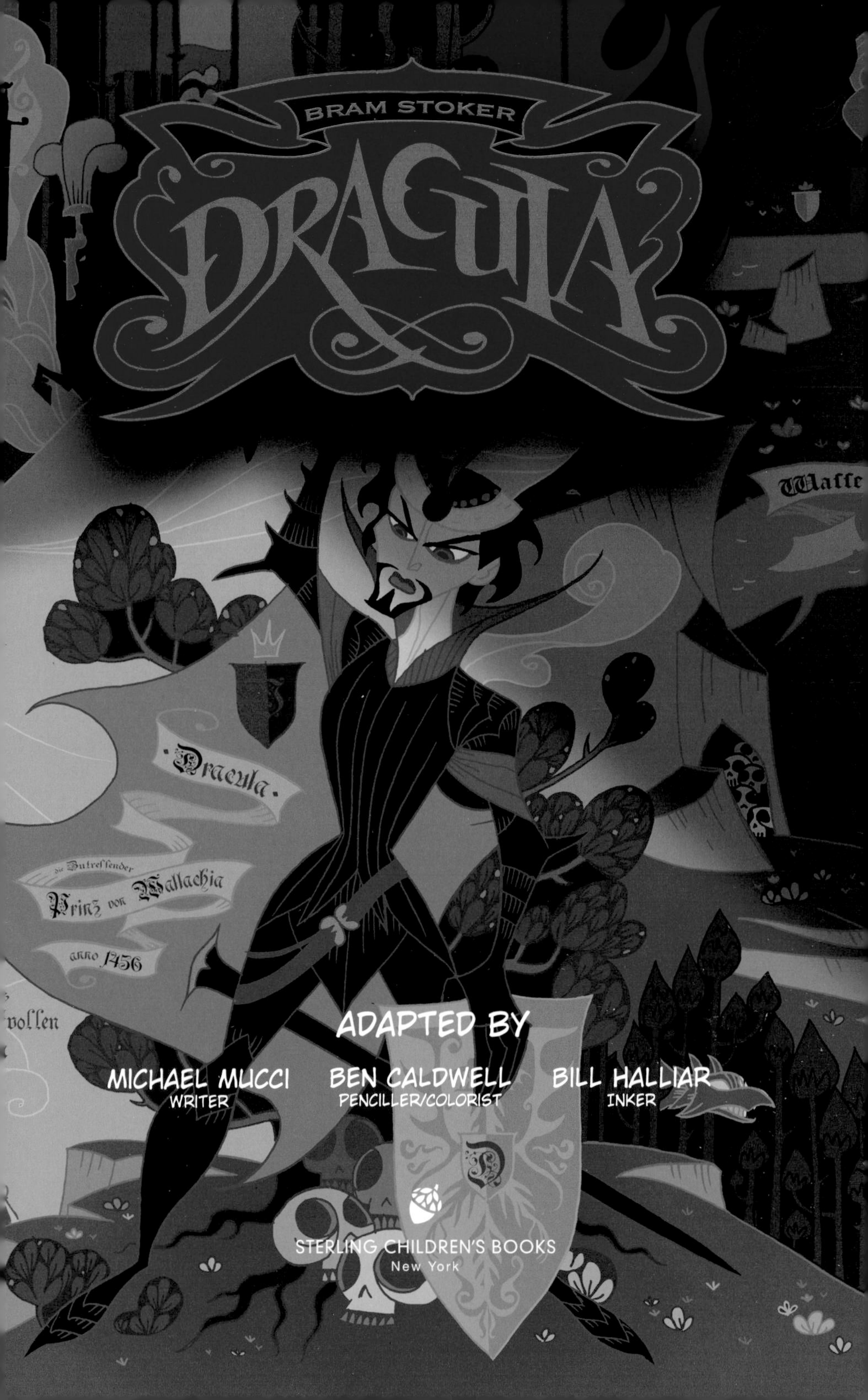

Waffe
Dracula
Prinz von Wallachia
anno 1456
vollen

ADAPTED BY

MICHAEL MUCCI
WRITER

BEN CALDWELL
PENCILLER/COLORIST

BILL HALLIAR
INKER

STERLING CHILDREN'S BOOKS
New York

FOR MY FOLKS,
WHO ALWAYS EMBRACED
THE IDEA OF MONSTERS
IN THE CLOSETS AND
TENTACLES UNDER
THE BEDS. I WILL BE
FOREVER GRATEFUL.
- M. M.

FOR DAVID MOORE, WHO
TAUGHT ME TO LOVE
HISTORY.
- B. C.

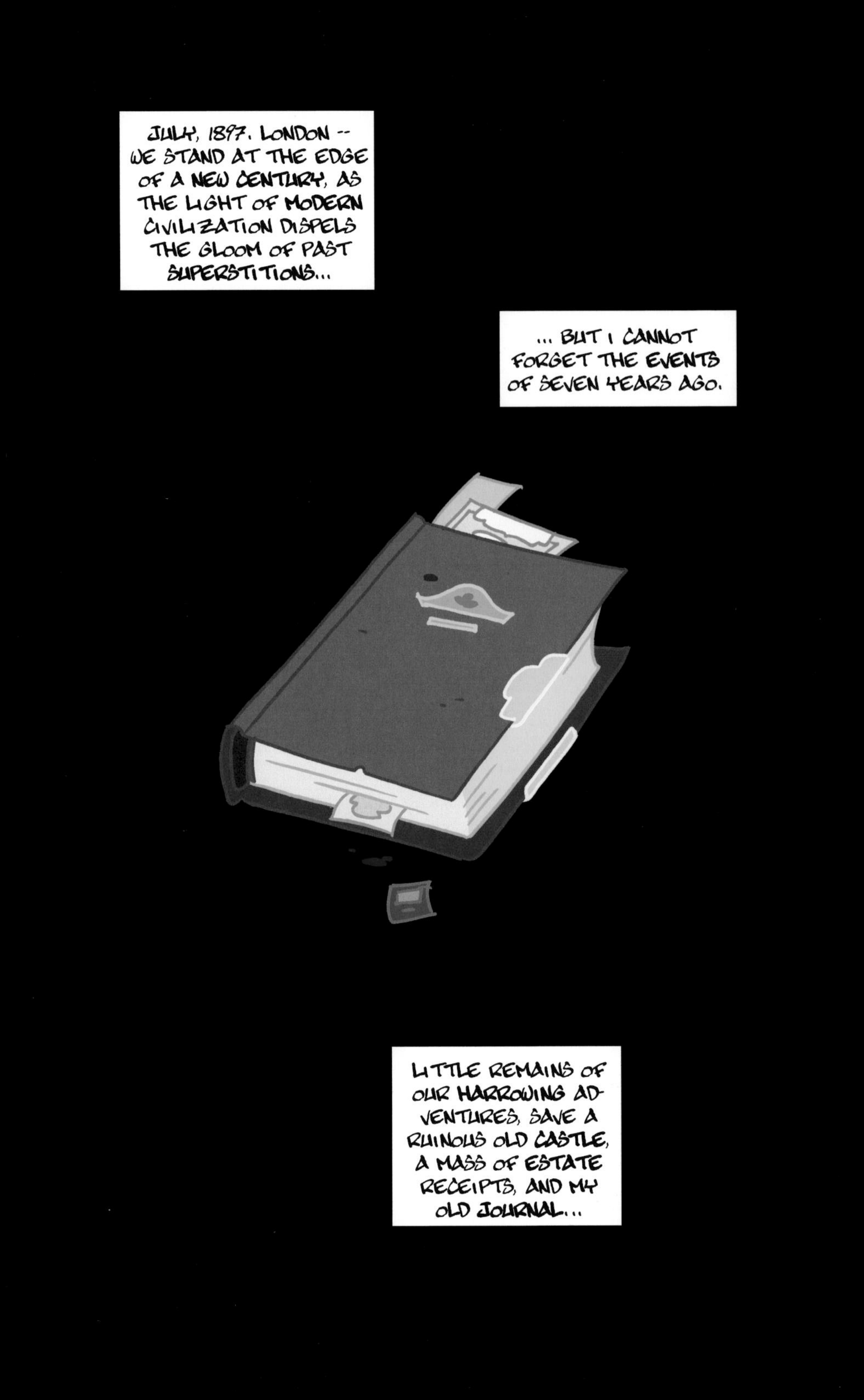
JULY, 1897. LONDON -- WE STAND AT THE EDGE OF A NEW CENTURY, AS THE LIGHT OF MODERN CIVILIZATION DISPELS THE GLOOM OF PAST SUPERSTITIONS...
... BUT I CANNOT FORGET THE EVENTS OF SEVEN YEARS AGO.
LITTLE REMAINS OF OUR HARROWING AD-VENTURES, SAVE A RUINOUS OLD CASTLE, A MASS OF ESTATE RECEIPTS, AND MY OLD JOURNAL...

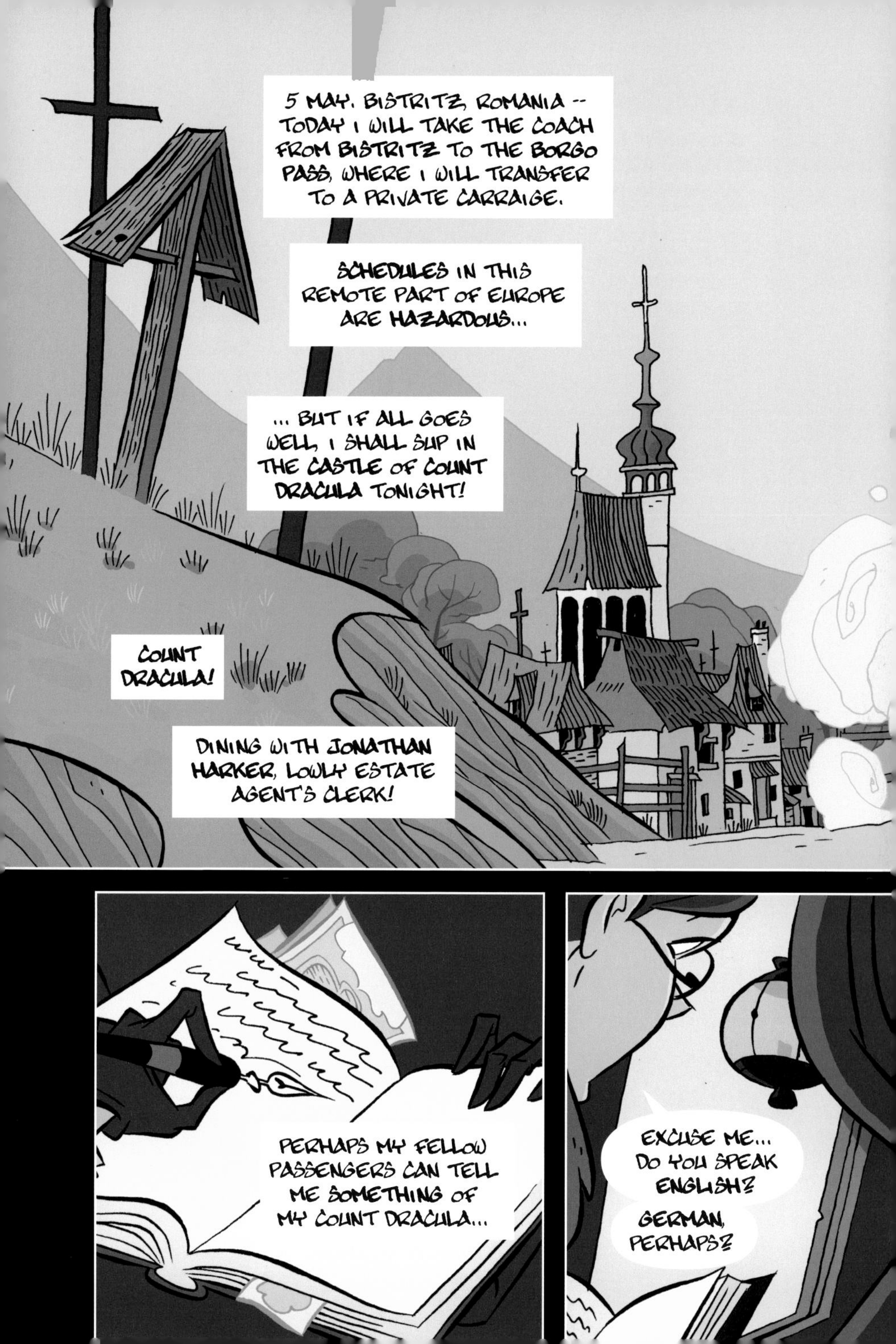
5 MAY. BISTRITZ, ROMANIA -- TODAY I WILL TAKE THE COACH FROM BISTRITZ TO THE BORGO PASS, WHERE I WILL TRANSFER TO A PRIVATE CARRAIGE.
SCHEDULES IN THIS REMOTE PART OF EUROPE ARE HAZARDOUS...
... BUT IF ALL GOES WELL, I SHALL SUP IN THE CASTLE OF COUNT DRACULA TONIGHT!
COUNT DRACULA!
DINING WITH JONATHAN HARKER, LOWLY ESTATE AGENT'S CLERK!
PERHAPS MY FELLOW PASSENGERS CAN TELL ME SOMETHING OF MY COUNT DRACULA...
EXCUSE ME... DO YOU SPEAK ENGLISH?
GERMAN, PERHAPS?

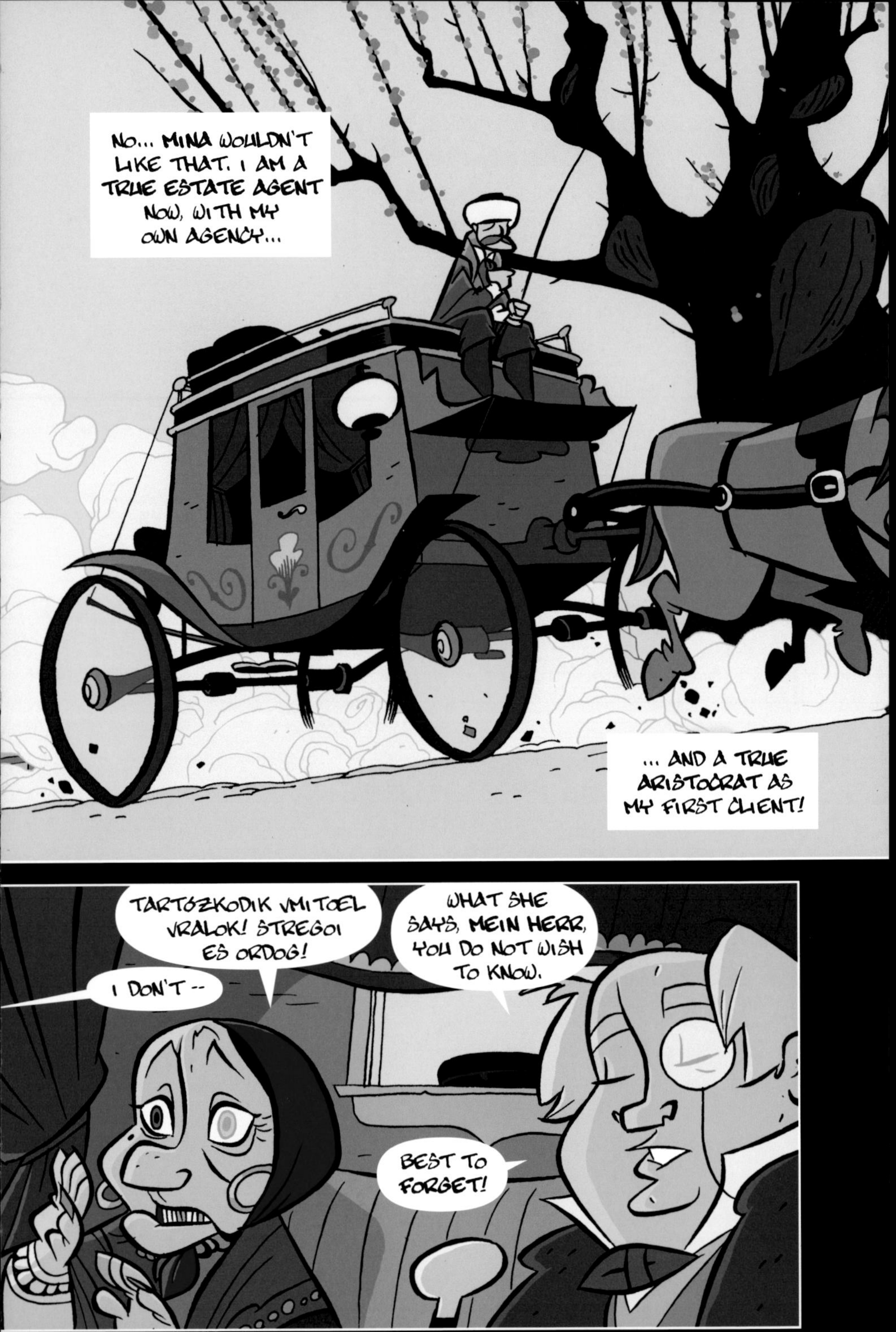
NO... MINA WOULDN'T LIKE THAT. I AM A TRUE ESTATE AGENT NOW, WITH MY OWN AGENCY...
... AND A TRUE ARISTOCRAT AS MY FIRST CLIENT!
I DON'T --
TARTOZKODIK VMI TOEL VRALOK! STREGOI ES ORDOG!
WHAT SHE SAYS, MEIN HERR, YOU DO NOT WISH TO KNOW.
BEST TO FORGET!

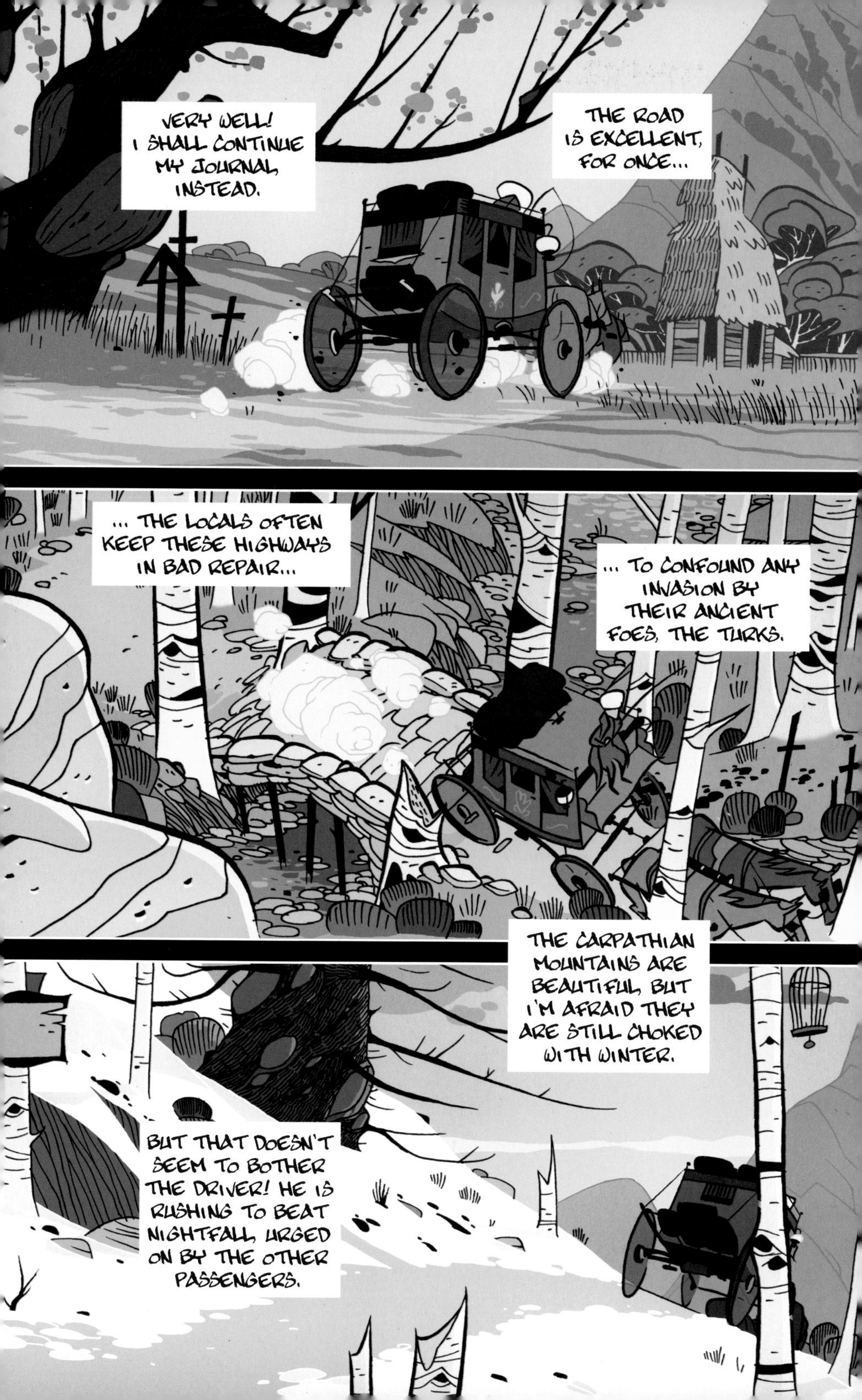
VERY WELL! I SHALL CONTINUE MY JOURNAL INSTEAD.
THE ROAD IS EXCELLENT, FOR ONCE...
... THE LOCALS OFTEN KEEP THESE HIGHWAYS IN BAD REPAIR...
... TO CONFOUND ANY INVASION BY THEIR ANCIENT FOES, THE TURKS.
THE CARPATHIAN MOUNTAINS ARE BEAUTIFUL, BUT I'M AFRAID THEY ARE STILL CHOKED WITH WINTER.
BUT THAT DOESN'T SEEM TO BOTHER THE DRIVER! HE IS RUSHING TO BEAT NIGHTFALL, URGED ON BY THE OTHER PASSENGERS.

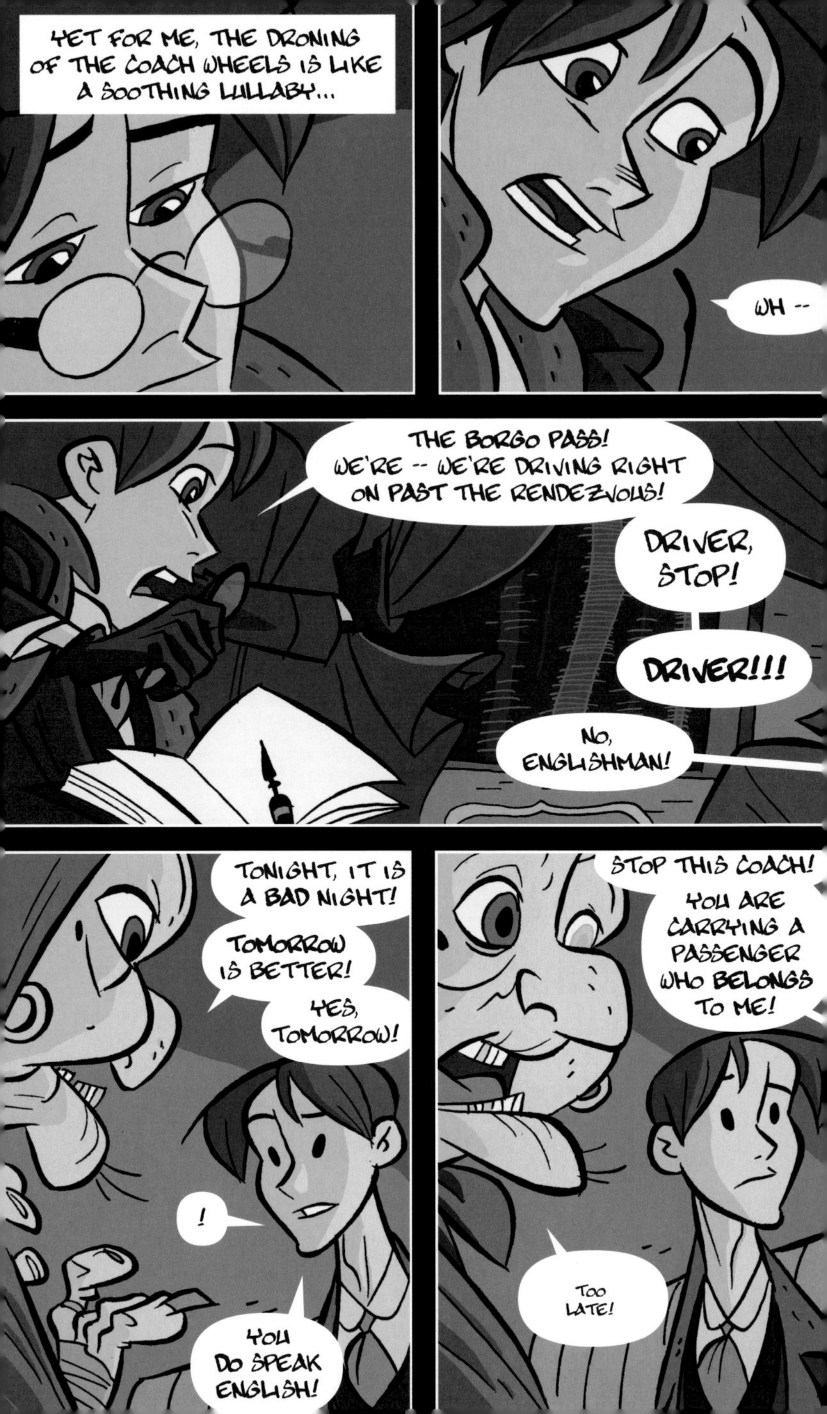
YET FOR ME, THE DRONING OF THE COACH WHEELS IS LIKE A SOOTHING LULLABY...
WH --
THE BORGO PASS! WE'RE -- WE'RE DRIVING RIGHT ON PAST THE RENDEZVOUS!
DRIVER, STOP!
DRIVER!!!
NO, ENGLISHMAN!
TONIGHT, IT IS A BAD NIGHT!
TOMORROW IS BETTER!
YES, TOMORROW!
!
YOU DO SPEAK ENGLISH!
STOP THIS COACH!
YOU ARE CARRYING A PASSENGER WHO BELONGS TO ME!
TOO LATE!

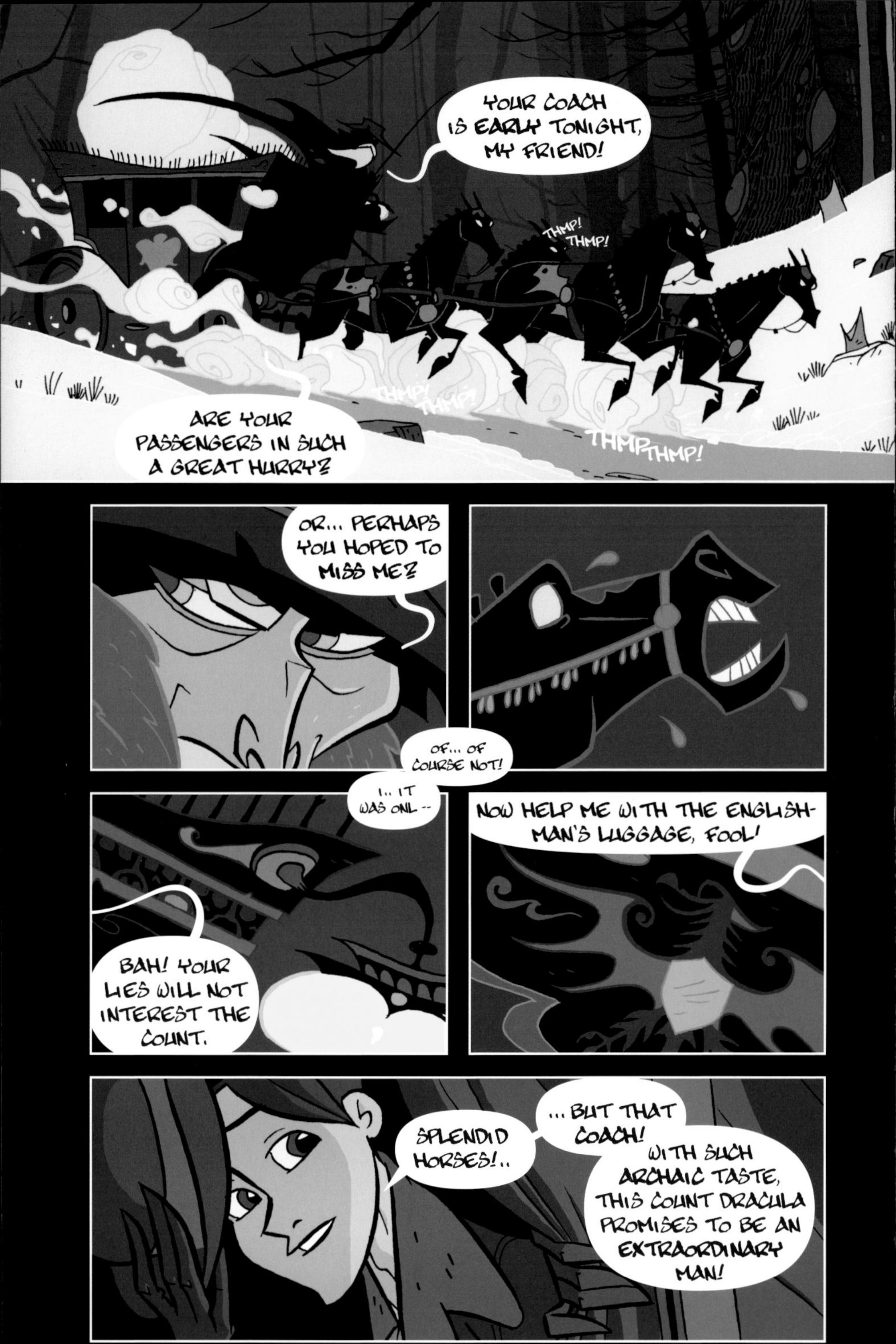
YOUR COACH IS EARLY TONIGHT, MY FRIEND!
THMP! THMP!
ARE YOUR PASSENGERS IN SUCH A GREAT HURRY?
THMP! THMP!
THMP THMP!
OR... PERHAPS YOU HOPED TO MISS ME?
OF... OF COURSE NOT!
I... IT WAS ONL --
BAH! YOUR LIES WILL NOT INTEREST THE COUNT.
NOW HELP ME WITH THE ENGLISH-MAN'S LUGGAGE, FOOL!
SPLENDID HORSES!..
... BUT THAT COACH!
WITH SUCH ARCHAIC TASTE, THIS COUNT DRACULA PROMISES TO BE AN EXTRAORDINARY MAN!

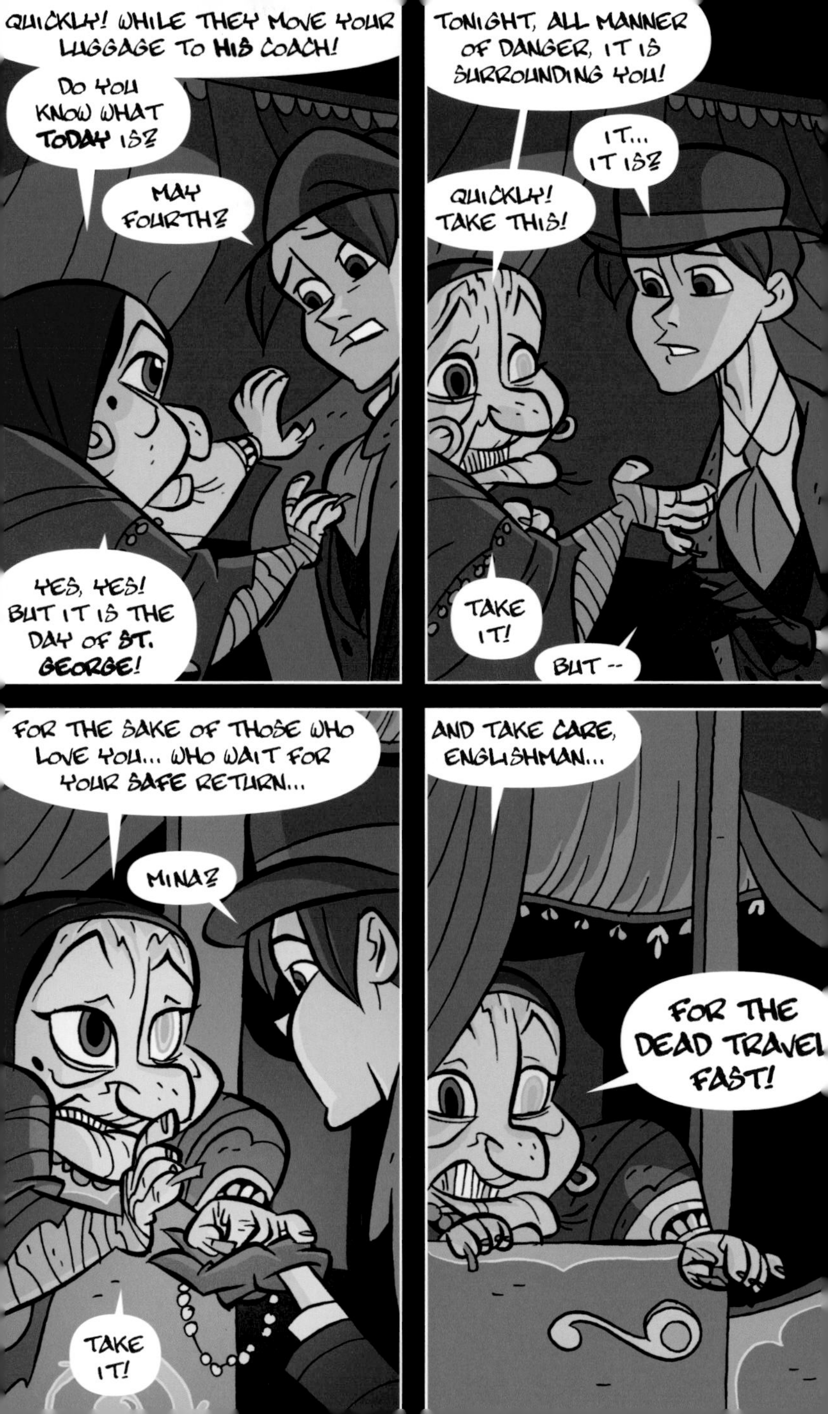
QUICKLY! WHILE THEY MOVE YOUR LUGGAGE TO HIS COACH!
DO YOU KNOW WHAT TODAY IS?
MAY FOURTH?
YES, YES! BUT IT IS THE DAY OF ST. GEORGE!
TONIGHT, ALL MANNER OF DANGER, IT IS SURROUNDING YOU!
IT... IT IS?
QUICKLY! TAKE THIS!
TAKE IT!
BUT --
FOR THE SAKE OF THOSE WHO LOVE YOU... WHO WAIT FOR YOUR SAFE RETURN...
MINA?
TAKE IT!
AND TAKE CARE, ENGLISHMAN...
FOR THE DEAD TRAVEL FAST!

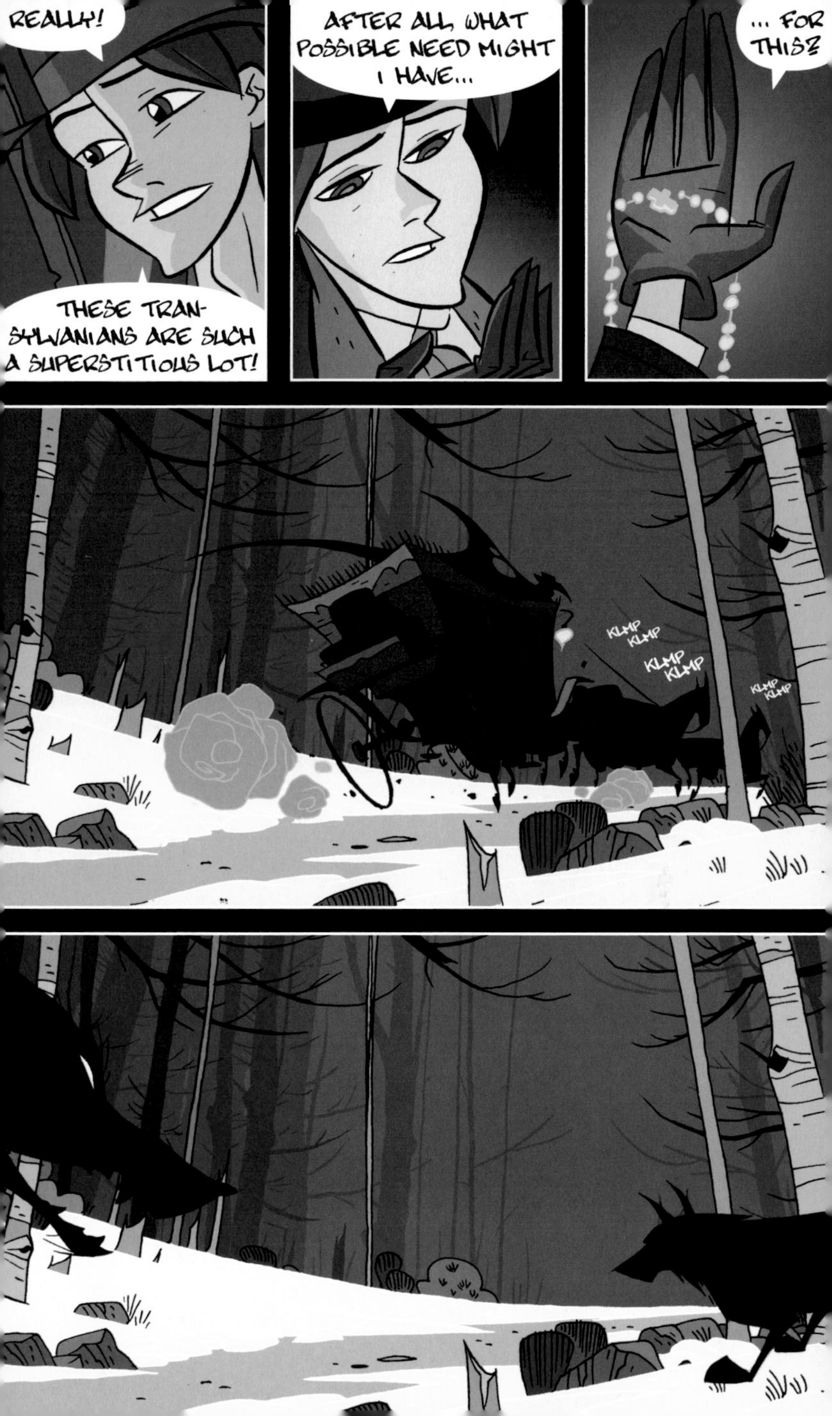
REALLY!
THESE TRAN-SYLVANIANS ARE SUCH A SUPERSTITIOUS LOT!
AFTER ALL, WHAT POSSIBLE NEED MIGHT I HAVE...
... FOR THIS?
KLMP KLMP
KLMP KLMP
KLMP KLMP

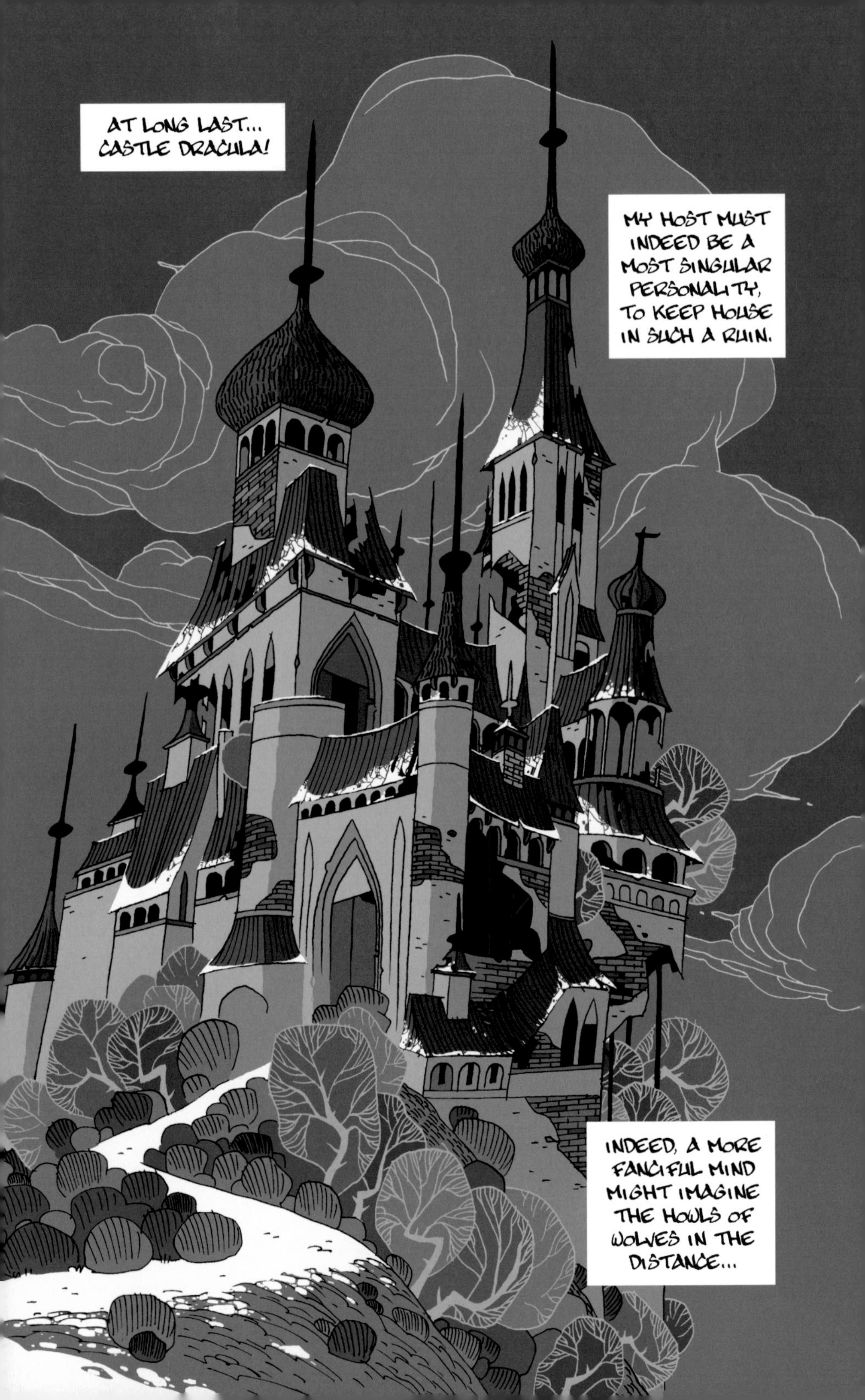
AT LONG LAST...
CASTLE DRACULA!
MY HOST MUST INDEED BE A MOST SINGULAR PERSONALITY, TO KEEP HOUSE IN SUCH A RUIN.
INDEED, A MORE FANCIFUL MIND MIGHT IMAGINE THE HOWLS OF WOLVES IN THE DISTANCE...

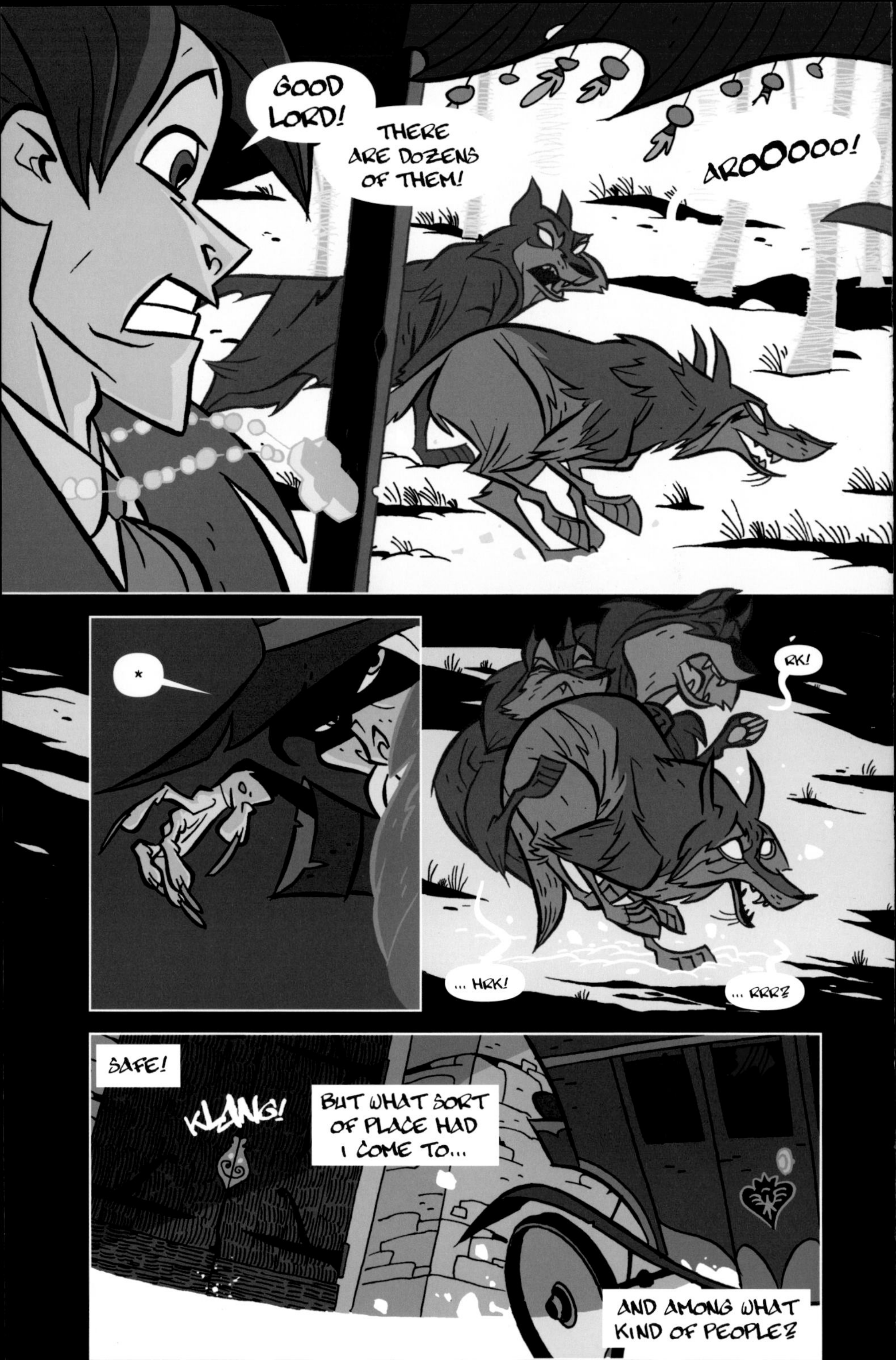
GOOD LORD!
THERE ARE DOZENS OF THEM!
AROOOOOO!
*
RK!
... HRK!
... RRR?
SAFE!
KLANG!
BUT WHAT SORT OF PLACE HAD I COME TO...
AND AMONG WHAT KIND OF PEOPLE?

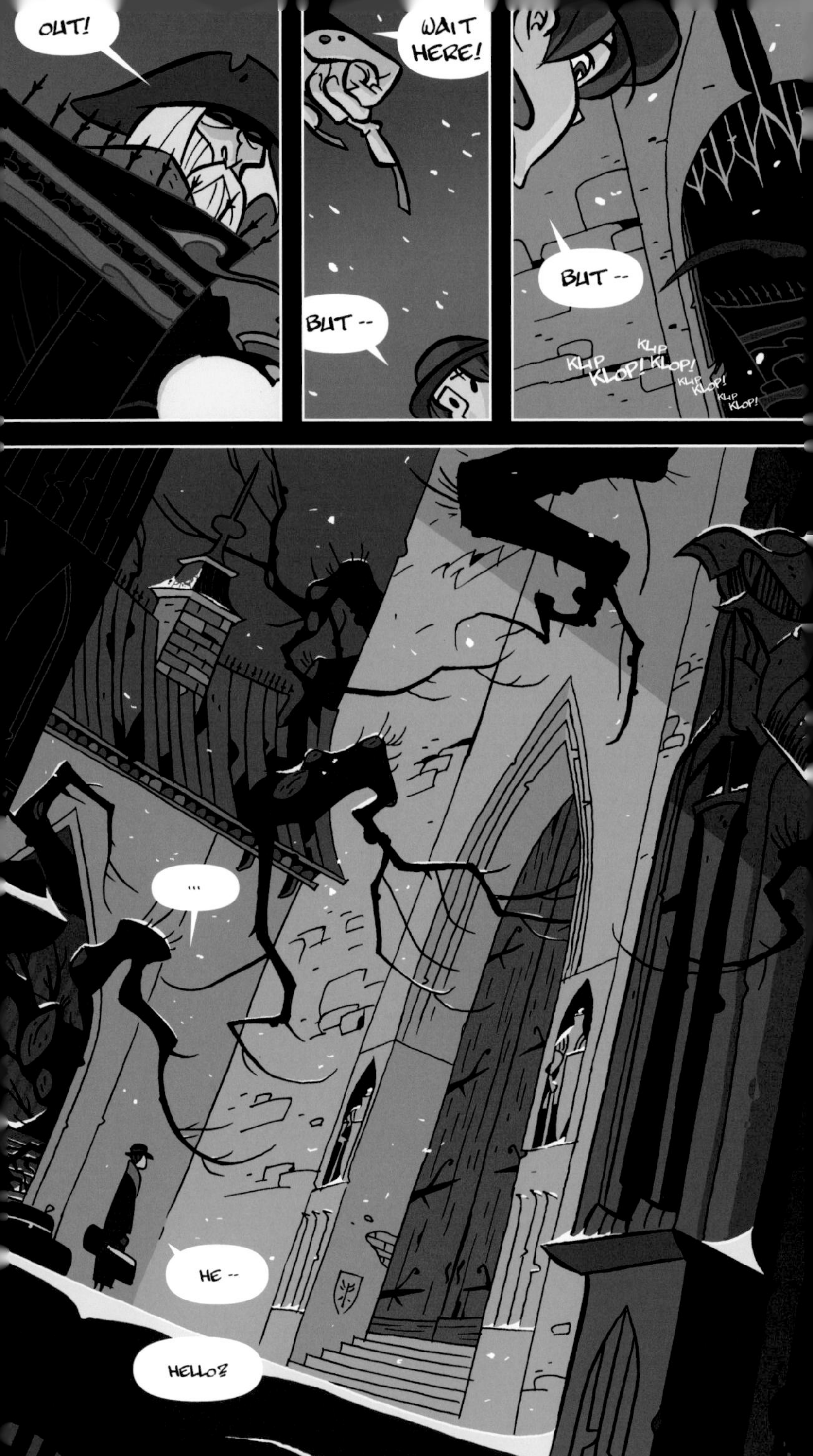
OUT!
WAIT HERE!
BUT --
BUT --
KLIP KLOP!
KLIP KLOP!
KLIP KLOP!
KLIP KLOP!
...
HE --
HELLO?

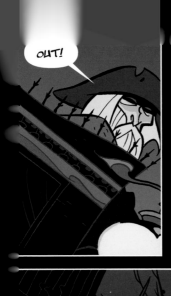

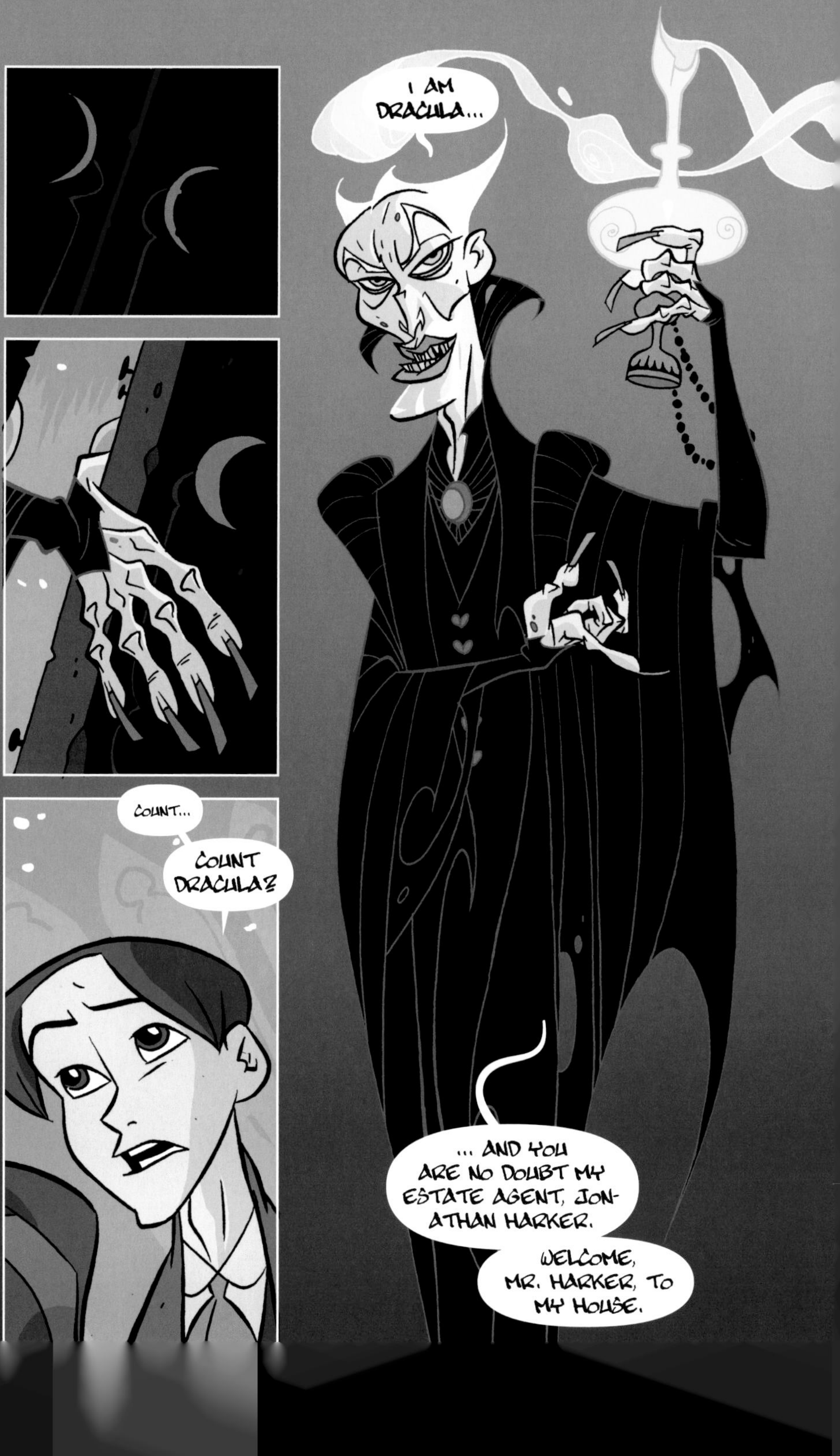
I AM DRACULA...
COUNT...
COUNT DRACULA?
... AND YOU ARE NO DOUBT MY ESTATE AGENT, JON-ATHAN HARKER.
WELCOME, MR. HARKER, TO MY HOUSE.

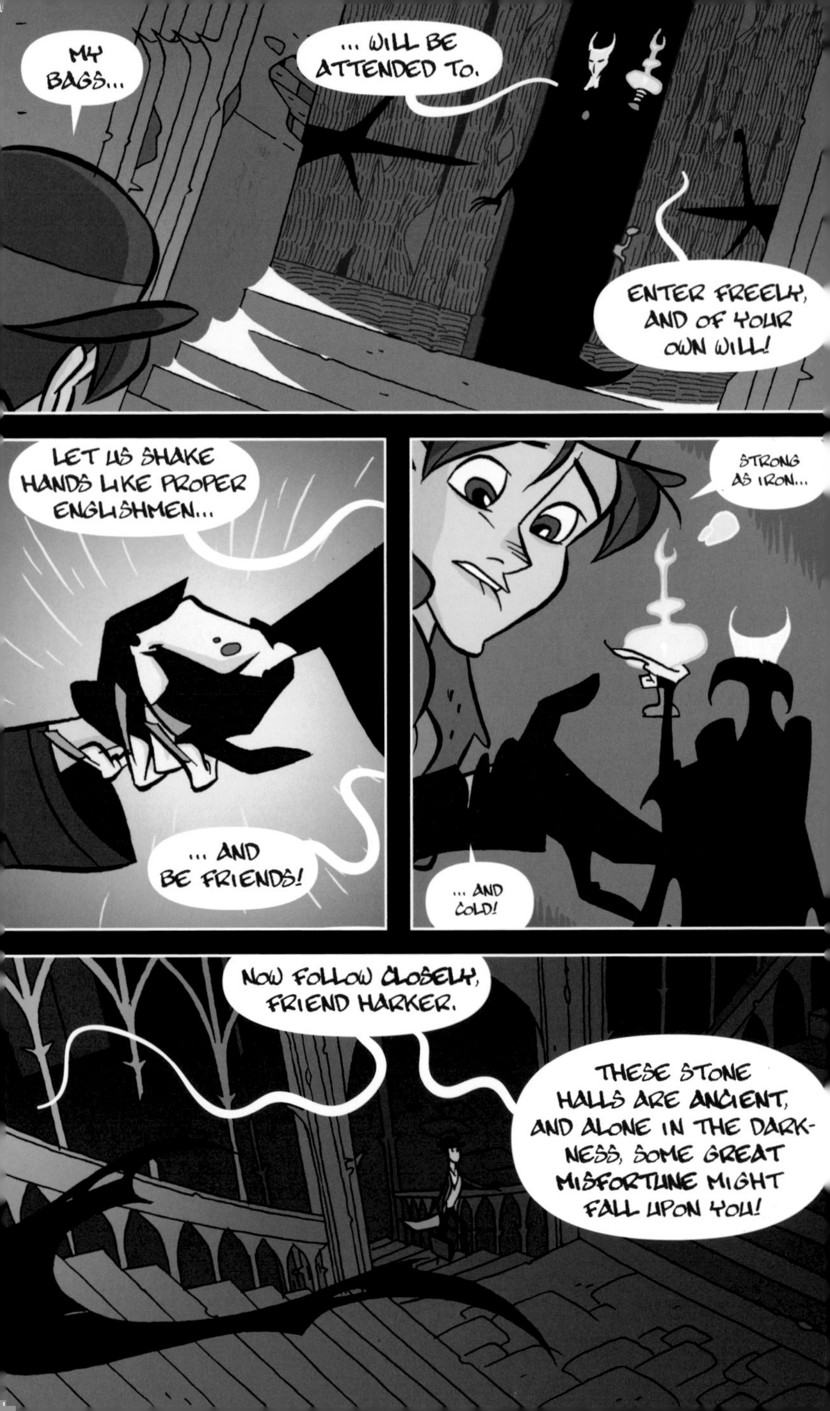
MY BAGS...
... WILL BE ATTENDED TO.
ENTER FREELY, AND OF YOUR OWN WILL!
LET US SHAKE HANDS LIKE PROPER ENGLISHMEN...
... AND BE FRIENDS!
STRONG AS IRON...
... AND COLD!
NOW FOLLOW CLOSELY, FRIEND HARKER.
THESE STONE HALLS ARE ANCIENT, AND ALONE IN THE DARK- NESS, SOME GREAT MISFORTUNE MIGHT FALL UPON YOU!

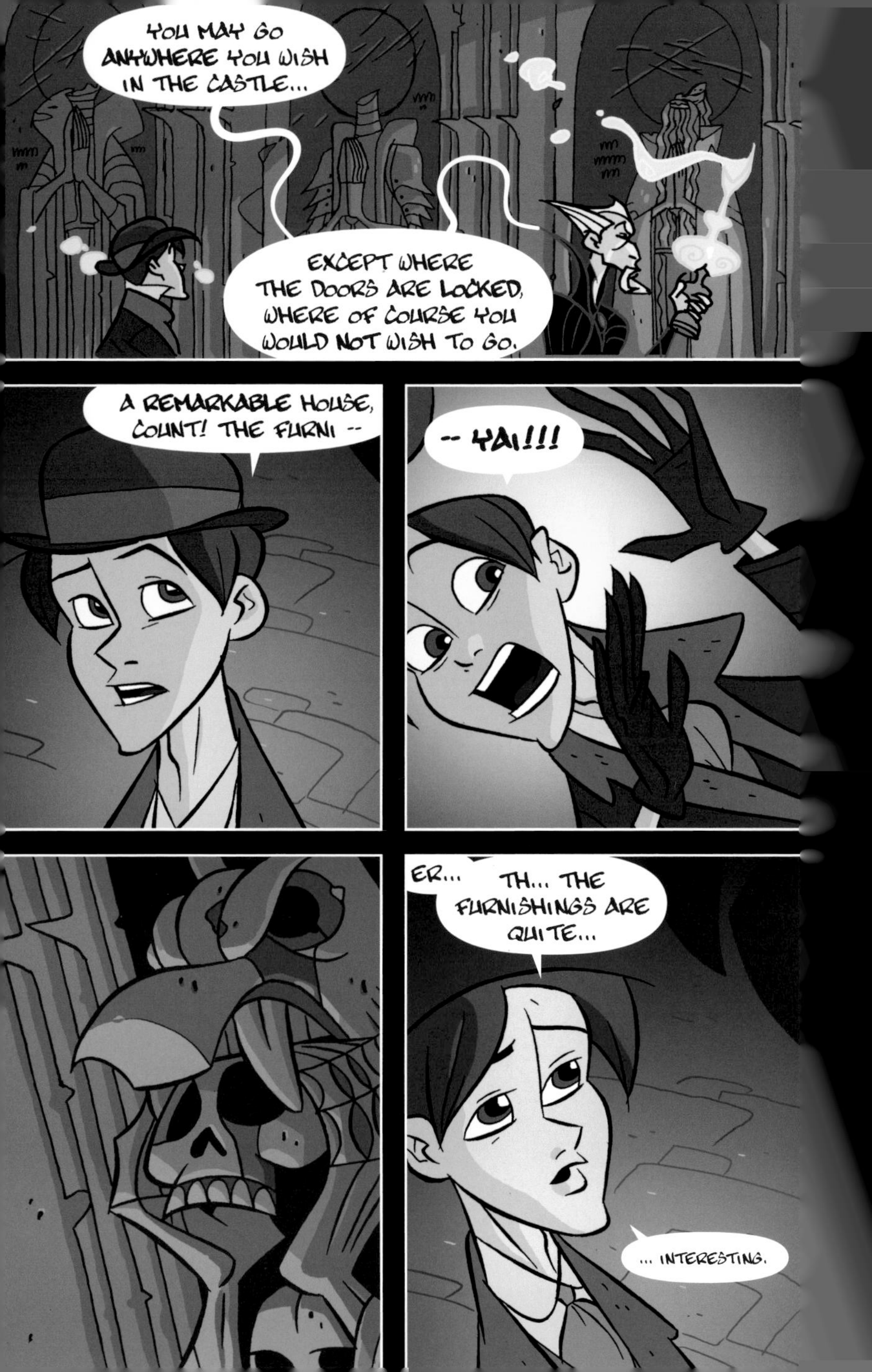
YOU MAY GO ANYWHERE YOU WISH IN THE CASTLE...
EXCEPT WHERE THE DOORS ARE LOCKED, WHERE OF COURSE YOU WOULD NOT WISH TO GO.
A REMARKABLE HOUSE, COUNT! THE FURNI --
-- YAI!!!
ER...
TH... THE FURNISHINGS ARE QUITE...
... INTERESTING.

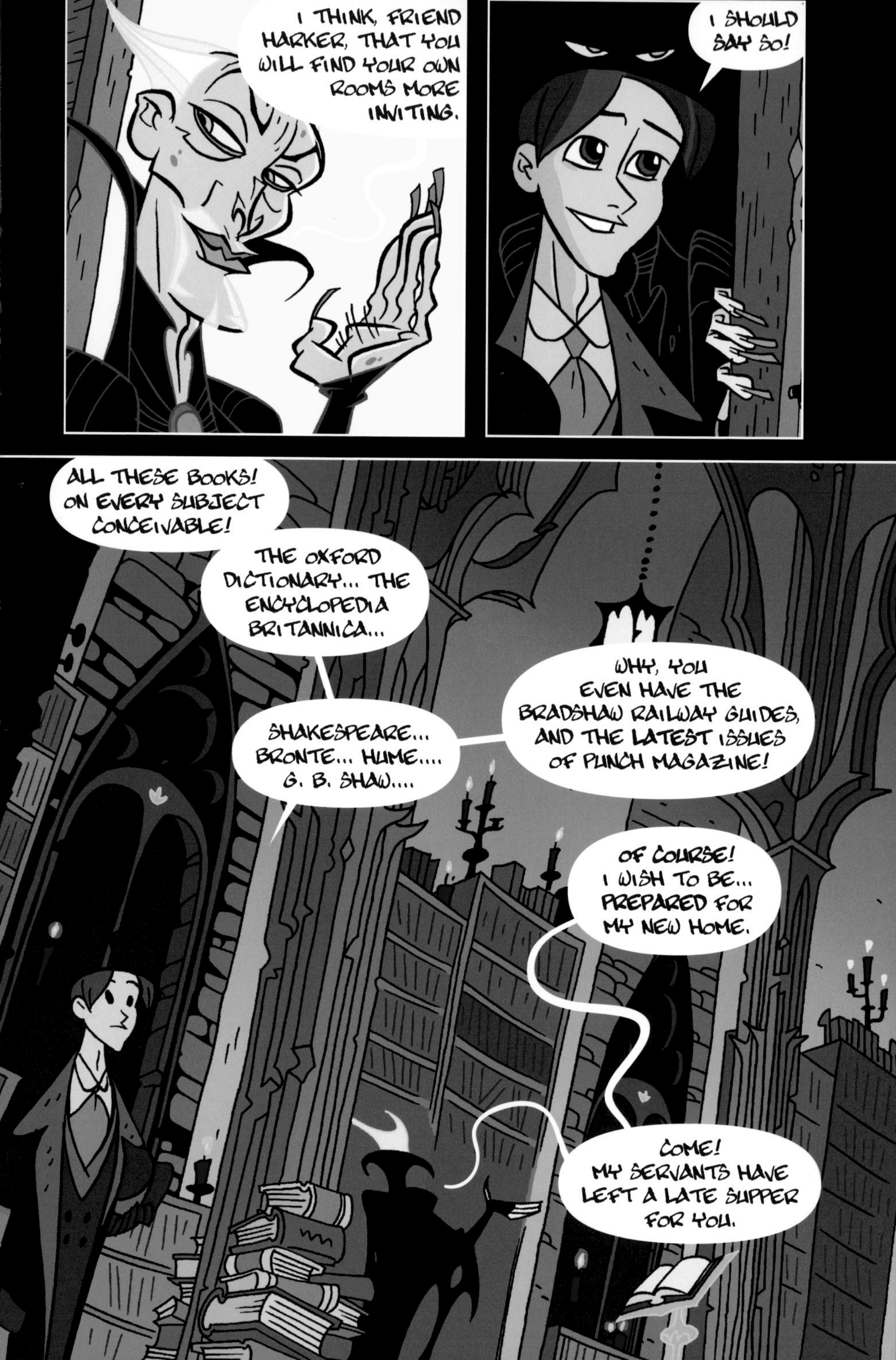
I THINK, FRIEND HARKER, THAT YOU WILL FIND YOUR OWN ROOMS MORE INVITING.
I SHOULD SAY SO!
ALL THESE BOOKS! ON EVERY SUBJECT CONCEIVABLE!
THE OXFORD DICTIONARY... THE ENCYCLOPEDIA BRITANNICA...
SHAKESPEARE... BRONTE... HUME.... G. B. SHAW....
WHY, YOU EVEN HAVE THE BRADSHAW RAILWAY GUIDES, AND THE LATEST ISSUES OF PUNCH MAGAZINE!
OF COURSE! I WISH TO BE... PREPARED FOR MY NEW HOME.
COME! MY SERVANTS HAVE LEFT A LATE SUPPER FOR YOU.

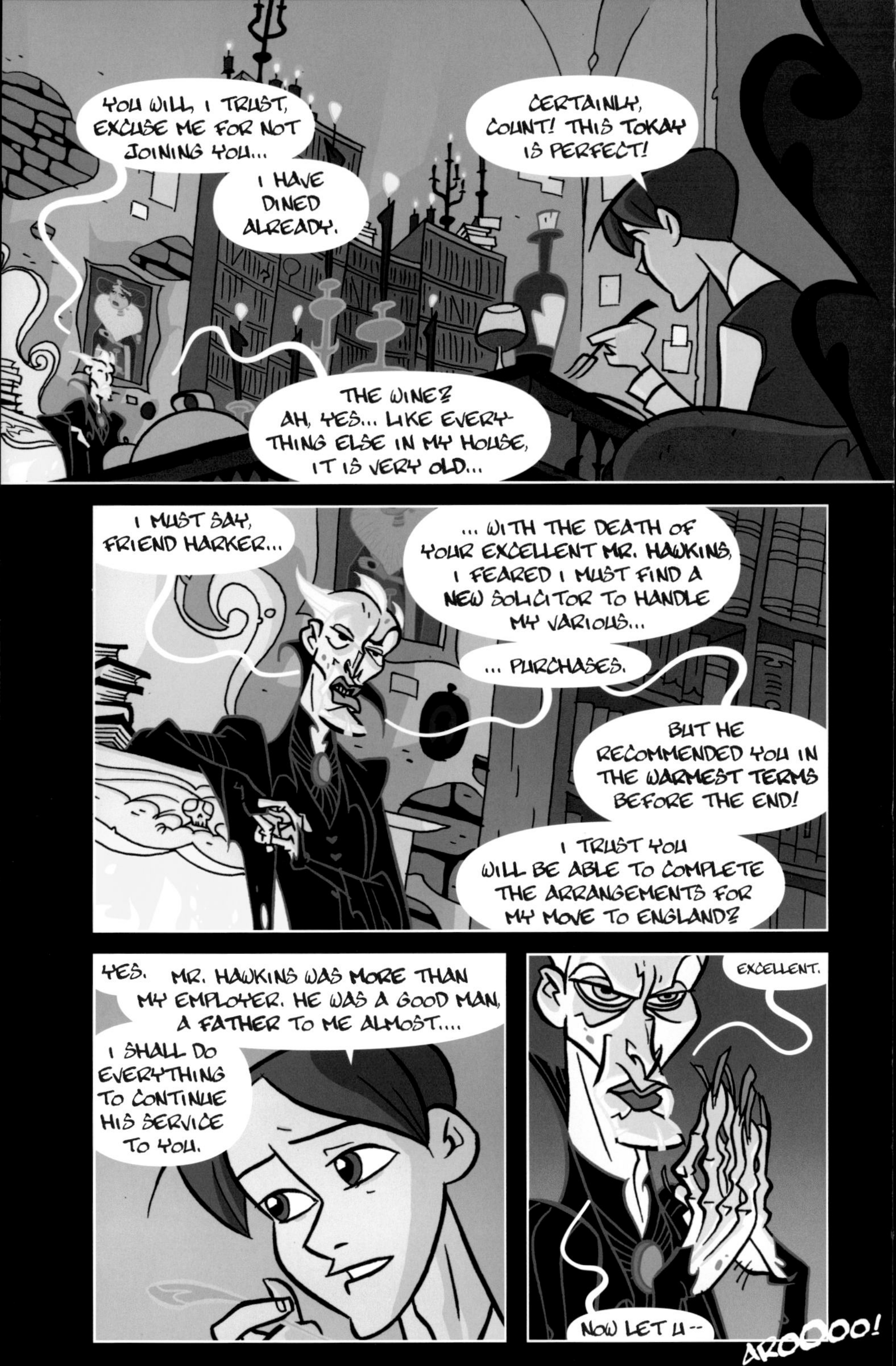

YOU WILL, I TRUST, EXCUSE ME FOR NOT JOINING YOU...
I HAVE DINED ALREADY.
CERTAINLY, COUNT! THIS TOKAY IS PERFECT!
THE WINE? AH, YES... LIKE EVERYTHING ELSE IN MY HOUSE, IT IS VERY OLD...
I MUST SAY, FRIEND HARKER...
... WITH THE DEATH OF YOUR EXCELLENT MR. HAWKINS, I FEARED I MUST FIND A NEW SOLICITOR TO HANDLE MY VARIOUS...
... PURCHASES.
BUT HE RECOMMENDED YOU IN THE WARMEST TERMS BEFORE THE END!
I TRUST YOU WILL BE ABLE TO COMPLETE THE ARRANGEMENTS FOR MY MOVE TO ENGLAND?
YES. MR. HAWKINS WAS MORE THAN MY EMPLOYER. HE WAS A GOOD MAN, A FATHER TO ME ALMOST....
I SHALL DO EVERYTHING TO CONTINUE HIS SERVICE TO YOU.
EXCELLENT.
NOW LET U--
AROOOOO!

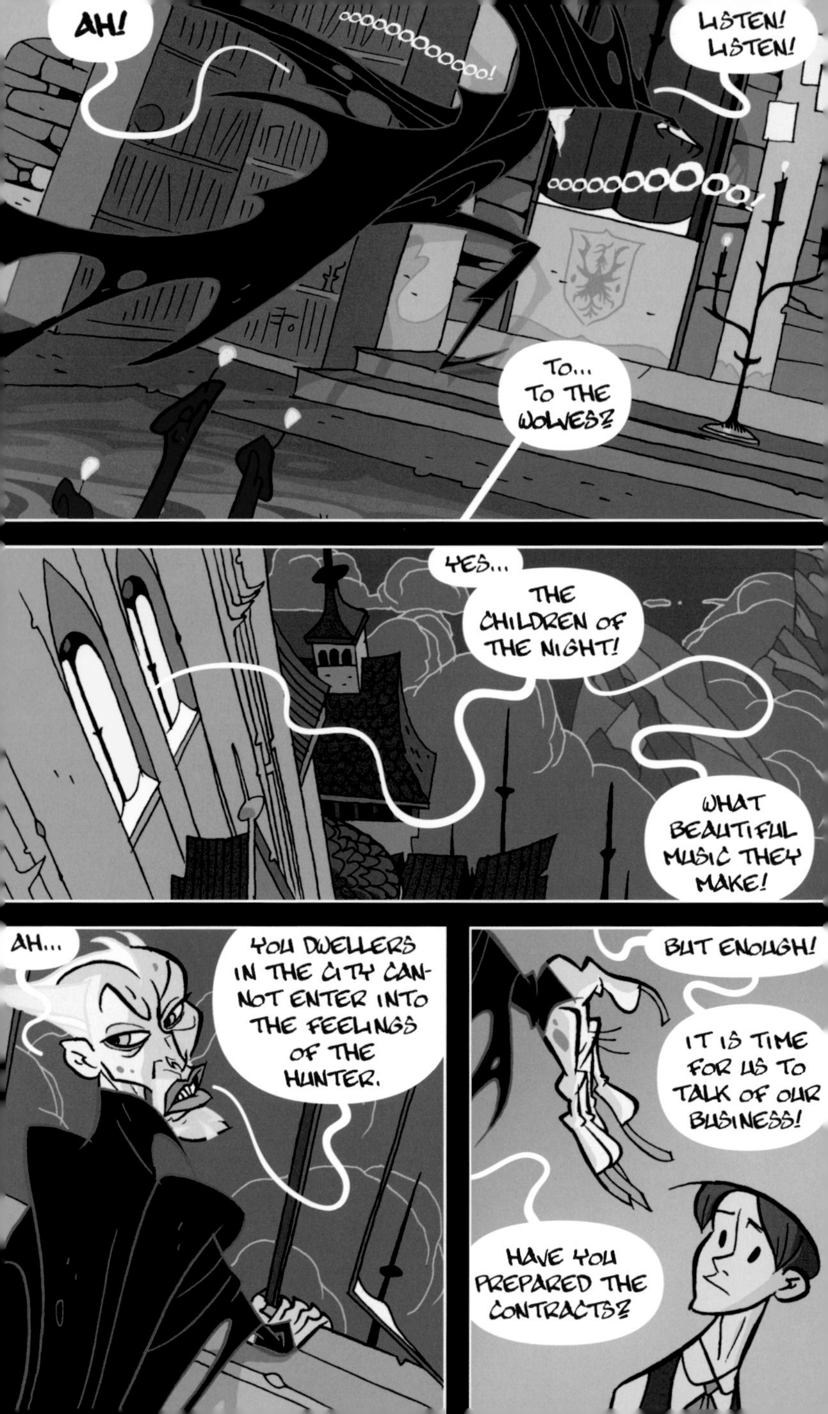
AH!
OOOOOOOOOOOOOOOO!
LISTEN! LISTEN!
OOOOOOOOOOOOO!
TO... TO THE WOLVES?
YES...
THE CHILDREN OF THE NIGHT!
WHAT BEAUTIFUL MUSIC THEY MAKE!
AH...
YOU DWELLERS IN THE CITY CANNOT ENTER INTO THE FEELINGS OF THE HUNTER.
BUT ENOUGH!
IT IS TIME FOR US TO TALK OF OUR BUSINESS!
HAVE YOU PREPARED THE CONTRACTS?

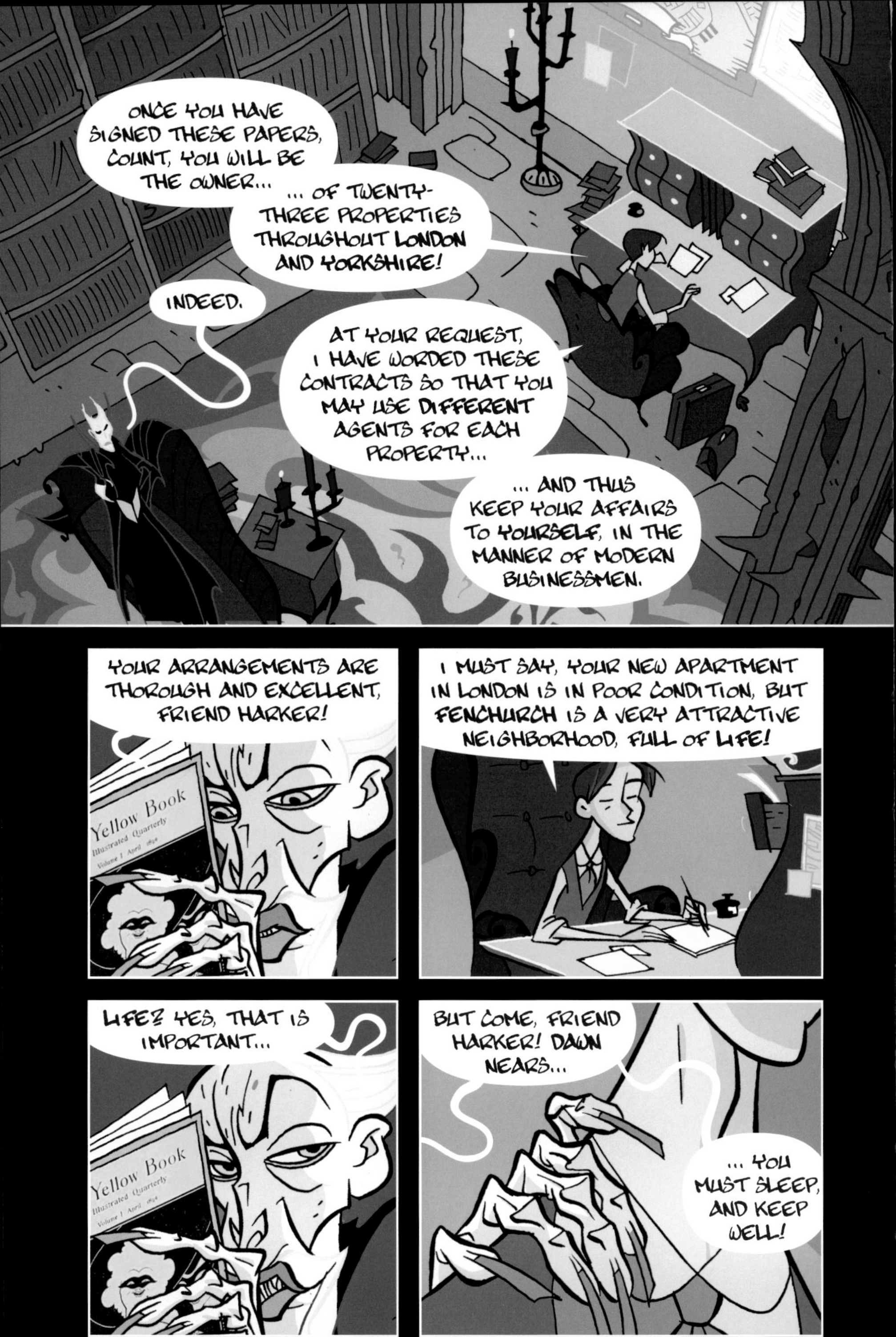
ONCE YOU HAVE SIGNED THESE PAPERS, COUNT, YOU WILL BE THE OWNER...
... OF TWENTY-THREE PROPERTIES THROUGHOUT LONDON AND YORKSHIRE!
INDEED.
AT YOUR REQUEST, I HAVE WORDED THESE CONTRACTS SO THAT YOU MAY USE DIFFERENT AGENTS FOR EACH PROPERTY...
... AND THUS KEEP YOUR AFFAIRS TO YOURSELF, IN THE MANNER OF MODERN BUSINESSMEN.
YOUR ARRANGEMENTS ARE THOROUGH AND EXCELLENT, FRIEND HARKER!
Yellow Book
Illustrated Quarterly
I MUST SAY, YOUR NEW APARTMENT IN LONDON IS IN POOR CONDITION, BUT FENCHURCH IS A VERY ATTRACTIVE NEIGHBORHOOD, FULL OF LIFE!
LIFE? YES, THAT IS IMPORTANT...
Yellow Book
Illustrated Quarterly
BUT COME, FRIEND HARKER! DAWN NEARS...
... YOU MUST SLEEP, AND KEEP WELL!

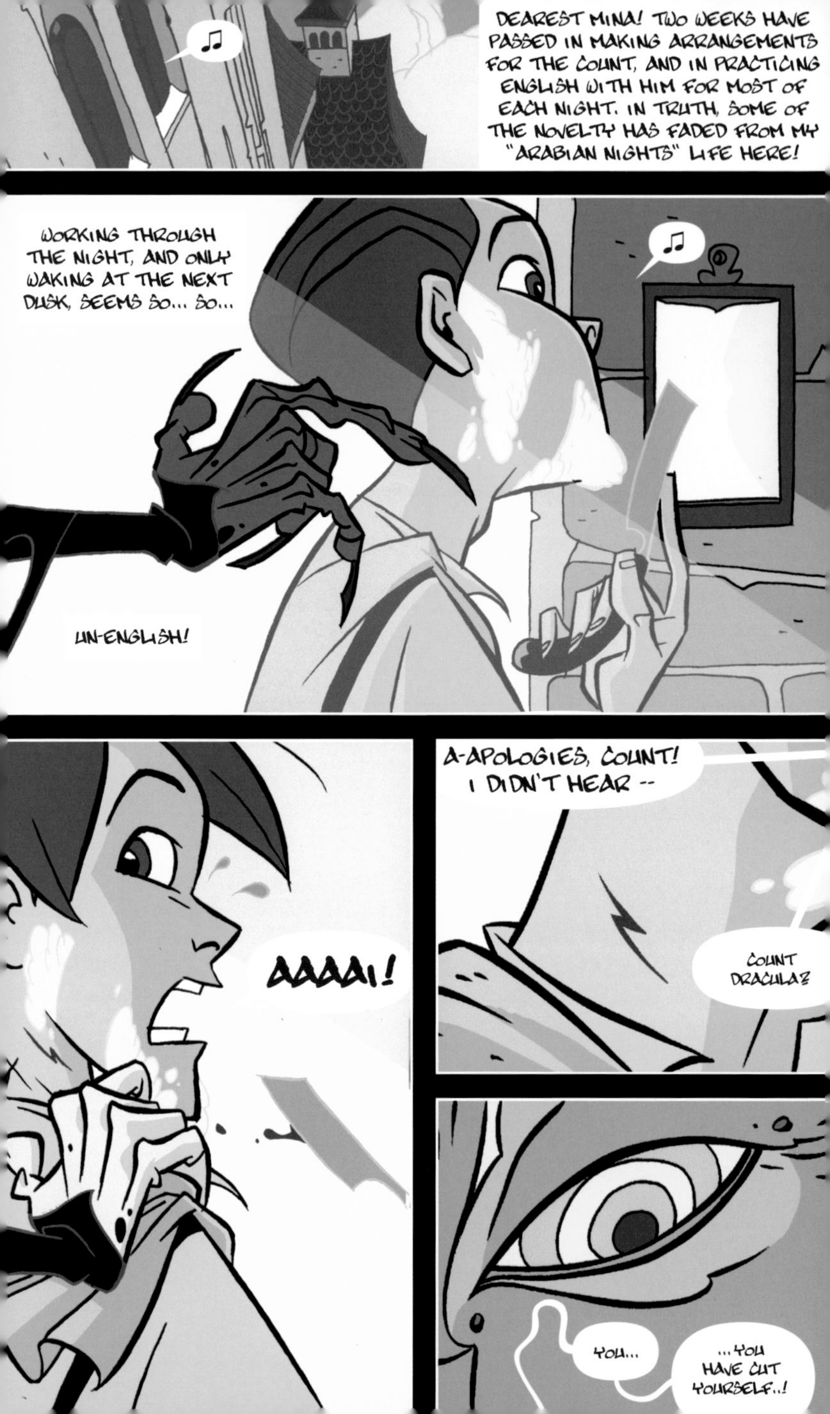

♫
DEAREST MINA! TWO WEEKS HAVE PASSED IN MAKING ARRANGEMENTS FOR THE COUNT, AND IN PRACTICING ENGLISH WITH HIM FOR MOST OF EACH NIGHT. IN TRUTH, SOME OF THE NOVELTY HAS FADED FROM MY "ARABIAN NIGHTS" LIFE HERE!
WORKING THROUGH THE NIGHT, AND ONLY WAKING AT THE NEXT DUSK, SEEMS SO... SO...
♫
UN-ENGLISH!
AAAAI!
A-APOLOGIES, COUNT! I DIDN'T HEAR --
COUNT DRACULA?
YOU...
...YOU HAVE CUT YOURSELF..!

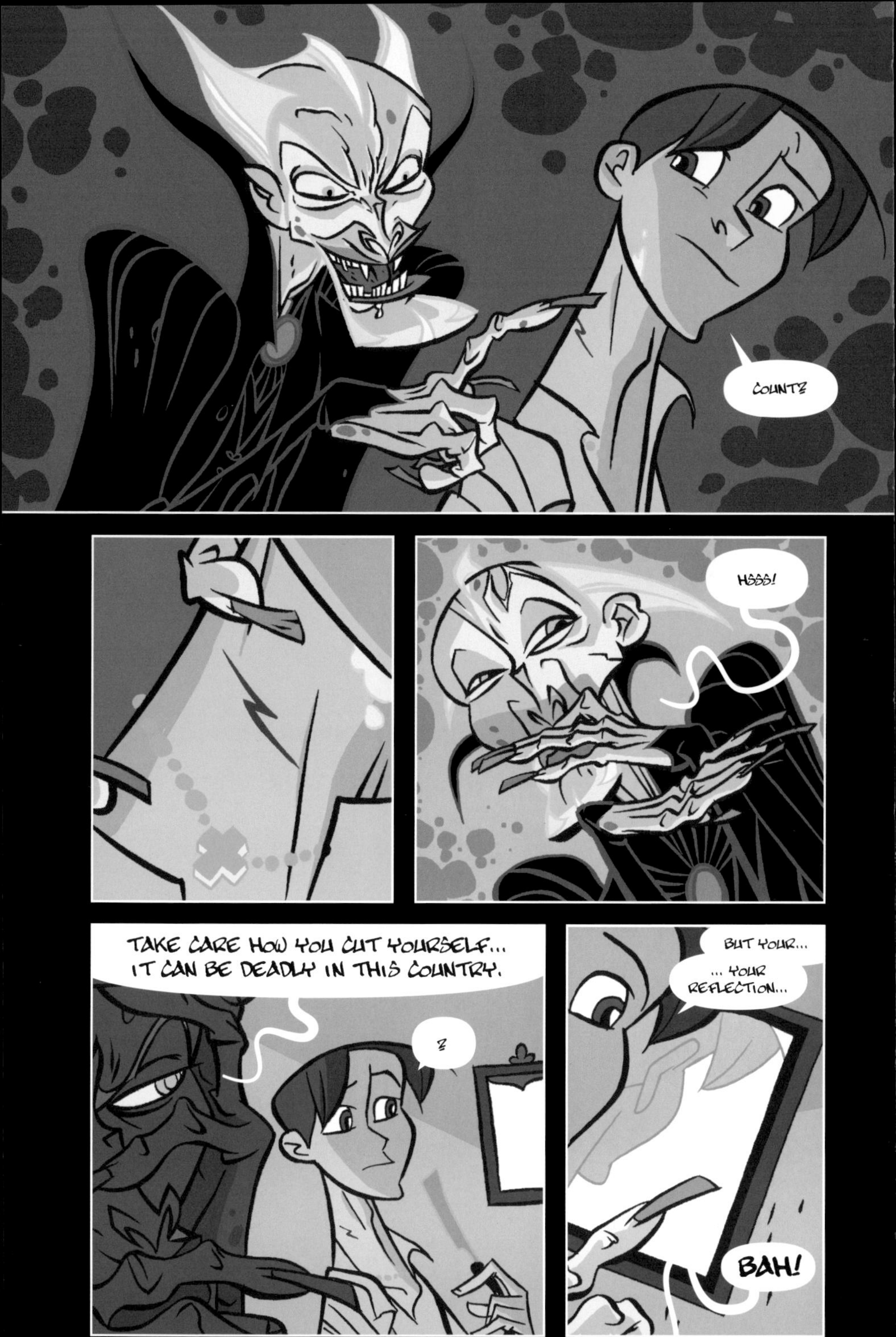
COUNT?
HSSS!
TAKE CARE HOW YOU CUT YOURSELF...
IT CAN BE DEADLY IN THIS COUNTRY.
?
BUT YOUR...
... YOUR REFLECTION...
BAH!

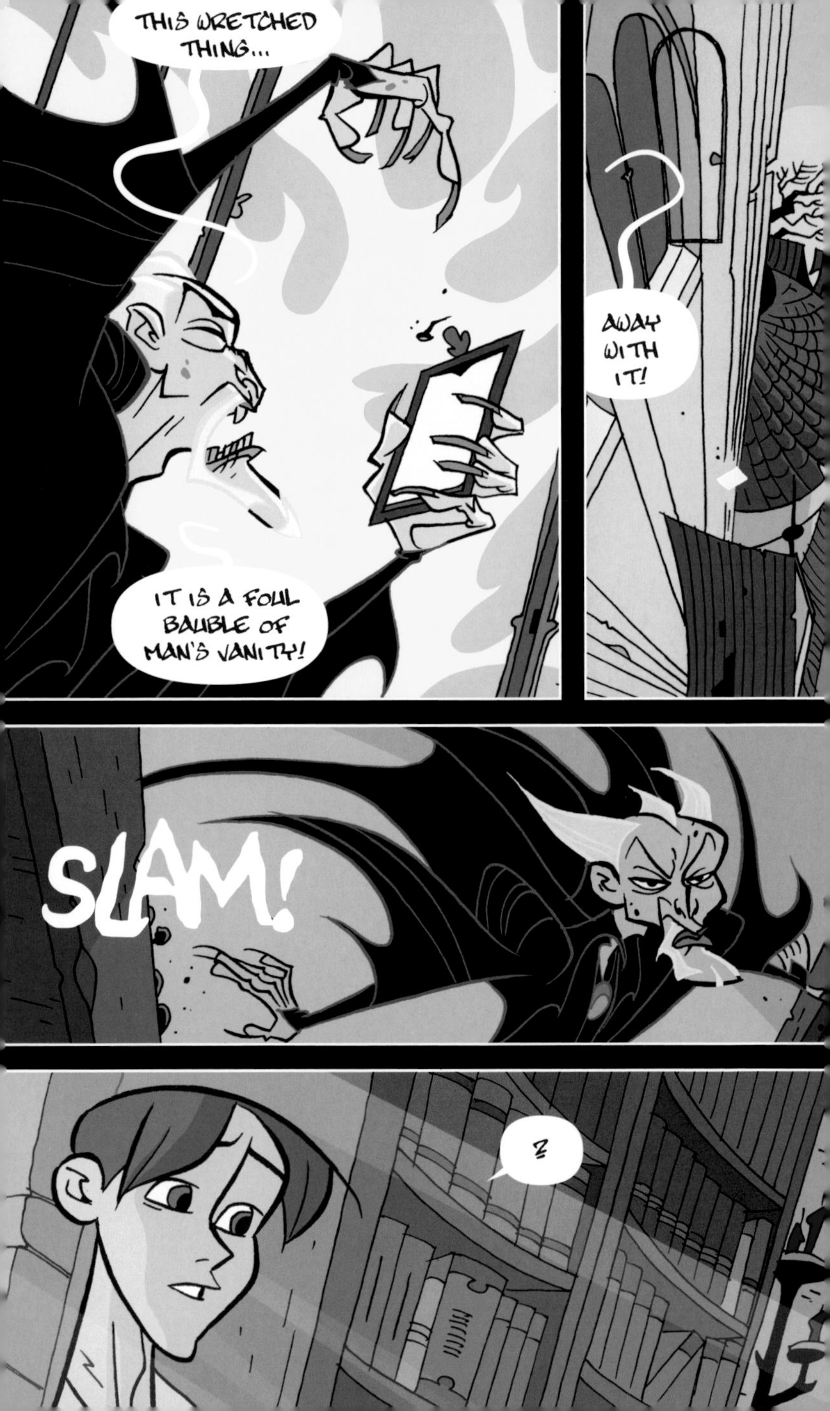
THIS WRETCHED THING...
IT IS A FOUL BAUBLE OF MAN'S VANITY!
AWAY WITH IT!
SLAM!
?

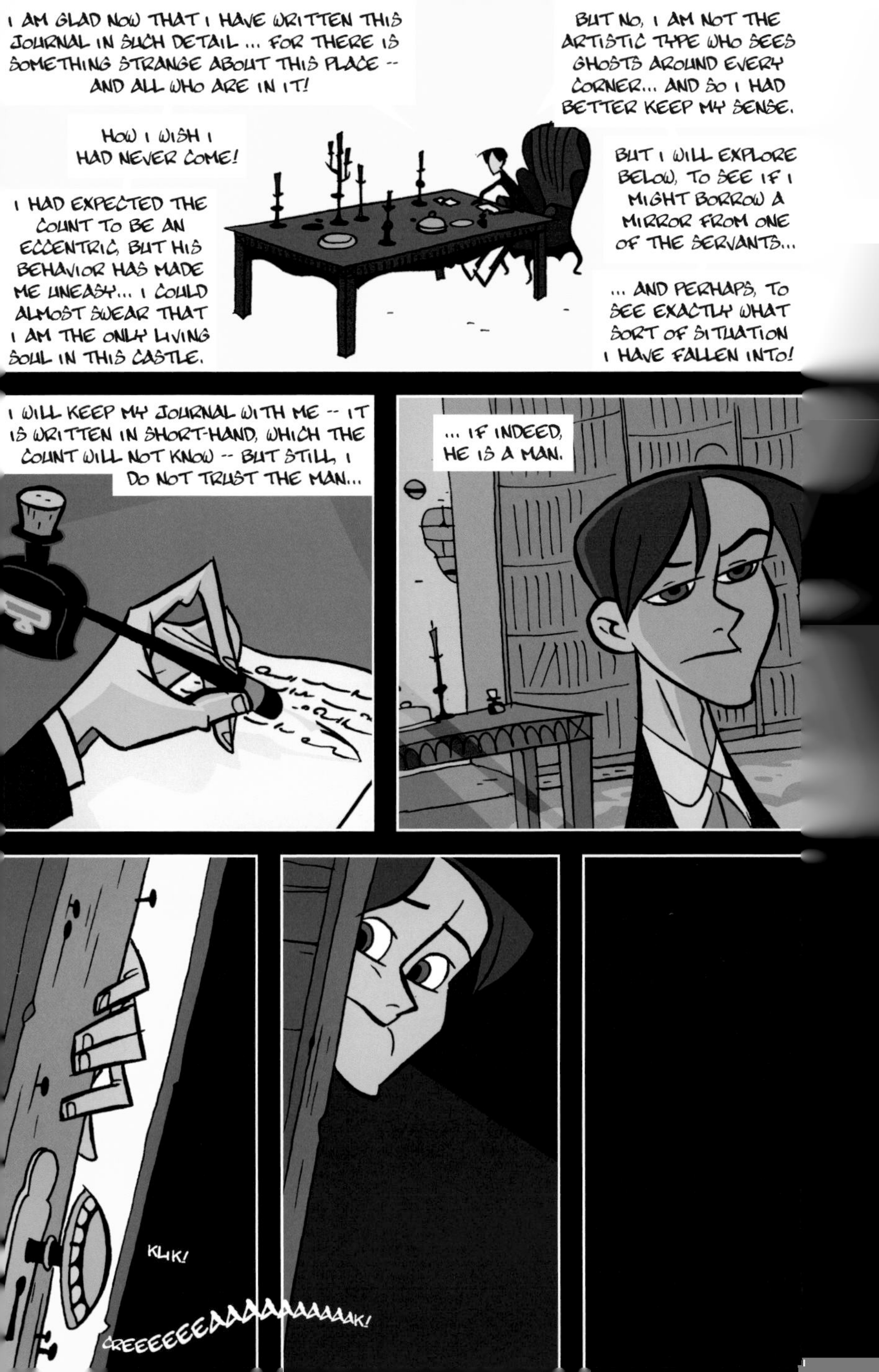
I AM GLAD NOW THAT I HAVE WRITTEN THIS JOURNAL IN SUCH DETAIL ... FOR THERE IS SOMETHING STRANGE ABOUT THIS PLACE -- AND ALL WHO ARE IN IT!
HOW I WISH I HAD NEVER COME!
I HAD EXPECTED THE COUNT TO BE AN ECCENTRIC, BUT HIS BEHAVIOR HAS MADE ME UNEASY... I COULD ALMOST SWEAR THAT I AM THE ONLY LIVING SOUL IN THIS CASTLE.
BUT NO, I AM NOT THE ARTISTIC TYPE WHO SEES GHOSTS AROUND EVERY CORNER... AND SO I HAD BETTER KEEP MY SENSE.
BUT I WILL EXPLORE BELOW, TO SEE IF I MIGHT BORROW A MIRROR FROM ONE OF THE SERVANTS...
... AND PERHAPS, TO SEE EXACTLY WHAT SORT OF SITUATION I HAVE FALLEN INTO!
I WILL KEEP MY JOURNAL WITH ME -- IT IS WRITTEN IN SHORT-HAND, WHICH THE COUNT WILL NOT KNOW -- BUT STILL, I DO NOT TRUST THE MAN...
... IF INDEED, HE IS A MAN.
KLIK!
CREEEEEEEAAAAAAAAAAAK!

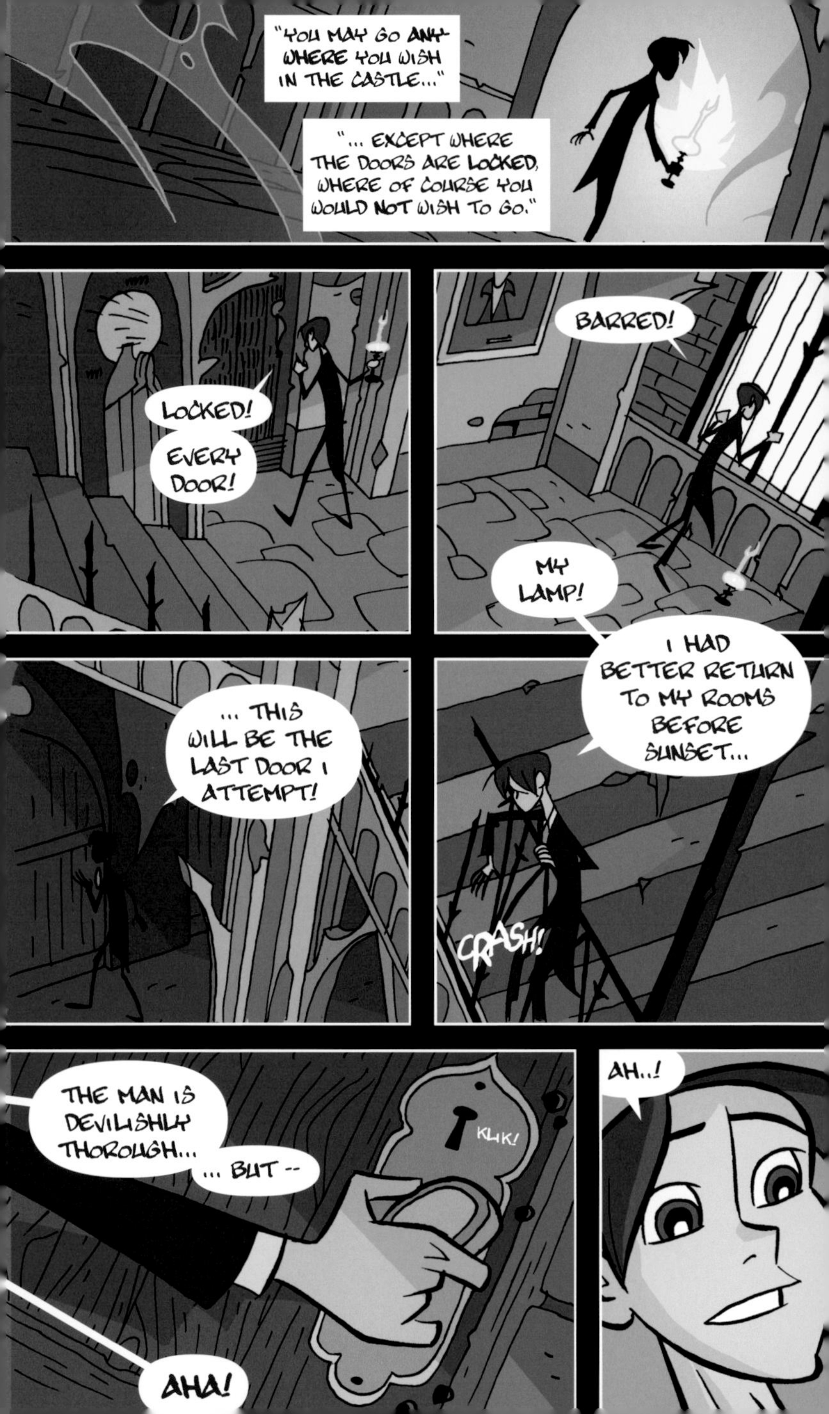
"YOU MAY GO ANY-WHERE YOU WISH IN THE CASTLE..."
"... EXCEPT WHERE THE DOORS ARE LOCKED, WHERE OF COURSE YOU WOULD NOT WISH TO GO."
LOCKED!
EVERY DOOR!
BARRED!
MY LAMP!
I HAD BETTER RETURN TO MY ROOMS BEFORE SUNSET...
... THIS WILL BE THE LAST DOOR I ATTEMPT!
CRASH!
THE MAN IS DEVILISHLY THOROUGH...
... BUT --
KLIK!
AHA!
AH..!

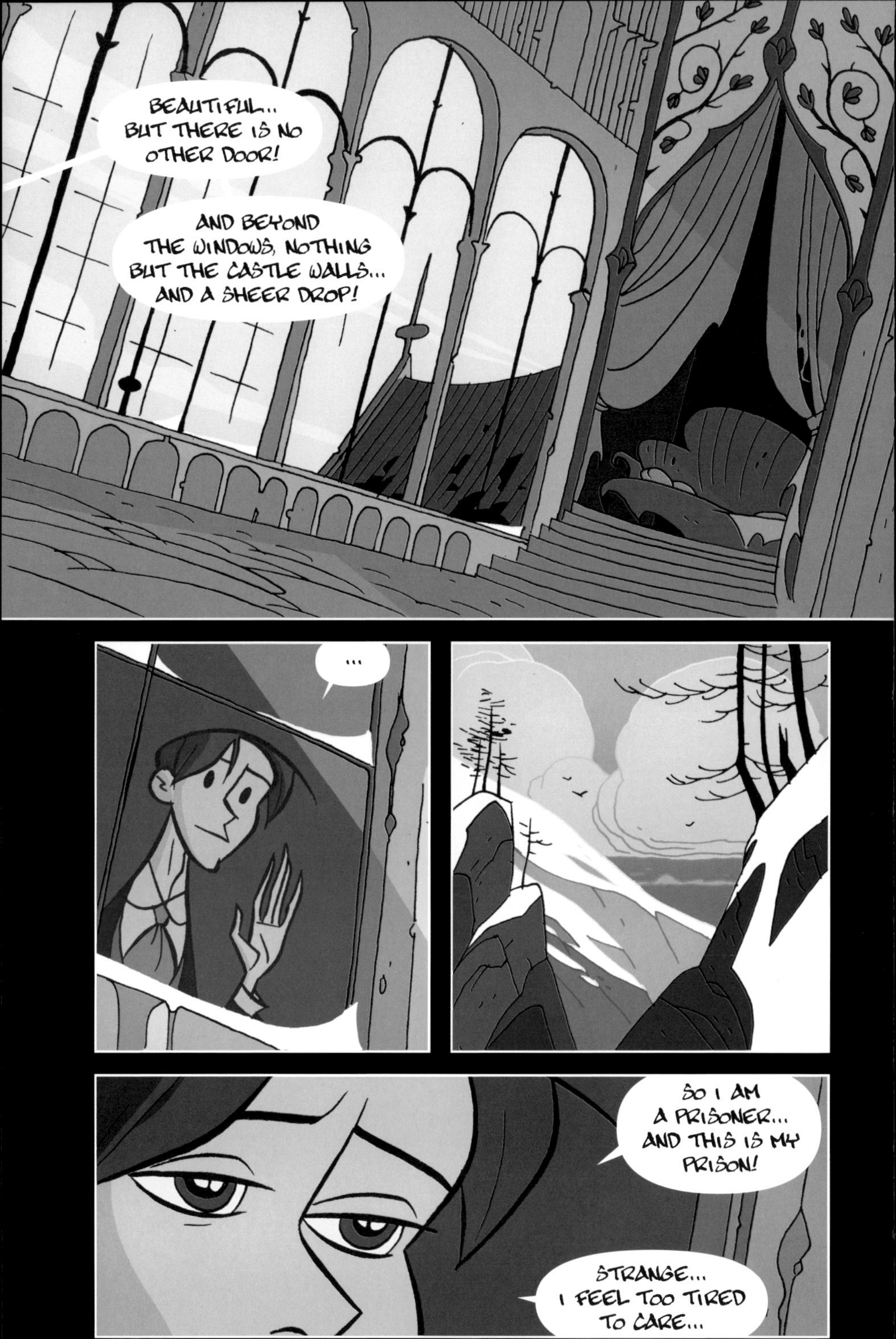
BEAUTIFUL... BUT THERE IS NO OTHER DOOR!
AND BEYOND THE WINDOWS, NOTHING BUT THE CASTLE WALLS... AND A SHEER DROP!
...
SO I AM A PRISONER... AND THIS IS MY PRISON!
STRANGE... I FEEL TOO TIRED TO CARE...

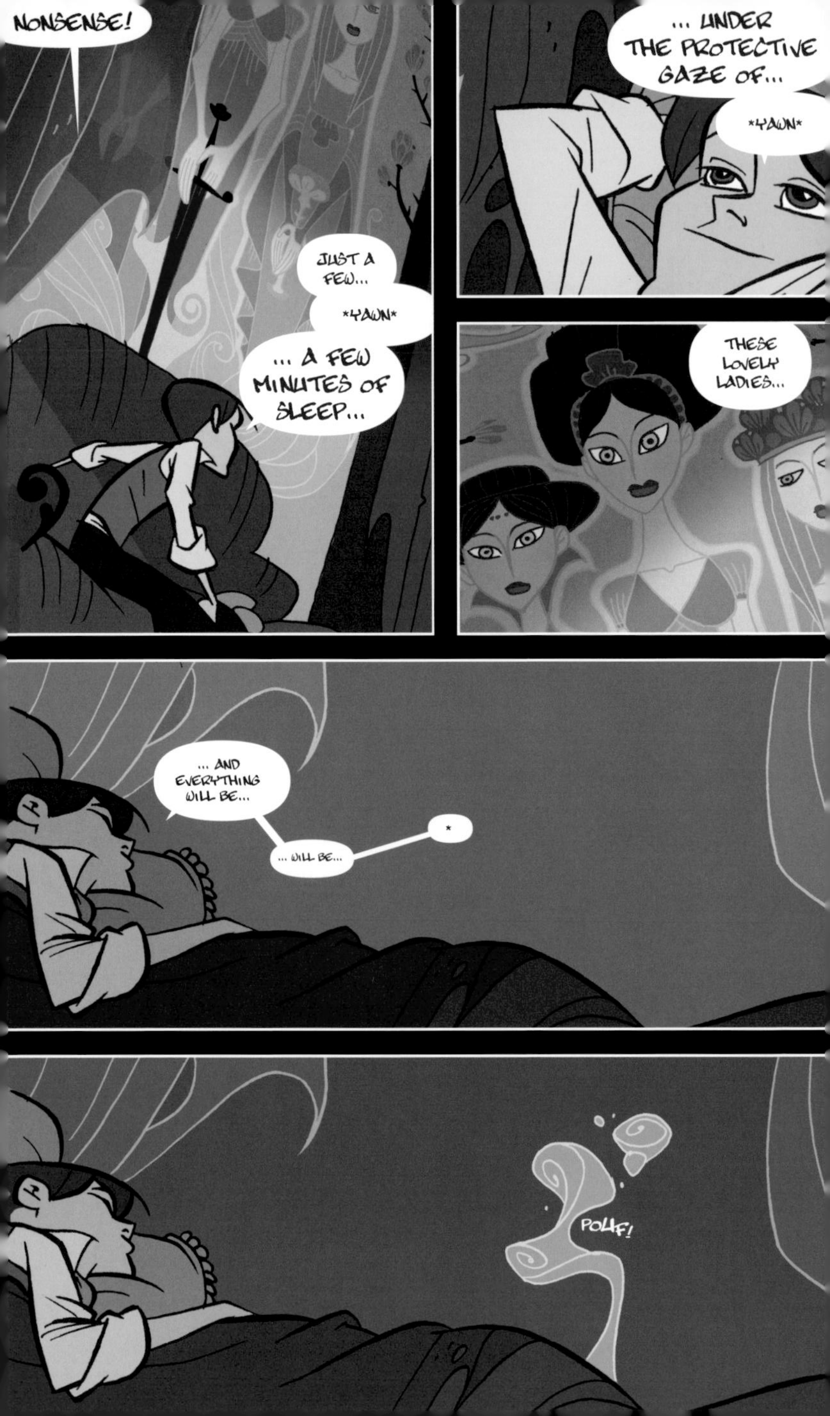
NONSENSE!
... UNDER THE PROTECTIVE GAZE OF...
YAWN
JUST A FEW...
YAWN
... A FEW MINUTES OF SLEEP...
THESE LOVELY LADIES...
... AND EVERYTHING WILL BE...
... WILL BE...
*
POUF!

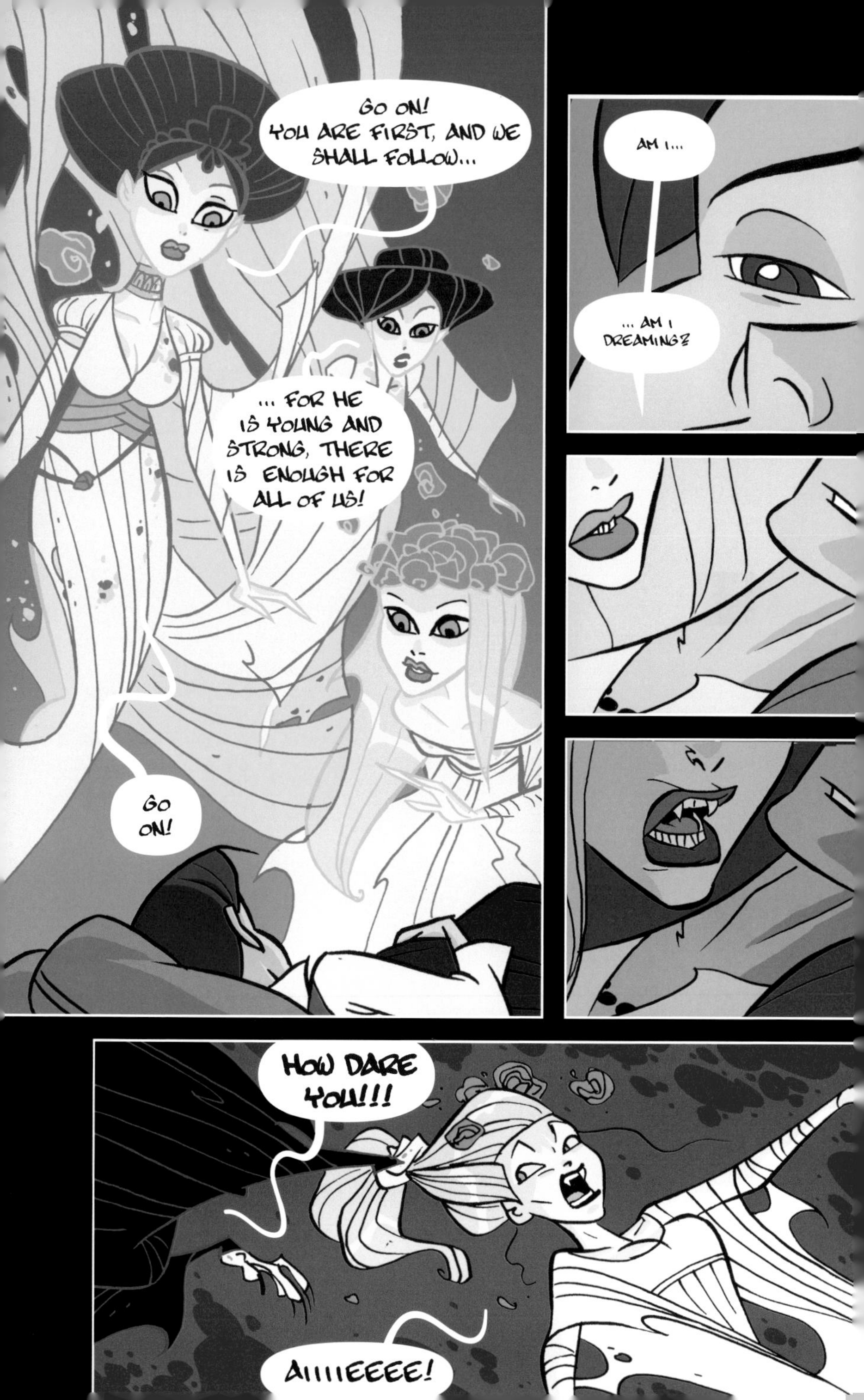
GO ON!
YOU ARE FIRST, AND WE SHALL FOLLOW...
... FOR HE IS YOUNG AND STRONG, THERE IS ENOUGH FOR ALL OF US!
GO ON!
AM I...
... AM I DREAMING?
HOW DARE YOU!!!
AIIIIEEEE!

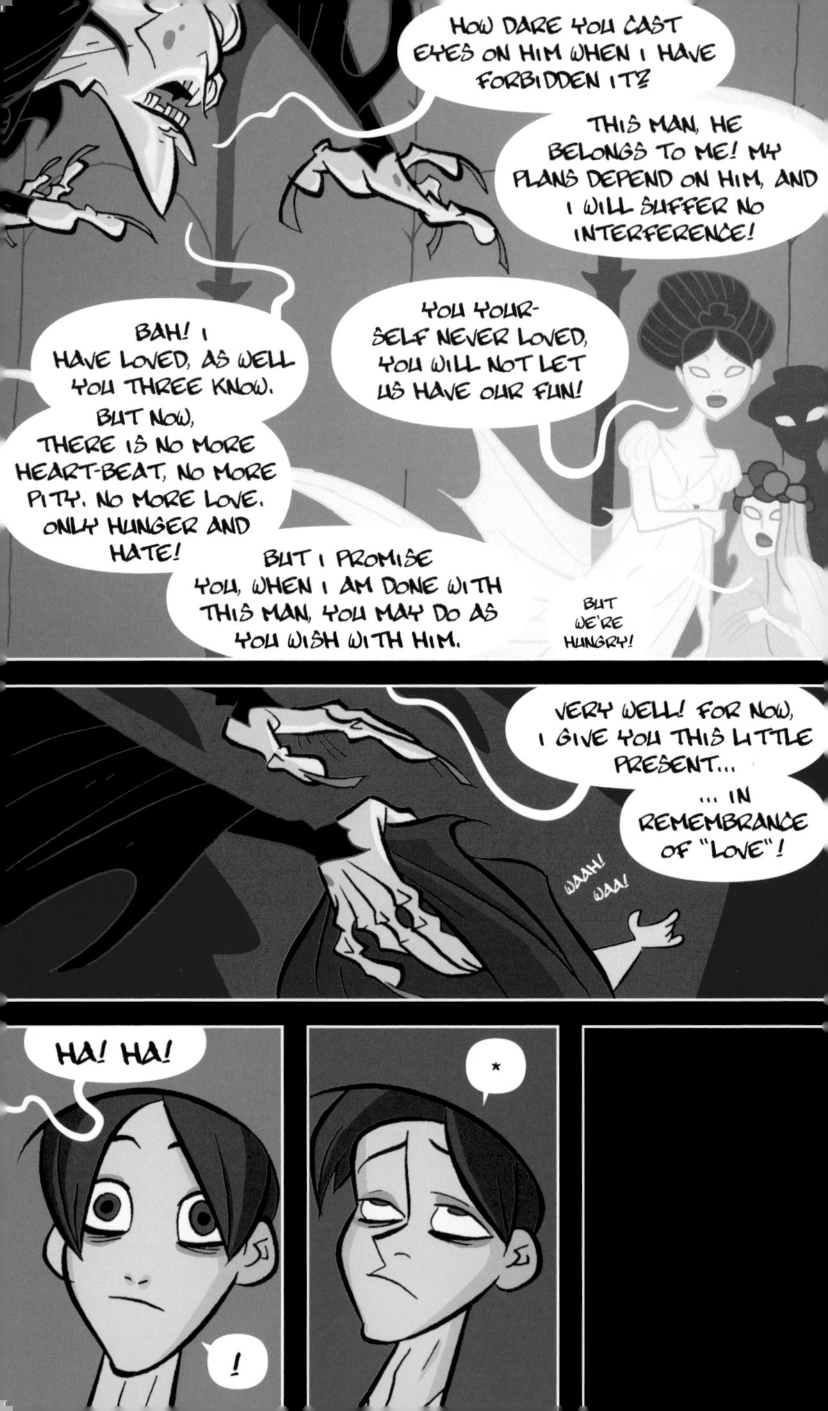
HOW DARE YOU CAST EYES ON HIM WHEN I HAVE FORBIDDEN IT?
THIS MAN, HE BELONGS TO ME! MY PLANS DEPEND ON HIM, AND I WILL SUFFER NO INTERFERENCE!
YOU YOURSELF NEVER LOVED, YOU WILL NOT LET US HAVE OUR FUN!
BAH! I HAVE LOVED, AS WELL YOU THREE KNOW.
BUT NOW, THERE IS NO MORE HEART-BEAT, NO MORE PITY. NO MORE LOVE. ONLY HUNGER AND HATE!
BUT I PROMISE YOU, WHEN I AM DONE WITH THIS MAN, YOU MAY DO AS YOU WISH WITH HIM.
BUT WE'RE HUNGRY!
VERY WELL! FOR NOW, I GIVE YOU THIS LITTLE PRESENT...
... IN REMEMBRANCE OF "LOVE"!
WAAH! WAA!
HA! HA!
!
*

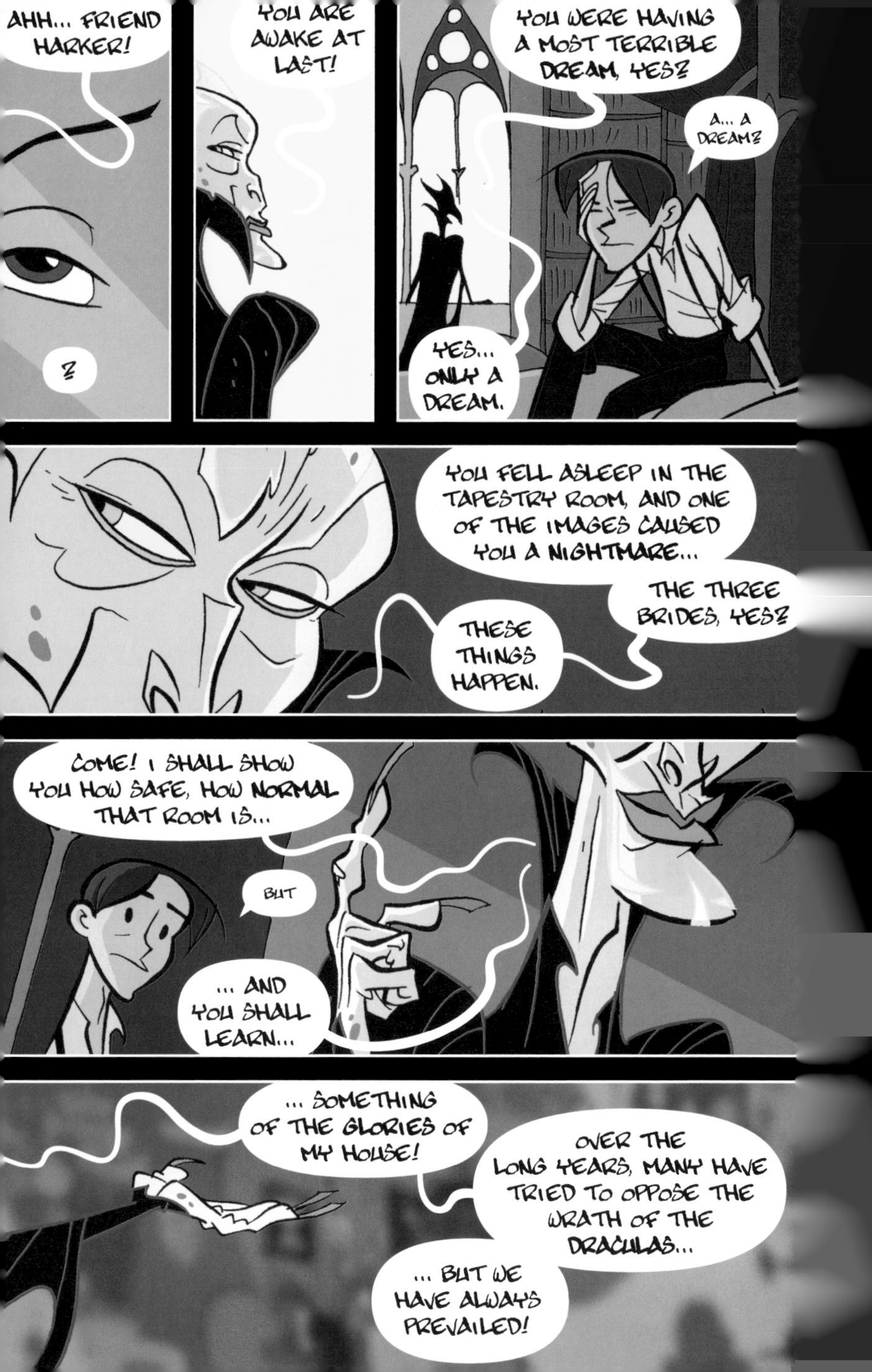
AHH... FRIEND HARKER!
?
YOU ARE AWAKE AT LAST!
YOU WERE HAVING A MOST TERRIBLE DREAM, YES?
A... A DREAM?
YES... ONLY A DREAM.
YOU FELL ASLEEP IN THE TAPESTRY ROOM, AND ONE OF THE IMAGES CAUSED YOU A NIGHTMARE...
THE THREE BRIDES, YES?
THESE THINGS HAPPEN.
COME! I SHALL SHOW YOU HOW SAFE, HOW NORMAL THAT ROOM IS...
BUT
... AND YOU SHALL LEARN...
... SOMETHING OF THE GLORIES OF MY HOUSE!
OVER THE LONG YEARS, MANY HAVE TRIED TO OPPOSE THE WRATH OF THE DRACULAS...
... BUT WE HAVE ALWAYS PREVAILED!

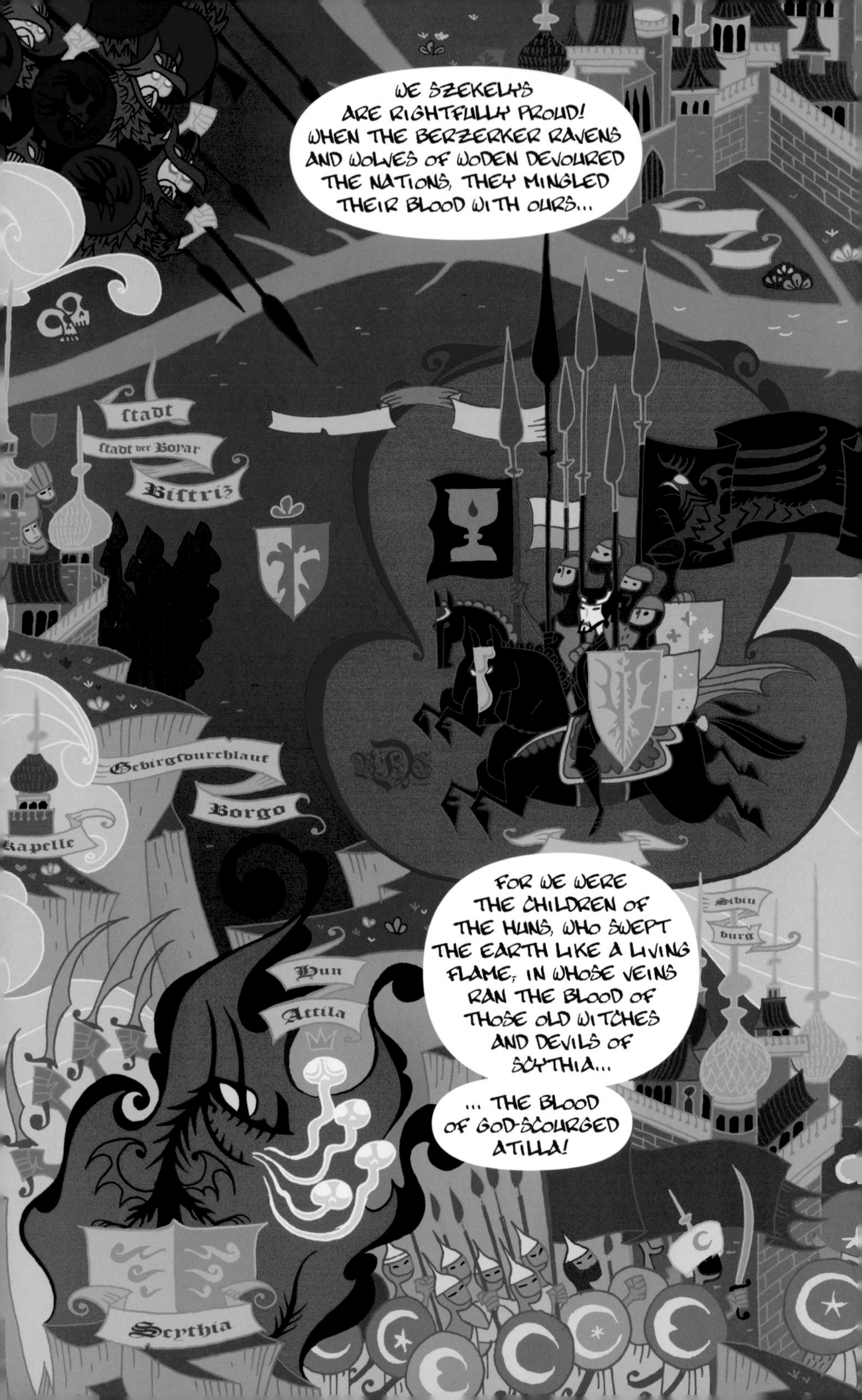

WE SZEKELYS ARE RIGHTFULLY PROUD! WHEN THE BERZERKER RAVENS AND WOLVES OF WODEN DEVOURED THE NATIONS, THEY MINGLED THEIR BLOOD WITH OURS...
ſtadt
ſtadt der Boyar
Biſtriz
Gebirgſdurchlauf
Borgo
Kapelle
FOR WE WERE THE CHILDREN OF THE HUNS, WHO SWEPT THE EARTH LIKE A LIVING FLAME; IN WHOSE VEINS RAN THE BLOOD OF THOSE OLD WITCHES AND DEVILS OF SCYTHIA...
Sibiu
burg
Hun
Attila
... THE BLOOD OF GOD-SCOURGED ATILLA!
Scythia

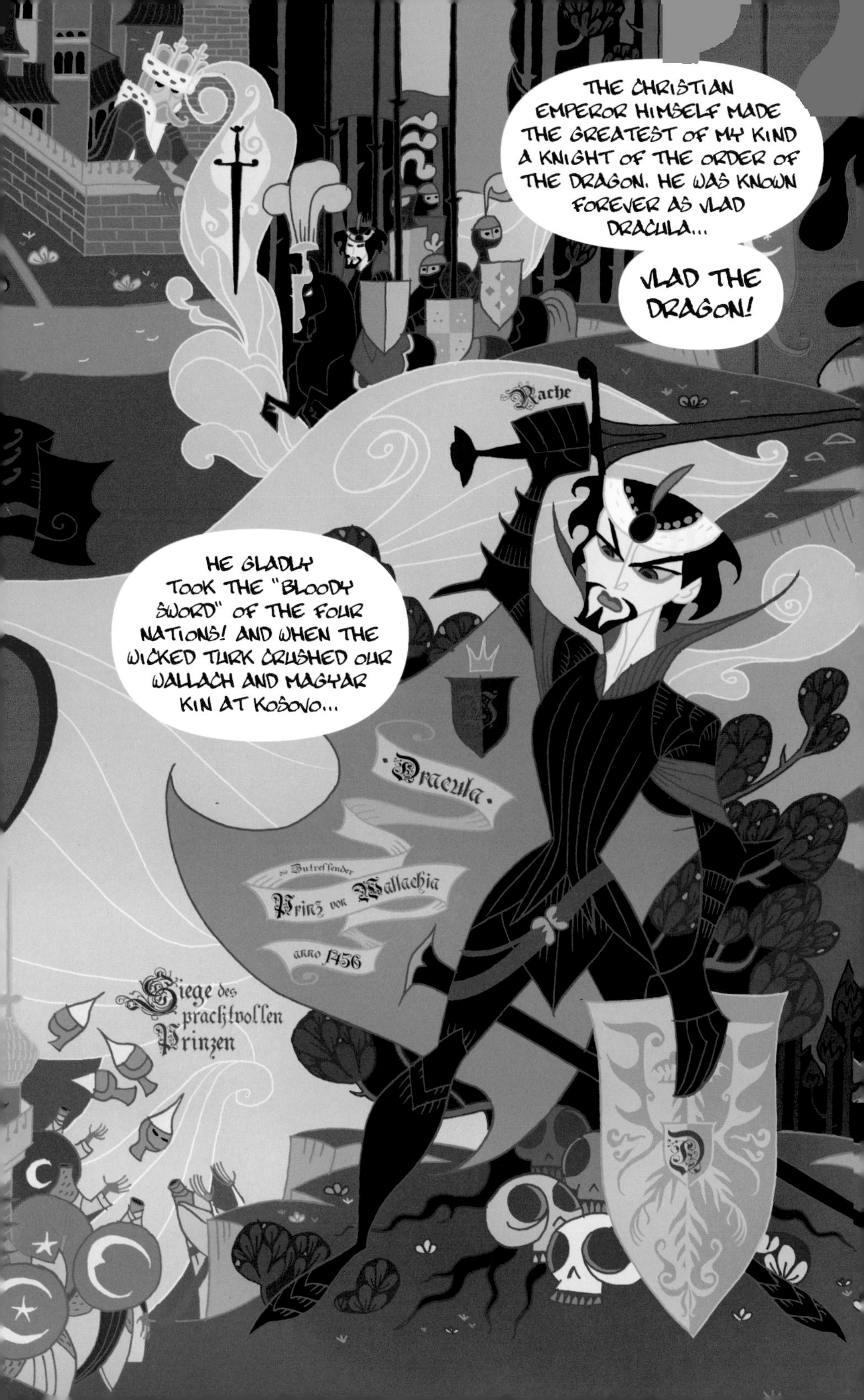
THE CHRISTIAN EMPEROR HIMSELF MADE THE GREATEST OF MY KIND A KNIGHT OF THE ORDER OF THE DRAGON. HE WAS KNOWN FOREVER AS VLAD DRACULA...
VLAD THE DRAGON!
Rache
HE GLADLY TOOK THE "BLOODY SWORD" OF THE FOUR NATIONS! AND WHEN THE WICKED TURK CRUSHED OUR WALLACH AND MAGYAR KIN AT KOSOVO...
Dracula
Prinz von Wallachia
anno 1456
Siege des prachtvollen Prinzen

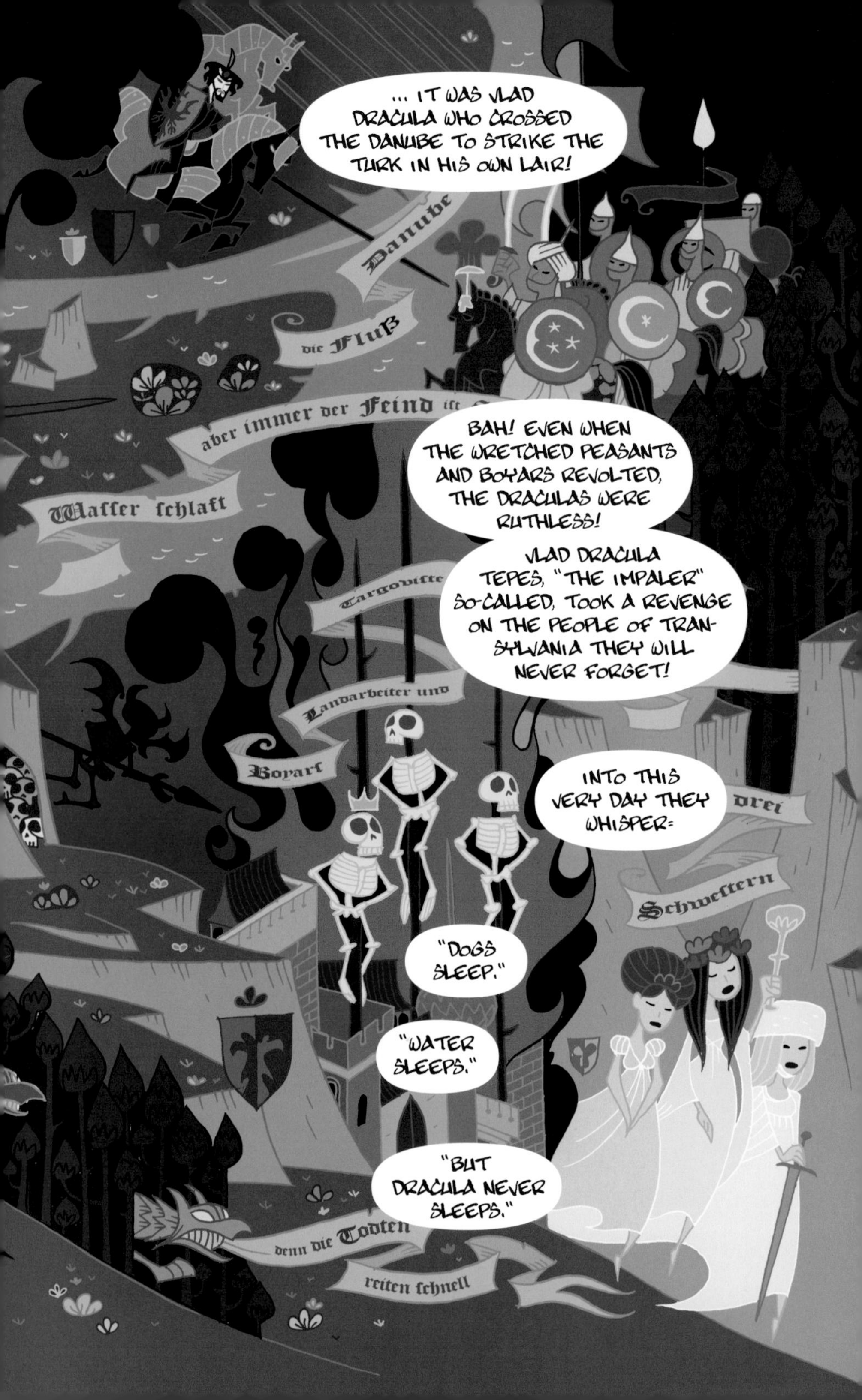
... IT WAS VLAD DRACULA WHO CROSSED THE DANUBE TO STRIKE THE TURK IN HIS OWN LAIR!
Danube
die Fluß
aber immer der Feind ist
Waſſer ſchlaft
BAH! EVEN WHEN THE WRETCHED PEASANTS AND BOYARS REVOLTED, THE DRACULAS WERE RUTHLESS!
VLAD DRACULA TEPES, "THE IMPALER" SO-CALLED, TOOK A REVENGE ON THE PEOPLE OF TRANSYLVANIA THEY WILL NEVER FORGET!
Targoviſte
Landarbeiter und
Boyarſ
INTO THIS VERY DAY THEY WHISPER:
drei
Schweſtern
"DOGS SLEEP."
"WATER SLEEPS."
"BUT DRACULA NEVER SLEEPS."
denn die Todten
reiten ſchnell

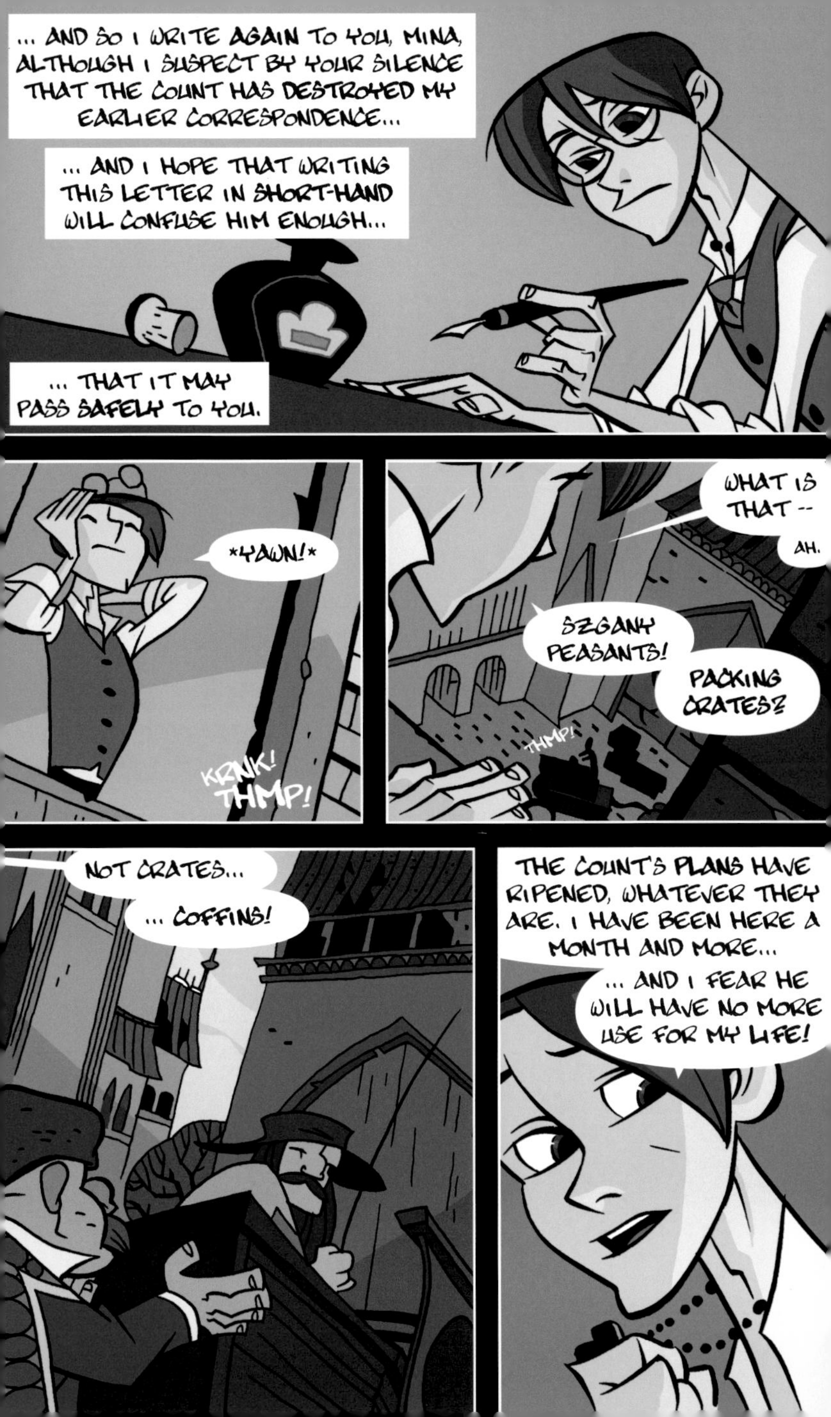
... AND SO I WRITE AGAIN TO YOU, MINA, ALTHOUGH I SUSPECT BY YOUR SILENCE THAT THE COUNT HAS DESTROYED MY EARLIER CORRESPONDENCE...
... AND I HOPE THAT WRITING THIS LETTER IN SHORT-HAND WILL CONFUSE HIM ENOUGH...
... THAT IT MAY PASS SAFELY TO YOU.
YAWN!
KRNK! THMP!
WHAT IS THAT --
AH.
SZGANY PEASANTS!
PACKING CRATES?
THMP!
NOT CRATES...
... COFFINS!
THE COUNT'S PLANS HAVE RIPENED, WHATEVER THEY ARE. I HAVE BEEN HERE A MONTH AND MORE...
... AND I FEAR HE WILL HAVE NO MORE USE FOR MY LIFE!

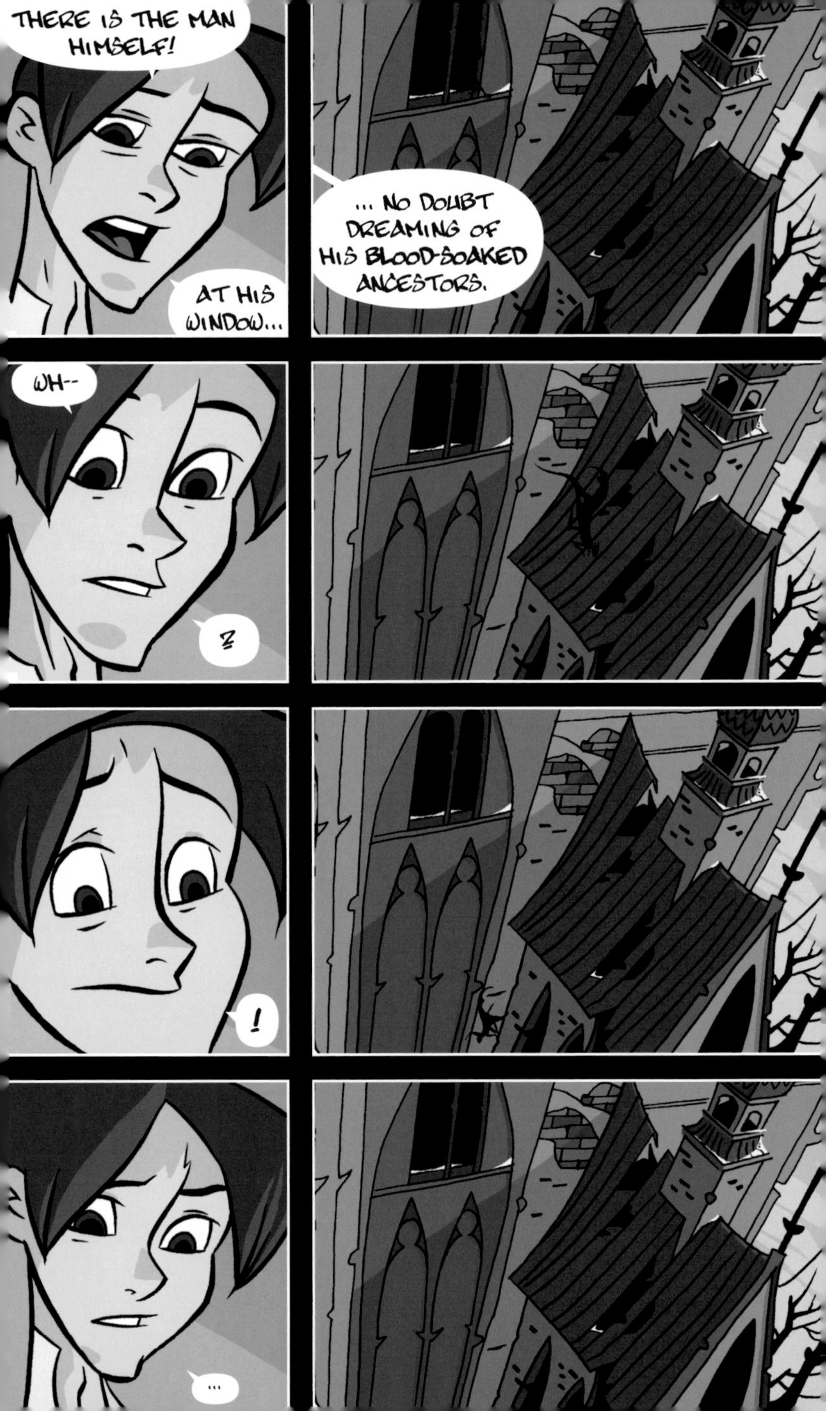
THERE IS THE MAN HIMSELF!
AT HIS WINDOW...
... NO DOUBT DREAMING OF HIS BLOOD-SOAKED ANCESTORS.
WH--
?
!
...

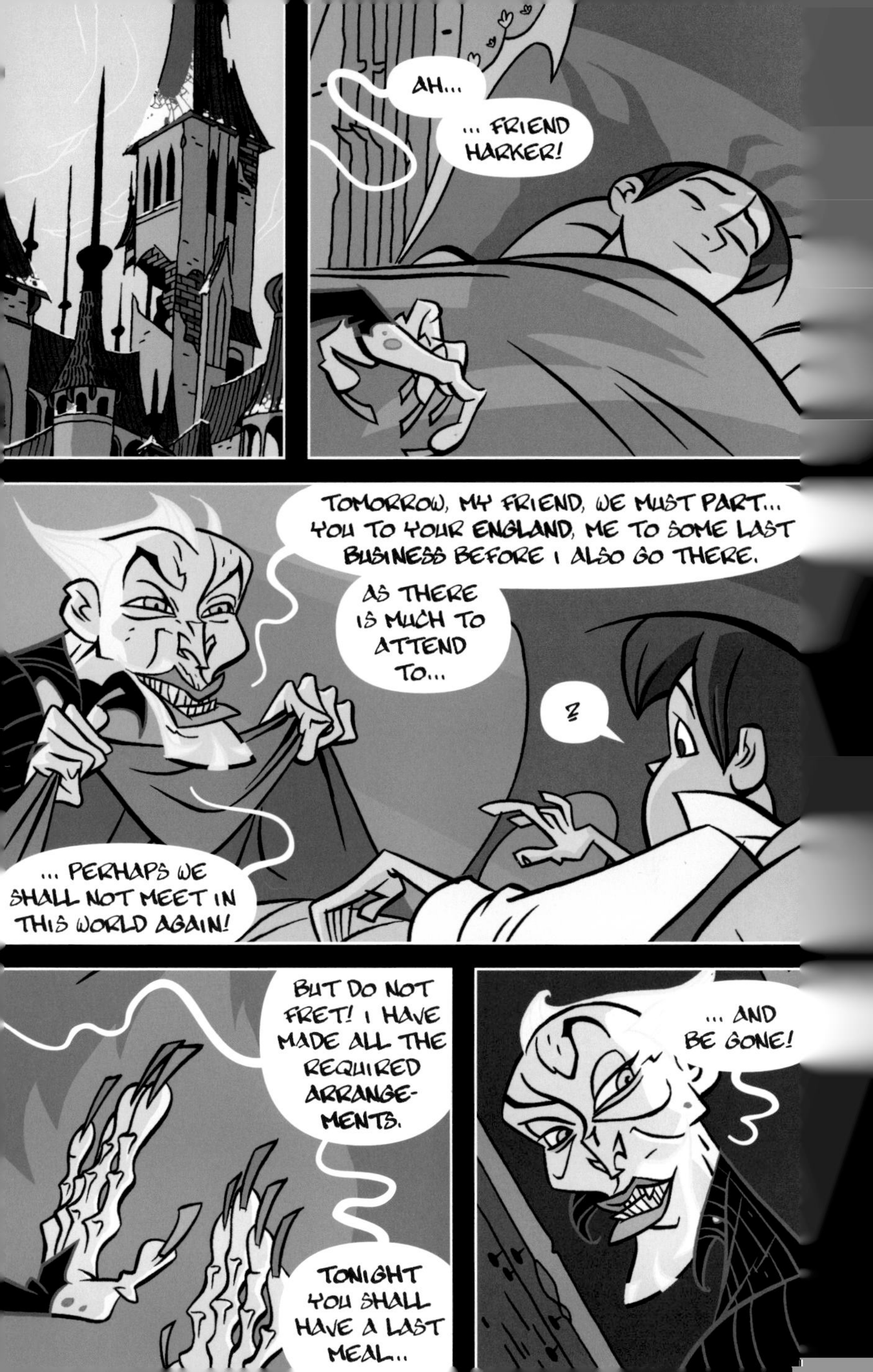
AH...
... FRIEND HARKER!
TOMORROW, MY FRIEND, WE MUST PART... YOU TO YOUR ENGLAND, ME TO SOME LAST BUSINESS BEFORE I ALSO GO THERE.
AS THERE IS MUCH TO ATTEND TO...
?
... PERHAPS WE SHALL NOT MEET IN THIS WORLD AGAIN!
BUT DO NOT FRET! I HAVE MADE ALL THE REQUIRED ARRANGE-MENTS.
TONIGHT YOU SHALL HAVE A LAST MEAL...
... AND BE GONE!

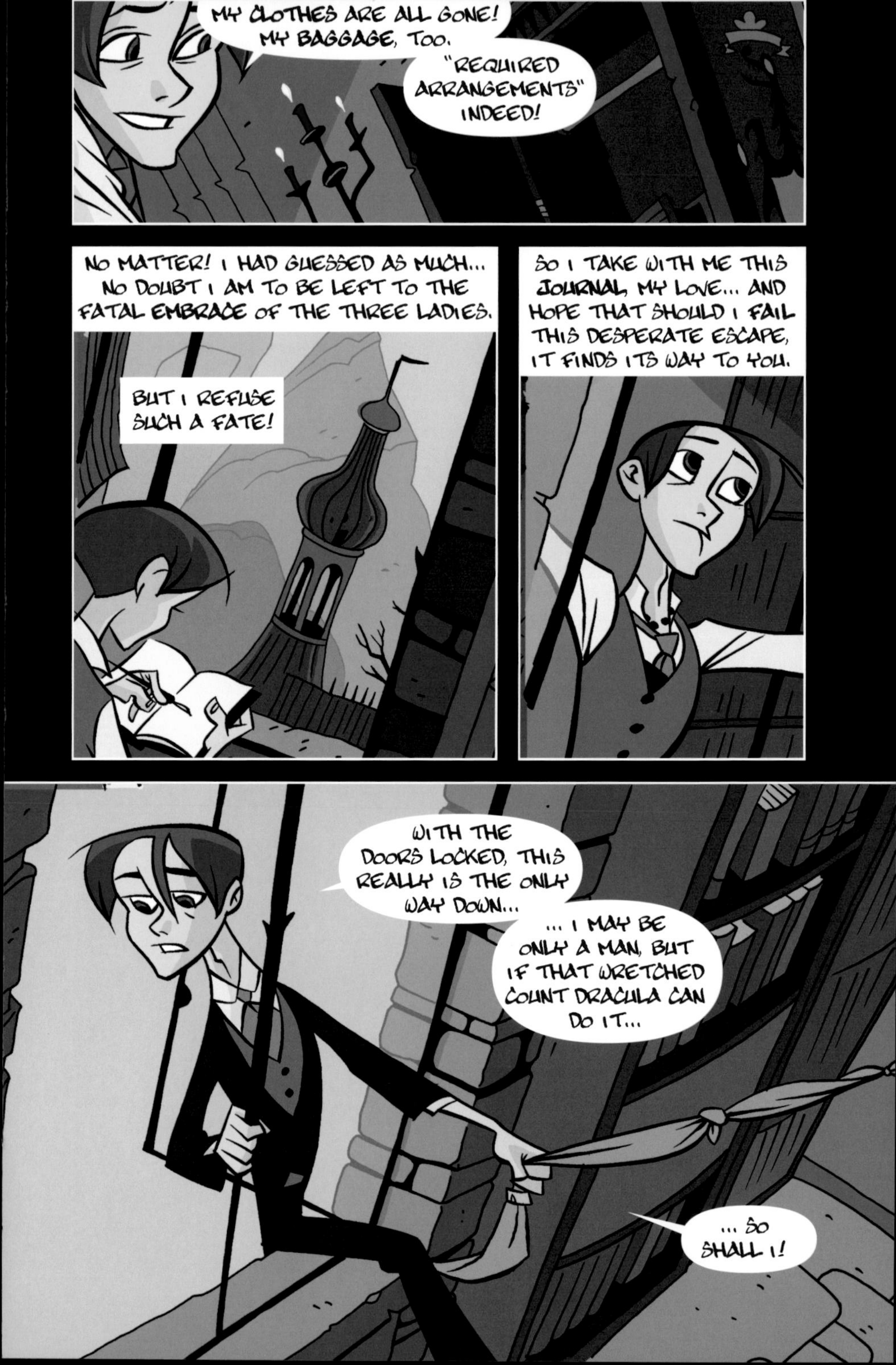
MY CLOTHES ARE ALL GONE! MY BAGGAGE, TOO.
"REQUIRED ARRANGEMENTS" INDEED!
NO MATTER! I HAD GUESSED AS MUCH... NO DOUBT I AM TO BE LEFT TO THE FATAL EMBRACE OF THE THREE LADIES.
BUT I REFUSE SUCH A FATE!
SO I TAKE WITH ME THIS JOURNAL, MY LOVE... AND HOPE THAT SHOULD I FAIL THIS DESPERATE ESCAPE, IT FINDS ITS WAY TO YOU.
WITH THE DOORS LOCKED, THIS REALLY IS THE ONLY WAY DOWN...
... I MAY BE ONLY A MAN, BUT IF THAT WRETCHED COUNT DRACULA CAN DO IT...
... SO SHALL I!

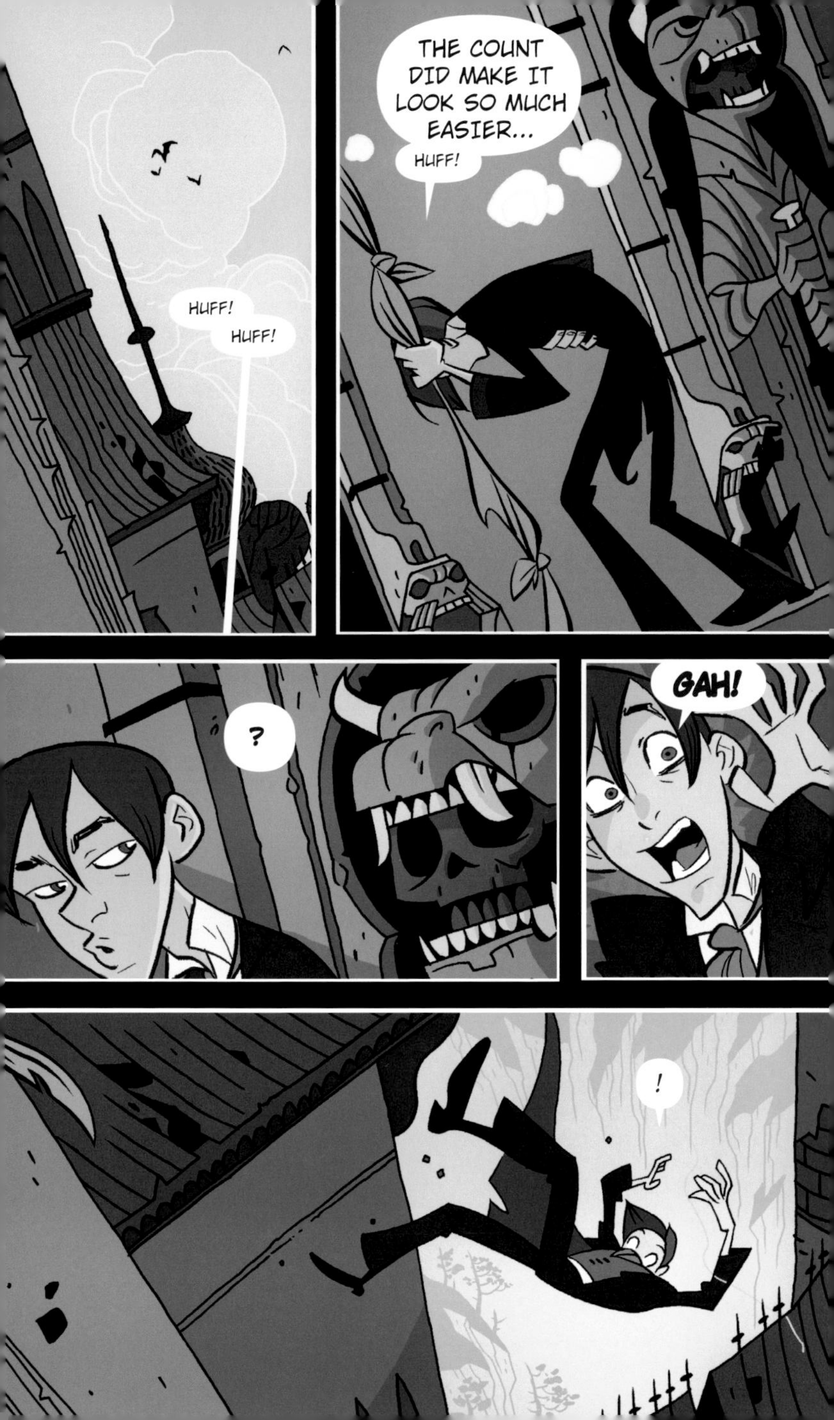
HUFF!
HUFF!
THE COUNT DID MAKE IT LOOK SO MUCH EASIER...
HUFF!
?
GAH!
!

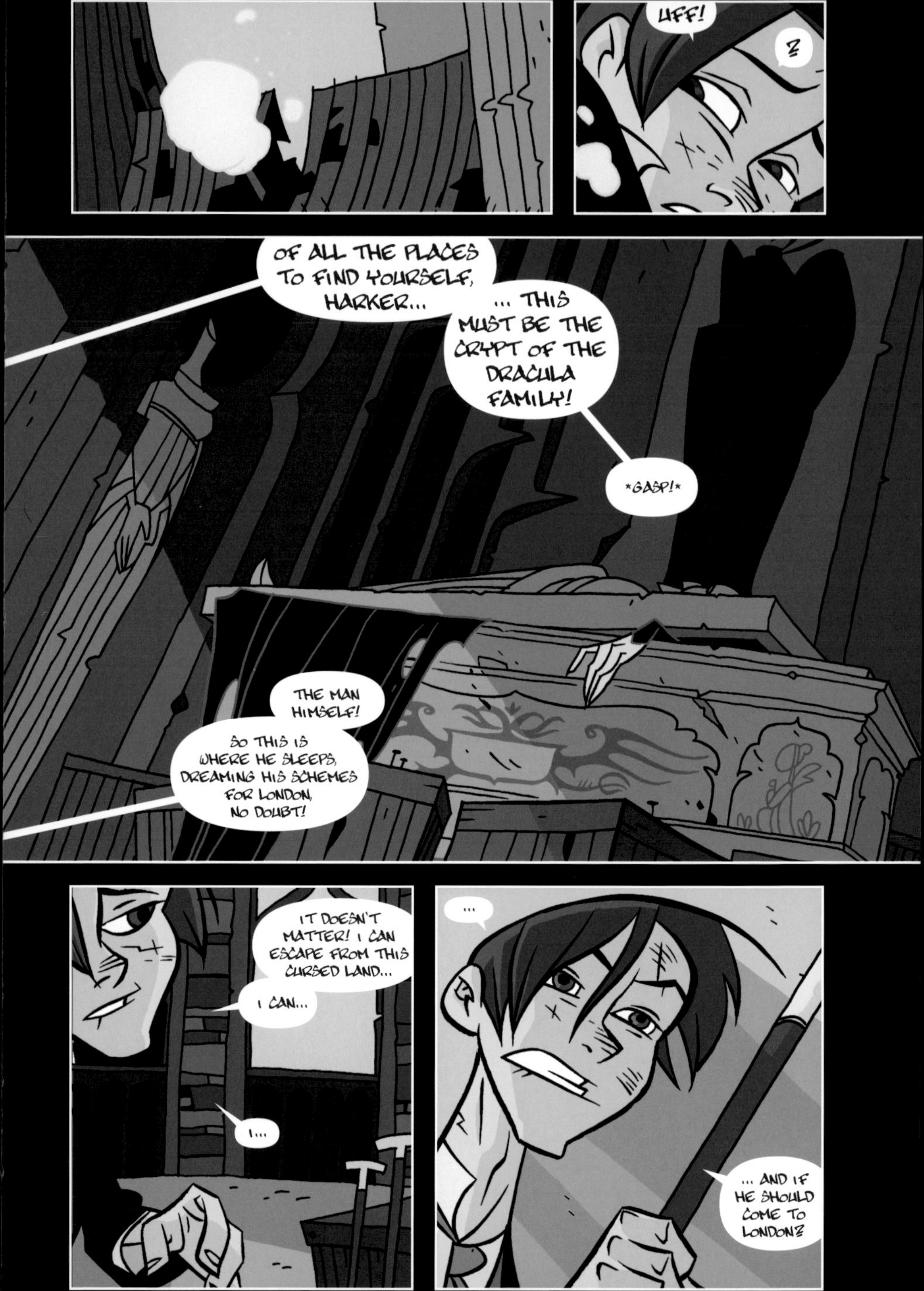
UFF!
?
OF ALL THE PLACES TO FIND YOURSELF, HARKER...
... THIS MUST BE THE CRYPT OF THE DRACULA FAMILY!
GASP!
THE MAN HIMSELF!
SO THIS IS WHERE HE SLEEPS, DREAMING HIS SCHEMES FOR LONDON, NO DOUBT!
IT DOESN'T MATTER! I CAN ESCAPE FROM THIS CURSED LAND...
I CAN...
I...
...
... AND IF HE SHOULD COME TO LONDON?

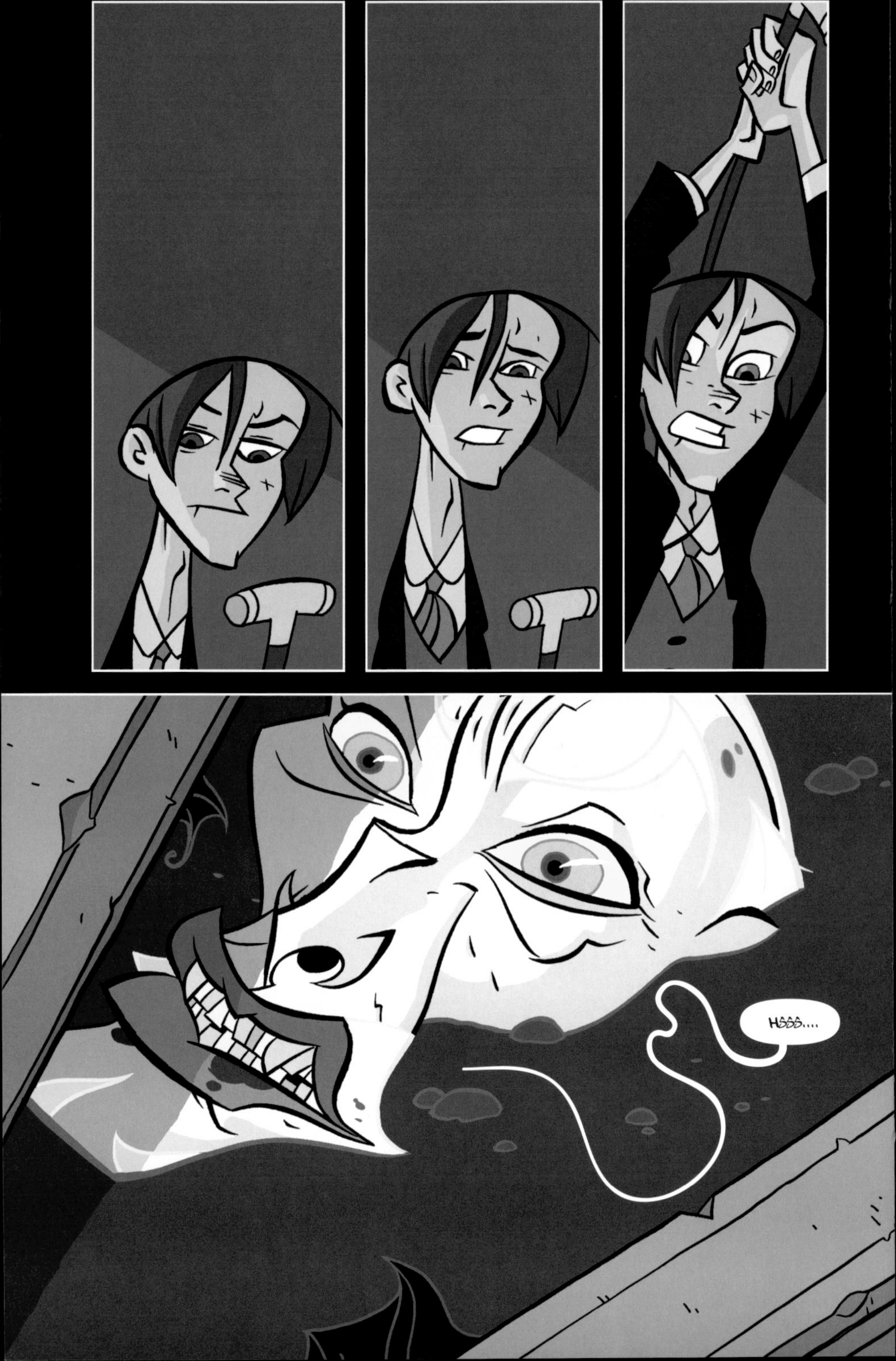
HSSS....

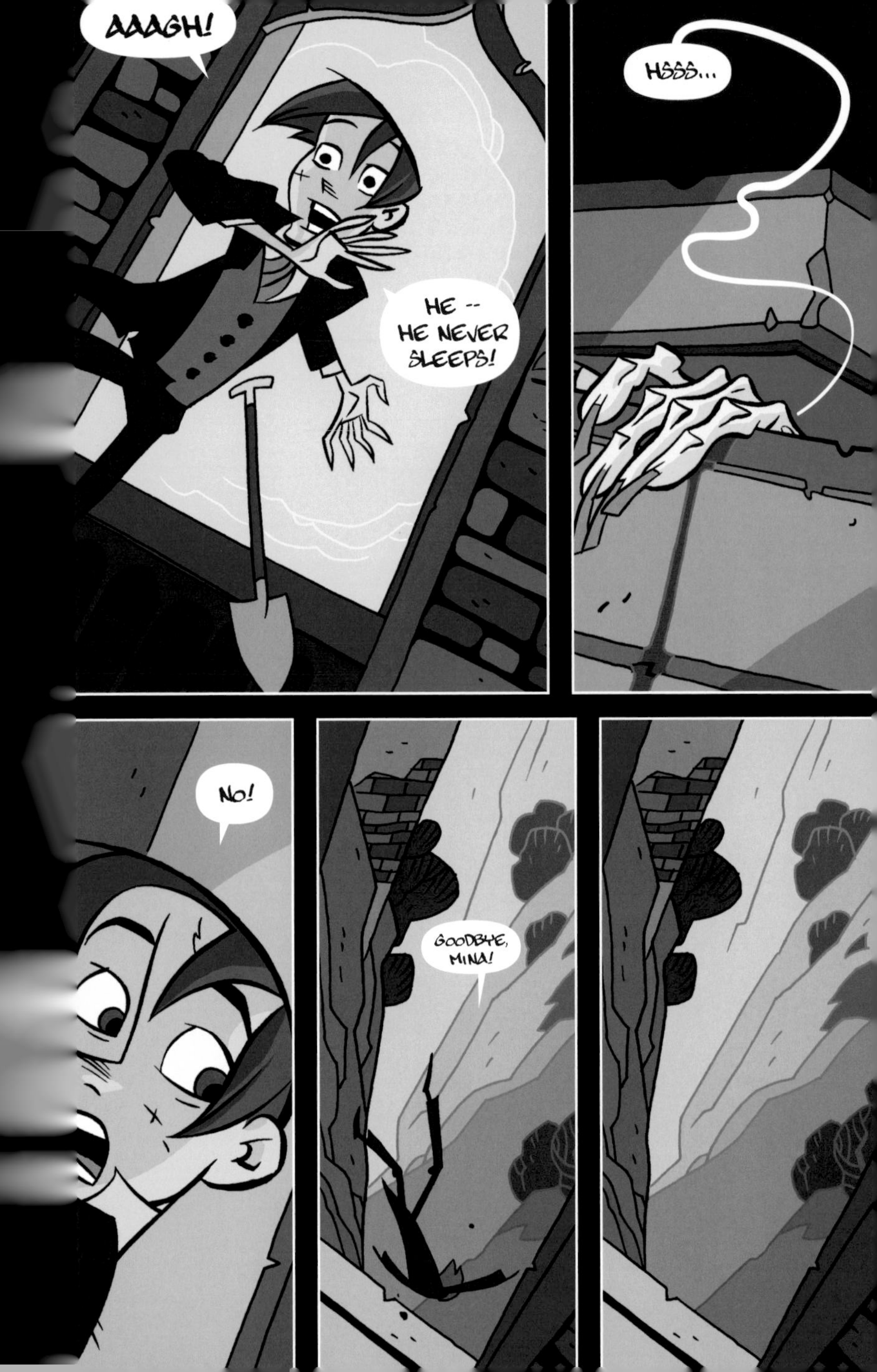
AAAGH!
HE -- HE NEVER SLEEPS!
HSSS...
NO!
GOODBYE, MINA!

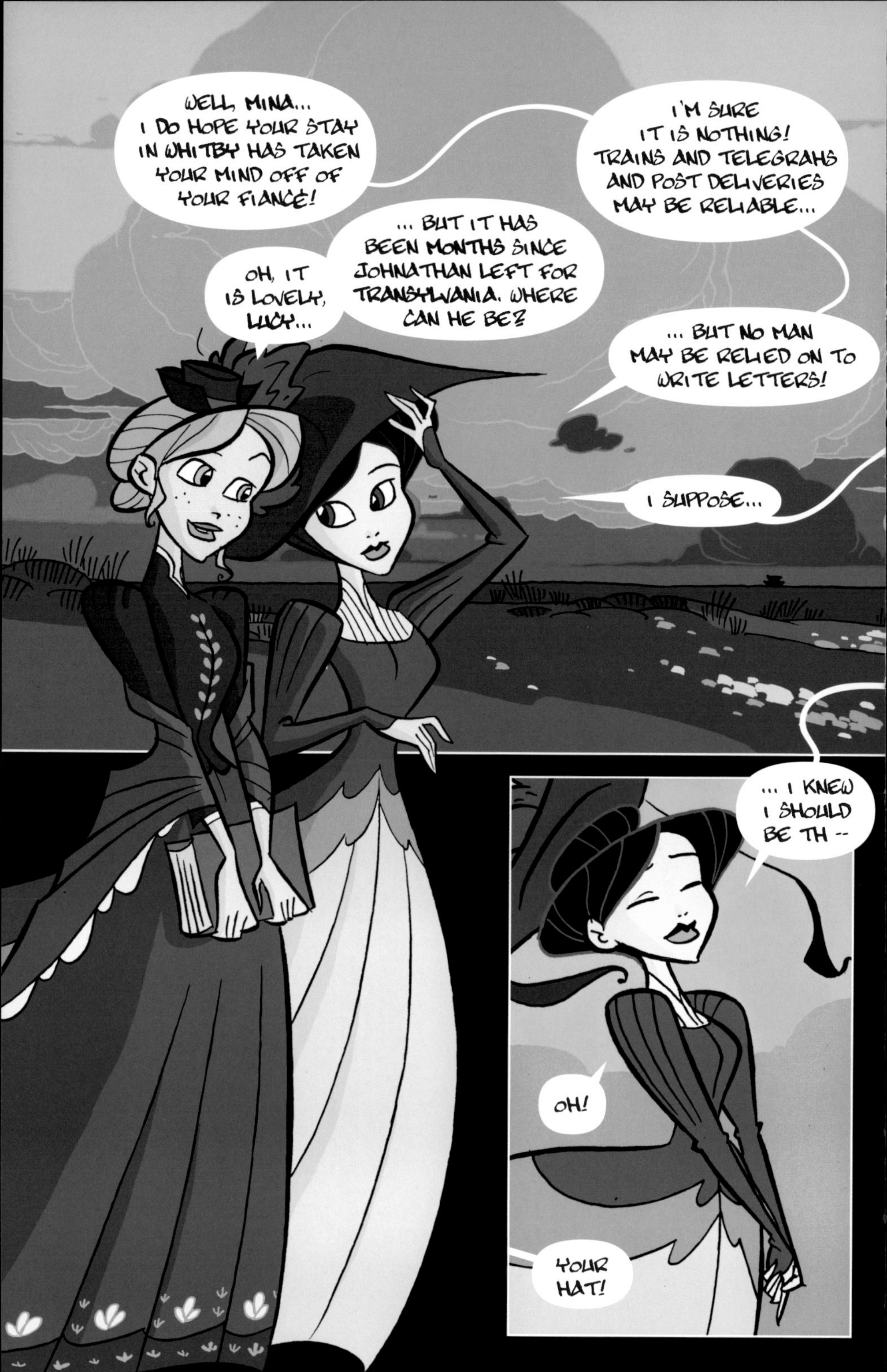
WELL, MINA...
I DO HOPE YOUR STAY IN WHITBY HAS TAKEN YOUR MIND OFF OF YOUR FIANCÉ!
OH, IT IS LOVELY, LUCY...
... BUT IT HAS BEEN MONTHS SINCE JOHNATHAN LEFT FOR TRANSYLVANIA. WHERE CAN HE BE?
I'M SURE IT IS NOTHING! TRAINS AND TELEGRAHS AND POST DELIVERIES MAY BE RELIABLE...
... BUT NO MAN MAY BE RELIED ON TO WRITE LETTERS!
I SUPPOSE...
... I KNEW I SHOULD BE TH --
OH!
YOUR HAT!

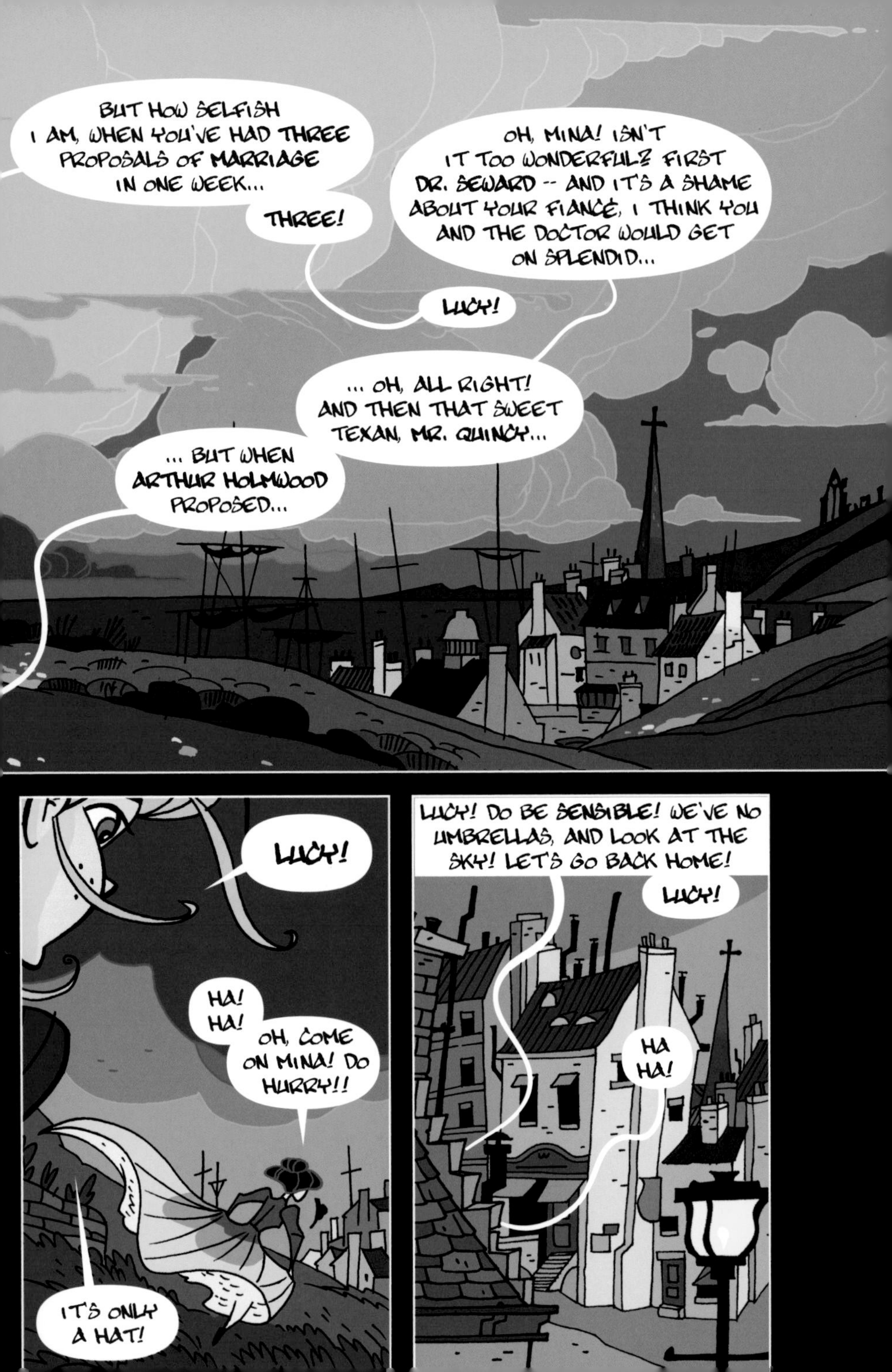
BUT HOW SELFISH I AM, WHEN YOU'VE HAD THREE PROPOSALS OF MARRIAGE IN ONE WEEK...
THREE!
OH, MINA! ISN'T IT TOO WONDERFUL? FIRST DR. SEWARD -- AND IT'S A SHAME ABOUT YOUR FIANCÉ, I THINK YOU AND THE DOCTOR WOULD GET ON SPLENDID...
LUCY!
... OH, ALL RIGHT! AND THEN THAT SWEET TEXAN, MR. QUINCY...
... BUT WHEN ARTHUR HOLMWOOD PROPOSED...
LUCY!
HA! HA!
OH, COME ON MINA! DO HURRY!!
IT'S ONLY A HAT!
LUCY! DO BE SENSIBLE! WE'VE NO UMBRELLAS, AND LOOK AT THE SKY! LET'S GO BACK HOME!
LUCY!
HA HA!

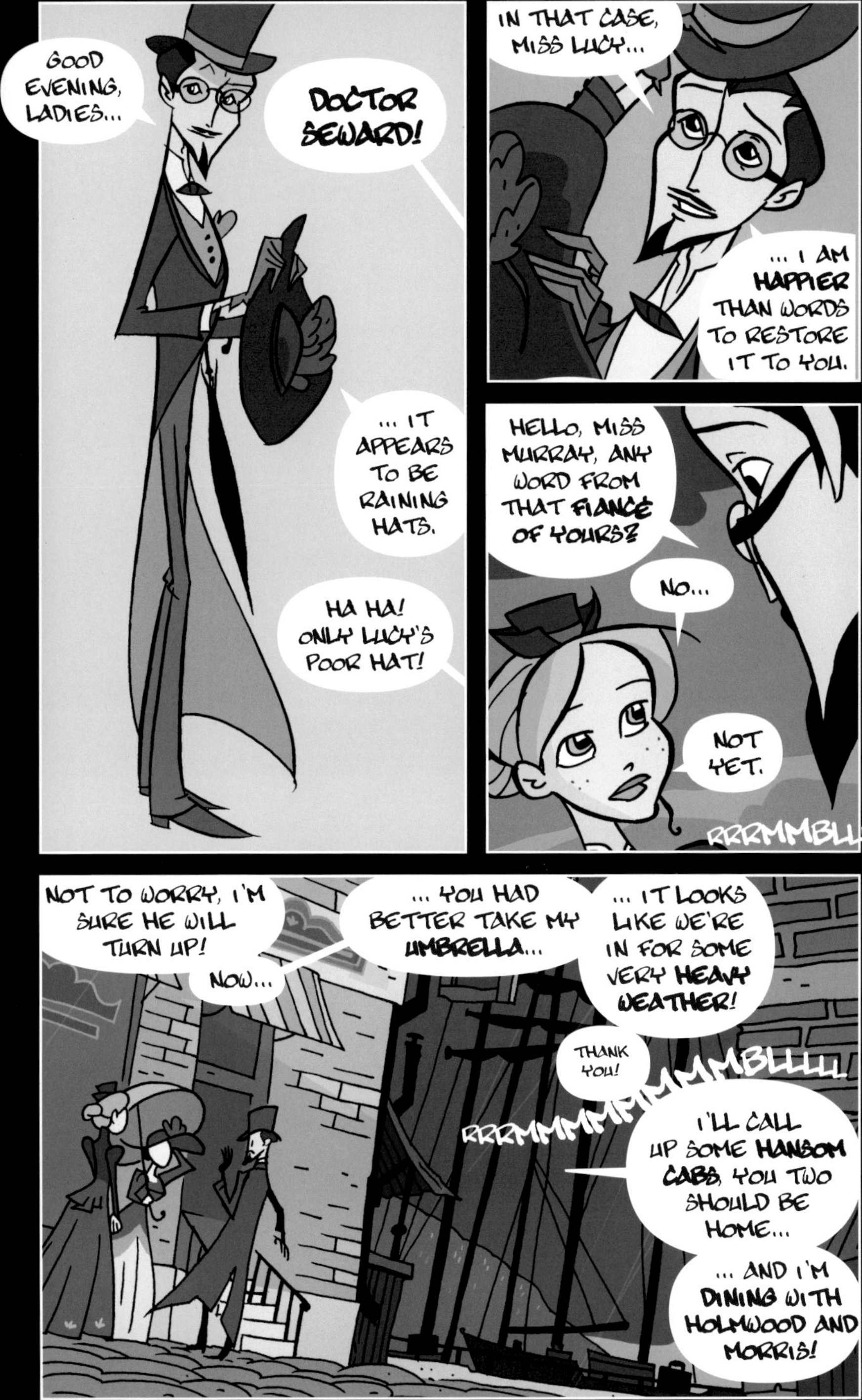
GOOD EVENING, LADIES...
DOCTOR SEWARD!
... IT APPEARS TO BE RAINING HATS.
HA HA! ONLY LUCY'S POOR HAT!
IN THAT CASE, MISS LUCY...
... I AM HAPPIER THAN WORDS TO RESTORE IT TO YOU.
HELLO, MISS MURRAY, ANY WORD FROM THAT FIANCÉ OF YOURS?
NO...
NOT YET.
RRRMMBLL
NOT TO WORRY, I'M SURE HE WILL TURN UP!
NOW...
... YOU HAD BETTER TAKE MY UMBRELLA...
... IT LOOKS LIKE WE'RE IN FOR SOME VERY HEAVY WEATHER!
THANK YOU!
RRRMMMMMMMMMMBLLLLL
I'LL CALL UP SOME HANSOM CABS, YOU TWO SHOULD BE HOME...
... AND I'M DINING WITH HOLMWOOD AND MORRIS!

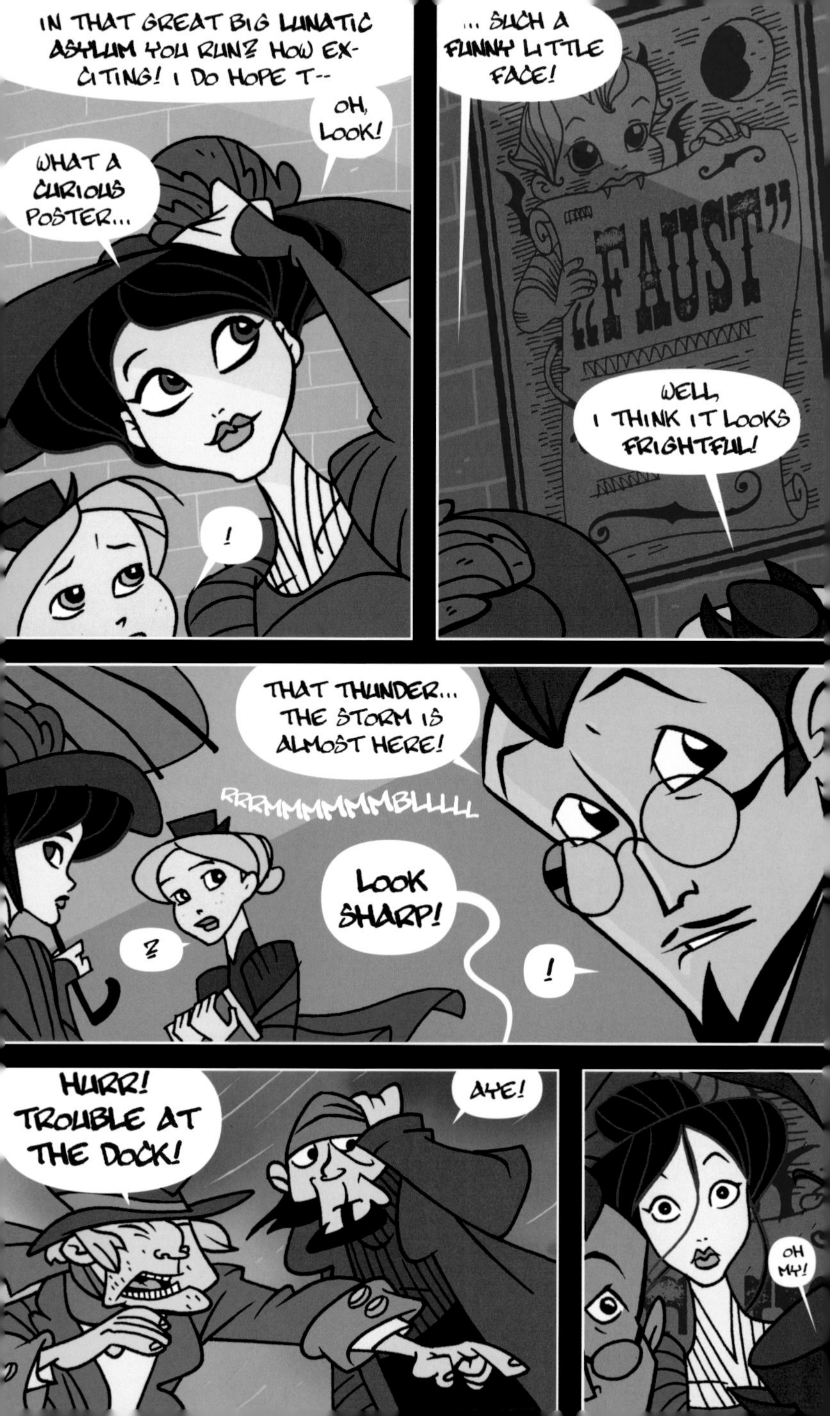
IN THAT GREAT BIG LUNATIC ASYLUM YOU RUN? HOW EXCITING! I DO HOPE T--
OH, LOOK!
WHAT A CURIOUS POSTER...
!
... SUCH A FUNNY LITTLE FACE!
"FAUST"
WELL, I THINK IT LOOKS FRIGHTFUL!
THAT THUNDER... THE STORM IS ALMOST HERE!
RRRMMMMMMBLLLLL
LOOK SHARP!
?
!
HURR! TROUBLE AT THE DOCK!
AYE!
OH MY!

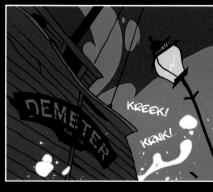

DEMETER

RUS...IA

KREEK!

KRNK!

KRASH!

DOUBLE QUICK!

BLASTED RAIN!

STEP LIVELY, LADS! THERE LOOKS TA' BE SURVIVORS! GRAB THEM LINES!

HEY!

WATCH THAT RIGGING! TIGHTER!

NOTHING BUT BOXES!

WAIT! OVER HERE!

DID... DID ANYONE JUST SEE THAT DOG?

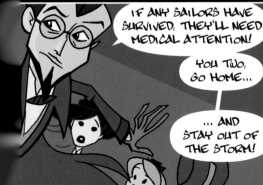

IF ANY SAILORS HAVE SURVIVED, THEY'LL NEED MEDICAL ATTENTION!

YOU TWO, GO HOME...

... AND STAY OUT OF THE STORM!

LET'S GO, LUCY...

LUCY?

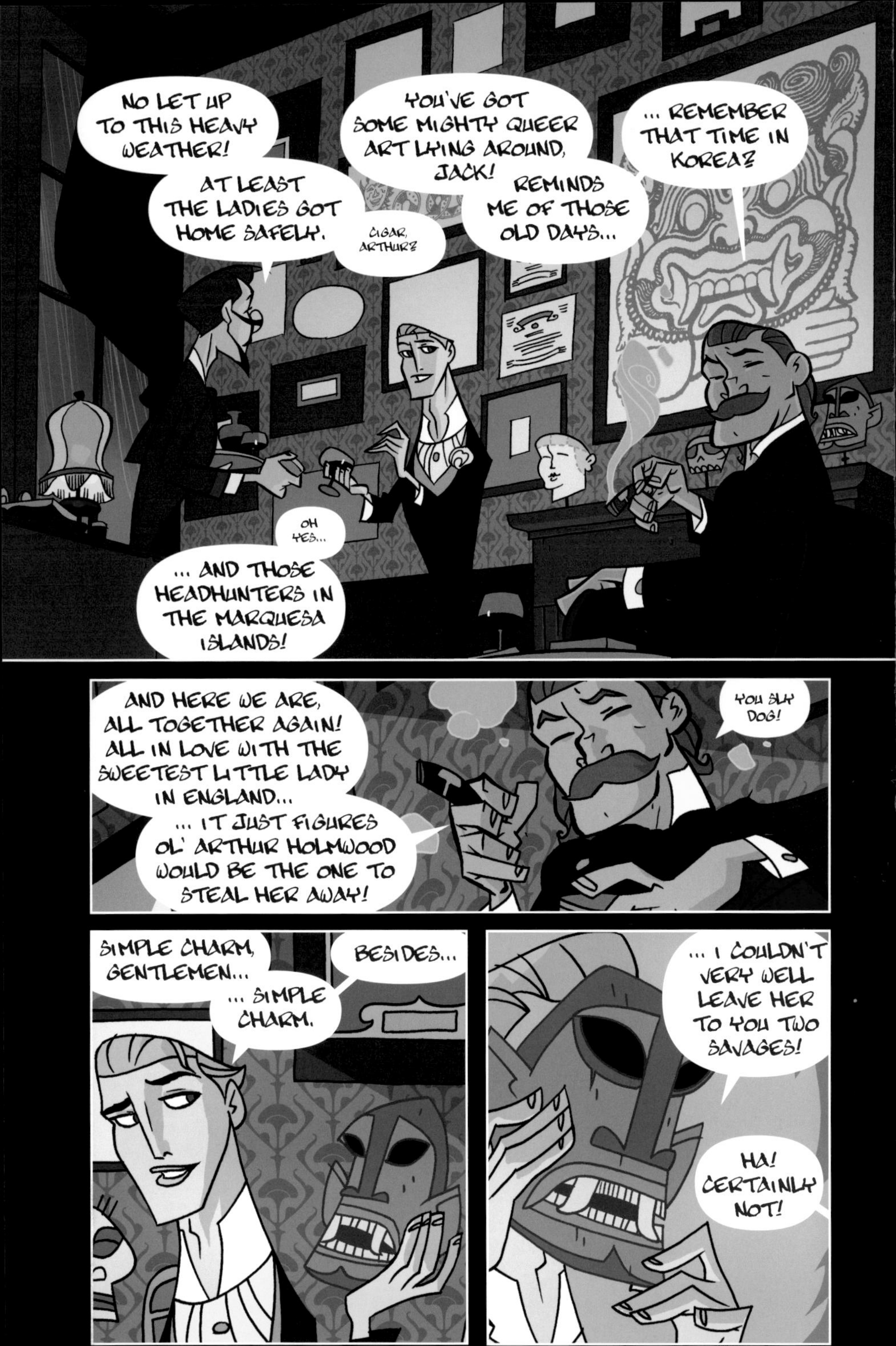
NO LET UP TO THIS HEAVY WEATHER!
AT LEAST THE LADIES GOT HOME SAFELY.
CIGAR, ARTHUR?
YOU'VE GOT SOME MIGHTY QUEER ART LYING AROUND, JACK!
REMINDS ME OF THOSE OLD DAYS...
... REMEMBER THAT TIME IN KOREA?
OH YES...
... AND THOSE HEADHUNTERS IN THE MARQUESA ISLANDS!
AND HERE WE ARE, ALL TOGETHER AGAIN! ALL IN LOVE WITH THE SWEETEST LITTLE LADY IN ENGLAND...
... IT JUST FIGURES OL' ARTHUR HOLMWOOD WOULD BE THE ONE TO STEAL HER AWAY!
YOU SLY DOG!
SIMPLE CHARM, GENTLEMEN...
... SIMPLE CHARM.
BESIDES...
... I COULDN'T VERY WELL LEAVE HER TO YOU TWO SAVAGES!
HA! CERTAINLY NOT!

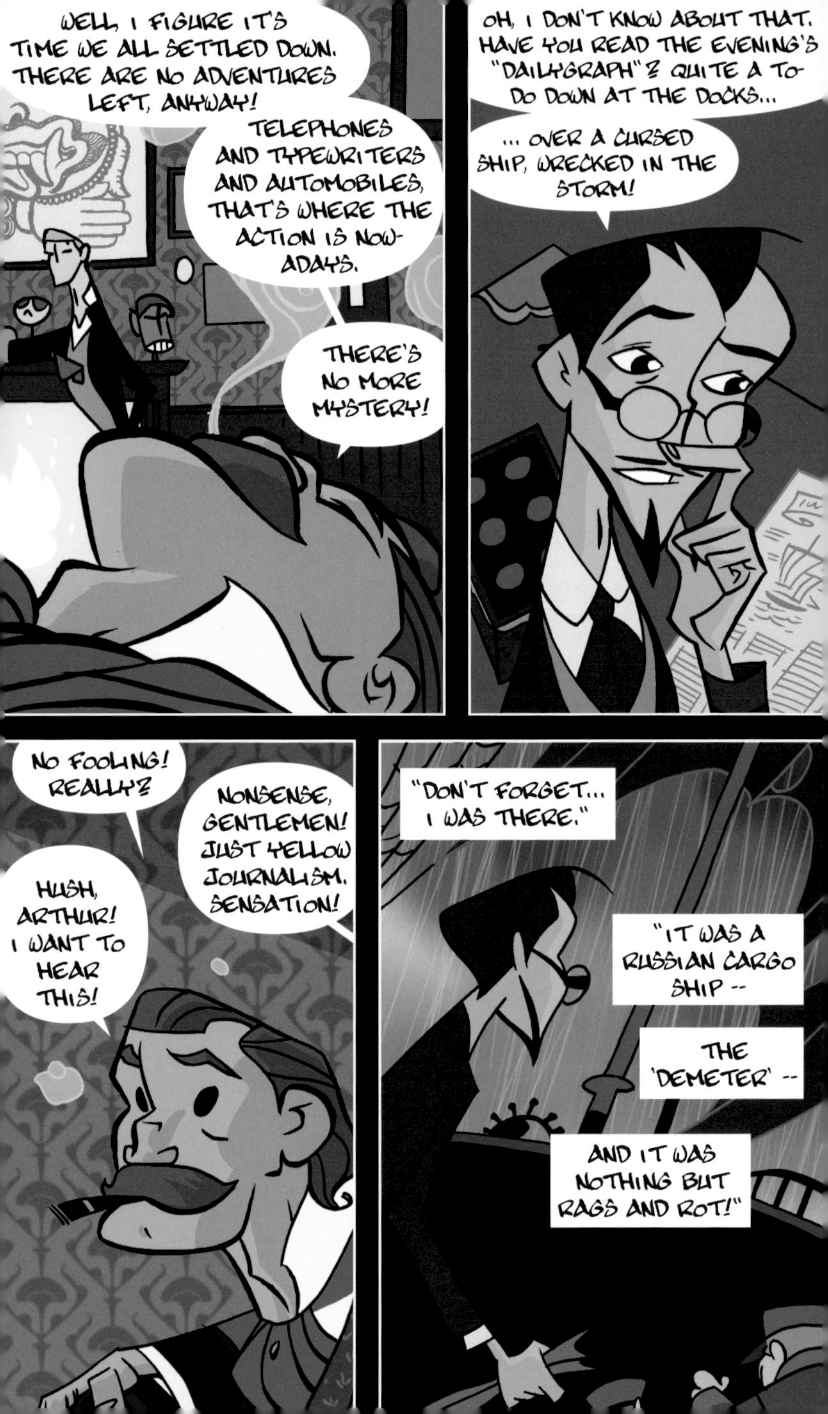
WELL, I FIGURE IT'S TIME WE ALL SETTLED DOWN. THERE ARE NO ADVENTURES LEFT, ANYWAY!
TELEPHONES AND TYPEWRITERS AND AUTOMOBILES, THAT'S WHERE THE ACTION IS NOW-ADAYS.
THERE'S NO MORE MYSTERY!
OH, I DON'T KNOW ABOUT THAT. HAVE YOU READ THE EVENING'S "DAILYGRAPH"? QUITE A TO-DO DOWN AT THE DOCKS...
... OVER A CURSED SHIP, WRECKED IN THE STORM!
NO FOOLING! REALLY?
NONSENSE, GENTLEMEN! JUST YELLOW JOURNALISM. SENSATION!
HUSH, ARTHUR! I WANT TO HEAR THIS!
"DON'T FORGET... I WAS THERE."
"IT WAS A RUSSIAN CARGO SHIP --
THE 'DEMETER' --
AND IT WAS NOTHING BUT RAGS AND ROT!"

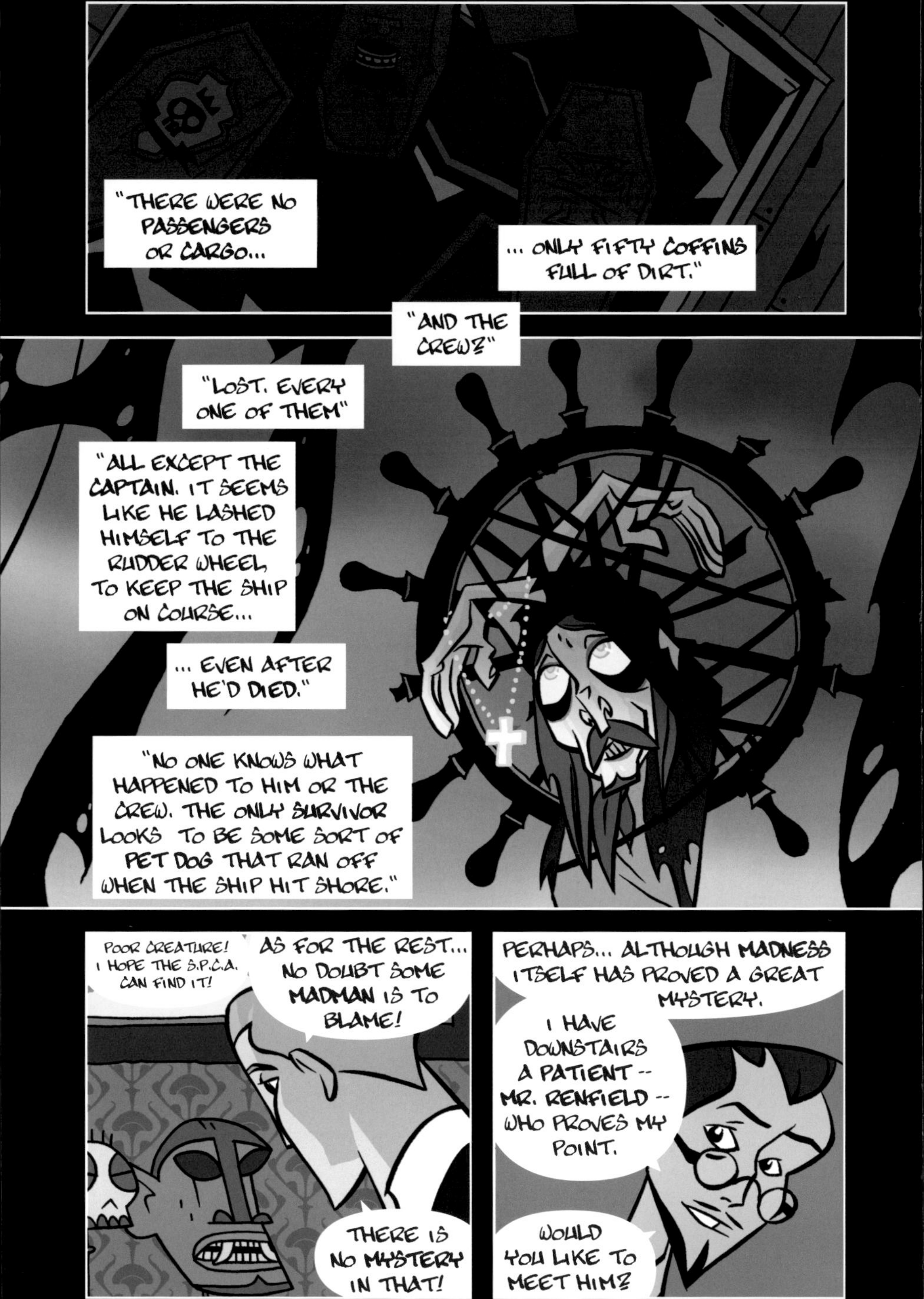
"THERE WERE NO PASSENGERS OR CARGO...
... ONLY FIFTY COFFINS FULL OF DIRT."
"AND THE CREW?"
"LOST. EVERY ONE OF THEM"
"ALL EXCEPT THE CAPTAIN. IT SEEMS LIKE HE LASHED HIMSELF TO THE RUDDER WHEEL, TO KEEP THE SHIP ON COURSE...
... EVEN AFTER HE'D DIED."
"NO ONE KNOWS WHAT HAPPENED TO HIM OR THE CREW. THE ONLY SURVIVOR LOOKS TO BE SOME SORT OF PET DOG THAT RAN OFF WHEN THE SHIP HIT SHORE."
POOR CREATURE! I HOPE THE S.P.C.A. CAN FIND IT!
AS FOR THE REST... NO DOUBT SOME MADMAN IS TO BLAME!
THERE IS NO MYSTERY IN THAT!
PERHAPS... ALTHOUGH MADNESS ITSELF HAS PROVED A GREAT MYSTERY.
I HAVE DOWNSTAIRS A PATIENT -- MR. RENFIELD -- WHO PROVES MY POINT.
WOULD YOU LIKE TO MEET HIM?

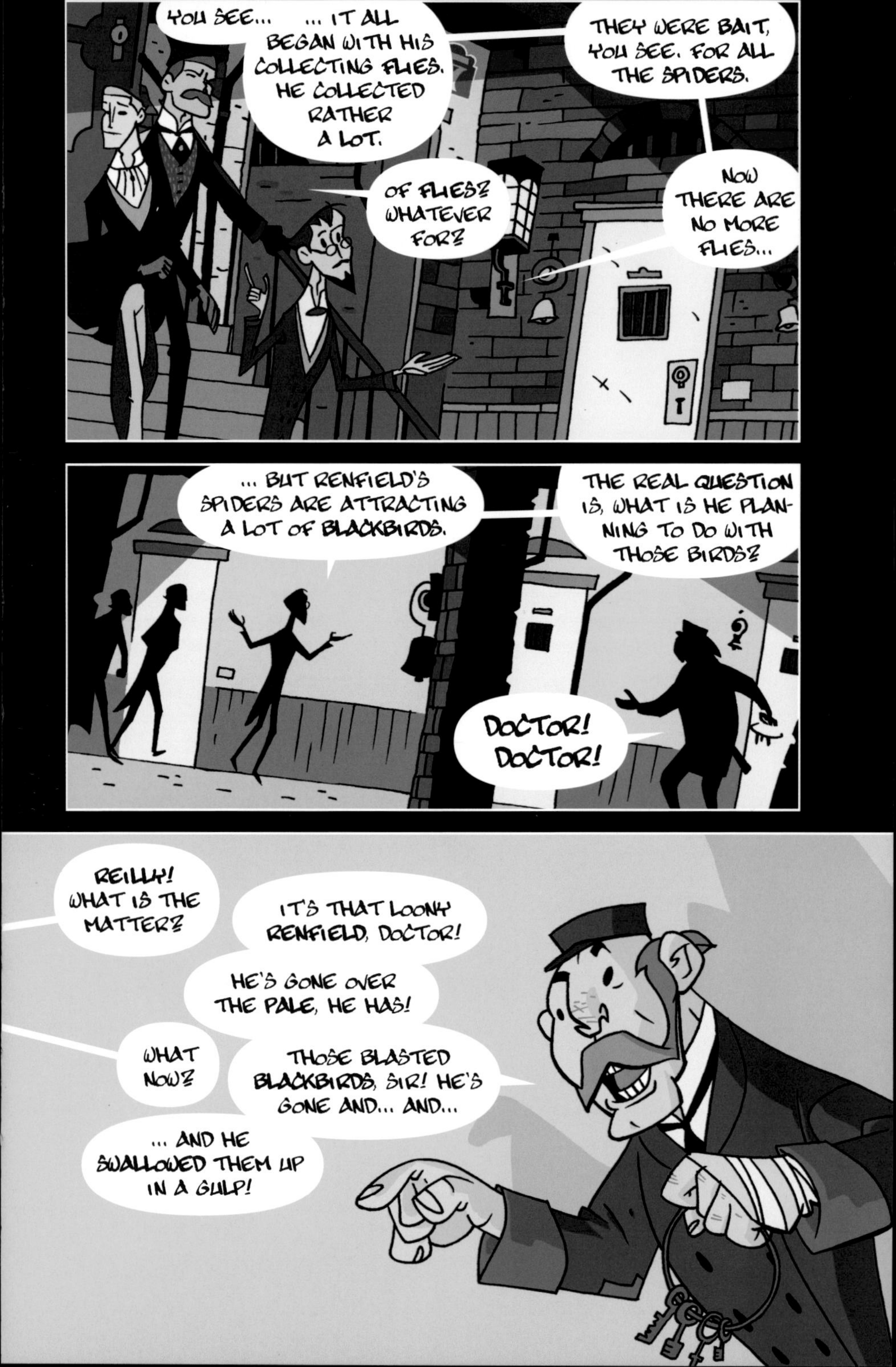
YOU SEE... ... IT ALL BEGAN WITH HIS COLLECTING FLIES. HE COLLECTED RATHER A LOT.
OF FLIES? WHATEVER FOR?
THEY WERE BAIT, YOU SEE. FOR ALL THE SPIDERS.
NOW THERE ARE NO MORE FLIES...
... BUT RENFIELD'S SPIDERS ARE ATTRACTING A LOT OF BLACKBIRDS.
THE REAL QUESTION IS, WHAT IS HE PLAN-NING TO DO WITH THOSE BIRDS?
DOCTOR! DOCTOR!
REILLY! WHAT IS THE MATTER?
IT'S THAT LOONY RENFIELD, DOCTOR!
HE'S GONE OVER THE PALE, HE HAS!
WHAT NOW?
THOSE BLASTED BLACKBIRDS, SIR! HE'S GONE AND... AND...
... AND HE SWALLOWED THEM UP IN A GULP!

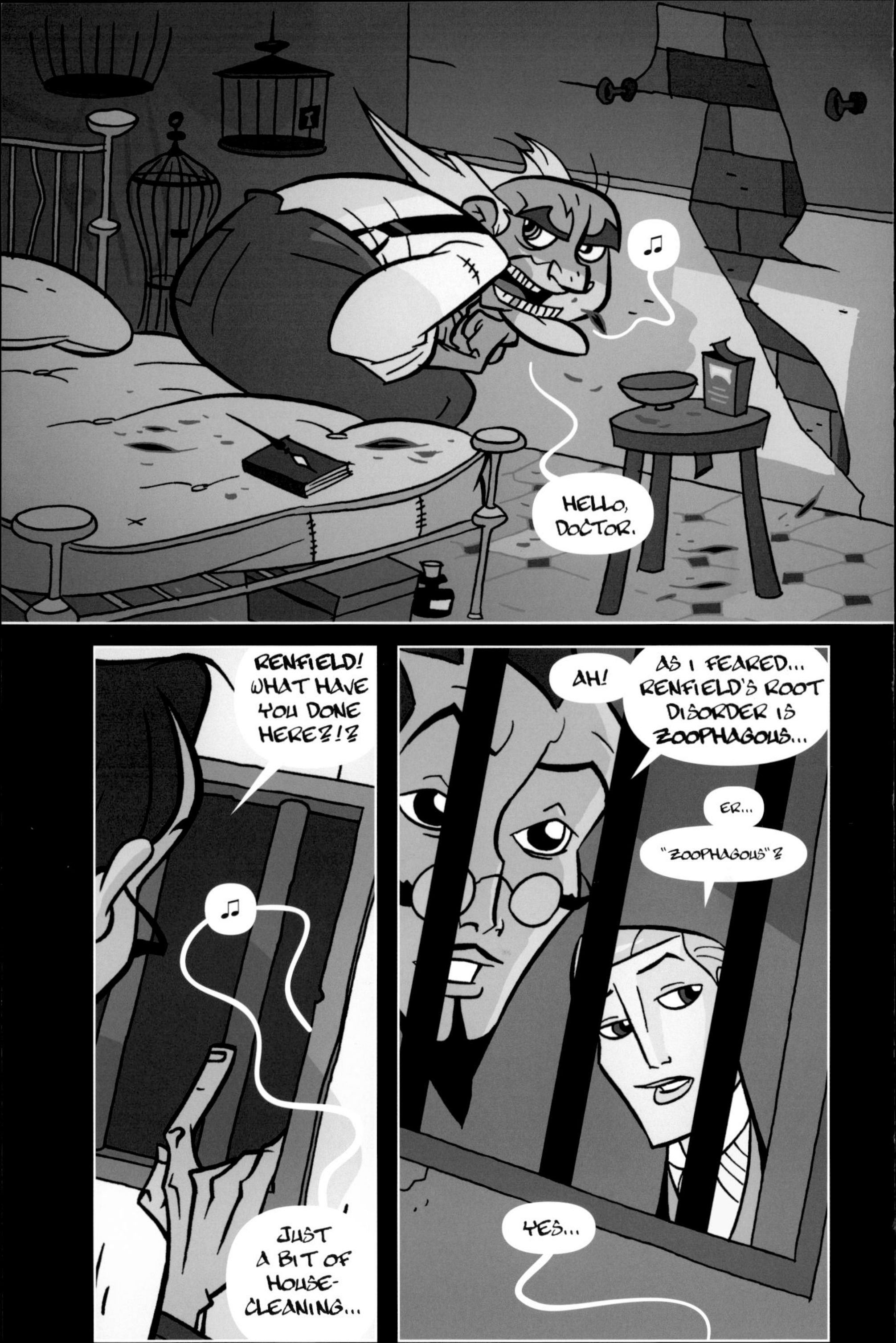
♫
HELLO, DOCTOR.
RENFIELD! WHAT HAVE YOU DONE HERE?!?
♫
JUST A BIT OF HOUSE-CLEANING...
AH!
AS I FEARED... RENFIELD'S ROOT DISORDER IS ZOOPHAGOUS...
ER...
"ZOOPHAGOUS"?
YES...

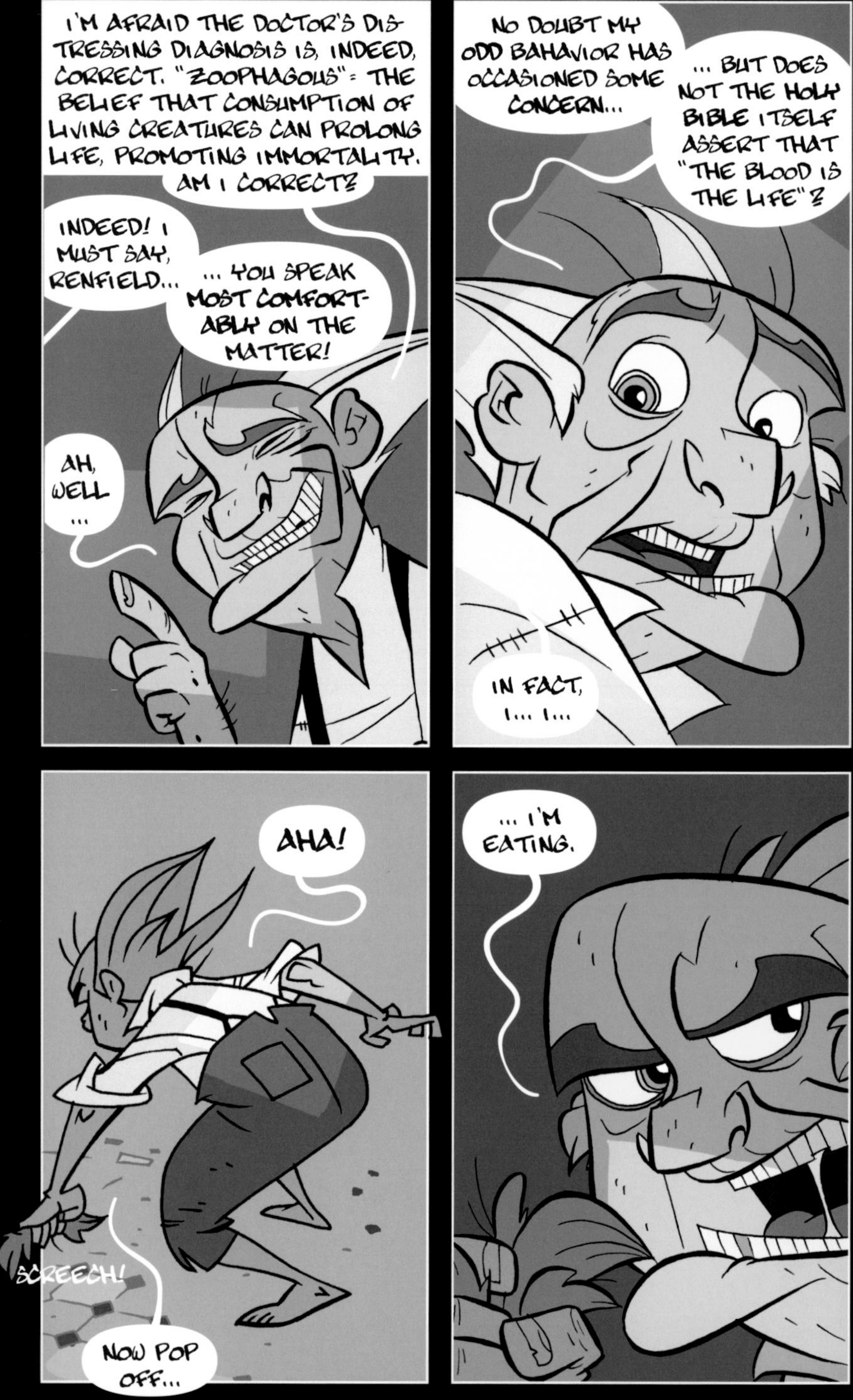
I'M AFRAID THE DOCTOR'S DIS-TRESSING DIAGNOSIS IS, INDEED, CORRECT. "ZOOPHAGOUS" = THE BELIEF THAT CONSUMPTION OF LIVING CREATURES CAN PROLONG LIFE, PROMOTING IMMORTALITY. AM I CORRECT?
INDEED! I MUST SAY, RENFIELD...
... YOU SPEAK MOST COMFORT-ABLY ON THE MATTER!
AH, WELL ...
NO DOUBT MY ODD BAHAVIOR HAS OCCASIONED SOME CONCERN...
... BUT DOES NOT THE HOLY BIBLE ITSELF ASSERT THAT "THE BLOOD IS THE LIFE"?
IN FACT, I... I...
AHA!
SCREECH!
NOW POP OFF...
... I'M EATING.

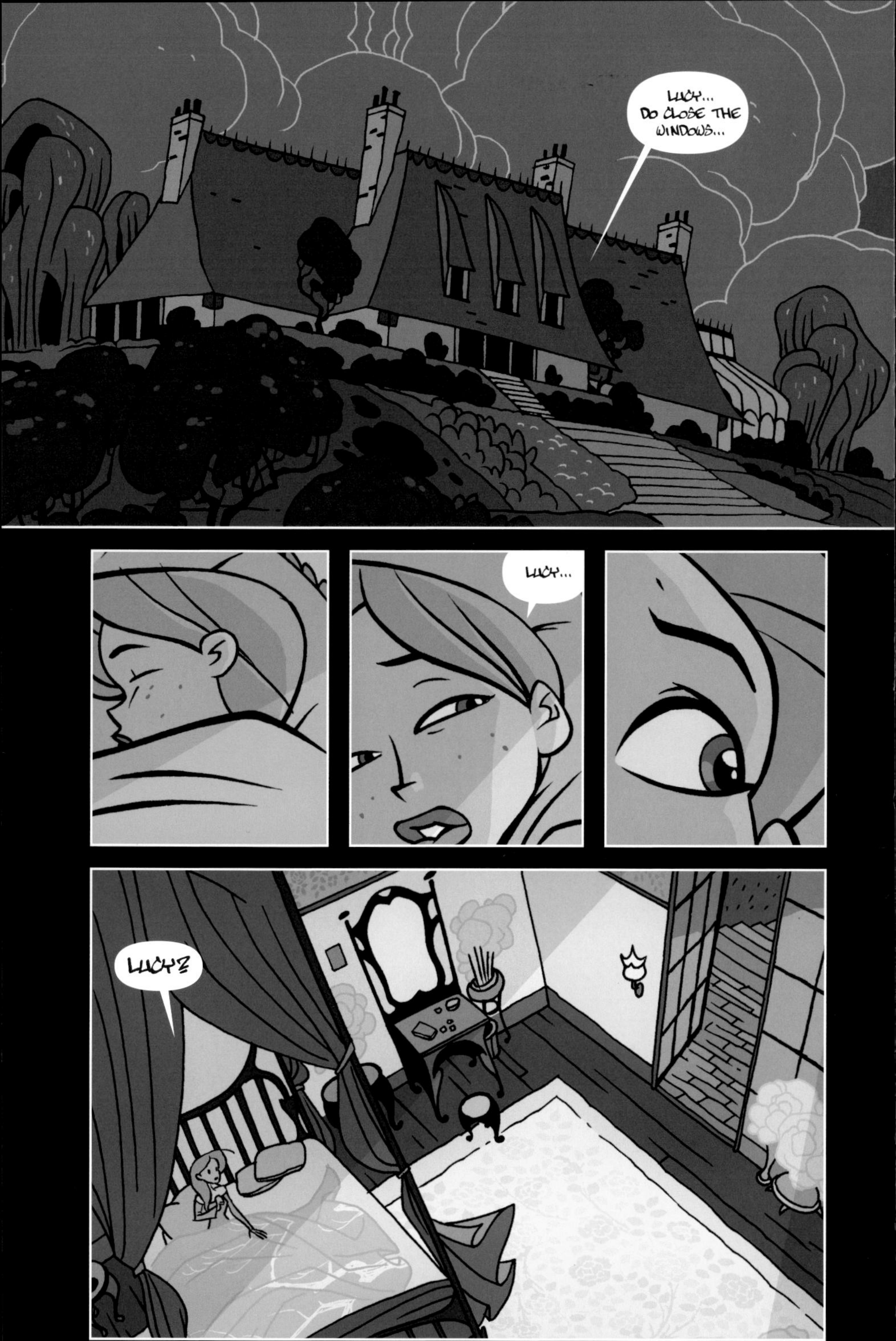
LUCY... DO CLOSE THE WINDOWS...
LUCY...
LUCY?

OH, DEAR!

IF SHE'S BEEN SLEEPWALKING AGAIN, SHE MIGHT BE ANYWHERE!

AT LEAST IT SHOULD BE EASY TO SPOT HER IN THIS MOONLIGHT...

YAWN!

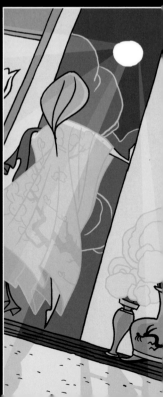

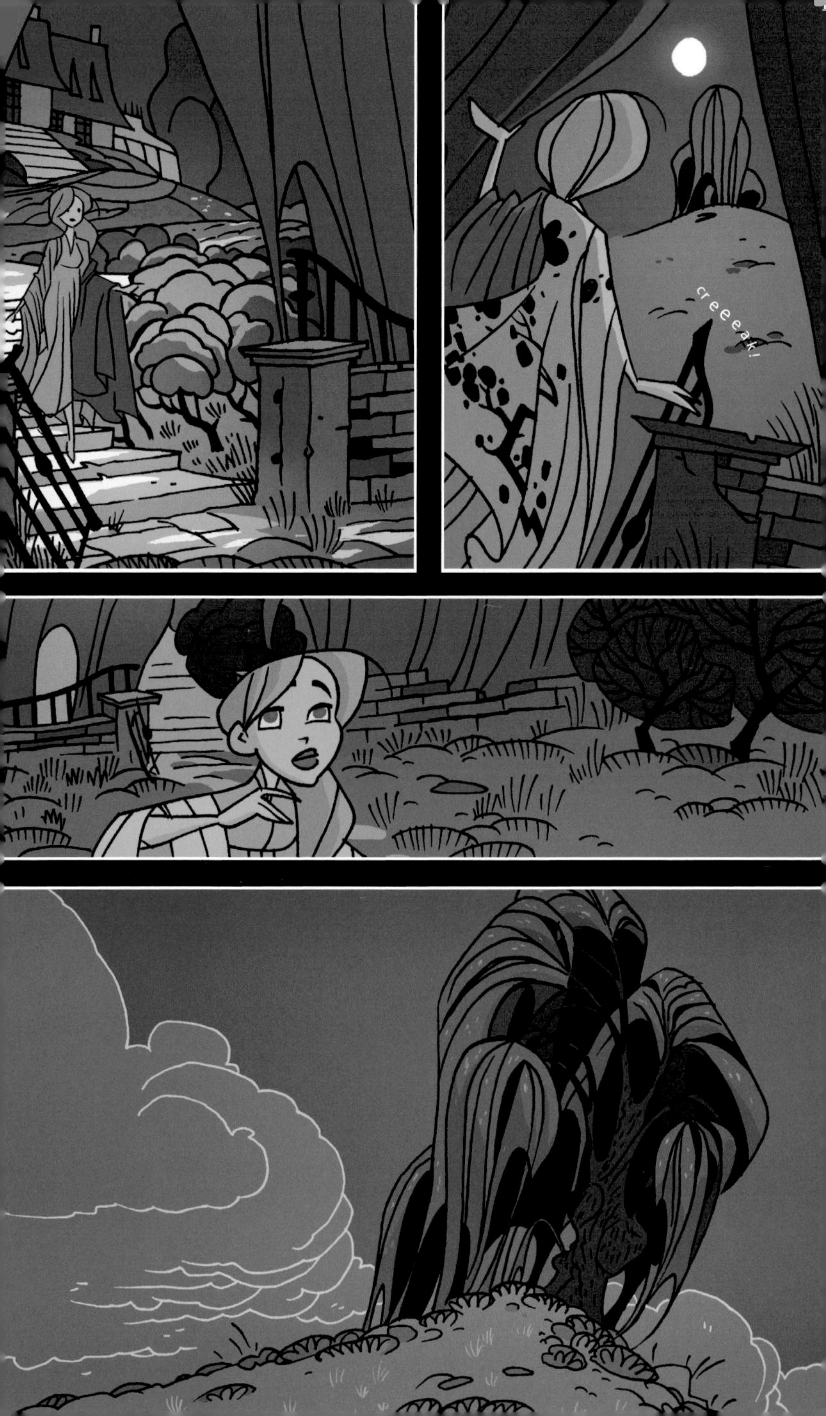
creeeak!

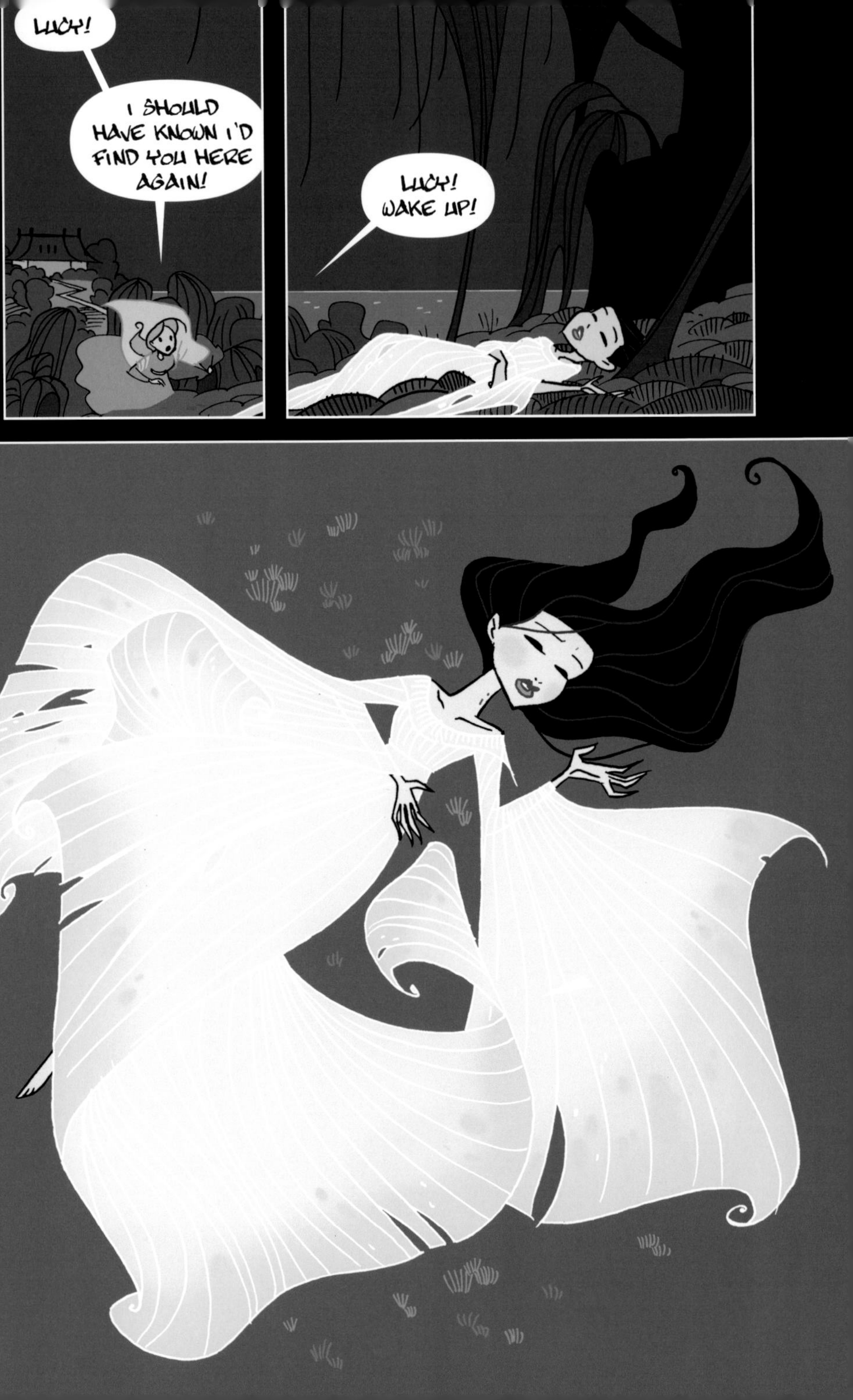
LUCY!
I SHOULD HAVE KNOWN I'D FIND YOU HERE AGAIN!
LUCY! WAKE UP!

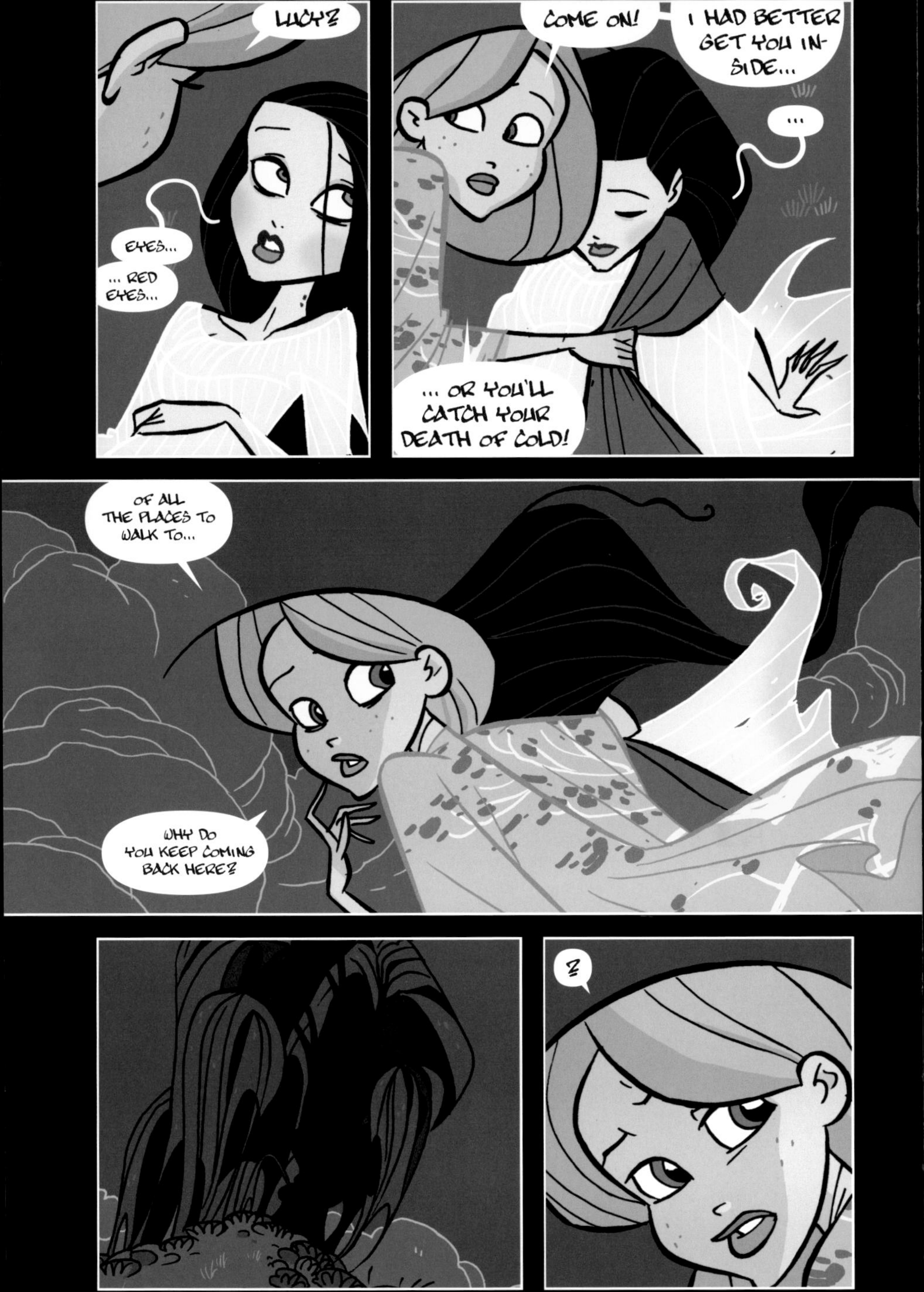
LUCY?
EYES...
... RED EYES...
COME ON!
I HAD BETTER GET YOU IN-SIDE...
...
... OR YOU'LL CATCH YOUR DEATH OF COLD!
OF ALL THE PLACES TO WALK TO...
WHY DO YOU KEEP COMING BACK HERE?
?

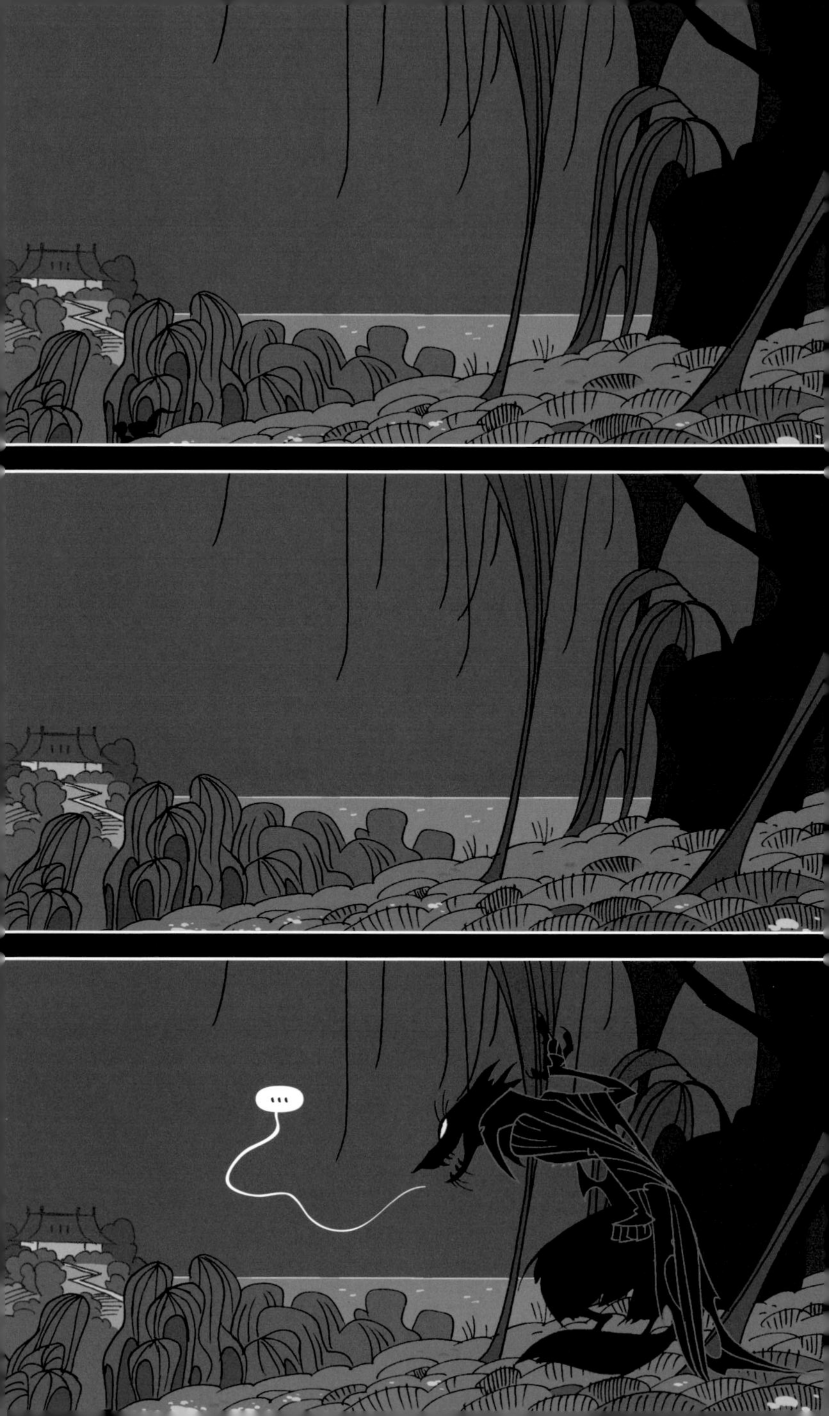
...

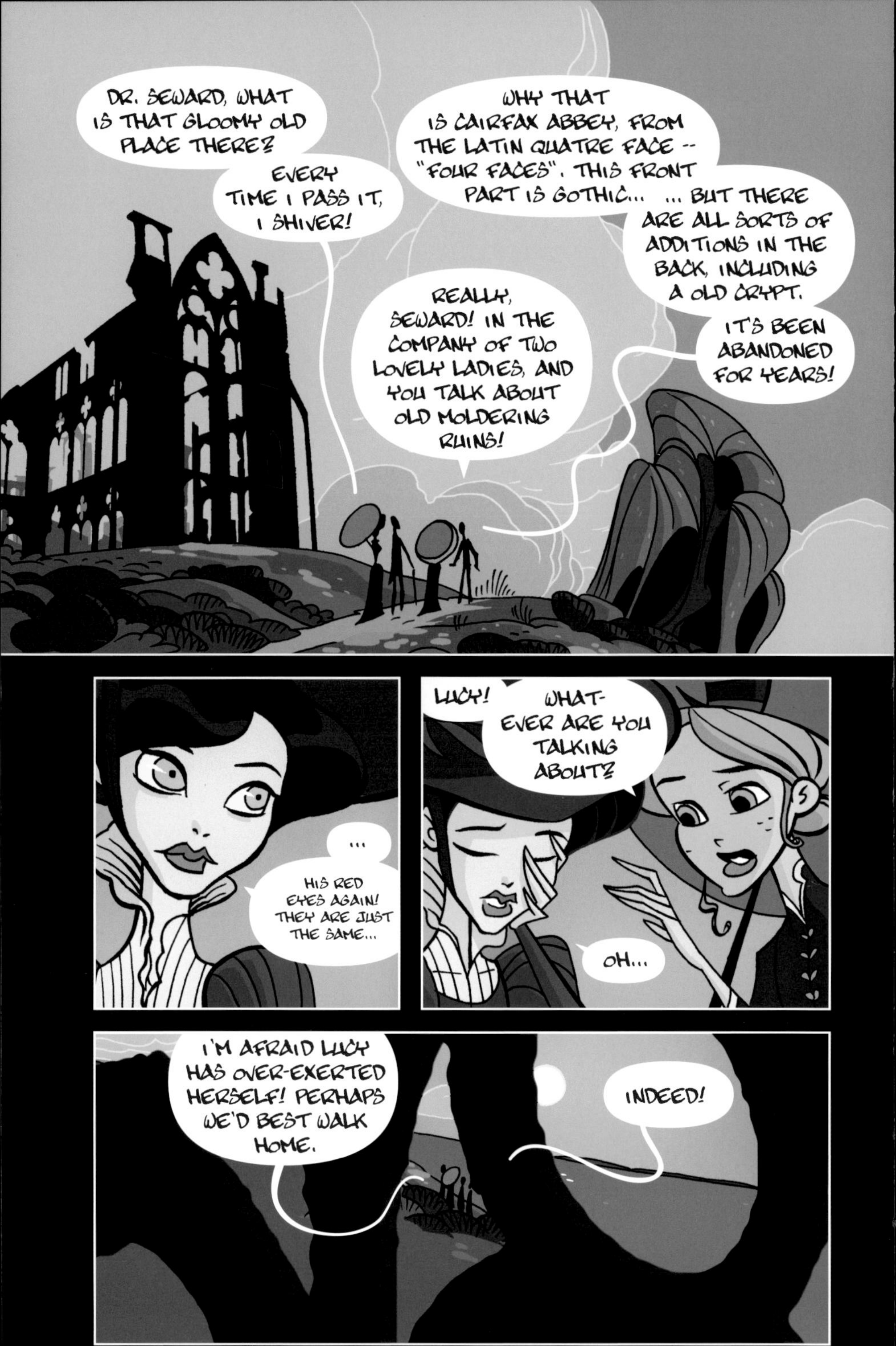
DR. SEWARD, WHAT IS THAT GLOOMY OLD PLACE THERE?
EVERY TIME I PASS IT, I SHIVER!
WHY THAT IS CAIRFAX ABBEY, FROM THE LATIN QUATRE FACE -- "FOUR FACES". THIS FRONT PART IS GOTHIC...
... BUT THERE ARE ALL SORTS OF ADDITIONS IN THE BACK, INCLUDING A OLD CRYPT.
IT'S BEEN ABANDONED FOR YEARS!
REALLY, SEWARD! IN THE COMPANY OF TWO LOVELY LADIES, AND YOU TALK ABOUT OLD MOLDERING RUINS!
...
HIS RED EYES AGAIN! THEY ARE JUST THE SAME...
LUCY!
WHATEVER ARE YOU TALKING ABOUT?
OH...
I'M AFRAID LUCY HAS OVER-EXERTED HERSELF! PERHAPS WE'D BEST WALK HOME.
INDEED!

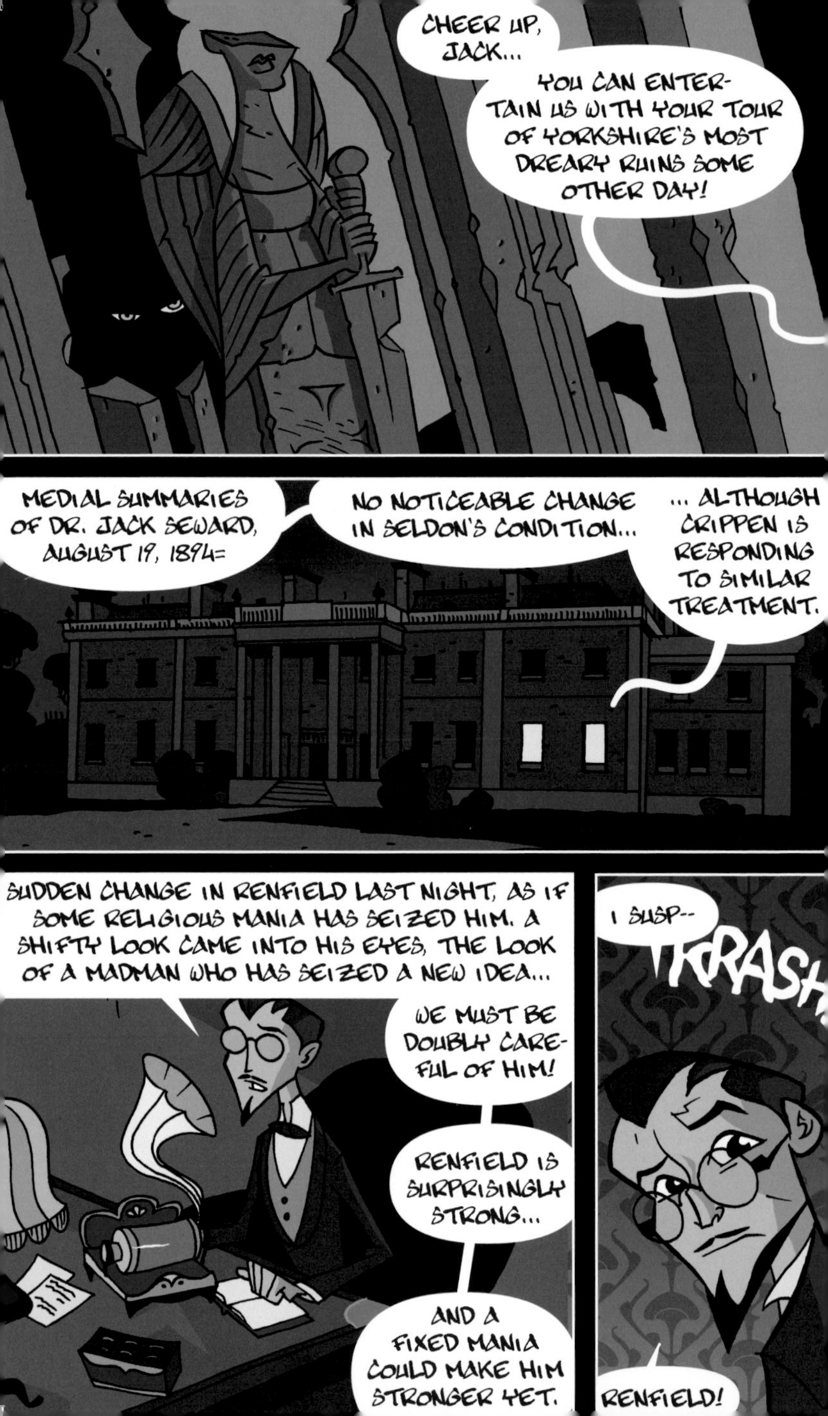
CHEER UP, JACK...
YOU CAN ENTERTAIN US WITH YOUR TOUR OF YORKSHIRE'S MOST DREARY RUINS SOME OTHER DAY!
MEDIAL SUMMARIES OF DR. JACK SEWARD, AUGUST 19, 1894=
NO NOTICEABLE CHANGE IN SELDON'S CONDITION...
... ALTHOUGH CRIPPEN IS RESPONDING TO SIMILAR TREATMENT.
SUDDEN CHANGE IN RENFIELD LAST NIGHT, AS IF SOME RELIGIOUS MANIA HAS SEIZED HIM. A SHIFTY LOOK CAME INTO HIS EYES, THE LOOK OF A MADMAN WHO HAS SEIZED A NEW IDEA...
WE MUST BE DOUBLY CAREFUL OF HIM!
RENFIELD IS SURPRISINGLY STRONG...
AND A FIXED MANIA COULD MAKE HIM STRONGER YET.
I SUSP--
KRASH
RENFIELD!

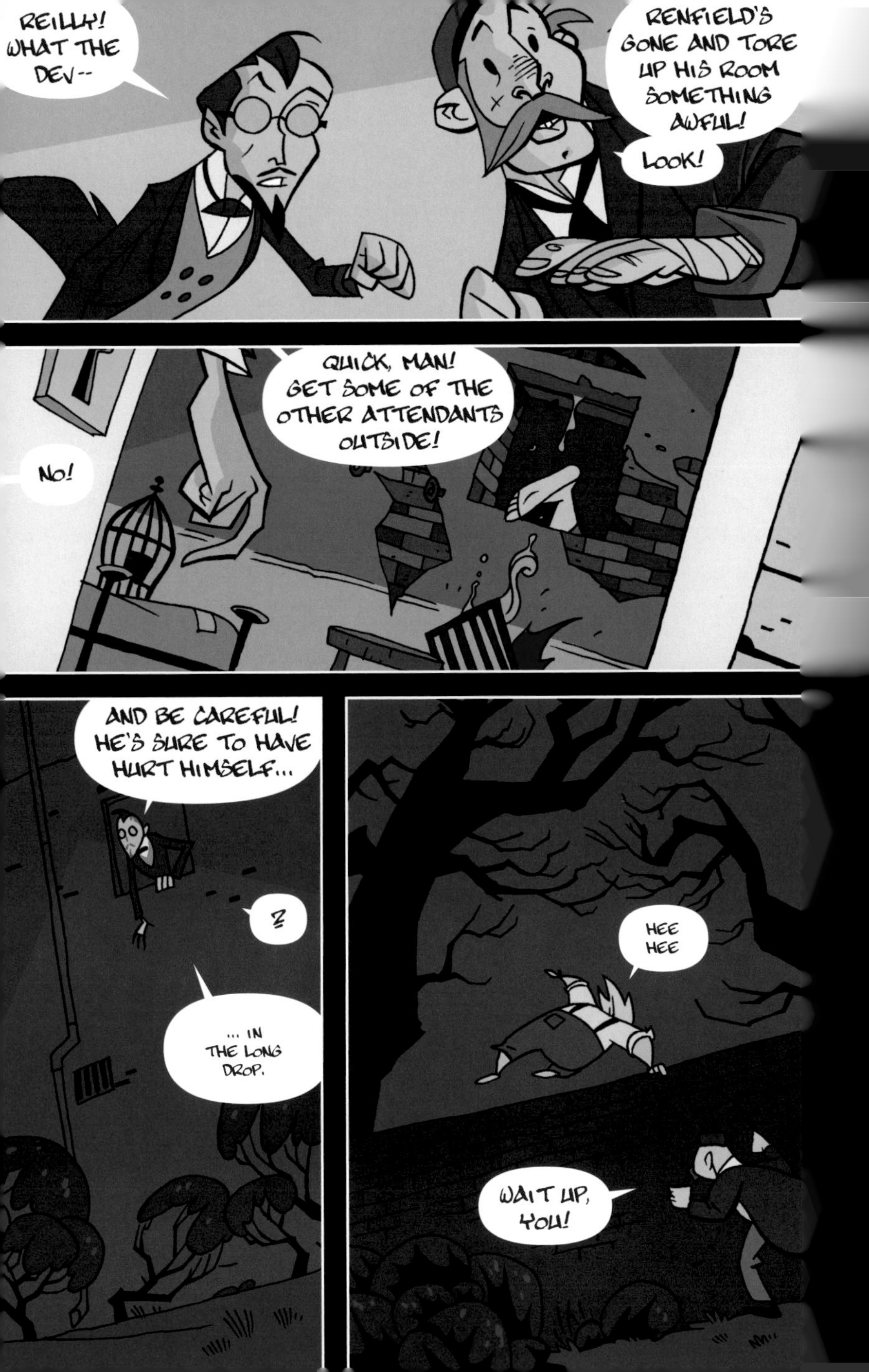
REILLY! WHAT THE DEV--
RENFIELD'S GONE AND TORE UP HIS ROOM SOMETHING AWFUL!
LOOK!
QUICK, MAN! GET SOME OF THE OTHER ATTENDANTS OUTSIDE!
NO!
AND BE CAREFUL! HE'S SURE TO HAVE HURT HIMSELF...
?
... IN THE LONG DROP.
HEE HEE
WAIT UP, YOU!

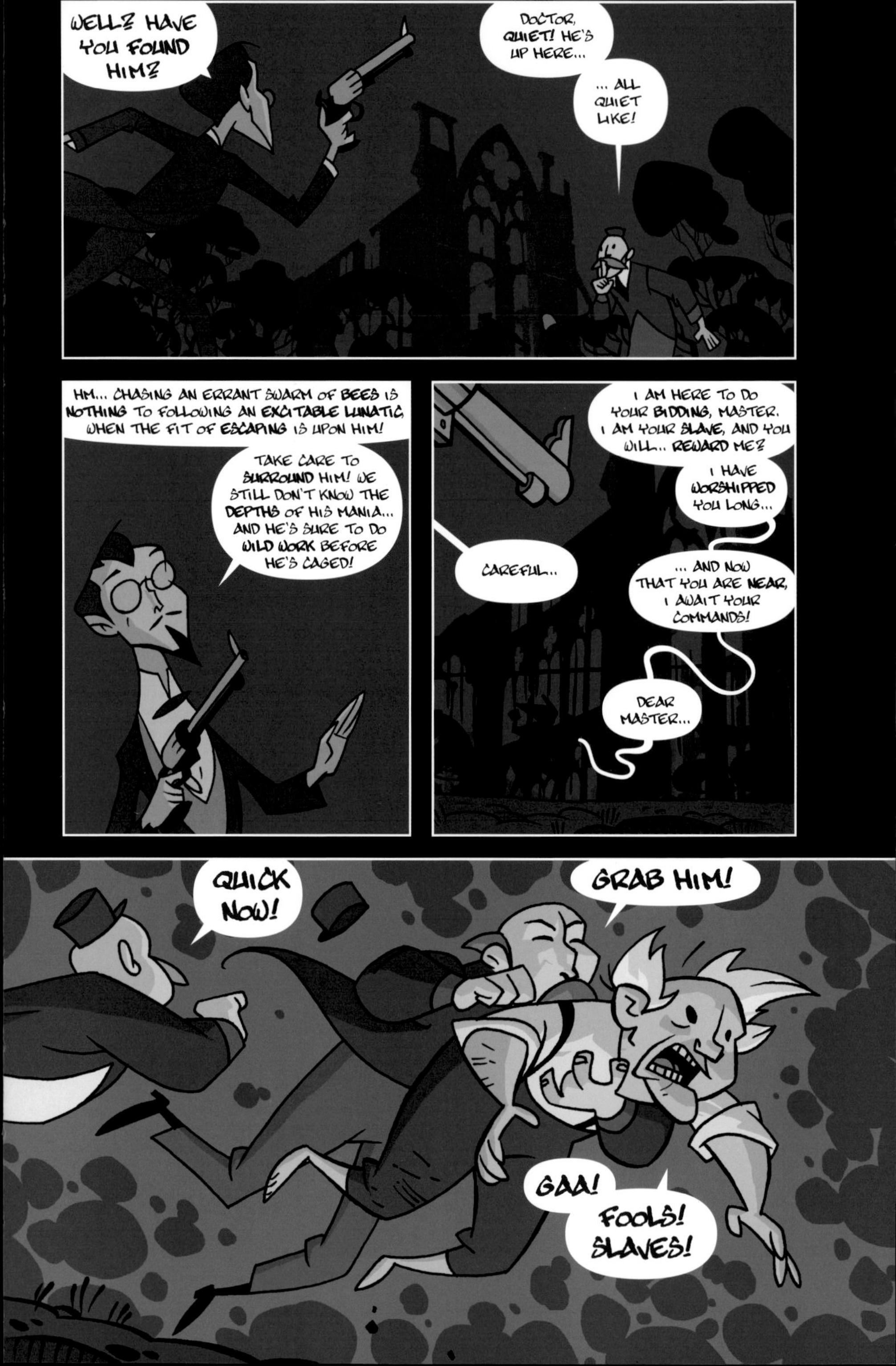
WELL? HAVE YOU FOUND HIM?
DOCTOR, QUIET! HE'S UP HERE...
... ALL QUIET LIKE!
HM... CHASING AN ERRANT SWARM OF BEES IS NOTHING TO FOLLOWING AN EXCITABLE LUNATIC WHEN THE FIT OF ESCAPING IS UPON HIM!
TAKE CARE TO SURROUND HIM! WE STILL DON'T KNOW THE DEPTHS OF HIS MANIA... AND HE'S SURE TO DO WILD WORK BEFORE HE'S CAGED!
I AM HERE TO DO YOUR BIDDING, MASTER. I AM YOUR SLAVE, AND YOU WILL... REWARD ME?
I HAVE WORSHIPPED YOU LONG...
CAREFUL...
... AND NOW THAT YOU ARE NEAR, I AWAIT YOUR COMMANDS!
DEAR MASTER...
QUICK NOW!
GRAB HIM!
GAA!
FOOLS! SLAVES!

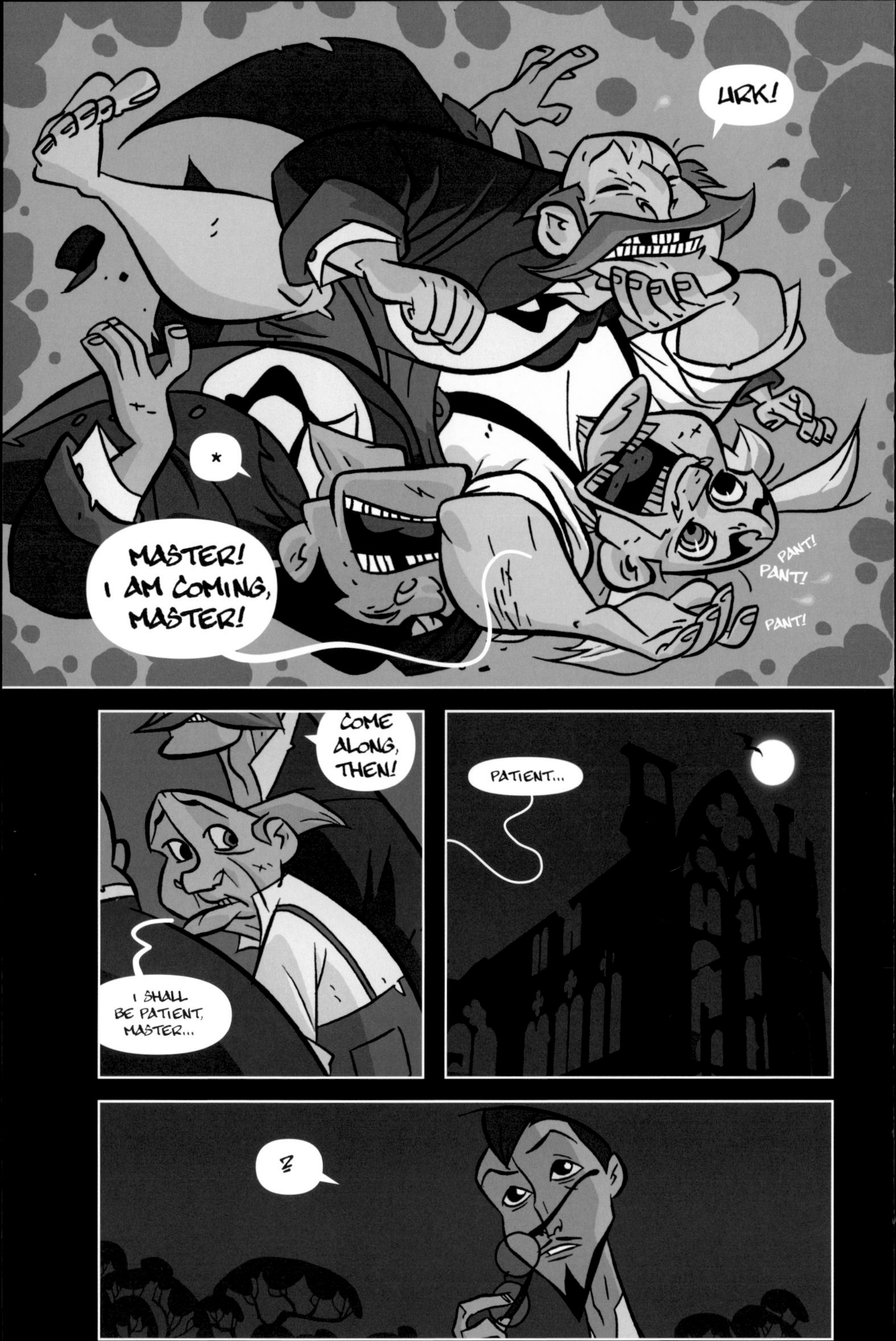
URK!
*
MASTER! I AM COMING, MASTER!
PANT!
PANT!
PANT!
COME ALONG, THEN!
I SHALL BE PATIENT, MASTER...
PATIENT...

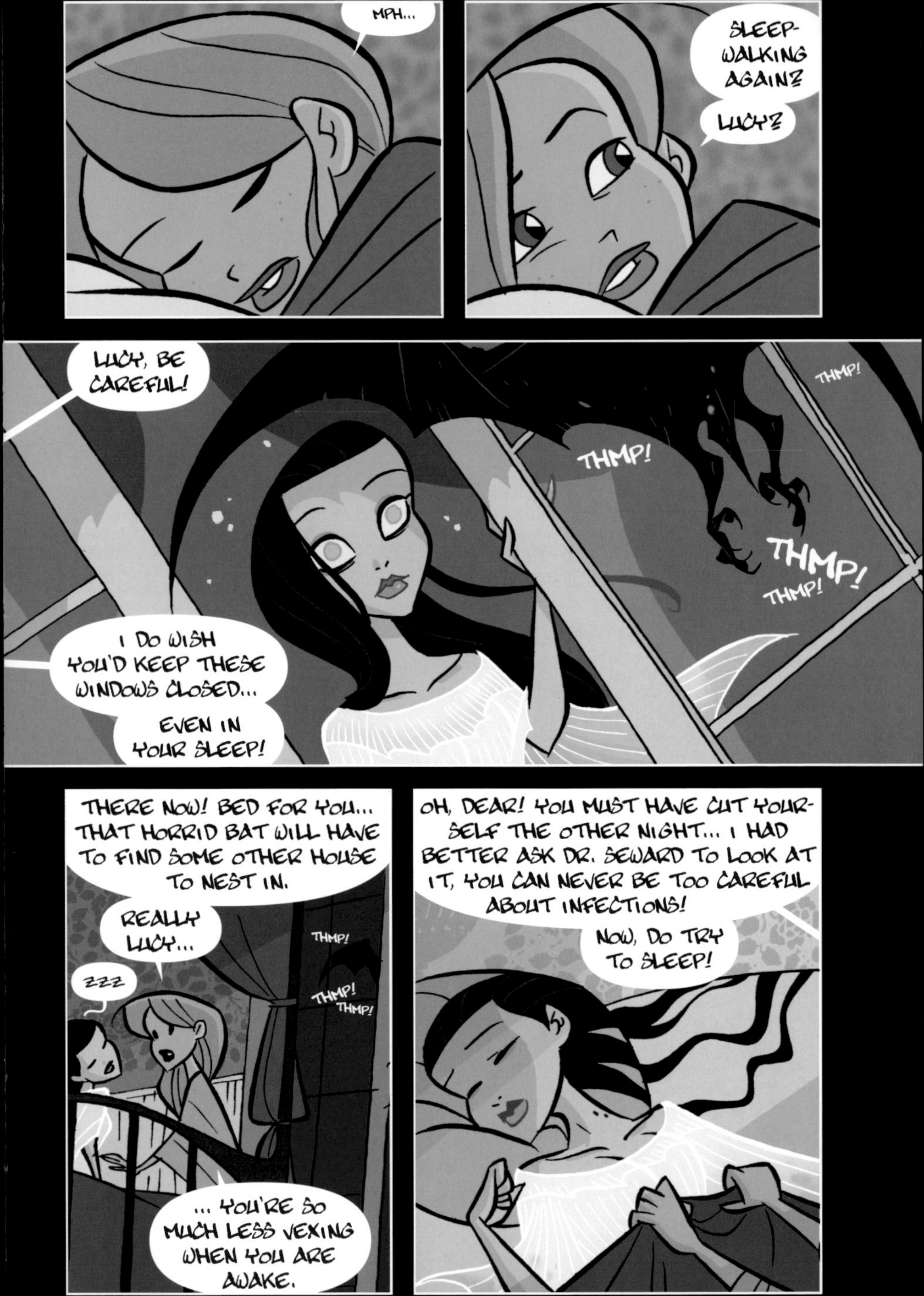
MPH...
SLEEP-WALKING AGAIN?
LUCY?
LUCY, BE CAREFUL!
THMP!
THMP!
THMP!
THMP!
I DO WISH YOU'D KEEP THESE WINDOWS CLOSED...
EVEN IN YOUR SLEEP!
THERE NOW! BED FOR YOU... THAT HORRID BAT WILL HAVE TO FIND SOME OTHER HOUSE TO NEST IN.
REALLY LUCY...
ZZZ
THMP!
THMP!
THMP!
... YOU'RE SO MUCH LESS VEXING WHEN YOU ARE AWAKE.
OH, DEAR! YOU MUST HAVE CUT YOURSELF THE OTHER NIGHT... I HAD BETTER ASK DR. SEWARD TO LOOK AT IT, YOU CAN NEVER BE TOO CAREFUL ABOUT INFECTIONS!
NOW, DO TRY TO SLEEP!

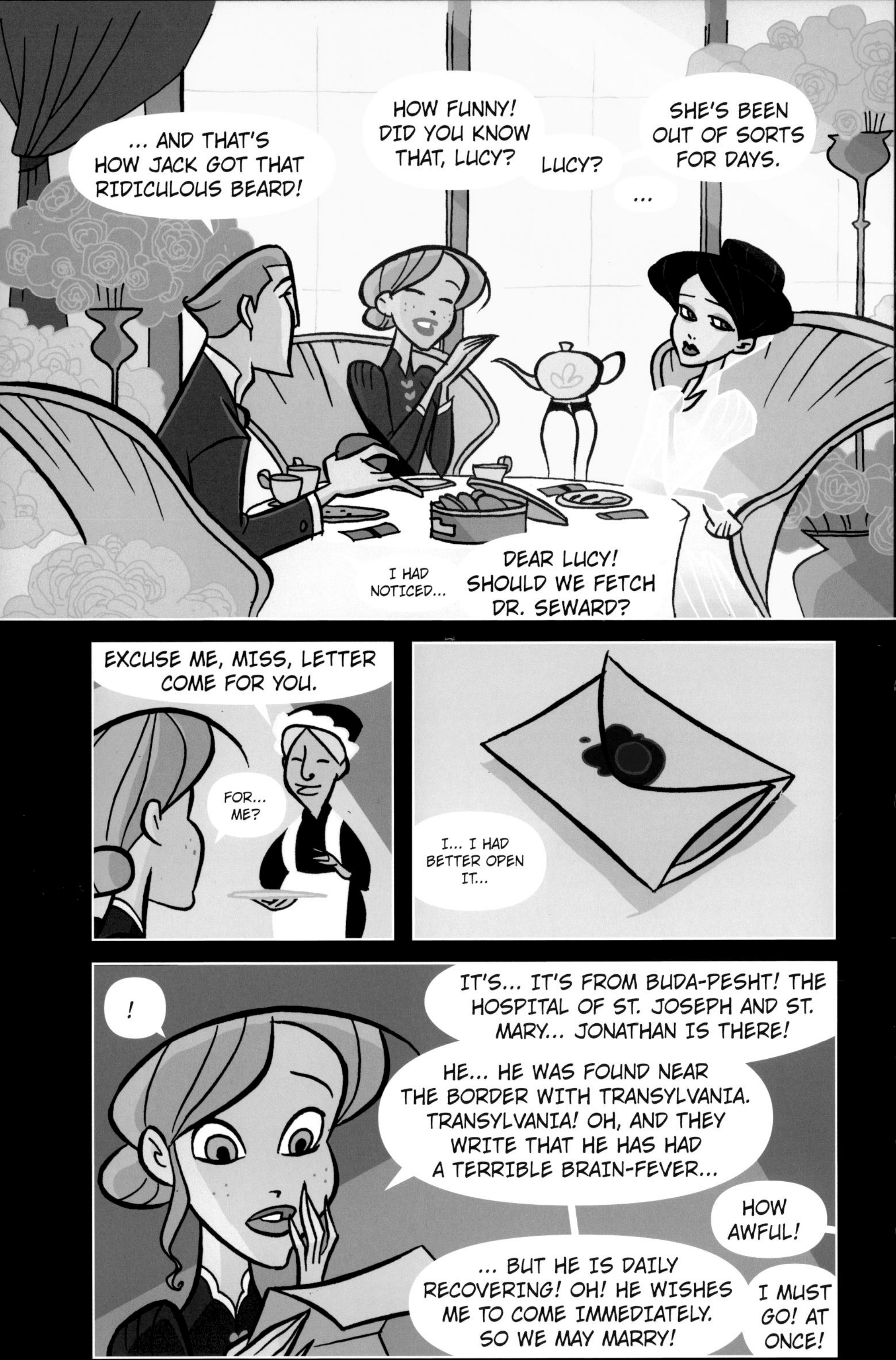
... AND THAT'S HOW JACK GOT THAT RIDICULOUS BEARD!
HOW FUNNY! DID YOU KNOW THAT, LUCY?
LUCY?
SHE'S BEEN OUT OF SORTS FOR DAYS.
...
I HAD NOTICED...
DEAR LUCY! SHOULD WE FETCH DR. SEWARD?
EXCUSE ME, MISS, LETTER COME FOR YOU.
FOR... ME?
I... I HAD BETTER OPEN IT...
!
IT'S... IT'S FROM BUDA-PESHT! THE HOSPITAL OF ST. JOSEPH AND ST. MARY... JONATHAN IS THERE!
HE... HE WAS FOUND NEAR THE BORDER WITH TRANSYLVANIA. TRANSYLVANIA! OH, AND THEY WRITE THAT HE HAS HAD A TERRIBLE BRAIN-FEVER...
HOW AWFUL!
... BUT HE IS DAILY RECOVERING! OH! HE WISHES ME TO COME IMMEDIATELY. SO WE MAY MARRY!
I MUST GO! AT ONCE!

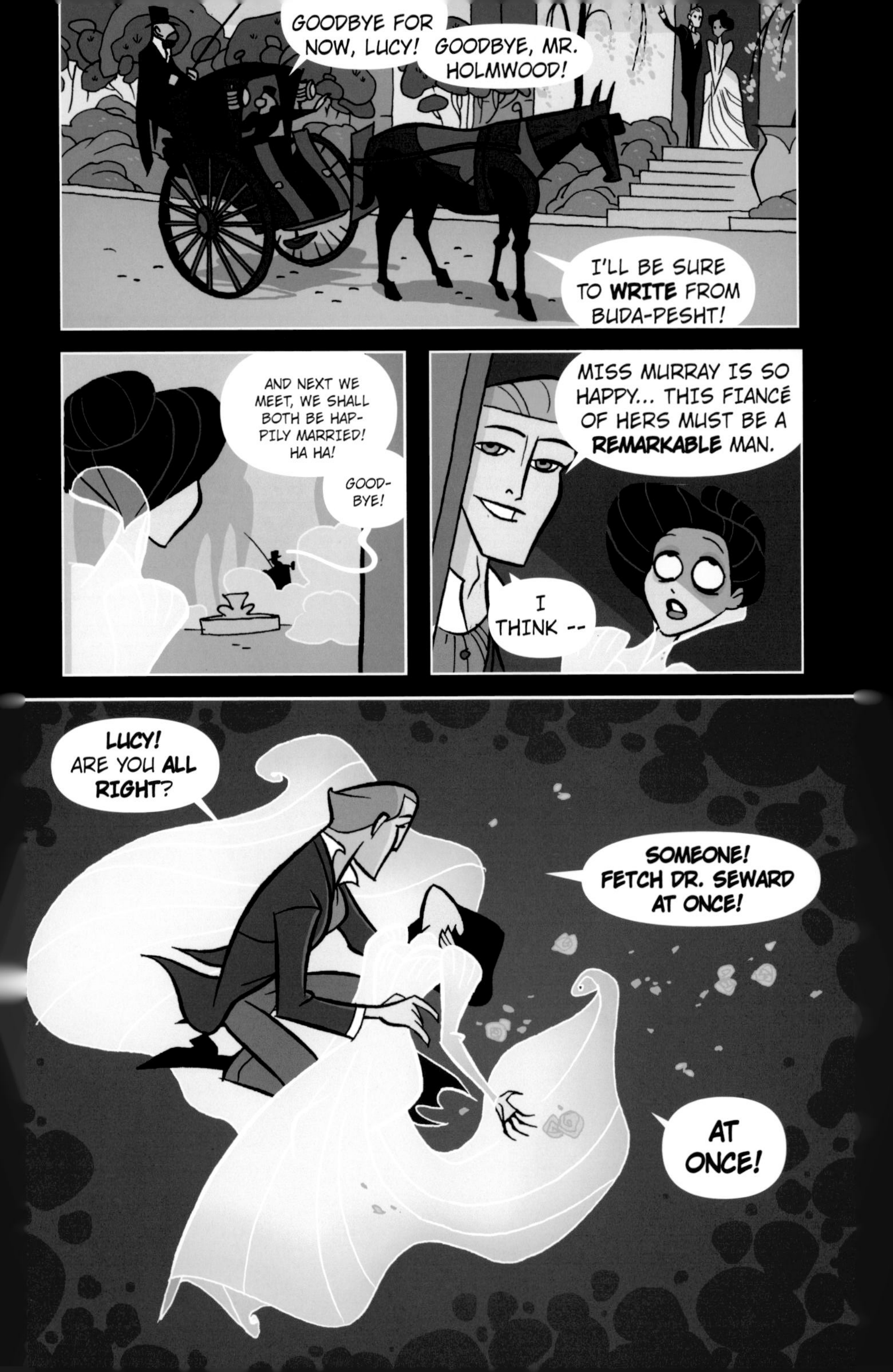
GOODBYE FOR NOW, LUCY!
GOODBYE, MR. HOLMWOOD!
I'LL BE SURE TO WRITE FROM BUDA-PESHT!
AND NEXT WE MEET, WE SHALL BOTH BE HAP-PILY MARRIED! HA HA!
GOOD-BYE!
MISS MURRAY IS SO HAPPY... THIS FIANCÉ OF HERS MUST BE A REMARKABLE MAN.
I THINK --
LUCY! ARE YOU ALL RIGHT?
SOMEONE! FETCH DR. SEWARD AT ONCE!
AT ONCE!

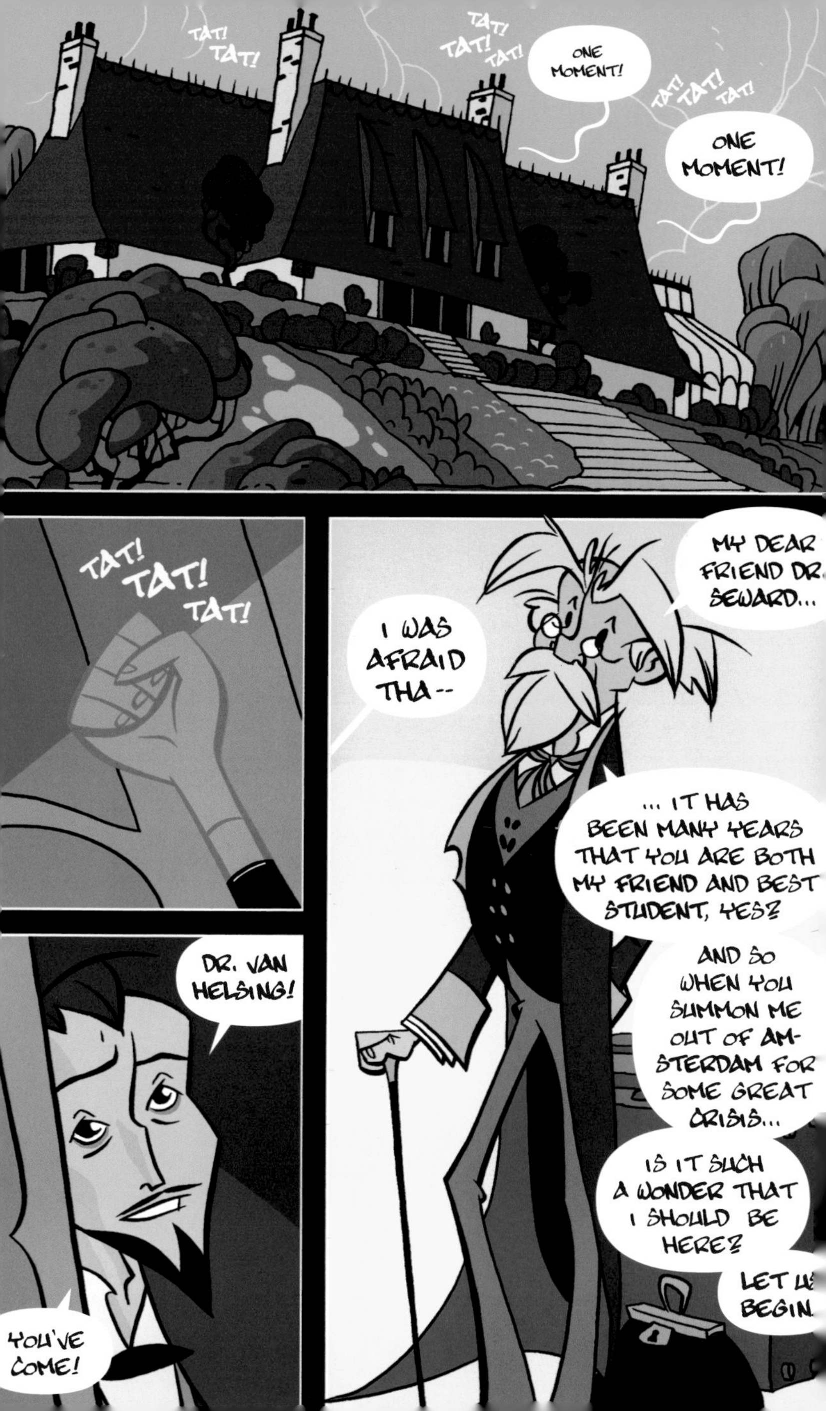
TAT! TAT!
TAT! TAT! TAT!
ONE MOMENT!
TAT! TAT! TAT!
ONE MOMENT!
TAT! TAT! TAT!
DR. VAN HELSING!
YOU'VE COME!
I WAS AFRAID THA--
MY DEAR FRIEND DR. SEWARD...
... IT HAS BEEN MANY YEARS THAT YOU ARE BOTH MY FRIEND AND BEST STUDENT, YES?
AND SO WHEN YOU SUMMON ME OUT OF AM-STERDAM FOR SOME GREAT CRISIS...
IS IT SUCH A WONDER THAT I SHOULD BE HERE?
LET US BEGIN.

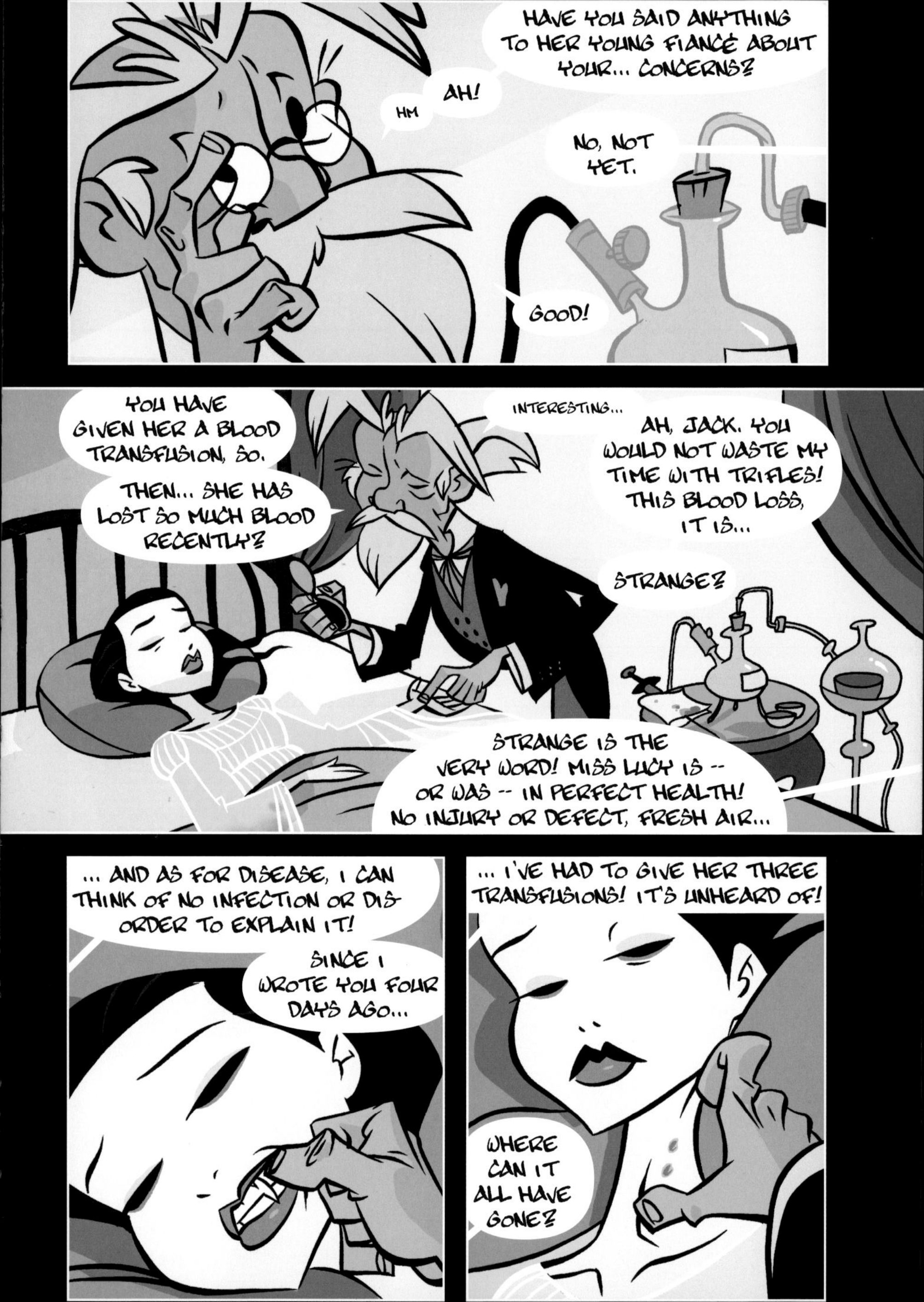
HAVE YOU SAID ANYTHING TO HER YOUNG FIANCÉ ABOUT YOUR... CONCERNS?
HM
AH!
NO, NOT YET.
GOOD!
YOU HAVE GIVEN HER A BLOOD TRANSFUSION, SO.
THEN... SHE HAS LOST SO MUCH BLOOD RECENTLY?
INTERESTING...
AH, JACK. YOU WOULD NOT WASTE MY TIME WITH TRIFLES! THIS BLOOD LOSS, IT IS...
STRANGE?
STRANGE IS THE VERY WORD! MISS LUCY IS -- OR WAS -- IN PERFECT HEALTH! NO INJURY OR DEFECT, FRESH AIR...
... AND AS FOR DISEASE, I CAN THINK OF NO INFECTION OR DIS-ORDER TO EXPLAIN IT!
SINCE I WROTE YOU FOUR DAYS AGO...
... I'VE HAD TO GIVE HER THREE TRANSFUSIONS! IT'S UNHEARD OF!
WHERE CAN IT ALL HAVE GONE?

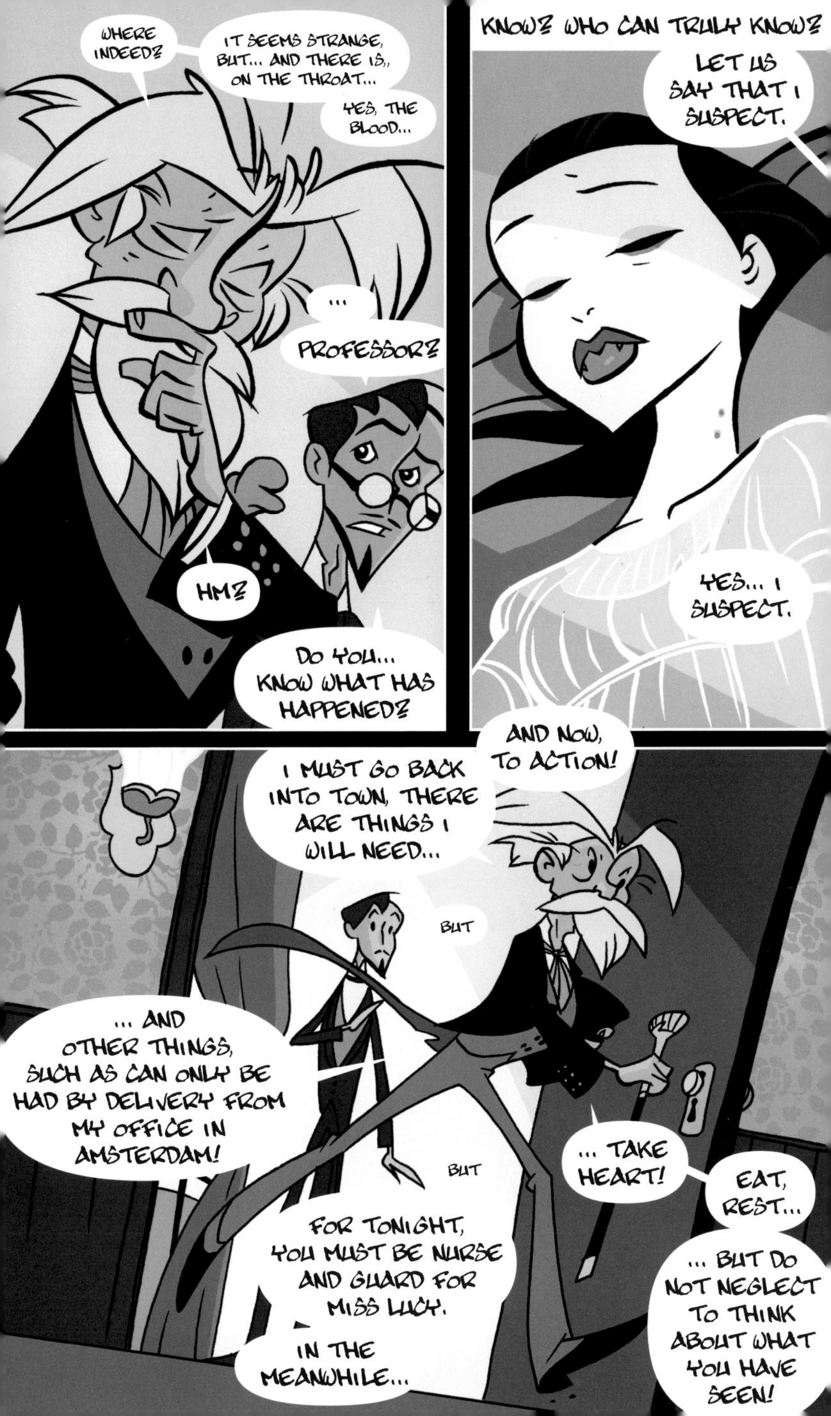

WHERE INDEED?
IT SEEMS STRANGE, BUT... AND THERE IS,, ON THE THROAT...
YES, THE BLOOD...
...
PROFESSOR?
HM?
DO YOU... KNOW WHAT HAS HAPPENED?
KNOW? WHO CAN TRULY KNOW?
LET US SAY THAT I SUSPECT.
YES... I SUSPECT.
AND NOW, TO ACTION!
I MUST GO BACK INTO TOWN, THERE ARE THINGS I WILL NEED...
BUT
... AND OTHER THINGS, SUCH AS CAN ONLY BE HAD BY DELIVERY FROM MY OFFICE IN AMSTERDAM!
BUT
FOR TONIGHT, YOU MUST BE NURSE AND GUARD FOR MISS LUCY.
IN THE MEANWHILE...
... TAKE HEART!
EAT, REST...
... BUT DO NOT NEGLECT TO THINK ABOUT WHAT YOU HAVE SEEN!

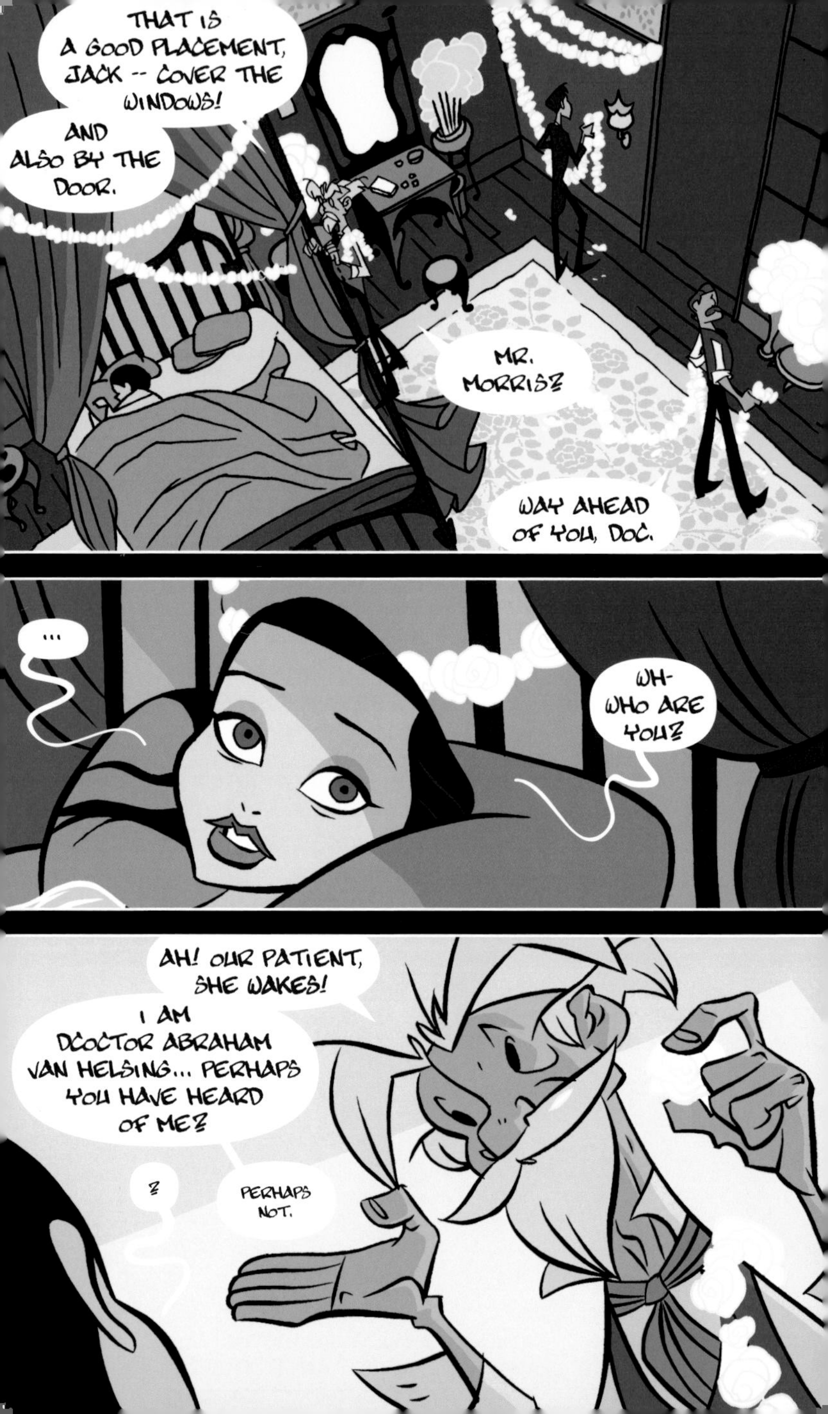
THAT IS A GOOD PLACEMENT, JACK -- COVER THE WINDOWS!
AND ALSO BY THE DOOR.
MR. MORRIS?
WAY AHEAD OF YOU, DOC.
...
WH- WHO ARE YOU?
AH! OUR PATIENT, SHE WAKES!
I AM DCOCTOR ABRAHAM VAN HELSING... PERHAPS YOU HAVE HEARD OF ME?
?
PERHAPS NOT.

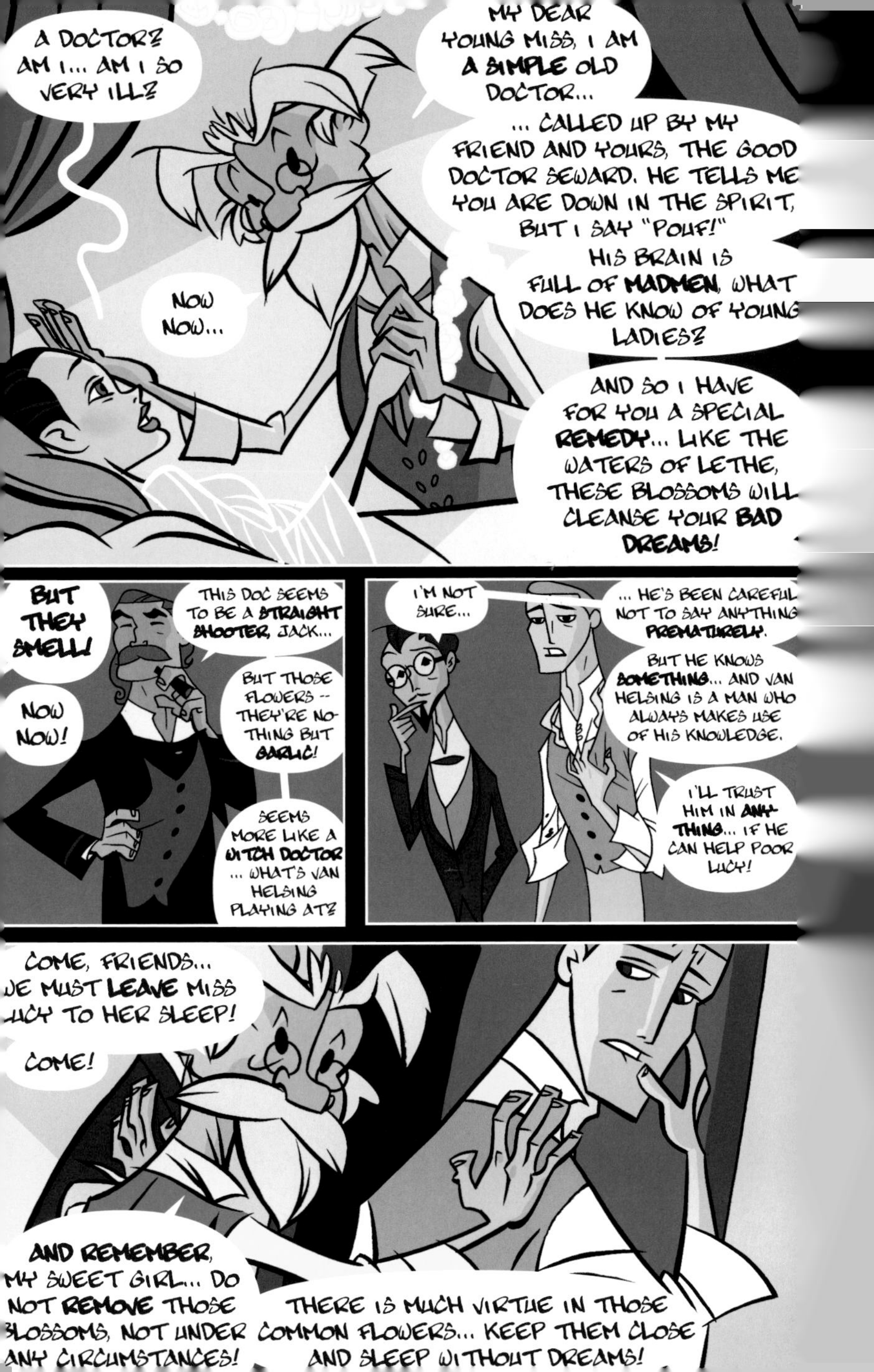
A DOCTOR? AM I... AM I SO VERY ILL?
MY DEAR YOUNG MISS, I AM A SIMPLE OLD DOCTOR...
... CALLED UP BY MY FRIEND AND YOURS, THE GOOD DOCTOR SEWARD. HE TELLS ME YOU ARE DOWN IN THE SPIRIT, BUT I SAY "POUF!"
NOW NOW...
HIS BRAIN IS FULL OF MADMEN, WHAT DOES HE KNOW OF YOUNG LADIES?
AND SO I HAVE FOR YOU A SPECIAL REMEDY... LIKE THE WATERS OF LETHE, THESE BLOSSOMS WILL CLEANSE YOUR BAD DREAMS!
BUT THEY SMELL!
NOW NOW!
THIS DOC SEEMS TO BE A STRAIGHT SHOOTER, JACK...
BUT THOSE FLOWERS -- THEY'RE NOTHING BUT GARLIC!
SEEMS MORE LIKE A WITCH DOCTOR ... WHAT'S VAN HELSING PLAYING AT?
I'M NOT SURE...
... HE'S BEEN CAREFUL NOT TO SAY ANYTHING PREMATURELY.
BUT HE KNOWS SOMETHING... AND VAN HELSING IS A MAN WHO ALWAYS MAKES USE OF HIS KNOWLEDGE.
I'LL TRUST HIM IN ANYTHING... IF HE CAN HELP POOR LUCY!
COME, FRIENDS... WE MUST LEAVE MISS LUCY TO HER SLEEP!
COME!
AND REMEMBER, MY SWEET GIRL... DO NOT REMOVE THOSE BLOSSOMS, NOT UNDER ANY CIRCUMSTANCES!
THERE IS MUCH VIRTUE IN THOSE COMMON FLOWERS... KEEP THEM CLOSE AND SLEEP WITHOUT DREAMS!

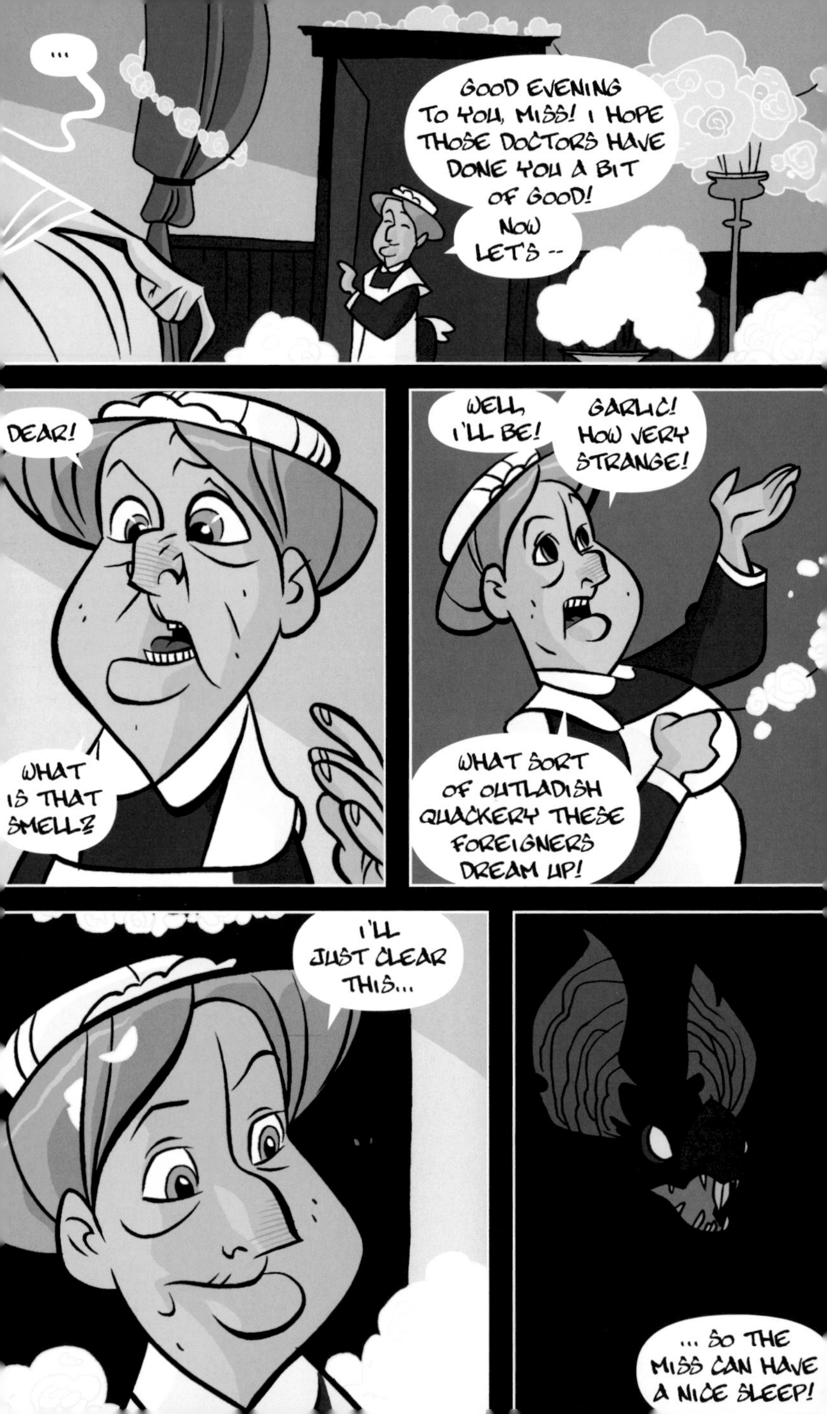
...
GOOD EVENING TO YOU, MISS! I HOPE THOSE DOCTORS HAVE DONE YOU A BIT OF GOOD!
NOW LET'S --
DEAR!
WHAT IS THAT SMELL?
WELL, I'LL BE!
GARLIC! HOW VERY STRANGE!
WHAT SORT OF OUTLADISH QUACKERY THESE FOREIGNERS DREAM UP!
I'LL JUST CLEAR THIS...
... SO THE MISS CAN HAVE A NICE SLEEP!

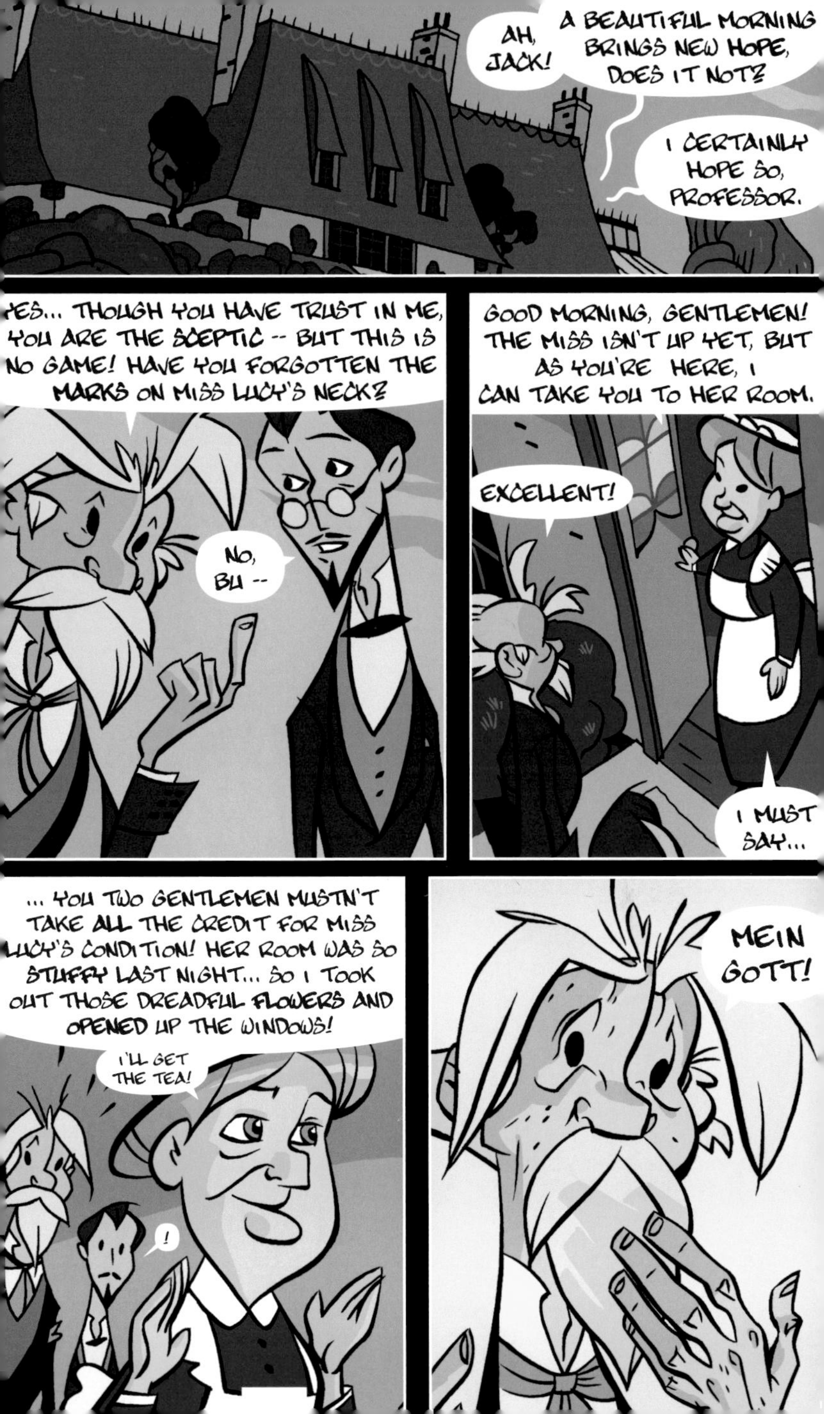
AH, JACK!
A BEAUTIFUL MORNING BRINGS NEW HOPE, DOES IT NOT?
I CERTAINLY HOPE SO, PROFESSOR.
YES... THOUGH YOU HAVE TRUST IN ME, YOU ARE THE SCEPTIC -- BUT THIS IS NO GAME! HAVE YOU FORGOTTEN THE MARKS ON MISS LUCY'S NECK?
NO, BU --
GOOD MORNING, GENTLEMEN! THE MISS ISN'T UP YET, BUT AS YOU'RE HERE, I CAN TAKE YOU TO HER ROOM.
EXCELLENT!
I MUST SAY...
... YOU TWO GENTLEMEN MUSTN'T TAKE ALL THE CREDIT FOR MISS LUCY'S CONDITION! HER ROOM WAS SO STUFFY LAST NIGHT... SO I TOOK OUT THOSE DREADFUL FLOWERS AND OPENED UP THE WINDOWS!
I'LL GET THE TEA!
!
MEIN GOTT!

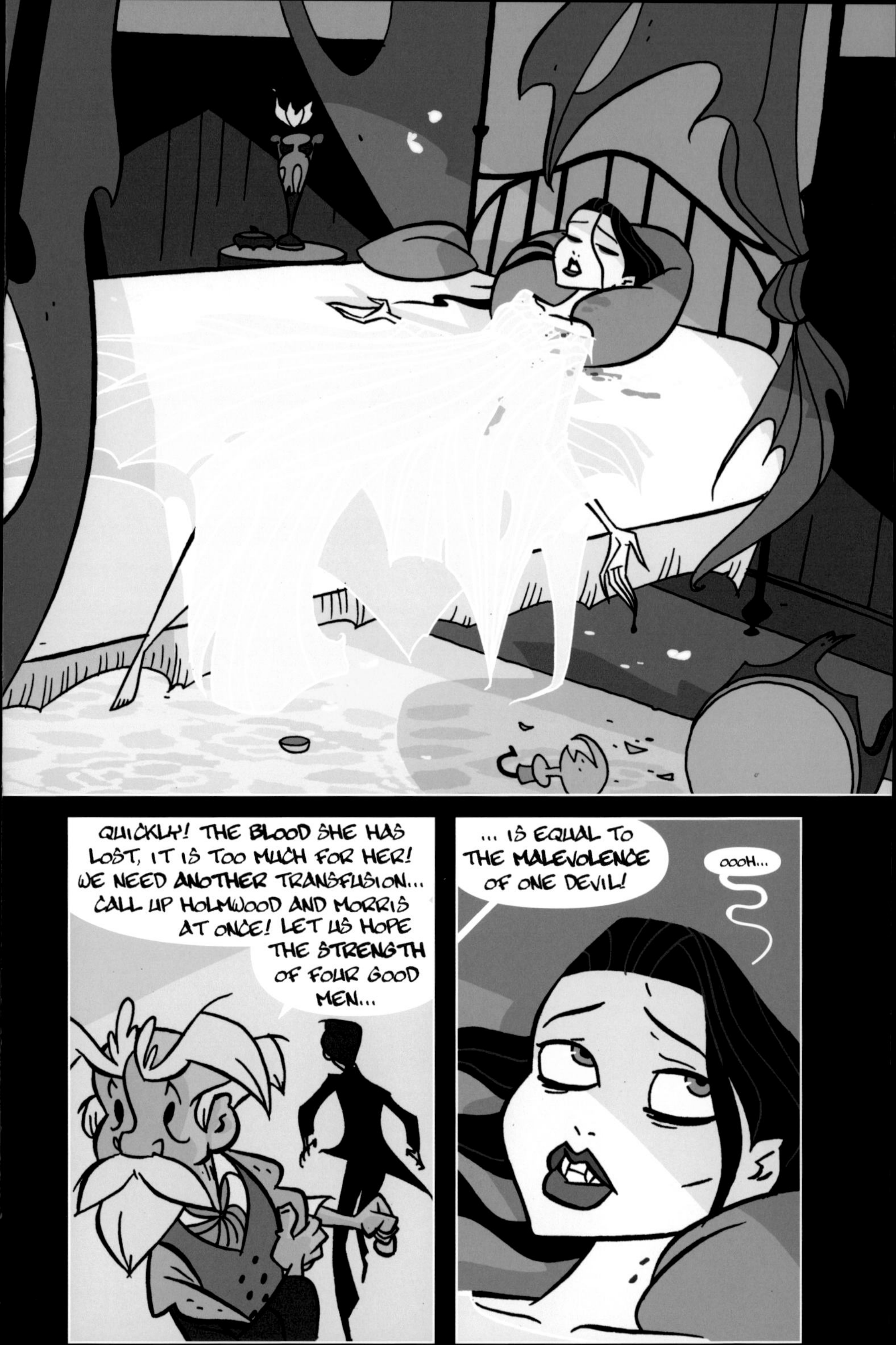
QUICKLY! THE BLOOD SHE HAS LOST, IT IS TOO MUCH FOR HER! WE NEED ANOTHER TRANSFUSION... CALL UP HOLMWOOD AND MORRIS AT ONCE! LET US HOPE THE STRENGTH OF FOUR GOOD MEN...
... IS EQUAL TO THE MALEVOLENCE OF ONE DEVIL!
OOOH...

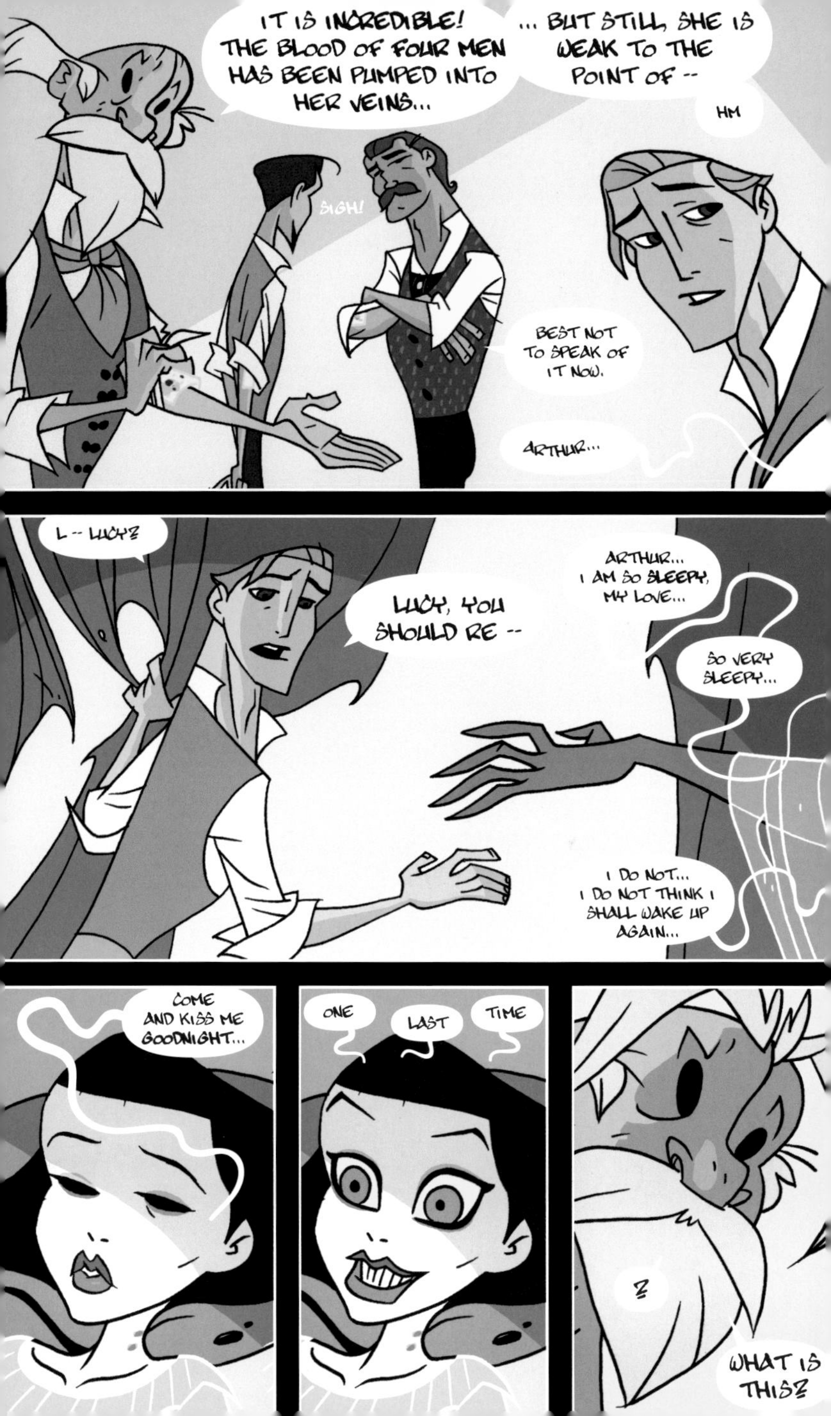
IT IS INCREDIBLE! THE BLOOD OF FOUR MEN HAS BEEN PUMPED INTO HER VEINS...
... BUT STILL, SHE IS WEAK TO THE POINT OF --
HM
SIGH!
BEST NOT TO SPEAK OF IT NOW.
ARTHUR...
L -- LUCY?
LUCY, YOU SHOULD RE --
ARTHUR... I AM SO SLEEPY, MY LOVE...
SO VERY SLEEPY...
I DO NOT... I DO NOT THINK I SHALL WAKE UP AGAIN...
COME AND KISS ME GOODNIGHT...
ONE
LAST
TIME
?
WHAT IS THIS?

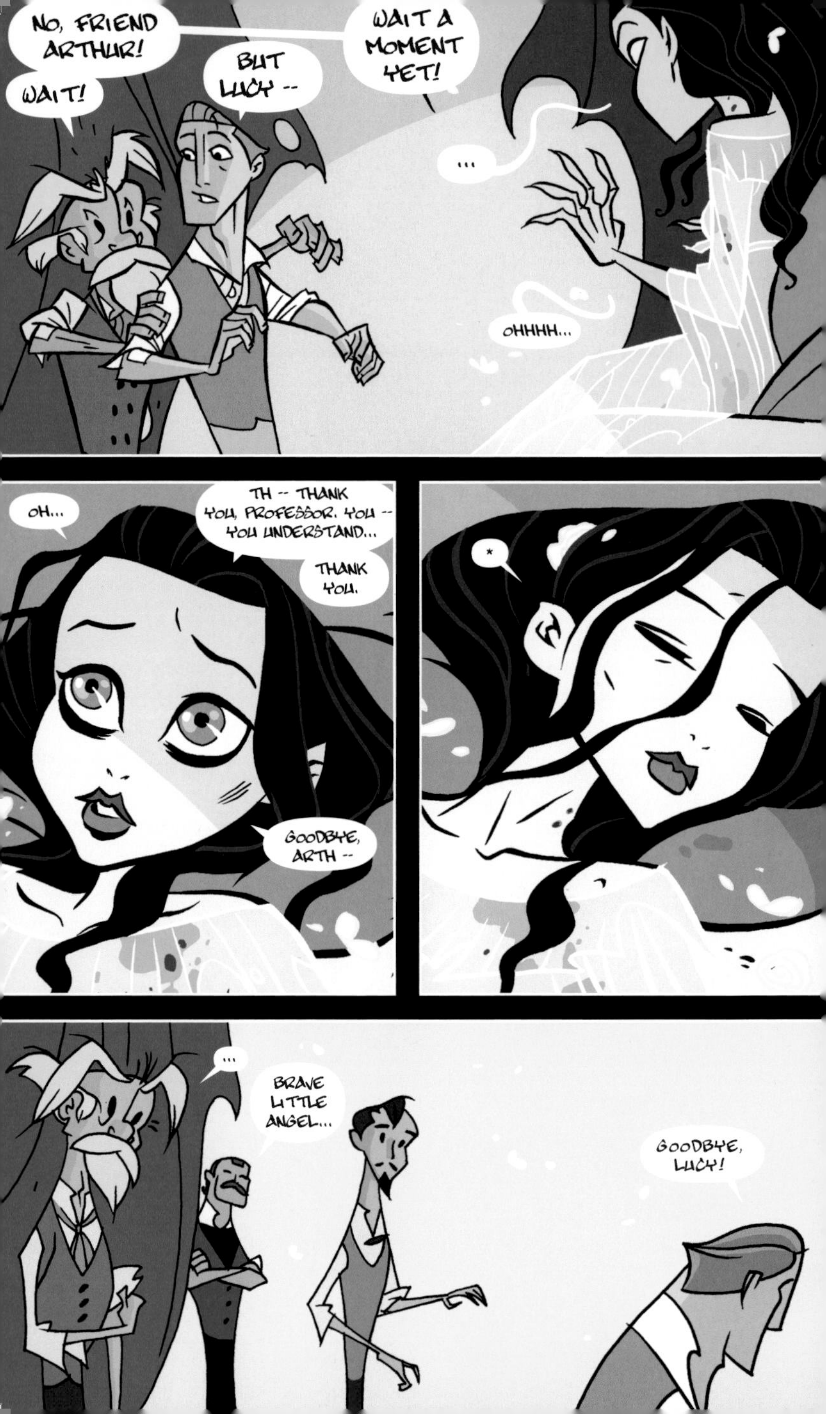
NO, FRIEND ARTHUR!
WAIT!
BUT LUCY --
WAIT A MOMENT YET!
...
OHHHH...
OH...
TH -- THANK YOU, PROFESSOR. YOU -- YOU UNDERSTAND...
THANK YOU.
GOODBYE, ARTH --
*
...
BRAVE LITTLE ANGEL...
GOODBYE, LUCY!

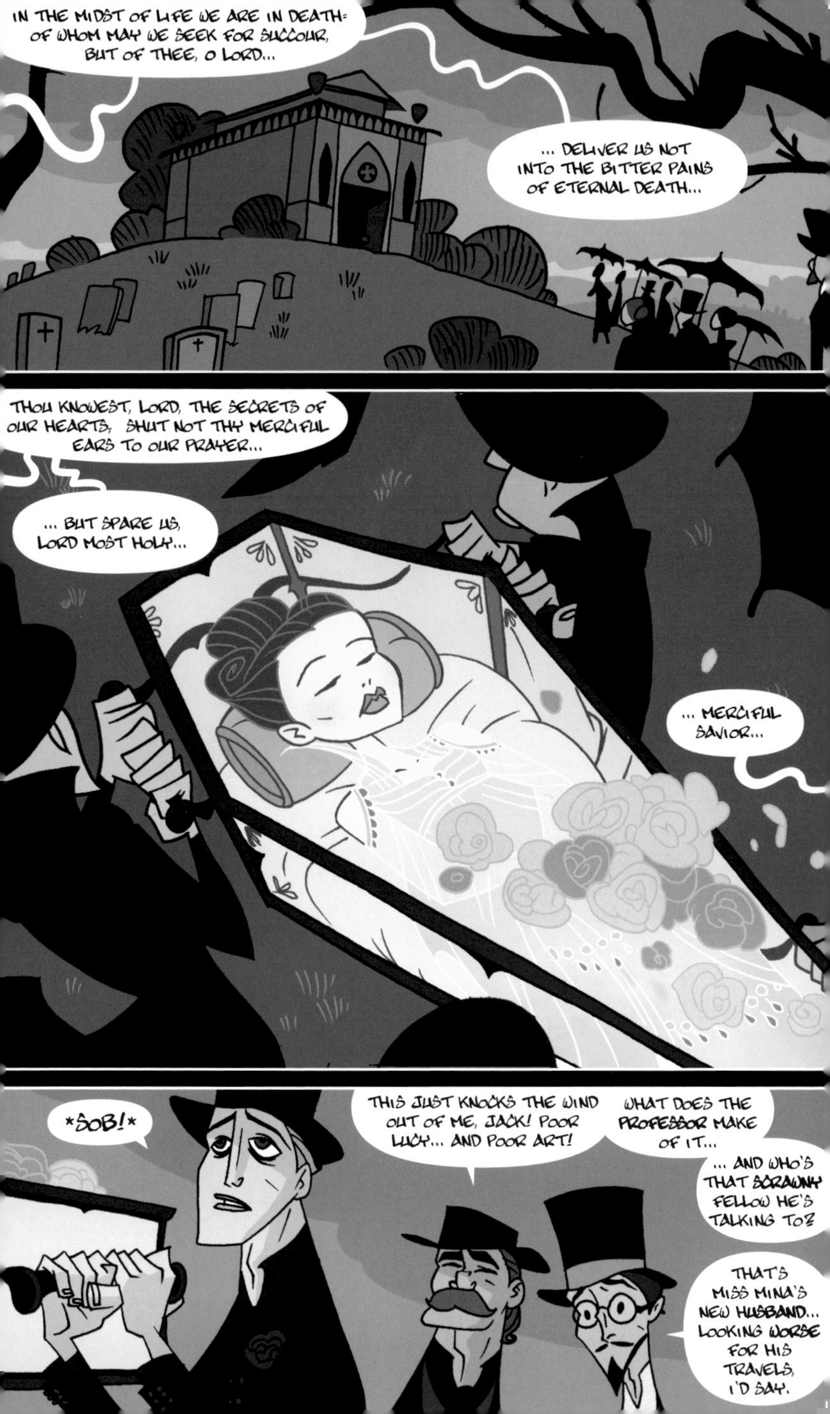
IN THE MIDST OF LIFE WE ARE IN DEATH: OF WHOM MAY WE SEEK FOR SUCCOUR, BUT OF THEE, O LORD...
... DELIVER US NOT INTO THE BITTER PAINS OF ETERNAL DEATH...
THOU KNOWEST, LORD, THE SECRETS OF OUR HEARTS; SHUT NOT THY MERCIFUL EARS TO OUR PRAYER...
... BUT SPARE US, LORD MOST HOLY...
... MERCIFUL SAVIOR...
SOB!
THIS JUST KNOCKS THE WIND OUT OF ME, JACK! POOR LUCY... AND POOR ART!
WHAT DOES THE PROFESSOR MAKE OF IT...
... AND WHO'S THAT SCRAWNY FELLOW HE'S TALKING TO?
THAT'S MISS MINA'S NEW HUSBAND... LOOKING WORSE FOR HIS TRAVELS, I'D SAY.

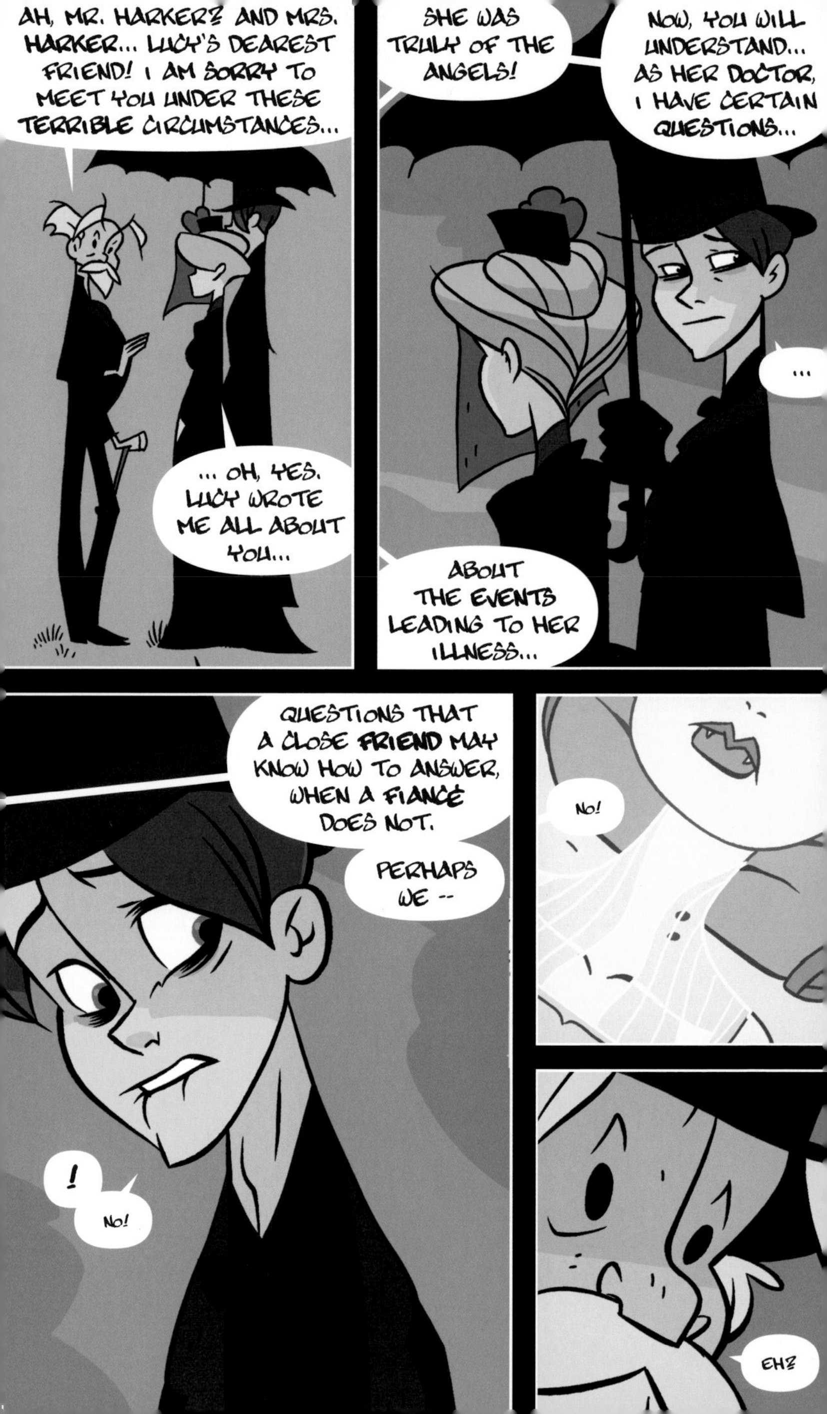
AH, MR. HARKER? AND MRS. HARKER... LUCY'S DEAREST FRIEND! I AM SORRY TO MEET YOU UNDER THESE TERRIBLE CIRCUMSTANCES...
... OH, YES. LUCY WROTE ME ALL ABOUT YOU...
SHE WAS TRULY OF THE ANGELS!
NOW, YOU WILL UNDERSTAND... AS HER DOCTOR, I HAVE CERTAIN QUESTIONS...
...
ABOUT THE EVENTS LEADING TO HER ILLNESS...
QUESTIONS THAT A CLOSE FRIEND MAY KNOW HOW TO ANSWER, WHEN A FIANCÉ DOES NOT.
PERHAPS WE --
!
NO!
NO!
EH?

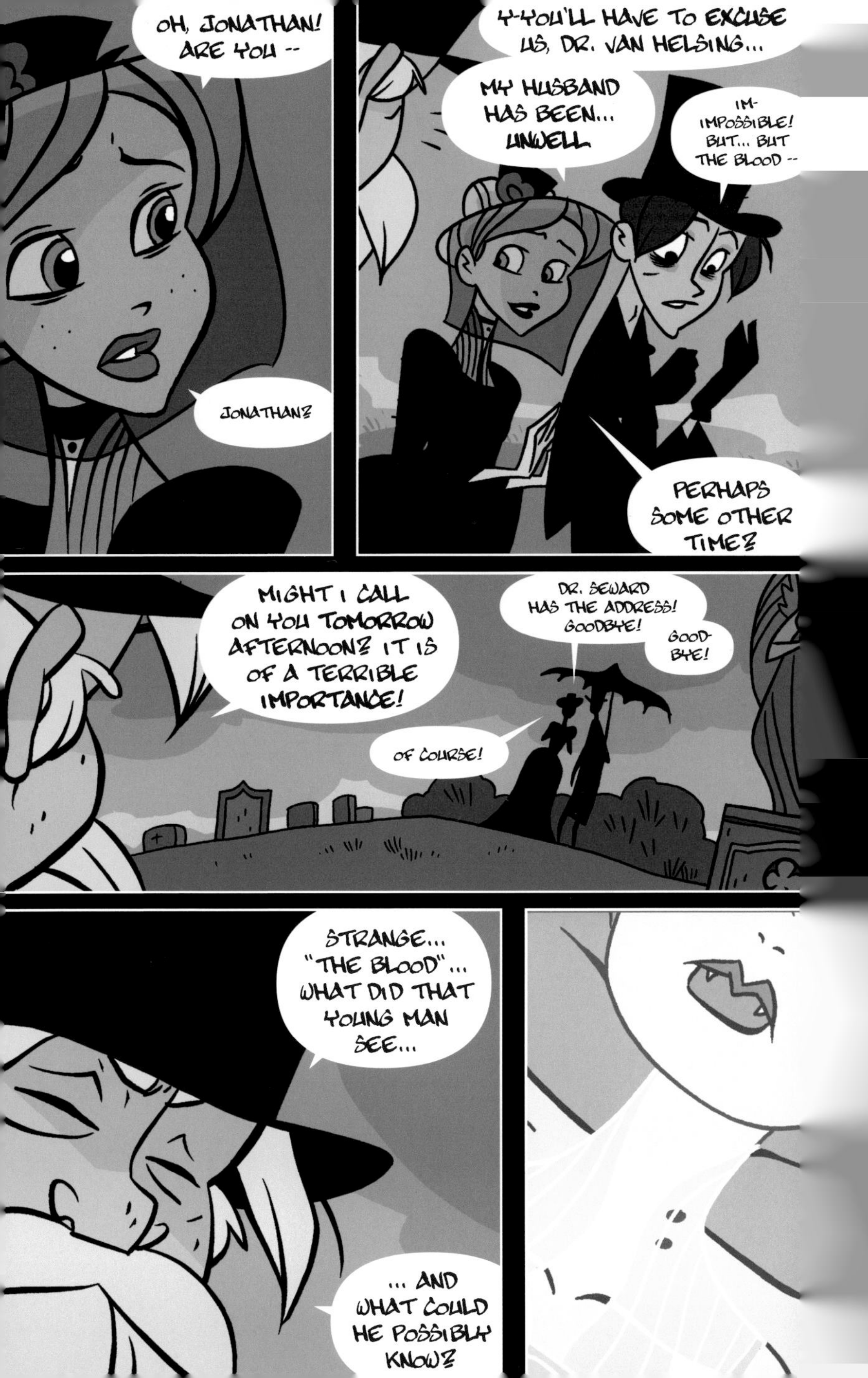
OH, JONATHAN! ARE YOU --
JONATHAN?
Y-YOU'LL HAVE TO EXCUSE US, DR. VAN HELSING...
MY HUSBAND HAS BEEN... UNWELL
IM-IMPOSSIBLE! BUT... BUT THE BLOOD --
PERHAPS SOME OTHER TIME?
MIGHT I CALL ON YOU TOMORROW AFTERNOON? IT IS OF A TERRIBLE IMPORTANCE!
OF COURSE!
DR. SEWARD HAS THE ADDRESS! GOODBYE!
GOOD-BYE!
STRANGE... "THE BLOOD"... WHAT DID THAT YOUNG MAN SEE...
... AND WHAT COULD HE POSSIBLY KNOW?

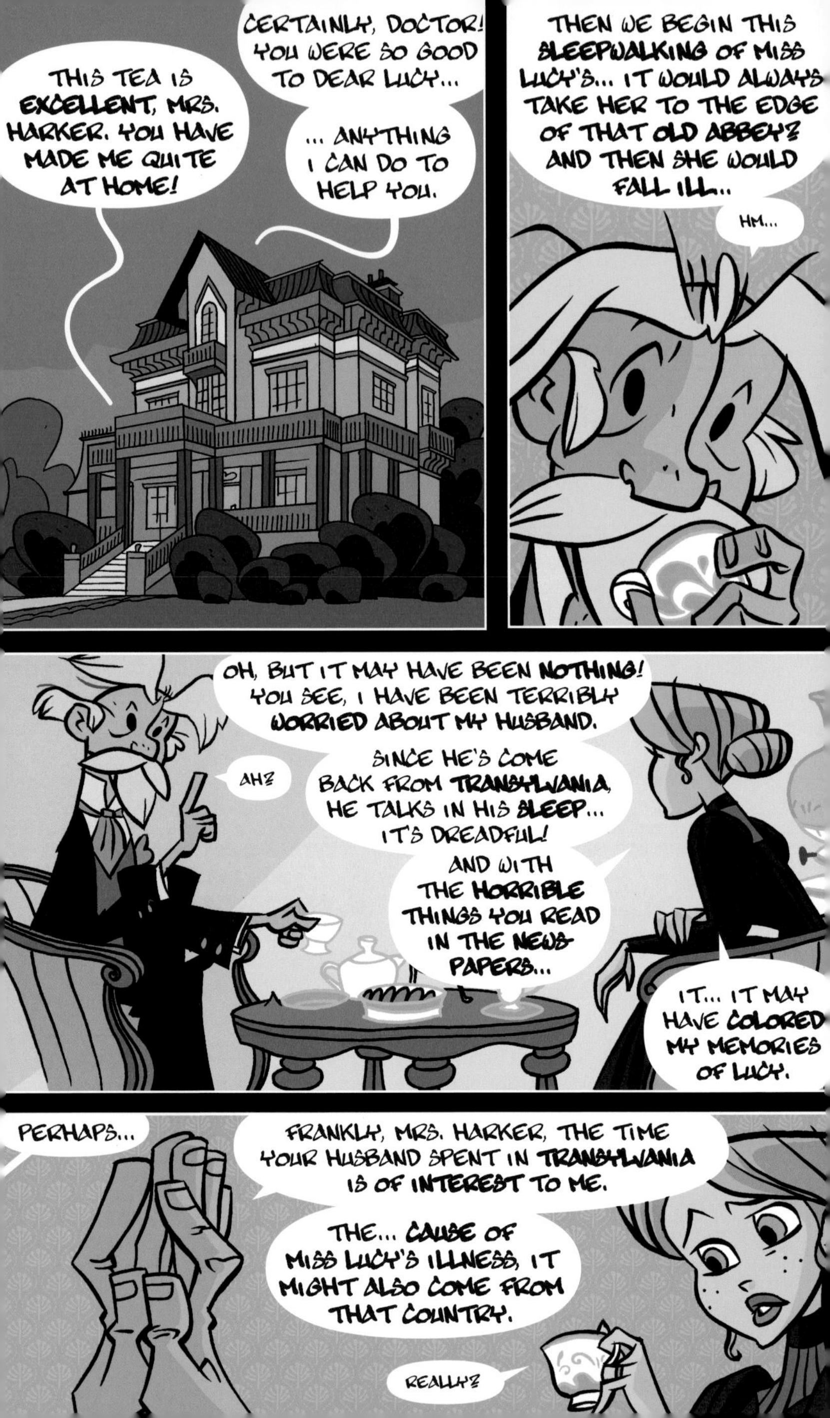
THIS TEA IS EXCELLENT, MRS. HARKER. YOU HAVE MADE ME QUITE AT HOME!
CERTAINLY, DOCTOR! YOU WERE SO GOOD TO DEAR LUCY...
... ANYTHING I CAN DO TO HELP YOU.
THEN WE BEGIN THIS SLEEPWALKING OF MISS LUCY'S... IT WOULD ALWAYS TAKE HER TO THE EDGE OF THAT OLD ABBEY? AND THEN SHE WOULD FALL ILL..
HM...
OH, BUT IT MAY HAVE BEEN NOTHING! YOU SEE, I HAVE BEEN TERRIBLY WORRIED ABOUT MY HUSBAND.
AH?
SINCE HE'S COME BACK FROM TRANSYLVANIA, HE TALKS IN HIS SLEEP... IT'S DREADFUL!
AND WITH THE HORRIBLE THINGS YOU READ IN THE NEWS-PAPERS...
IT... IT MAY HAVE COLORED MY MEMORIES OF LUCY.
PERHAPS...
FRANKLY, MRS. HARKER, THE TIME YOUR HUSBAND SPENT IN TRANSYLVANIA IS OF INTEREST TO ME.
THE... CAUSE OF MISS LUCY'S ILLNESS, IT MIGHT ALSO COME FROM THAT COUNTRY.
REALLY?

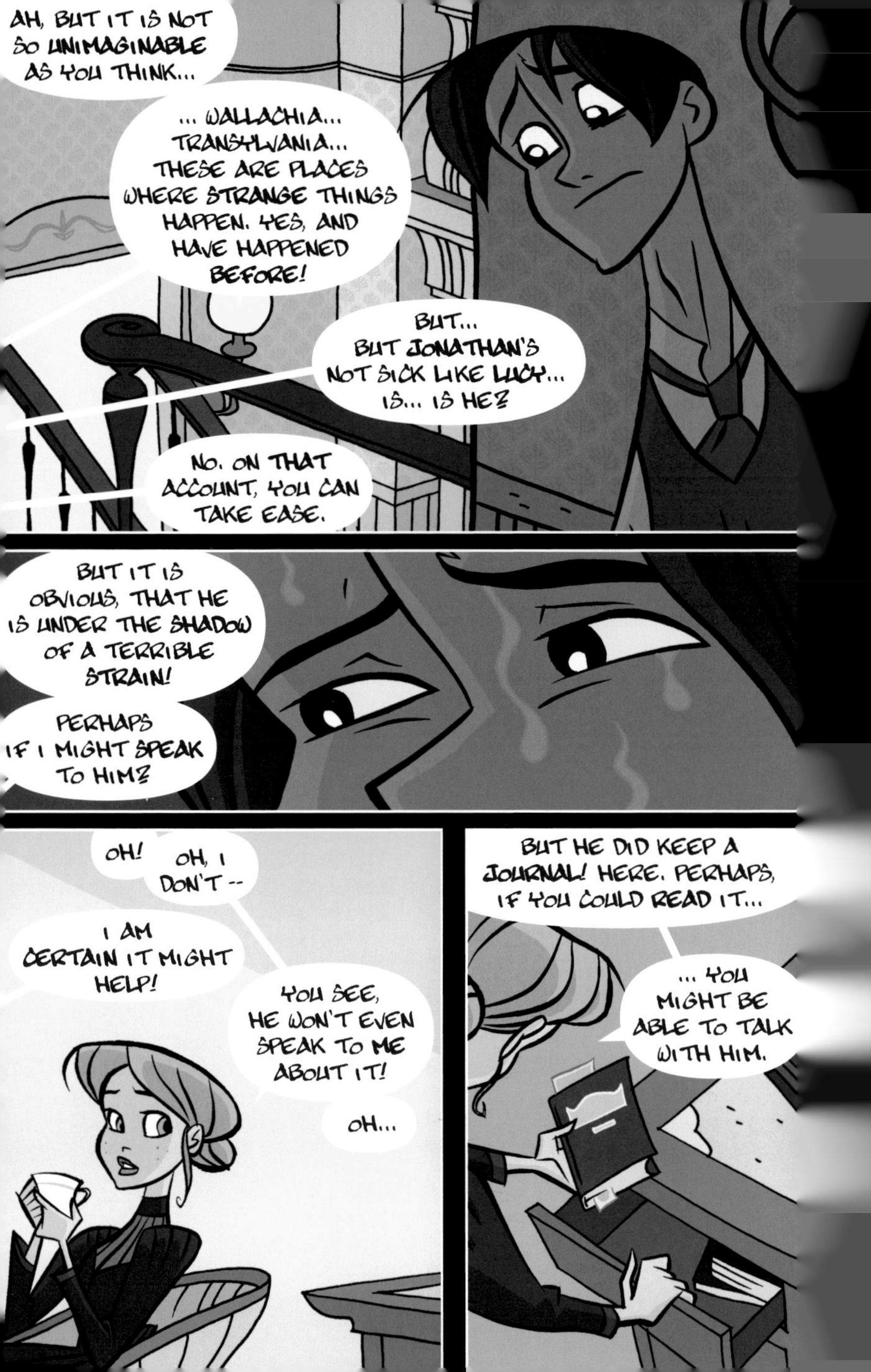
AH, BUT IT IS NOT SO UNIMAGINABLE AS YOU THINK...
... WALLACHIA... TRANSYLVANIA... THESE ARE PLACES WHERE STRANGE THINGS HAPPEN. YES, AND HAVE HAPPENED BEFORE!
BUT... BUT JONATHAN'S NOT SICK LIKE LUCY... IS... IS HE?
NO. ON THAT ACCOUNT, YOU CAN TAKE EASE.
BUT IT IS OBVIOUS, THAT HE IS UNDER THE SHADOW OF A TERRIBLE STRAIN!
PERHAPS IF I MIGHT SPEAK TO HIM?
OH!
OH, I DON'T --
I AM CERTAIN IT MIGHT HELP!
YOU SEE, HE WON'T EVEN SPEAK TO ME ABOUT IT!
OH...
BUT HE DID KEEP A JOURNAL! HERE. PERHAPS, IF YOU COULD READ IT...
... YOU MIGHT BE ABLE TO TALK WITH HIM.

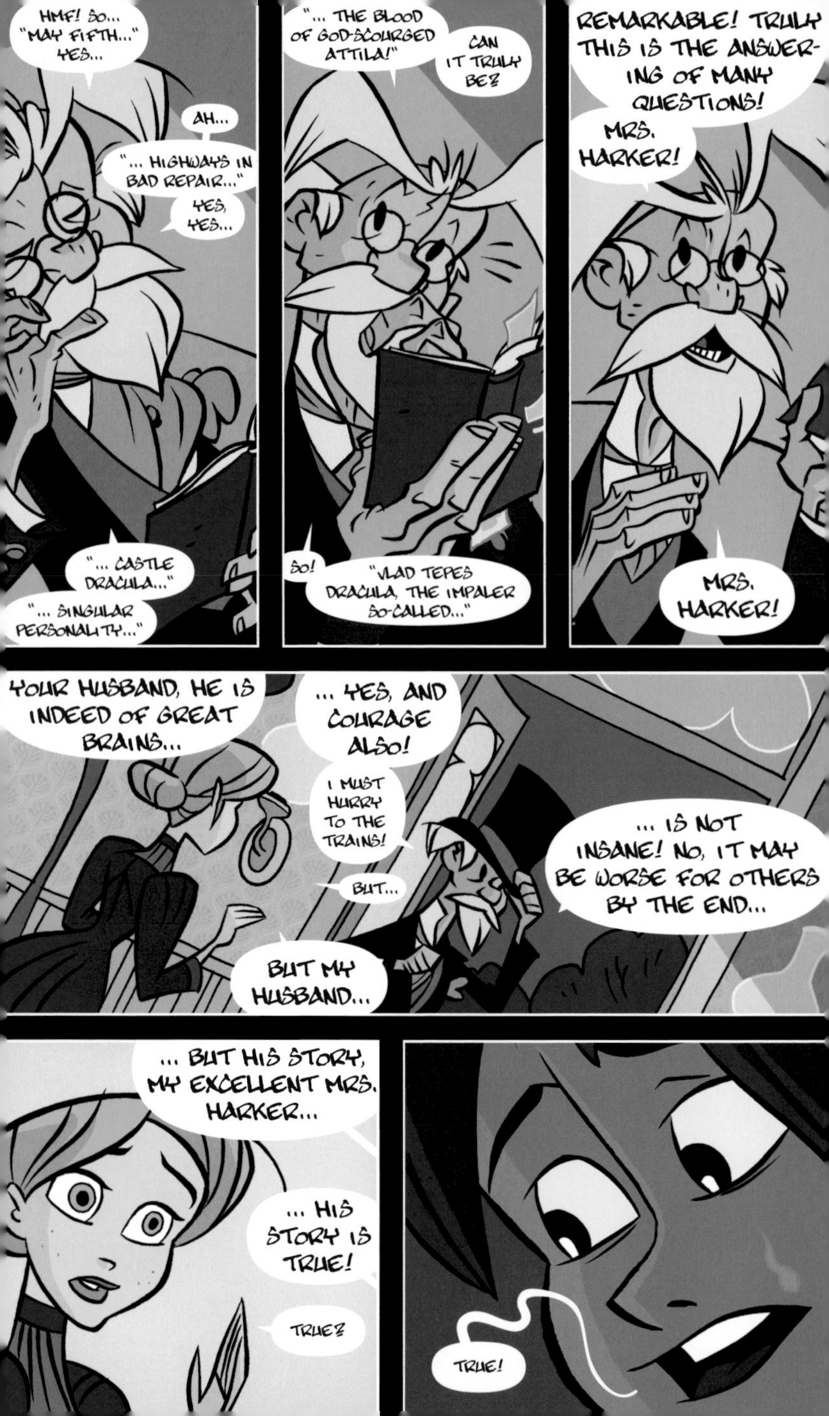

HMF! SO... "MAY FIFTH..." YES...
AH...
"... HIGHWAYS IN BAD REPAIR..."
YES, YES...
"... CASTLE DRACULA..."
"... SINGULAR PERSONALITY..."
"... THE BLOOD OF GOD-SCOURGED ATTILA!"
CAN IT TRULY BE?
SO!
"VLAD TEPES DRACULA, THE IMPALER SO-CALLED..."
REMARKABLE! TRULY THIS IS THE ANSWERING OF MANY QUESTIONS!
MRS. HARKER!
MRS. HARKER!
YOUR HUSBAND, HE IS INDEED OF GREAT BRAINS...
... YES, AND COURAGE ALSO!
I MUST HURRY TO THE TRAINS!
BUT...
BUT MY HUSBAND...
... IS NOT INSANE! NO, IT MAY BE WORSE FOR OTHERS BY THE END...
... BUT HIS STORY, MY EXCELLENT MRS. HARKER...
... HIS STORY IS TRUE!
TRUE?
TRUE!

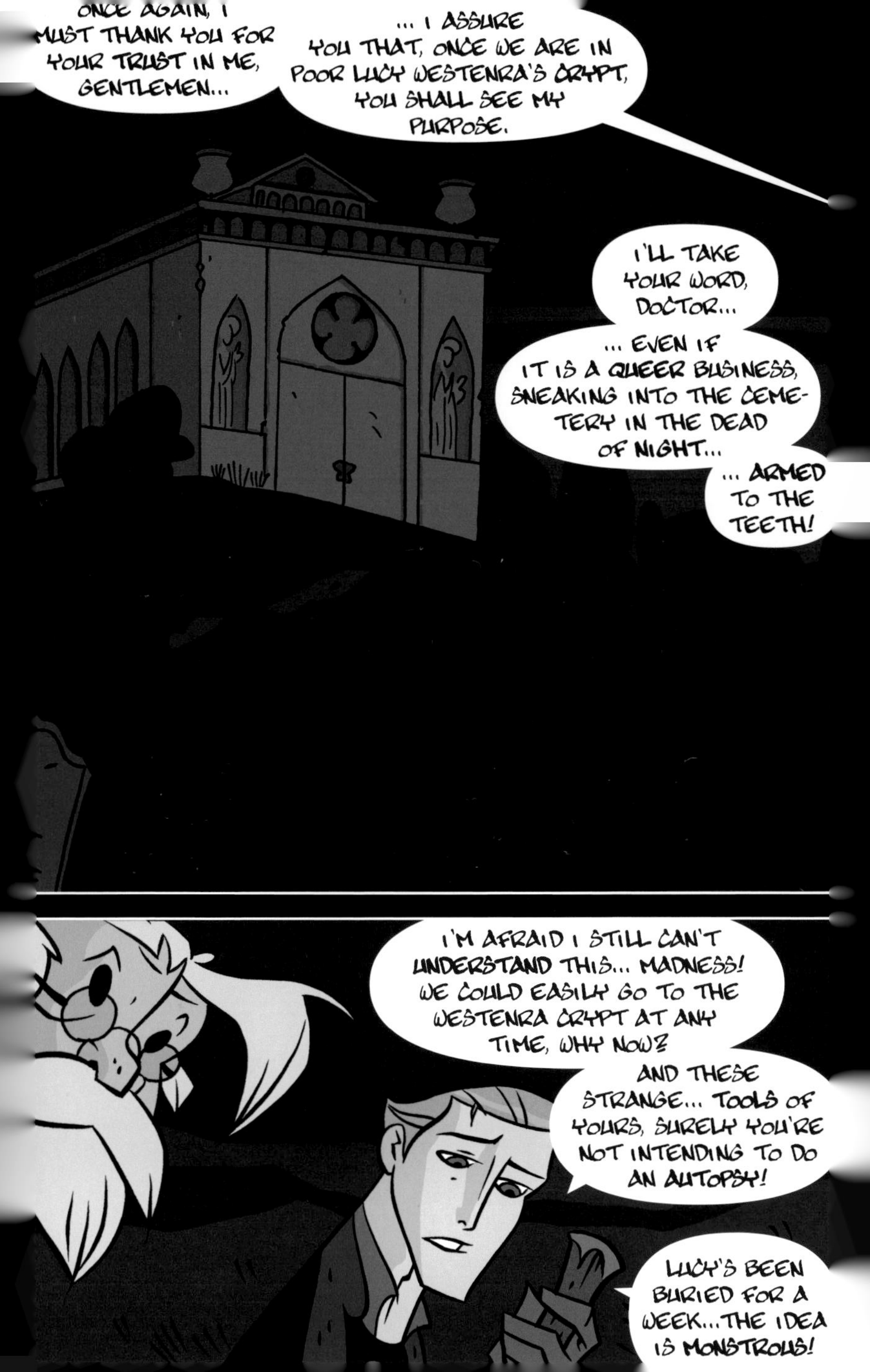
ONCE AGAIN, I MUST THANK YOU FOR YOUR TRUST IN ME, GENTLEMEN...
... I ASSURE YOU THAT, ONCE WE ARE IN POOR LUCY WESTENRA'S CRYPT, YOU SHALL SEE MY PURPOSE.
I'LL TAKE YOUR WORD, DOCTOR...
... EVEN IF IT IS A QUEER BUSINESS, SNEAKING INTO THE CEMETERY IN THE DEAD OF NIGHT...
... ARMED TO THE TEETH!
I'M AFRAID I STILL CAN'T UNDERSTAND THIS... MADNESS! WE COULD EASILY GO TO THE WESTENRA CRYPT AT ANY TIME, WHY NOW?
AND THESE STRANGE... TOOLS OF YOURS, SURELY YOU'RE NOT INTENDING TO DO AN AUTOPSY!
LUCY'S BEEN BURIED FOR A WEEK...THE IDEA IS MONSTROUS!

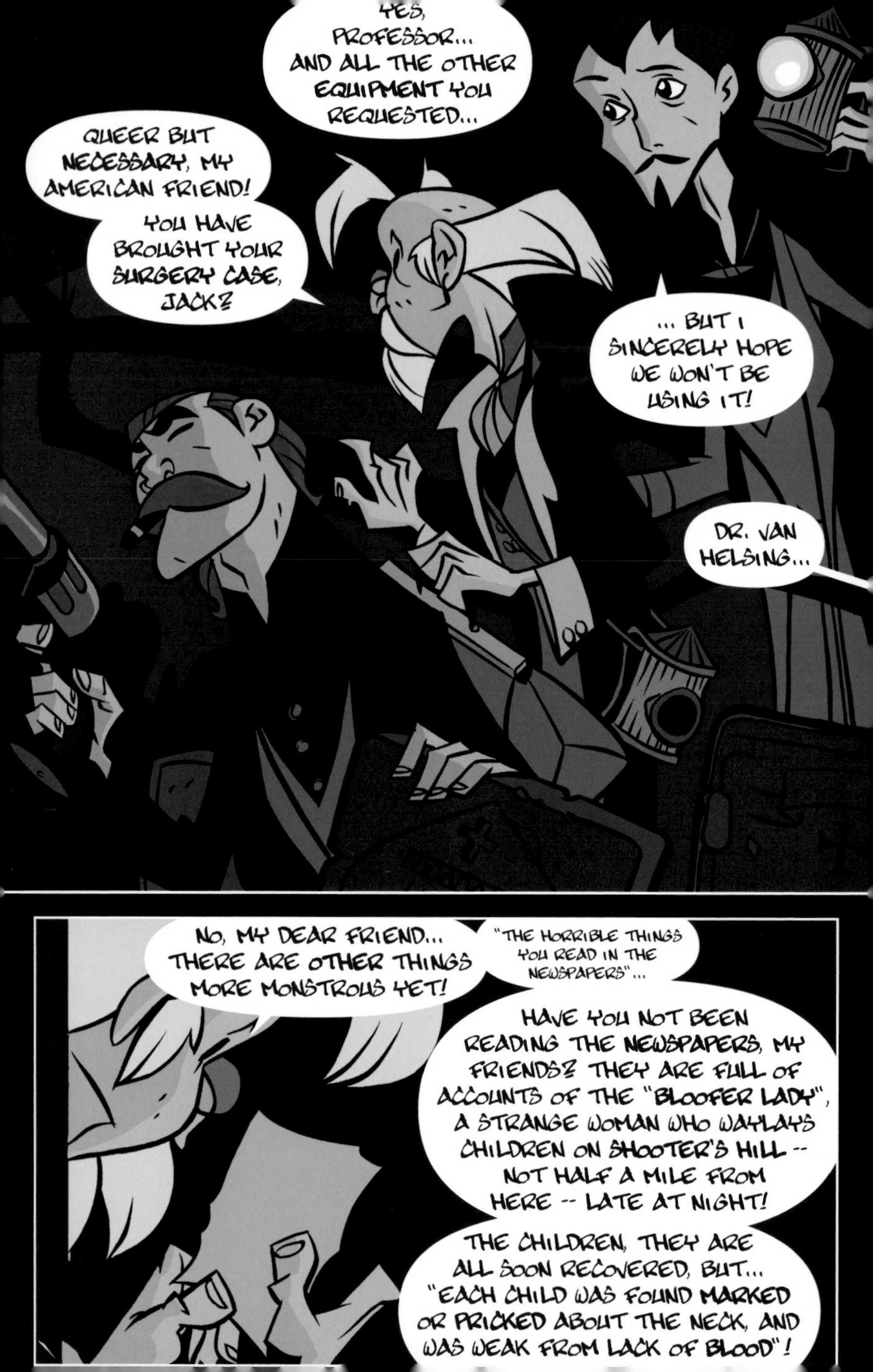
YES, PROFESSOR... AND ALL THE OTHER EQUIPMENT YOU REQUESTED...
QUEER BUT NECESSARY, MY AMERICAN FRIEND!
YOU HAVE BROUGHT YOUR SURGERY CASE, JACK?
... BUT I SINCERELY HOPE WE WON'T BE USING IT!
DR. VAN HELSING...
NO, MY DEAR FRIEND... THERE ARE OTHER THINGS MORE MONSTROUS YET!
"THE HORRIBLE THINGS YOU READ IN THE NEWSPAPERS"...
HAVE YOU NOT BEEN READING THE NEWSPAPERS, MY FRIENDS? THEY ARE FULL OF ACCOUNTS OF THE "BLOOFER LADY", A STRANGE WOMAN WHO WAYLAYS CHILDREN ON SHOOTER'S HILL -- NOT HALF A MILE FROM HERE -- LATE AT NIGHT!
THE CHILDREN, THEY ARE ALL SOON RECOVERED, BUT... "EACH CHILD WAS FOUND MARKED OR PRICKED ABOUT THE NECK, AND WAS WEAK FROM LACK OF BLOOD"!

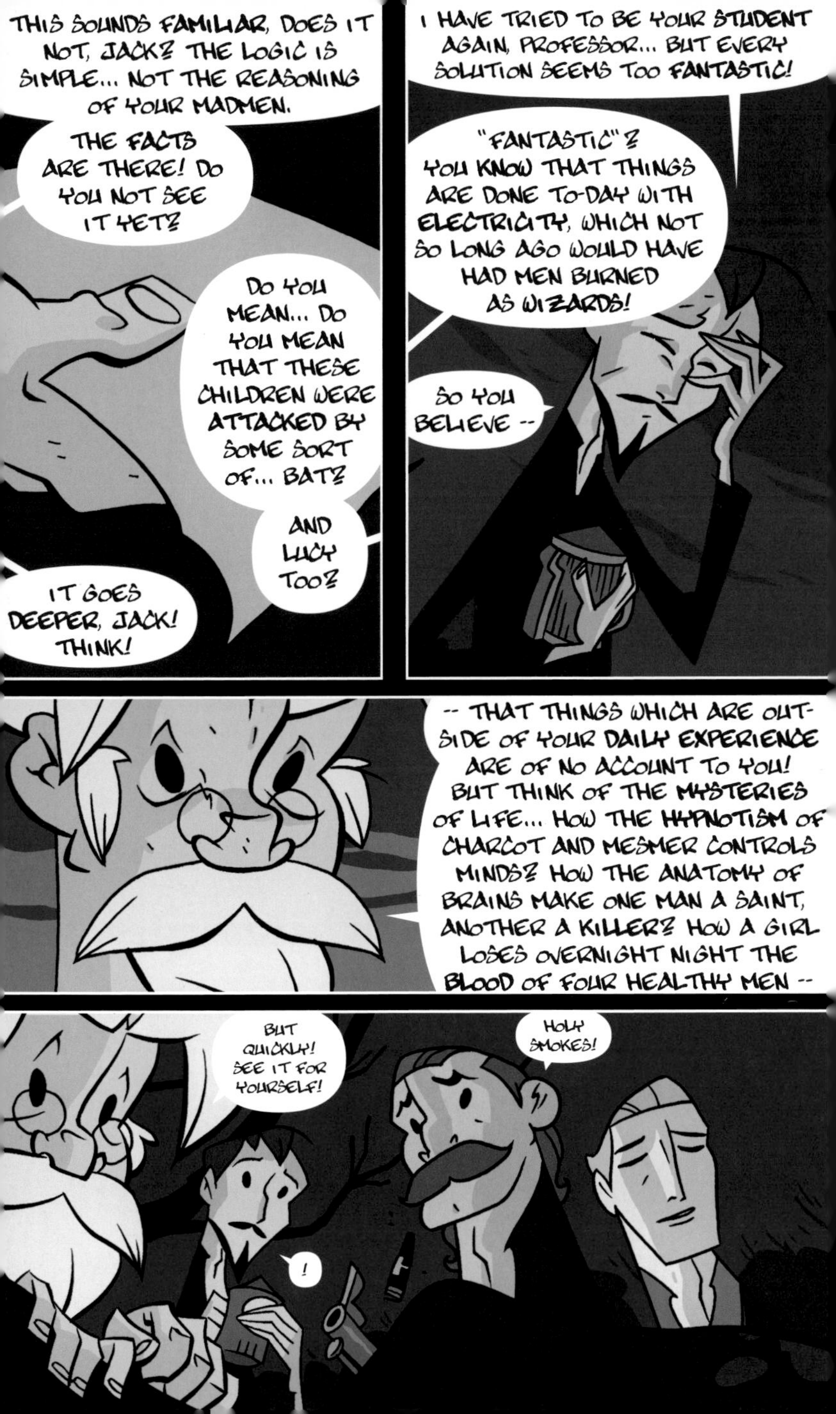
THIS SOUNDS FAMILIAR, DOES IT NOT, JACK? THE LOGIC IS SIMPLE... NOT THE REASONING OF YOUR MADMEN.
THE FACTS ARE THERE! DO YOU NOT SEE IT YET?
DO YOU MEAN... DO YOU MEAN THAT THESE CHILDREN WERE ATTACKED BY SOME SORT OF... BAT?
AND LUCY TOO?
IT GOES DEEPER, JACK! THINK!
I HAVE TRIED TO BE YOUR STUDENT AGAIN, PROFESSOR... BUT EVERY SOLUTION SEEMS TOO FANTASTIC!
"FANTASTIC"? YOU KNOW THAT THINGS ARE DONE TO-DAY WITH ELECTRICITY, WHICH NOT SO LONG AGO WOULD HAVE HAD MEN BURNED AS WIZARDS!
SO YOU BELIEVE --
-- THAT THINGS WHICH ARE OUT-SIDE OF YOUR DAILY EXPERIENCE ARE OF NO ACCOUNT TO YOU! BUT THINK OF THE MYSTERIES OF LIFE... HOW THE HYPNOTISM OF CHARCOT AND MESMER CONTROLS MINDS? HOW THE ANATOMY OF BRAINS MAKE ONE MAN A SAINT, ANOTHER A KILLER? HOW A GIRL LOSES OVERNIGHT NIGHT THE BLOOD OF FOUR HEALTHY MEN --
BUT QUICKLY! SEE IT FOR YOURSELF!
HOLY SMOKES!
!

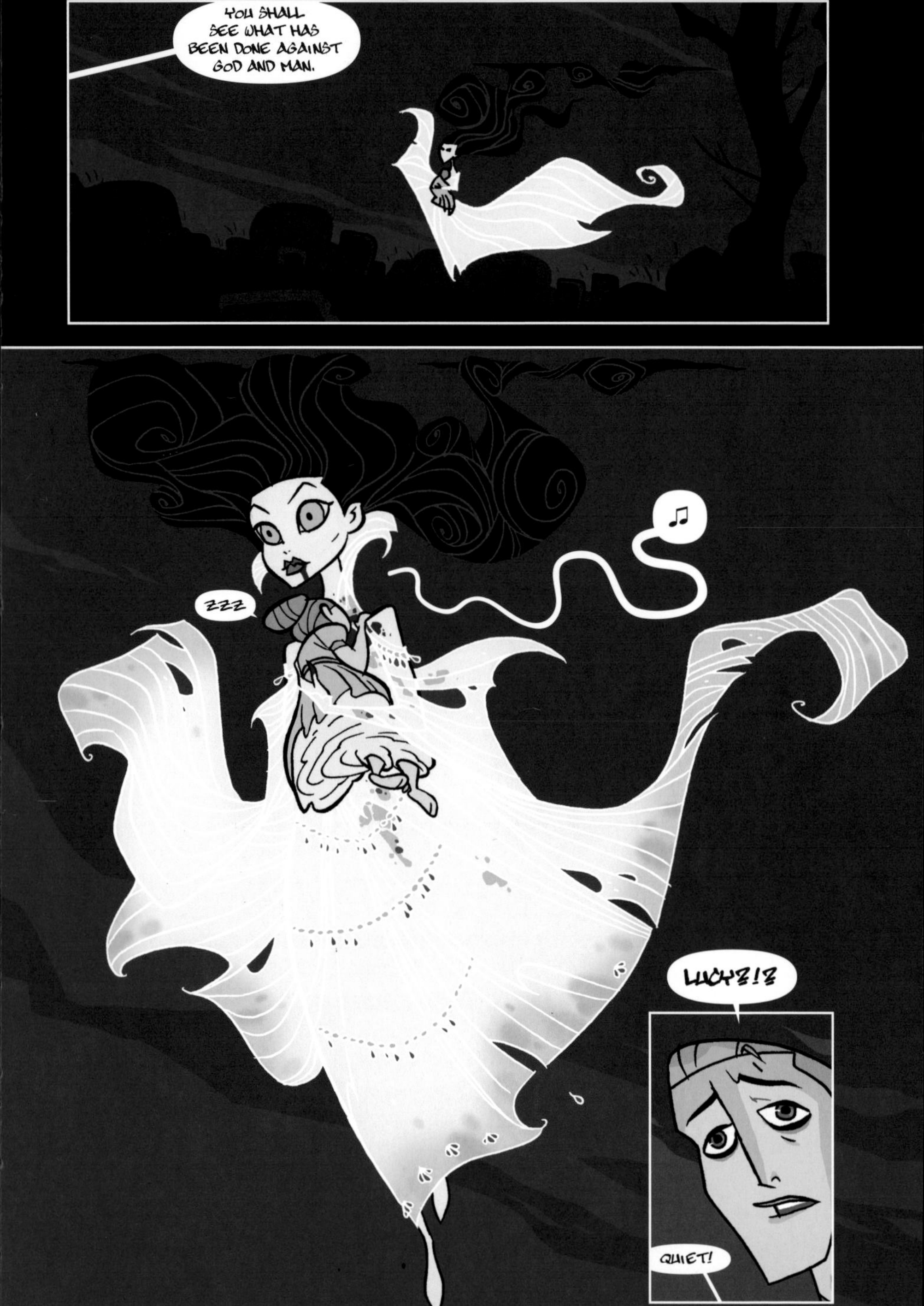
YOU SHALL SEE WHAT HAS BEEN DONE AGAINST GOD AND MAN.
ZZZ
♫
LUCY?!?
QUIET!

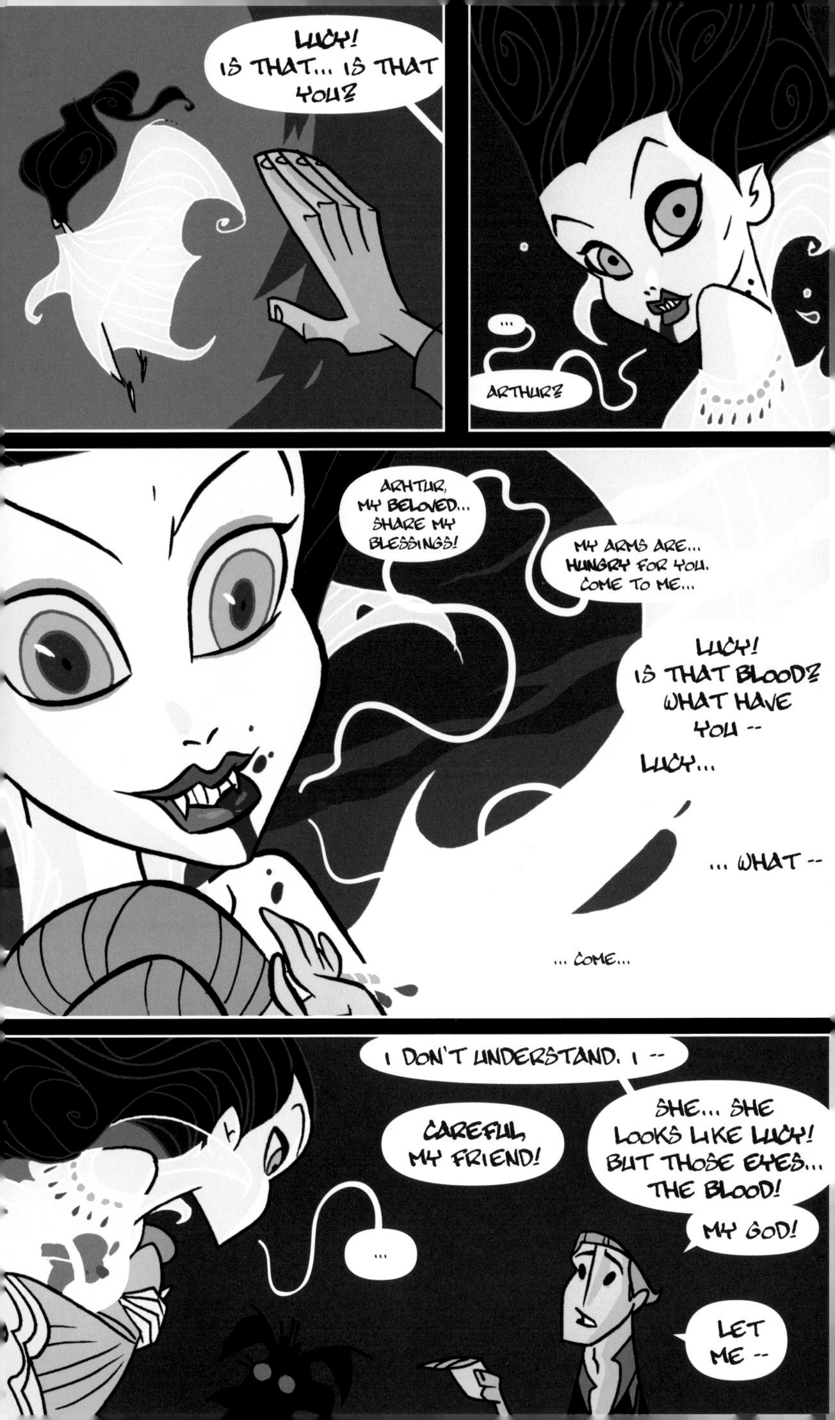
LUCY! IS THAT... IS THAT YOU?
...
ARTHUR?
ARHTUR, MY BELOVED... SHARE MY BLESSINGS!
MY ARMS ARE... HUNGRY FOR YOU. COME TO ME...
LUCY! IS THAT BLOOD? WHAT HAVE YOU --
LUCY...
... WHAT --
... COME...
I DON'T UNDERSTAND. I --
SHE... SHE LOOKS LIKE LUCY! BUT THOSE EYES... THE BLOOD!
MY GOD!
CAREFUL MY FRIEND!
...
LET ME --

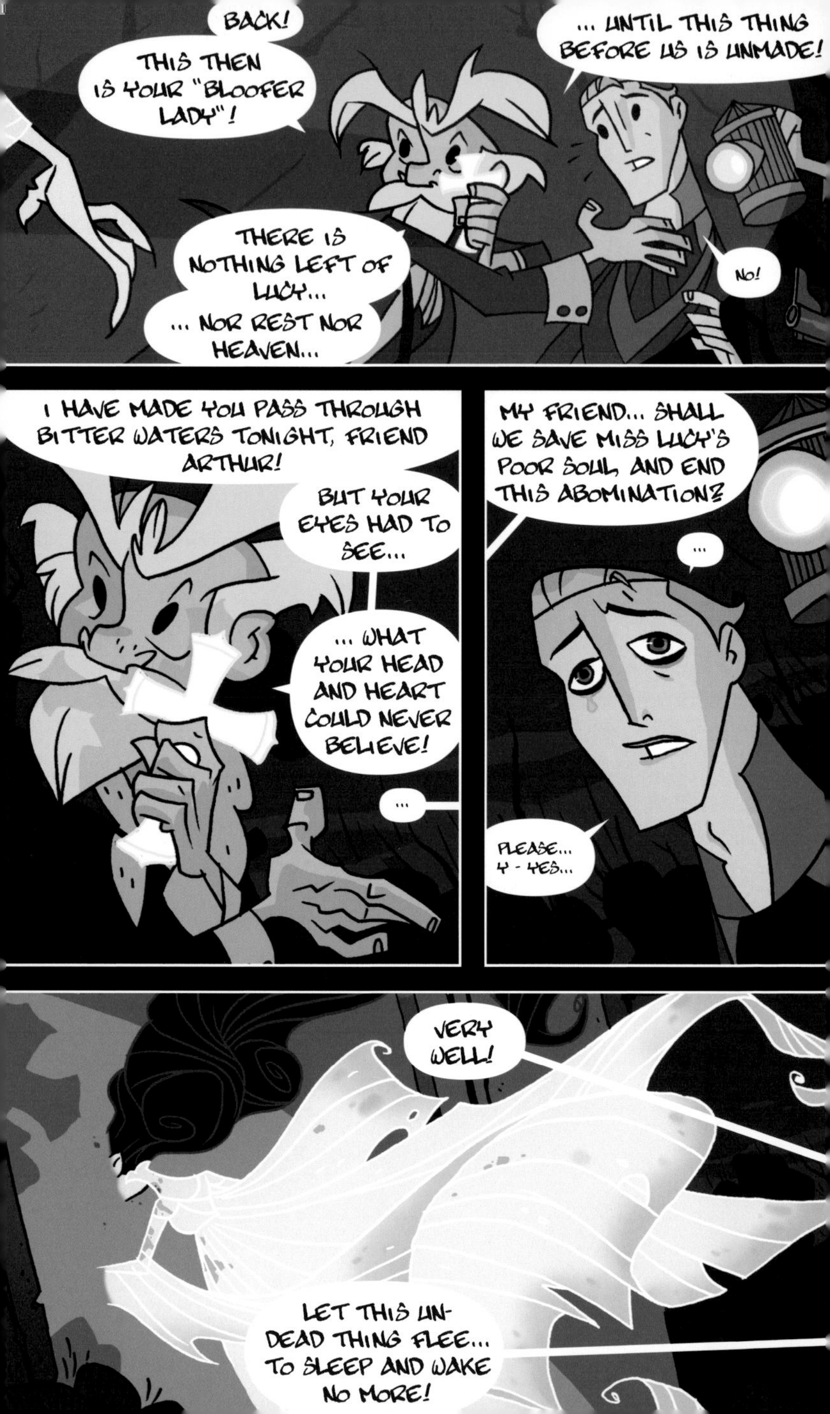
BACK!
THIS THEN IS YOUR "BLOOFER LADY"!
... UNTIL THIS THING BEFORE US IS UNMADE!
THERE IS NOTHING LEFT OF LUCY...
... NOR REST NOR HEAVEN...
NO!
I HAVE MADE YOU PASS THROUGH BITTER WATERS TONIGHT, FRIEND ARTHUR!
BUT YOUR EYES HAD TO SEE...
... WHAT YOUR HEAD AND HEART COULD NEVER BELIEVE!
...
MY FRIEND... SHALL WE SAVE MISS LUCY'S POOR SOUL, AND END THIS ABOMINATION?
...
PLEASE... Y - YES...
VERY WELL!
LET THIS UN-DEAD THING FLEE... TO SLEEP AND WAKE NO MORE!

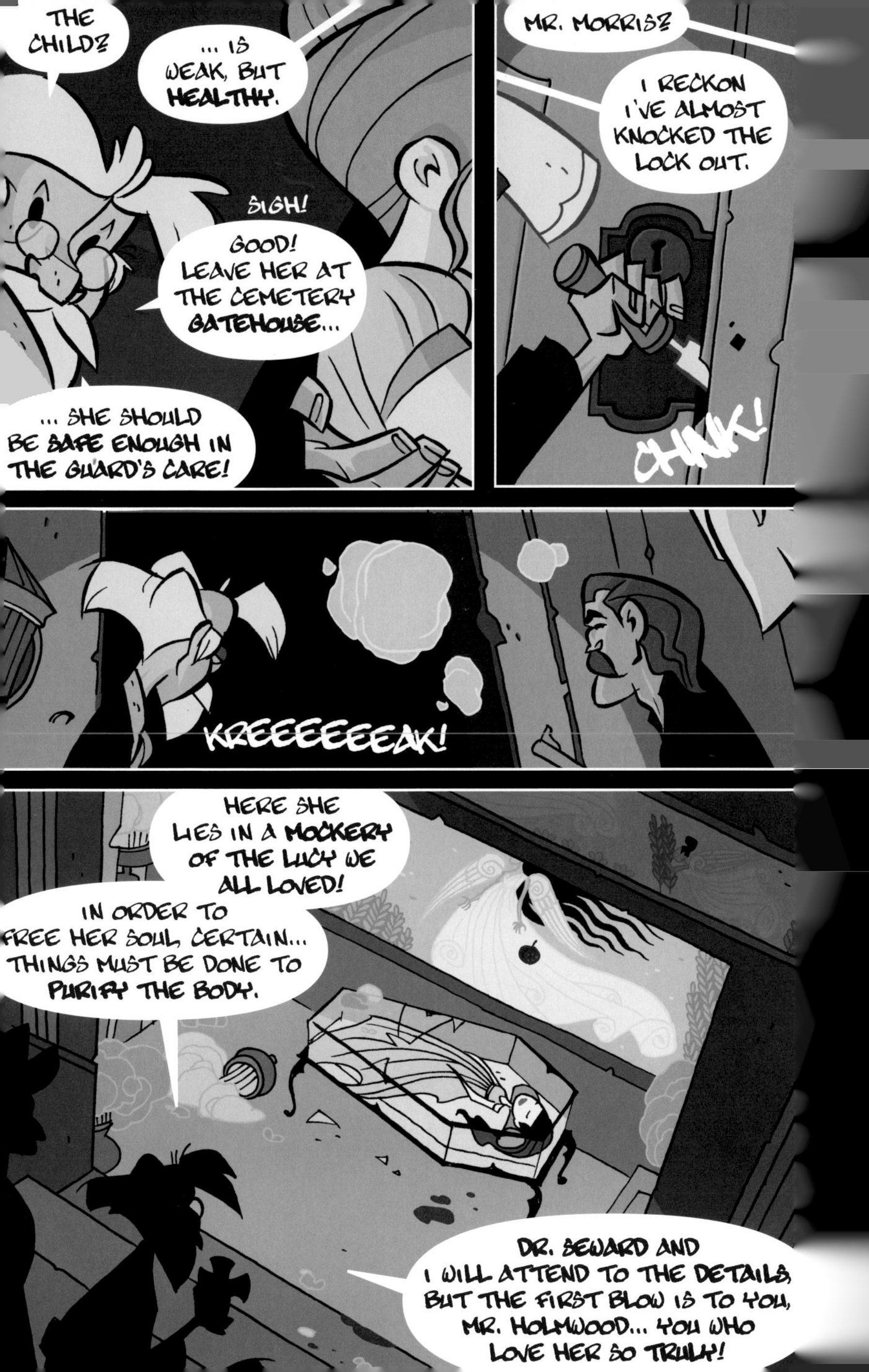
THE CHILD?
... IS WEAK, BUT HEALTHY.
SIGH!
GOOD! LEAVE HER AT THE CEMETERY GATEHOUSE...
... SHE SHOULD BE SAFE ENOUGH IN THE GUARD'S CARE!
MR. MORRIS?
I RECKON I'VE ALMOST KNOCKED THE LOCK OUT.
CHINK!
KREEEEEEEEAK!
HERE SHE LIES IN A MOCKERY OF THE LUCY WE ALL LOVED!
IN ORDER TO FREE HER SOUL, CERTAIN... THINGS MUST BE DONE TO PURIFY THE BODY.
DR. SEWARD AND I WILL ATTEND TO THE DETAILS, BUT THE FIRST BLOW IS TO YOU, MR. HOLMWOOD... YOU WHO LOVE HER SO TRULY!

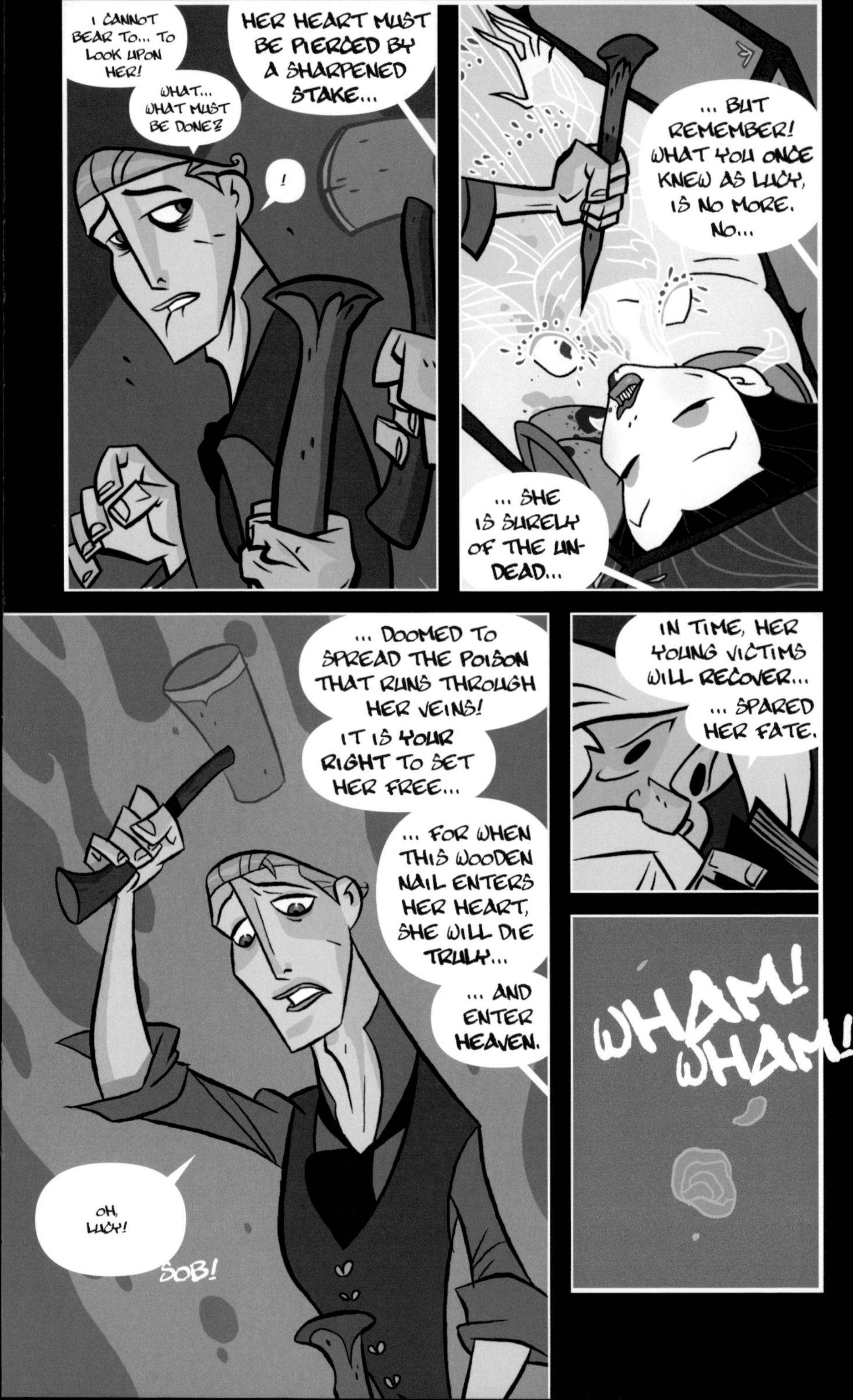
I CANNOT BEAR TO... TO LOOK UPON HER!
WHAT... WHAT MUST BE DONE?
HER HEART MUST BE PIERCED BY A SHARPENED STAKE...
!
... BUT REMEMBER! WHAT YOU ONCE KNEW AS LUCY, IS NO MORE. NO...
... SHE IS SURELY OF THE UN-DEAD...
... DOOMED TO SPREAD THE POISON THAT RUNS THROUGH HER VEINS!
IT IS YOUR RIGHT TO SET HER FREE...
... FOR WHEN THIS WOODEN NAIL ENTERS HER HEART, SHE WILL DIE TRULY...
... AND ENTER HEAVEN.
OH, LUCY!
SOB!
IN TIME, HER YOUNG VICTIMS WILL RECOVER...
... SPARED HER FATE.
WHAM!
WHAM!

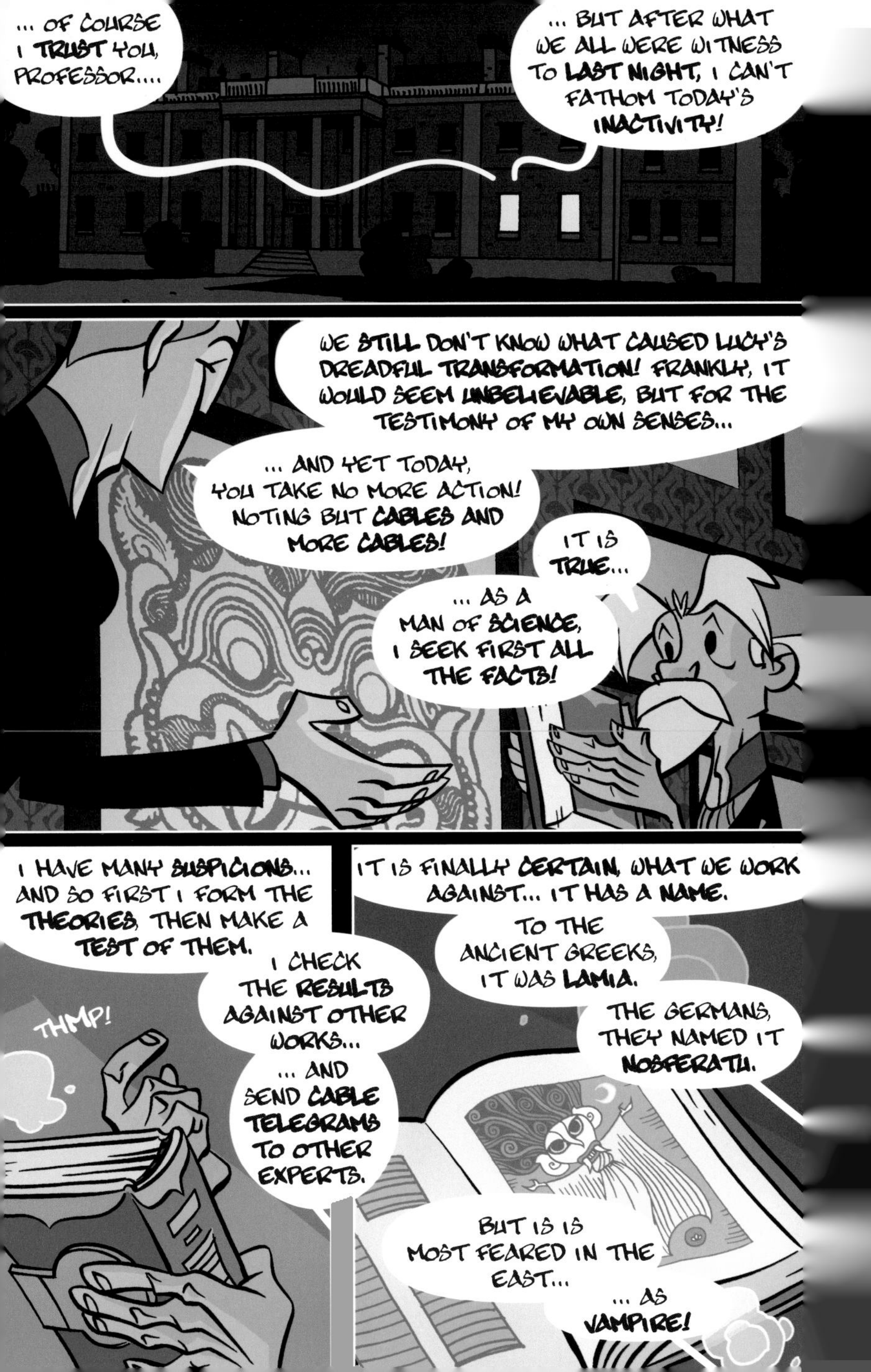
... OF COURSE I TRUST YOU, PROFESSOR....
... BUT AFTER WHAT WE ALL WERE WITNESS TO LAST NIGHT, I CAN'T FATHOM TODAY'S INACTIVITY!
WE STILL DON'T KNOW WHAT CAUSED LUCY'S DREADFUL TRANSFORMATION! FRANKLY, IT WOULD SEEM UNBELIEVABLE, BUT FOR THE TESTIMONY OF MY OWN SENSES...
... AND YET TODAY, YOU TAKE NO MORE ACTION! NOTING BUT CABLES AND MORE CABLES!
IT IS TRUE...
... AS A MAN OF SCIENCE, I SEEK FIRST ALL THE FACTS!
I HAVE MANY SUSPICIONS... AND SO FIRST I FORM THE THEORIES, THEN MAKE A TEST OF THEM.
I CHECK THE RESULTS AGAINST OTHER WORKS...
... AND SEND CABLE TELEGRAMS TO OTHER EXPERTS.
THMP!
IT IS FINALLY CERTAIN, WHAT WE WORK AGAINST... IT HAS A NAME.
TO THE ANCIENT GREEKS, IT WAS LAMIA.
THE GERMANS, THEY NAMED IT NOSFERATU.
BUT IS IS MOST FEARED IN THE EAST...
... AS VAMPIRE!

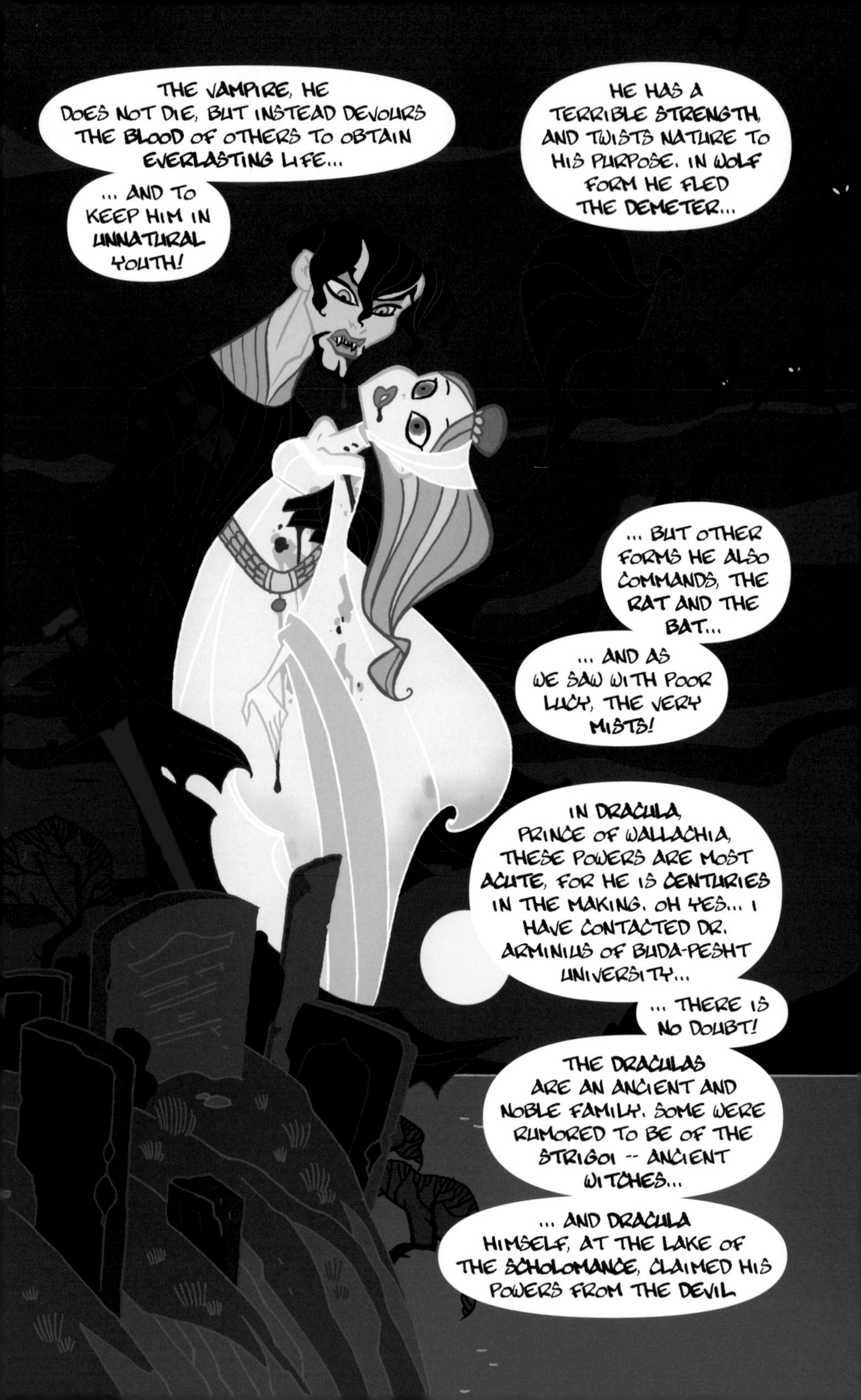
THE VAMPIRE, HE DOES NOT DIE, BUT INSTEAD DEVOURS THE BLOOD OF OTHERS TO OBTAIN EVERLASTING LIFE...
... AND TO KEEP HIM IN UNNATURAL YOUTH!
HE HAS A TERRIBLE STRENGTH, AND TWISTS NATURE TO HIS PURPOSE. IN WOLF FORM HE FLED THE DEMETER...
... BUT OTHER FORMS HE ALSO COMMANDS, THE RAT AND THE BAT...
... AND AS WE SAW WITH POOR LUCY, THE VERY MISTS!
IN DRACULA, PRINCE OF WALLACHIA, THESE POWERS ARE MOST ACUTE, FOR HE IS CENTURIES IN THE MAKING. OH YES... I HAVE CONTACTED DR. ARMINIUS OF BUDA-PESHT UNIVERSITY...
... THERE IS NO DOUBT!
THE DRACULAS ARE AN ANCIENT AND NOBLE FAMILY. SOME WERE RUMORED TO BE OF THE STRIGOI -- ANCIENT WITCHES...
... AND DRACULA HIMSELF, AT THE LAKE OF THE SCHOLOMANCE, CLAIMED HIS POWERS FROM THE DEVIL

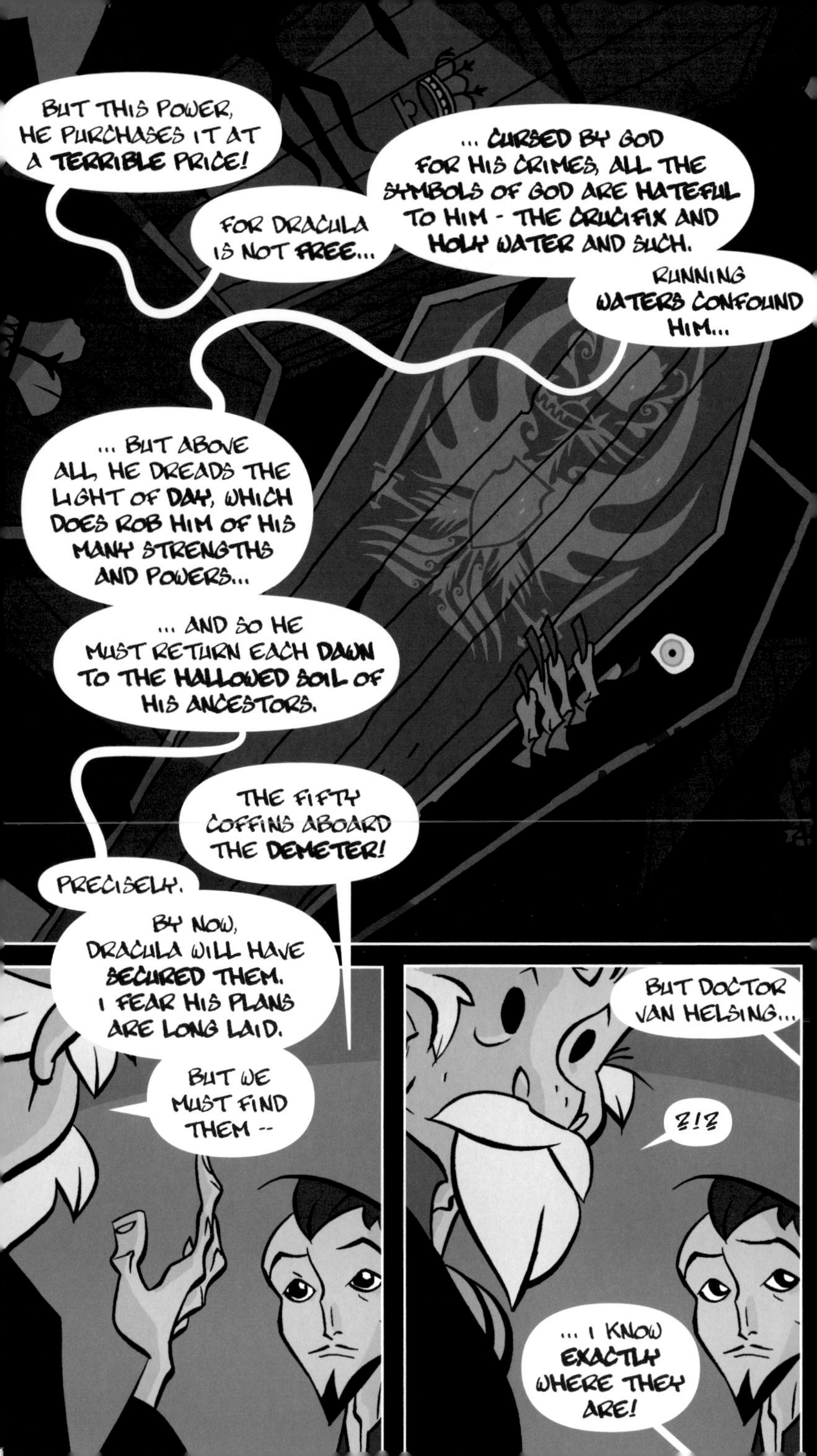
BUT THIS POWER, HE PURCHASES IT AT A TERRIBLE PRICE!
FOR DRACULA IS NOT FREE...
... CURSED BY GOD FOR HIS CRIMES, ALL THE SYMBOLS OF GOD ARE HATEFUL TO HIM - THE CRUCIFIX AND HOLY WATER AND SUCH.
RUNNING WATERS CONFOUND HIM...
... BUT ABOVE ALL, HE DREADS THE LIGHT OF DAY, WHICH DOES ROB HIM OF HIS MANY STRENGTHS AND POWERS...
... AND SO HE MUST RETURN EACH DAWN TO THE HALLOWED SOIL OF HIS ANCESTORS.
THE FIFTY COFFINS ABOARD THE DEMETER!
PRECISELY.
BY NOW, DRACULA WILL HAVE SECURED THEM. I FEAR HIS PLANS ARE LONG LAID.
BUT WE MUST FIND THEM --
BUT DOCTOR VAN HELSING...
?!?
... I KNOW EXACTLY WHERE THEY ARE!

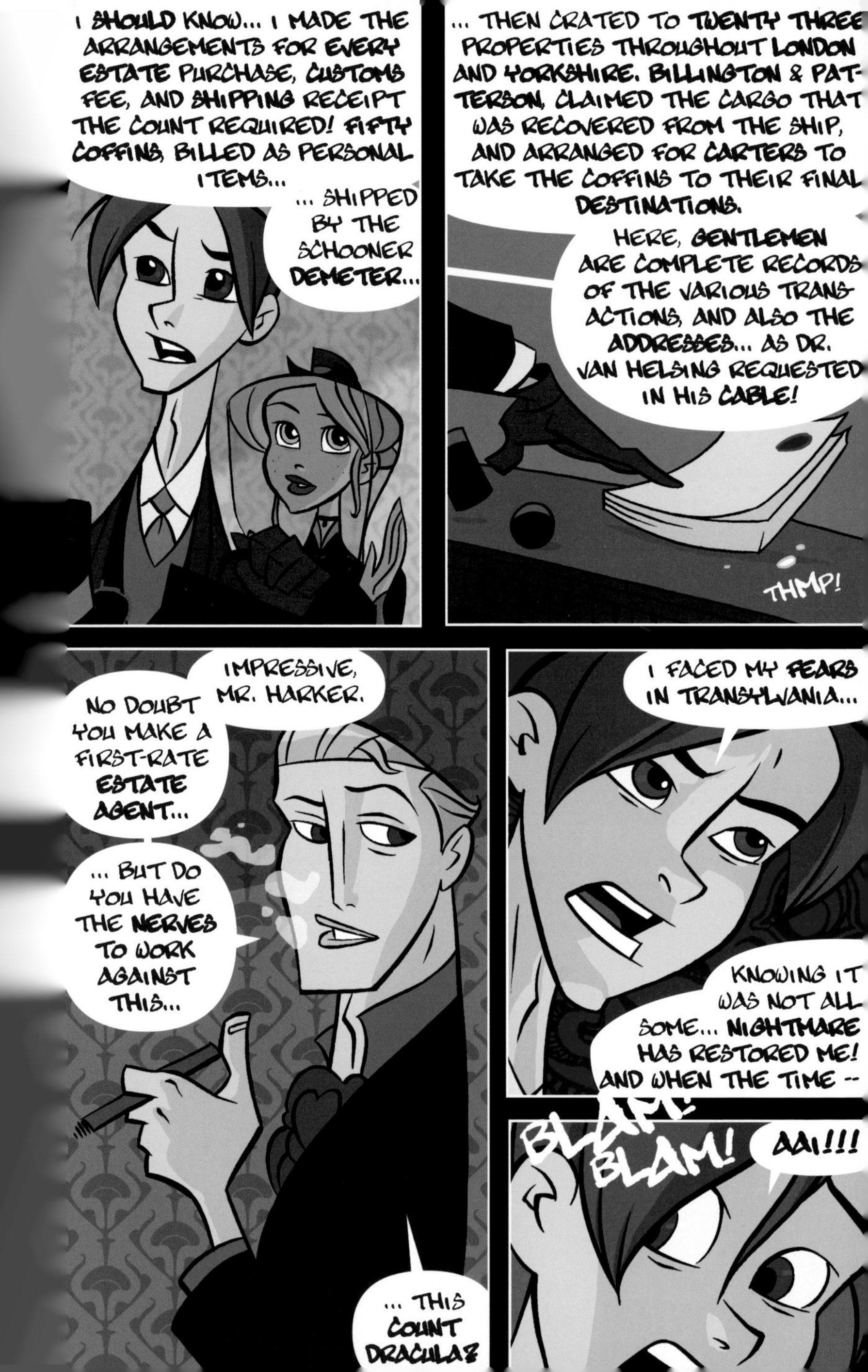
I SHOULD KNOW... I MADE THE ARRANGEMENTS FOR EVERY ESTATE PURCHASE, CUSTOMS FEE, AND SHIPPING RECEIPT THE COUNT REQUIRED! FIFTY COFFINS, BILLED AS PERSONAL ITEMS...
... SHIPPED BY THE SCHOONER DEMETER...
... THEN CRATED TO TWENTY THREE PROPERTIES THROUGHOUT LONDON AND YORKSHIRE. BILLINGTON & PATTERSON, CLAIMED THE CARGO THAT WAS RECOVERED FROM THE SHIP, AND ARRANGED FOR CARTERS TO TAKE THE COFFINS TO THEIR FINAL DESTINATIONS.
HERE, GENTLEMEN ARE COMPLETE RECORDS OF THE VARIOUS TRANSACTIONS, AND ALSO THE ADDRESSES... AS DR. VAN HELSING REQUESTED IN HIS CABLE!
THMP!
IMPRESSIVE, MR. HARKER.
NO DOUBT YOU MAKE A FIRST-RATE ESTATE AGENT...
... BUT DO YOU HAVE THE NERVES TO WORK AGAINST THIS...
... THIS COUNT DRACULA?
I FACED MY FEARS IN TRANSYLVANIA...
KNOWING IT WAS NOT ALL SOME... NIGHTMARE HAS RESTORED ME! AND WHEN THE TIME --
BLAM!
BLAM!
AAI!!!

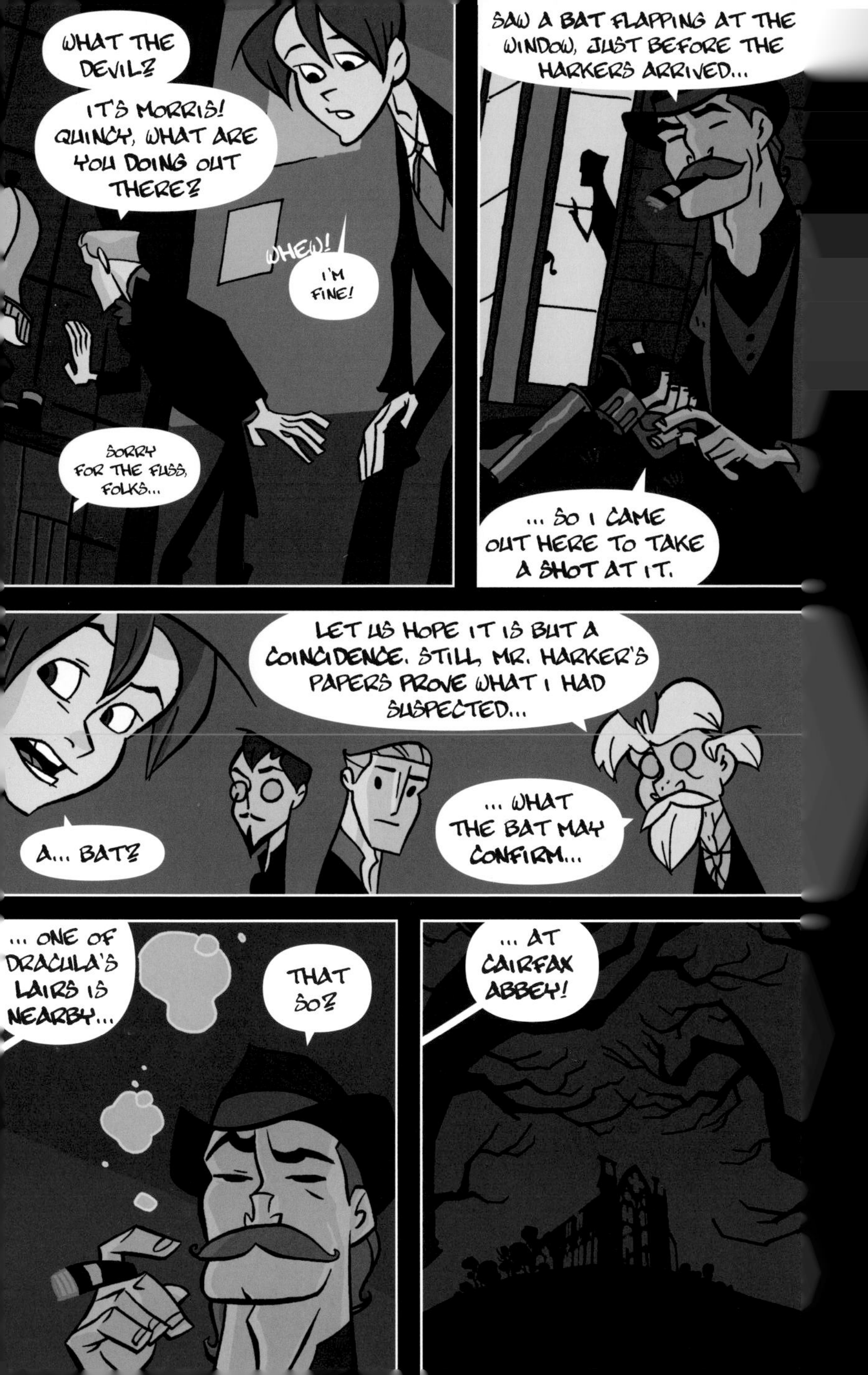
WHAT THE DEVIL?
IT'S MORRIS! QUINCY, WHAT ARE YOU DOING OUT THERE?
WHEW!
I'M FINE!
SORRY FOR THE FUSS, FOLKS...
SAW A BAT FLAPPING AT THE WINDOW, JUST BEFORE THE HARKERS ARRIVED...
... SO I CAME OUT HERE TO TAKE A SHOT AT IT.
LET US HOPE IT IS BUT A COINCIDENCE. STILL, MR. HARKER'S PAPERS PROVE WHAT I HAD SUSPECTED...
A... BAT?
... WHAT THE BAT MAY CONFIRM...
... ONE OF DRACULA'S LAIRS IS NEARBY...
THAT SO?
... AT CAIRFAX ABBEY!

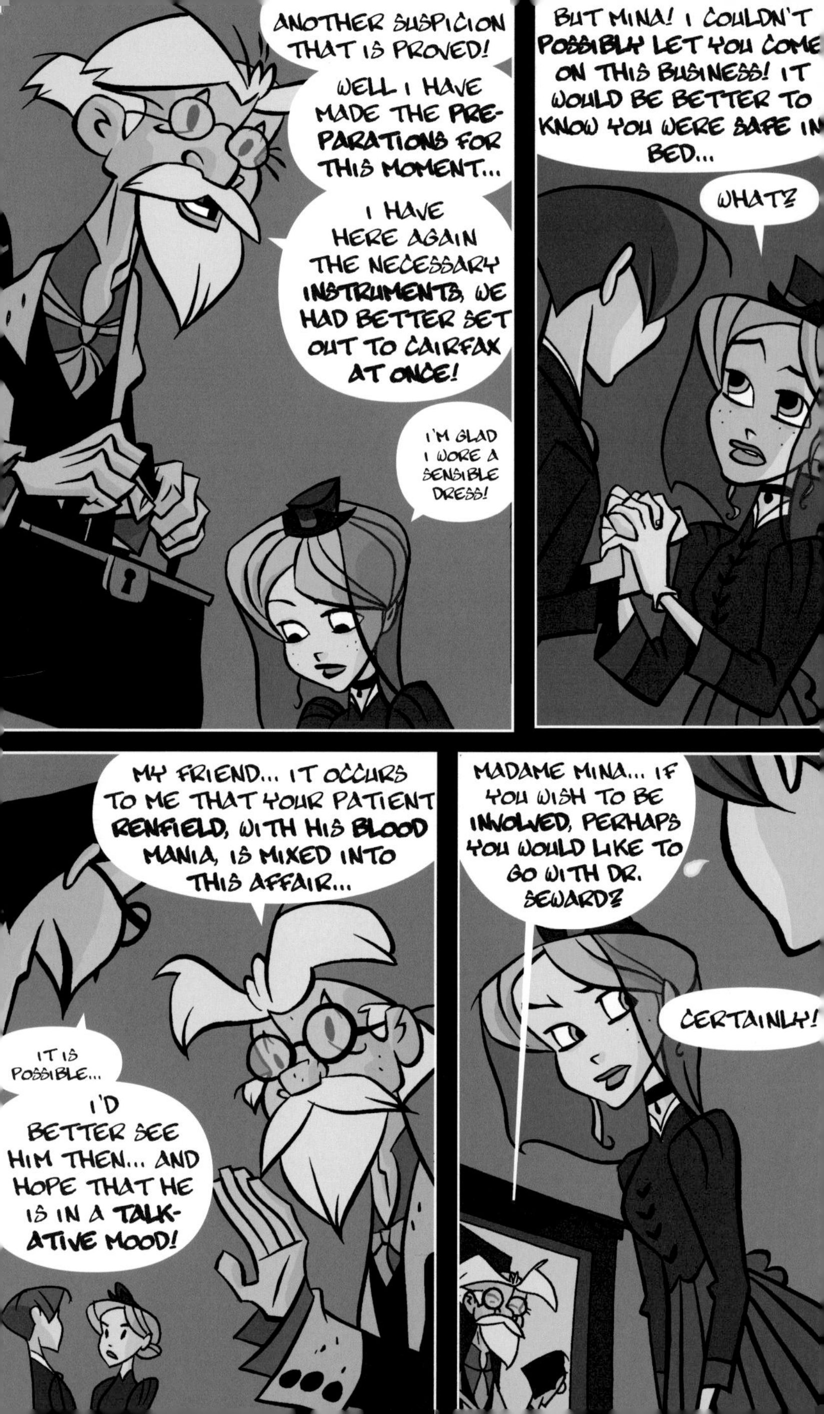
ANOTHER SUSPICION THAT IS PROVED!
WELL I HAVE MADE THE PREPARATIONS FOR THIS MOMENT...
I HAVE HERE AGAIN THE NECESSARY INSTRUMENTS, WE HAD BETTER SET OUT TO CAIRFAX AT ONCE!
I'M GLAD I WORE A SENSIBLE DRESS!
BUT MINA! I COULDN'T POSSIBLY LET YOU COME ON THIS BUSINESS! IT WOULD BE BETTER TO KNOW YOU WERE SAFE IN BED...
WHAT?
MY FRIEND... IT OCCURS TO ME THAT YOUR PATIENT RENFIELD, WITH HIS BLOOD MANIA, IS MIXED INTO THIS AFFAIR...
IT IS POSSIBLE...
I'D BETTER SEE HIM THEN... AND HOPE THAT HE IS IN A TALKATIVE MOOD!
MADAME MINA... IF YOU WISH TO BE INVOLVED, PERHAPS YOU WOULD LIKE TO GO WITH DR. SEWARD?
CERTAINLY!

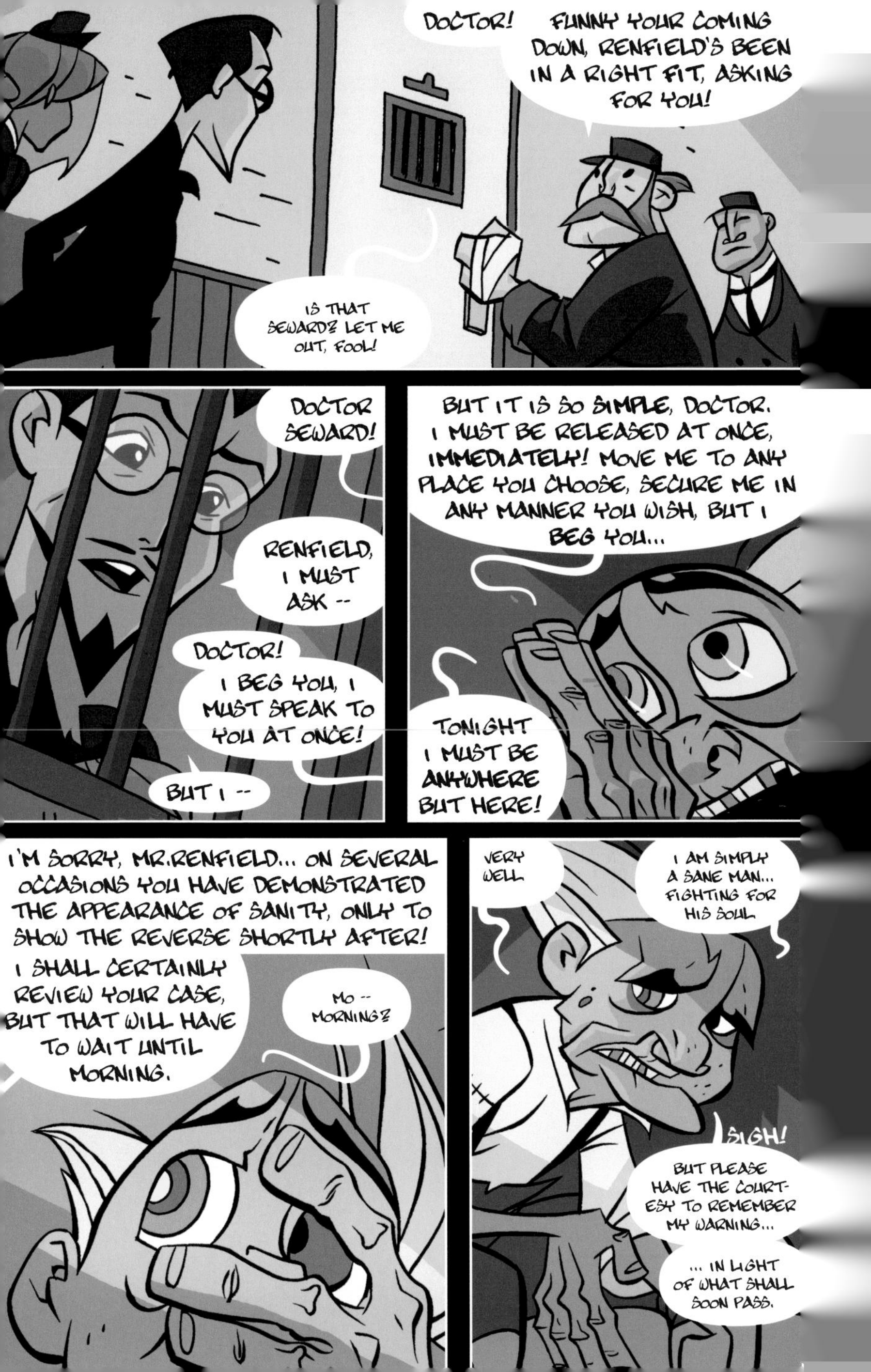
DOCTOR!
FUNNY YOUR COMING DOWN, RENFIELD'S BEEN IN A RIGHT FIT, ASKING FOR YOU!
IS THAT SEWARD? LET ME OUT, FOOL!
DOCTOR SEWARD!
RENFIELD, I MUST ASK --
DOCTOR!
I BEG YOU, I MUST SPEAK TO YOU AT ONCE!
BUT I --
BUT IT IS SO SIMPLE, DOCTOR. I MUST BE RELEASED AT ONCE, IMMEDIATELY! MOVE ME TO ANY PLACE YOU CHOOSE, SECURE ME IN ANY MANNER YOU WISH, BUT I BEG YOU...
TONIGHT I MUST BE ANYWHERE BUT HERE!
I'M SORRY, MR. RENFIELD... ON SEVERAL OCCASIONS YOU HAVE DEMONSTRATED THE APPEARANCE OF SANITY, ONLY TO SHOW THE REVERSE SHORTLY AFTER!
I SHALL CERTAINLY REVIEW YOUR CASE, BUT THAT WILL HAVE TO WAIT UNTIL MORNING.
MO -- MORNING?
VERY WELL.
I AM SIMPLY A SANE MAN... FIGHTING FOR HIS SOUL.
SIGH!
BUT PLEASE HAVE THE COURTESY TO REMEMBER MY WARNING...
... IN LIGHT OF WHAT SHALL SOON PASS.

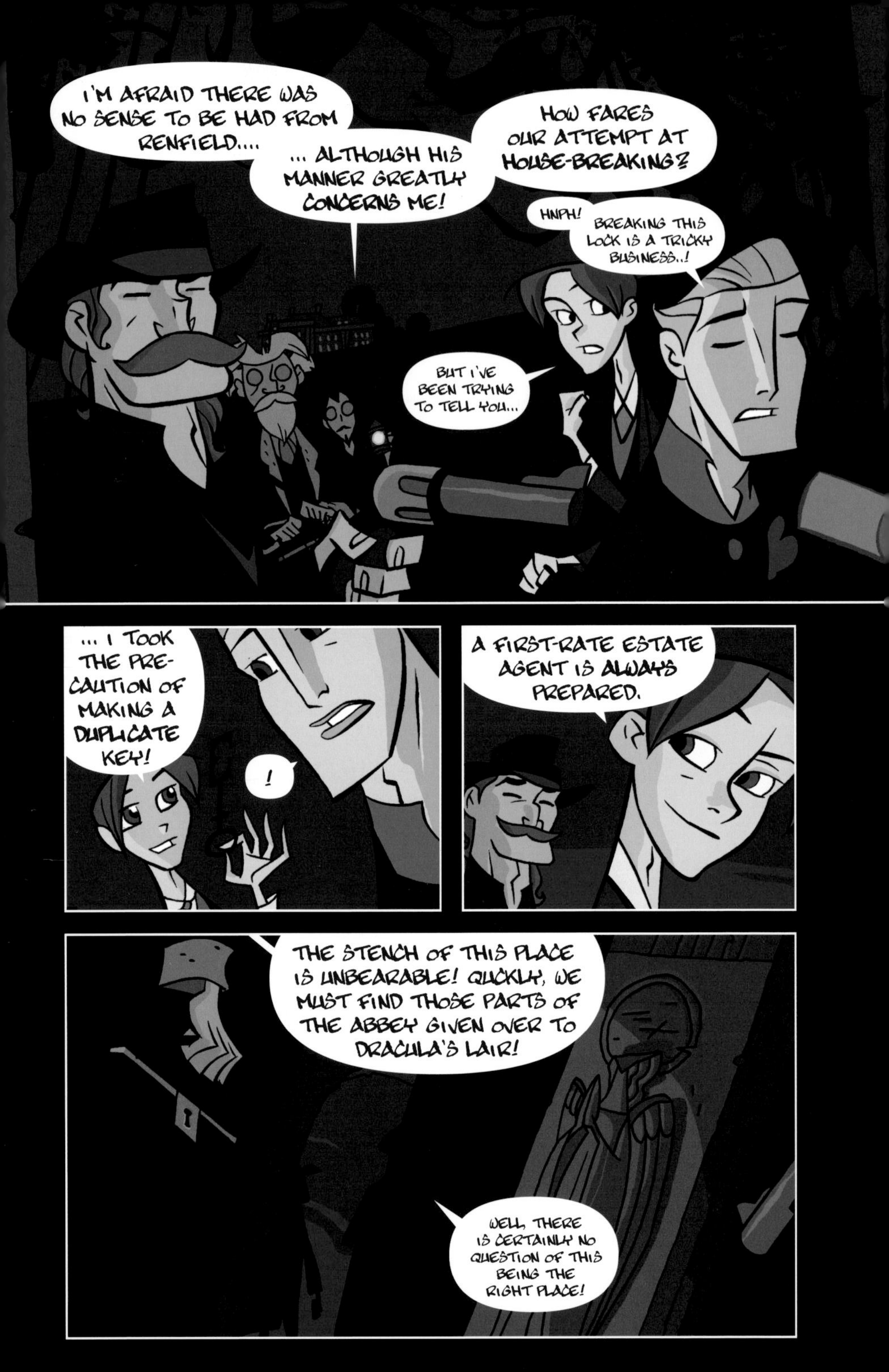
I'M AFRAID THERE WAS NO SENSE TO BE HAD FROM RENFIELD....
... ALTHOUGH HIS MANNER GREATLY CONCERNS ME!
HOW FARES OUR ATTEMPT AT HOUSE-BREAKING?
HNPH!
BREAKING THIS LOCK IS A TRICKY BUSINESS..!
BUT I'VE BEEN TRYING TO TELL YOU...
... I TOOK THE PRE-CAUTION OF MAKING A DUPLICATE KEY!
!
A FIRST-RATE ESTATE AGENT IS ALWAYS PREPARED.
THE STENCH OF THIS PLACE IS UNBEARABLE! QUICKLY, WE MUST FIND THOSE PARTS OF THE ABBEY GIVEN OVER TO DRACULA'S LAIR!
WELL, THERE IS CERTAINLY NO QUESTION OF THIS BEING THE RIGHT PLACE!

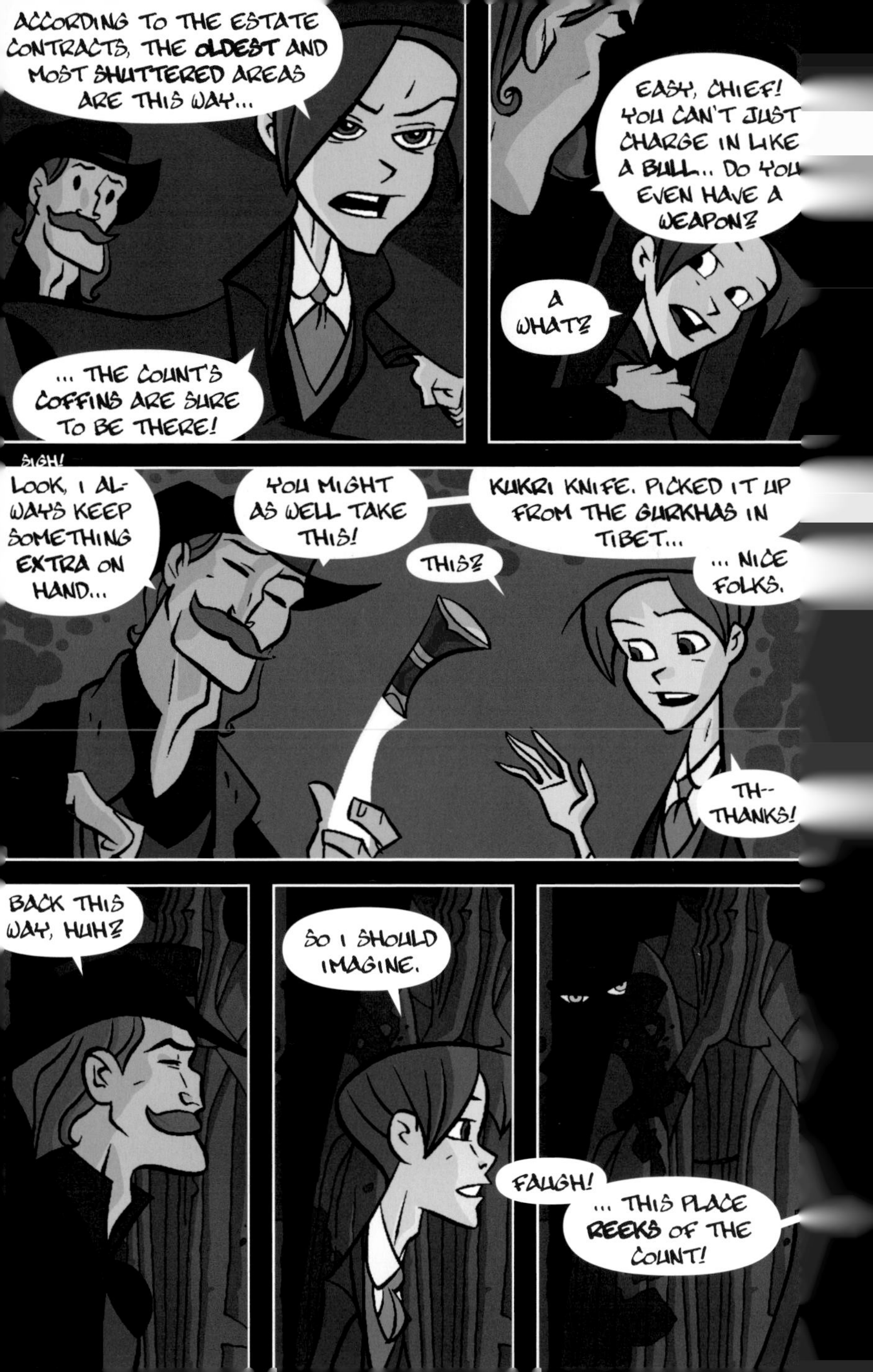
ACCORDING TO THE ESTATE CONTRACTS, THE OLDEST AND MOST SHUTTERED AREAS ARE THIS WAY...
... THE COUNT'S COFFINS ARE SURE TO BE THERE!
EASY, CHIEF! YOU CAN'T JUST CHARGE IN LIKE A BULL.. DO YOU EVEN HAVE A WEAPON?
A WHAT?
SIGH!
LOOK, I AL-WAYS KEEP SOMETHING EXTRA ON HAND...
YOU MIGHT AS WELL TAKE THIS!
KUKRI KNIFE. PICKED IT UP FROM THE GURKHAS IN TIBET...
THIS?
... NICE FOLKS.
TH-THANKS!
BACK THIS WAY, HUH?
SO I SHOULD IMAGINE.
FAUGH!
... THIS PLACE REEKS OF THE COUNT!

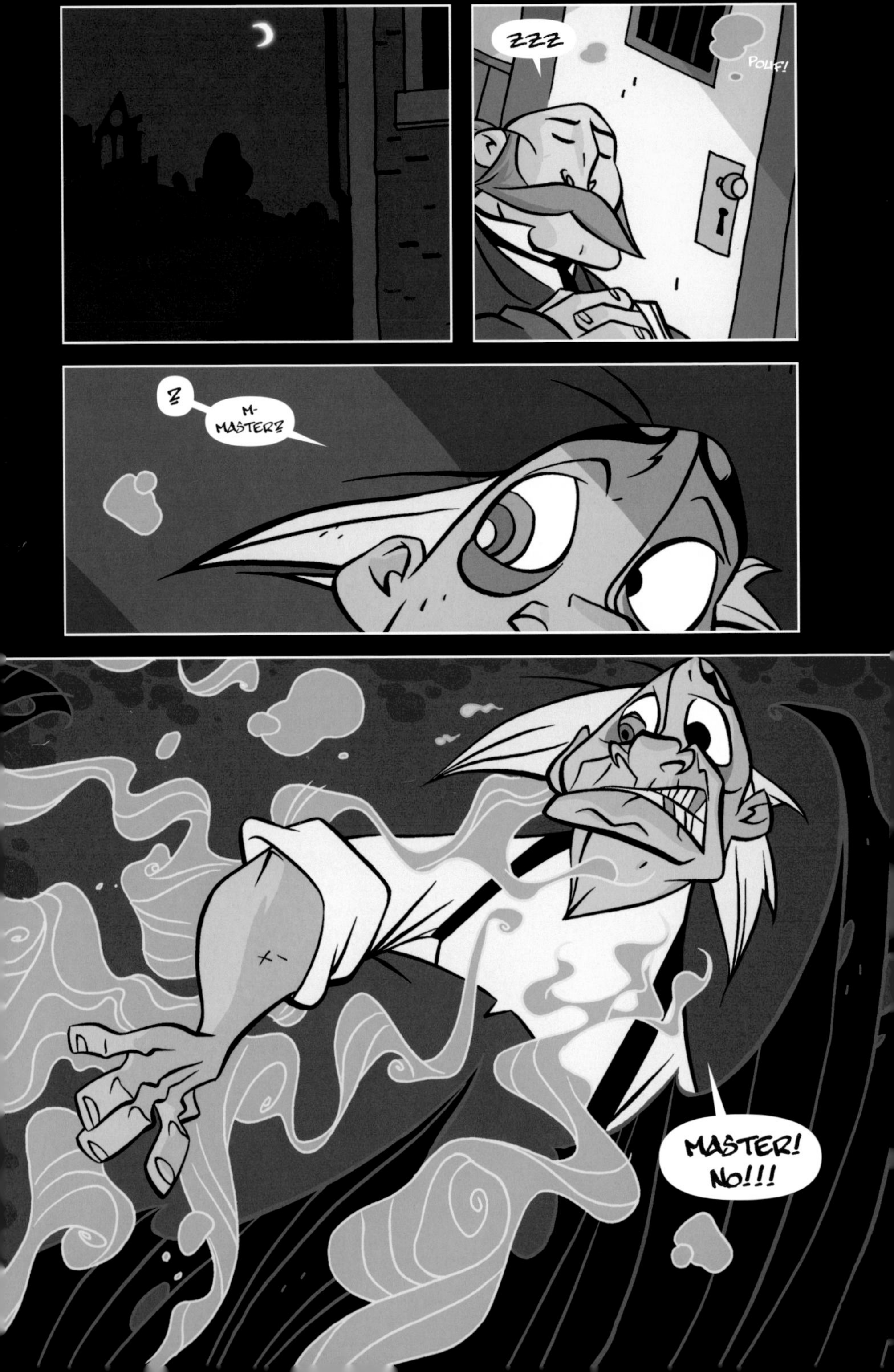
ZZZ
POUF!
Z
M-MASTER?
MASTER! NO!!!

GLK!

THEY HAVE FOUND MY HOME...

WHAT HAVE YOU TOLD THEM, SLAVE?

I HAVE PROMISED YOU MANY SPIDERS... YES, AND OTHER FLESH THAT IS GOOD... ... BUT YOU HAVE EARNED NOTHING!

WE'VE FOUND THEM! BACK HERE!

EXCELLENT!

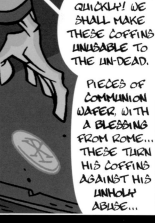

QUICKLY! WE SHALL MAKE THESE COFFINS UNUSABLE TO THE UN-DEAD.

PIECES OF COMMUNION WAFER, WITH A BLESSING FROM ROME... THESE TURN HIS COFFINS AGAINST HIS UNHOLY ABUSE...

BUT FURTHER, LET US TAKE THE STENCH OF UN-DEAD FROM THESE HALLS FOREVER!

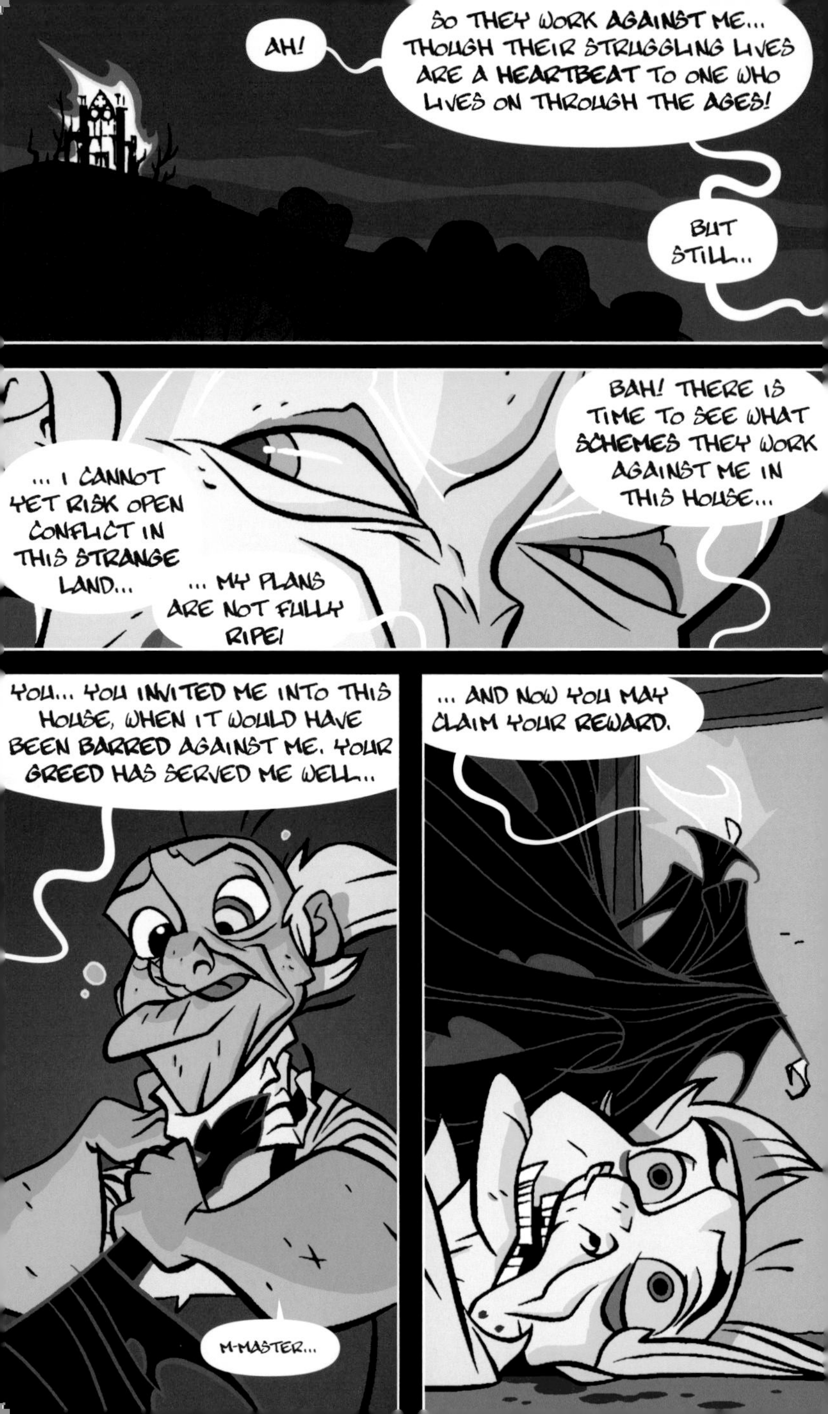
AH!
SO THEY WORK AGAINST ME... THOUGH THEIR STRUGGLING LIVES ARE A HEARTBEAT TO ONE WHO LIVES ON THROUGH THE AGES!
BUT STILL...
... I CANNOT YET RISK OPEN CONFLICT IN THIS STRANGE LAND...
... MY PLANS ARE NOT FULLY RIPE!
BAH! THERE IS TIME TO SEE WHAT SCHEMES THEY WORK AGAINST ME IN THIS HOUSE...
YOU... YOU INVITED ME INTO THIS HOUSE, WHEN IT WOULD HAVE BEEN BARRED AGAINST ME. YOUR GREED HAS SERVED ME WELL...
M-MASTER...
... AND NOW YOU MAY CLAIM YOUR REWARD.

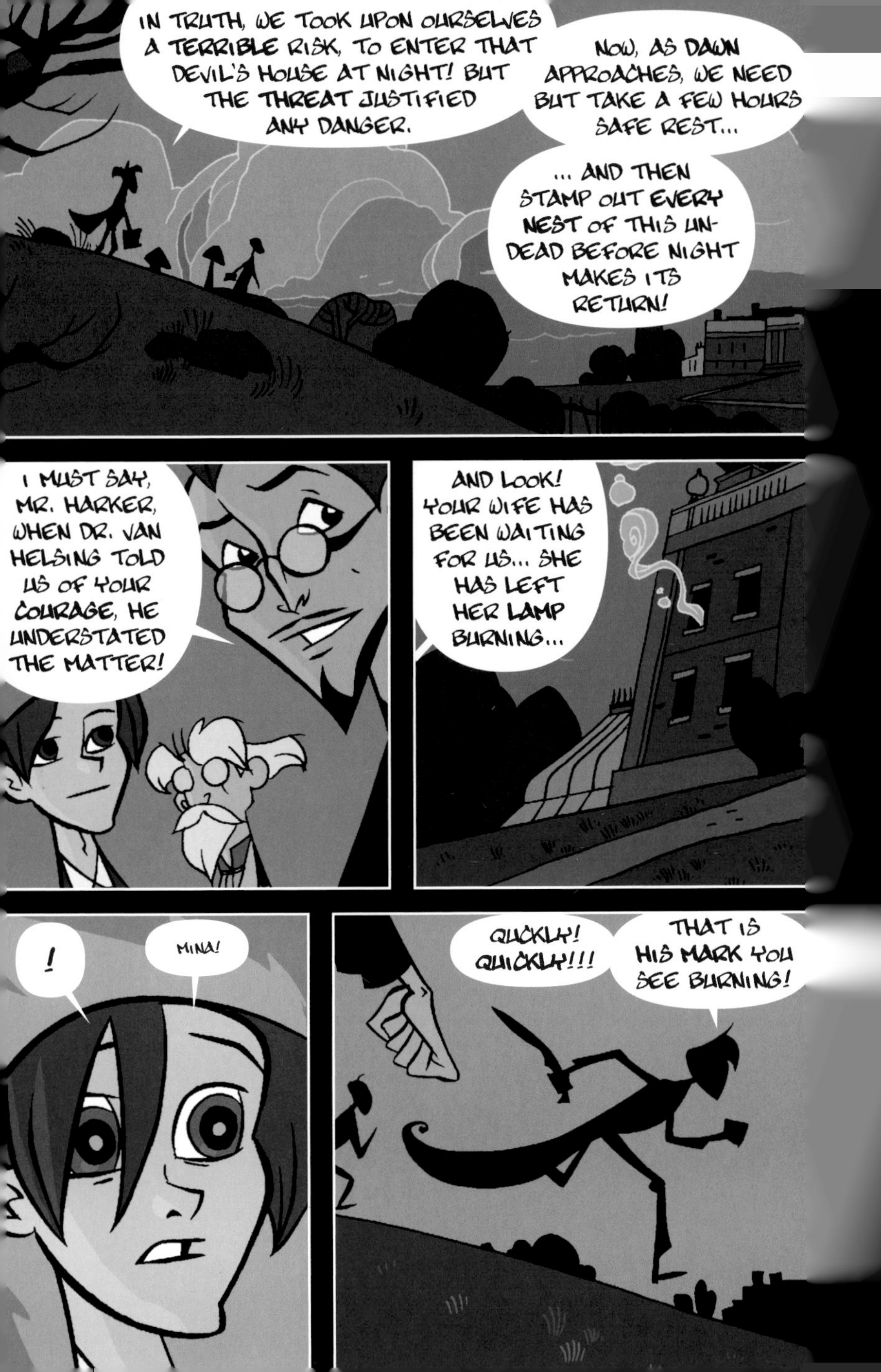
IN TRUTH, WE TOOK UPON OURSELVES A TERRIBLE RISK, TO ENTER THAT DEVIL'S HOUSE AT NIGHT! BUT THE THREAT JUSTIFIED ANY DANGER.
NOW, AS DAWN APPROACHES, WE NEED BUT TAKE A FEW HOURS SAFE REST...
... AND THEN STAMP OUT EVERY NEST OF THIS UN-DEAD BEFORE NIGHT MAKES ITS RETURN!
I MUST SAY, MR. HARKER, WHEN DR. VAN HELSING TOLD US OF YOUR COURAGE, HE UNDERSTATED THE MATTER!
AND LOOK! YOUR WIFE HAS BEEN WAITING FOR US... SHE HAS LEFT HER LAMP BURNING...
!
MINA!
THAT IS HIS MARK YOU SEE BURNING!
QUICKLY! QUICKLY!!!

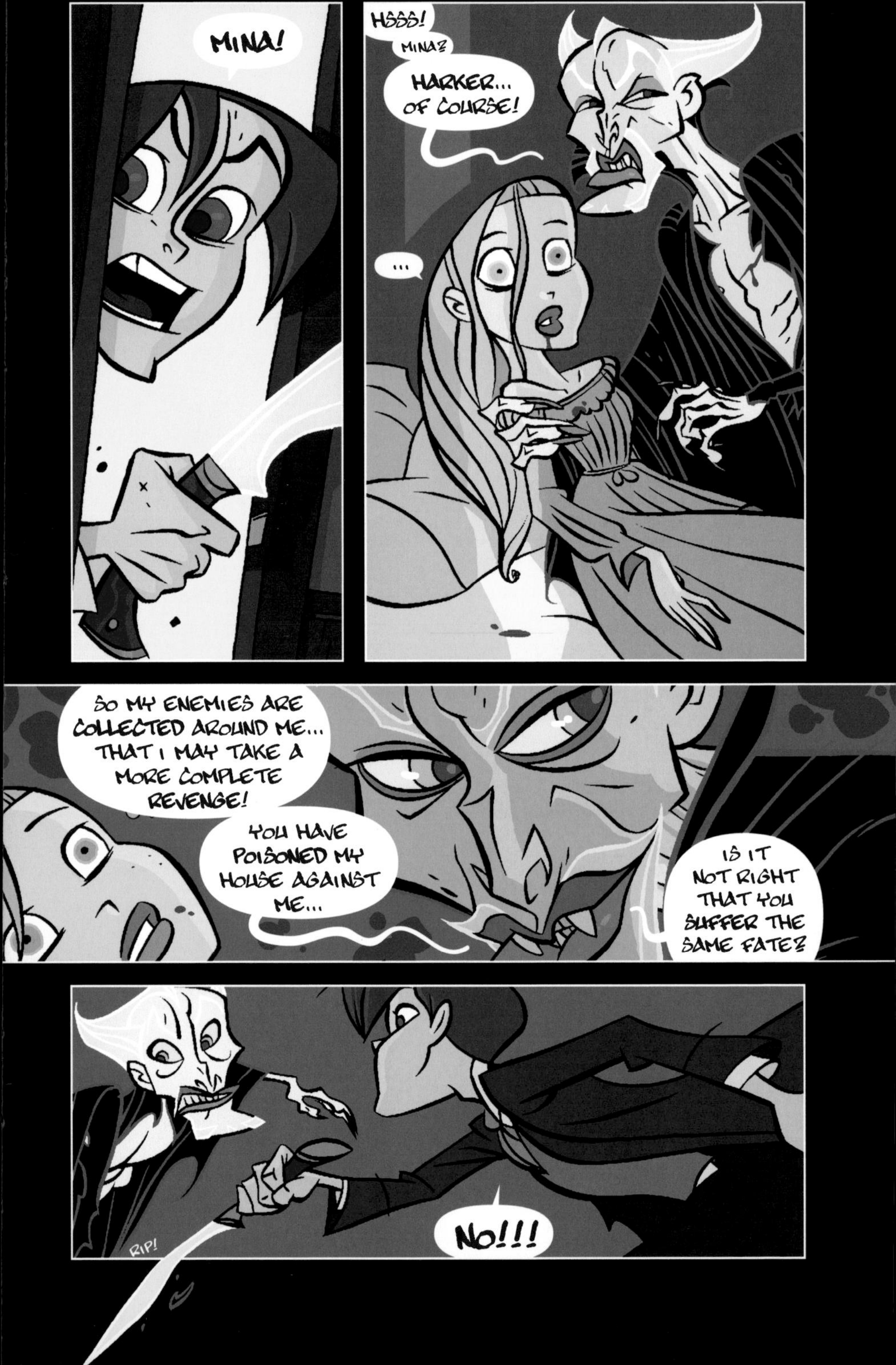
MINA!
HSSS!
MINA?
HARKER... OF COURSE!
...
SO MY ENEMIES ARE COLLECTED AROUND ME... THAT I MAY TAKE A MORE COMPLETE REVENGE!
YOU HAVE POISONED MY HOUSE AGAINST ME...
IS IT NOT RIGHT THAT YOU SUFFER THE SAME FATE?
NO!!!
RIP!

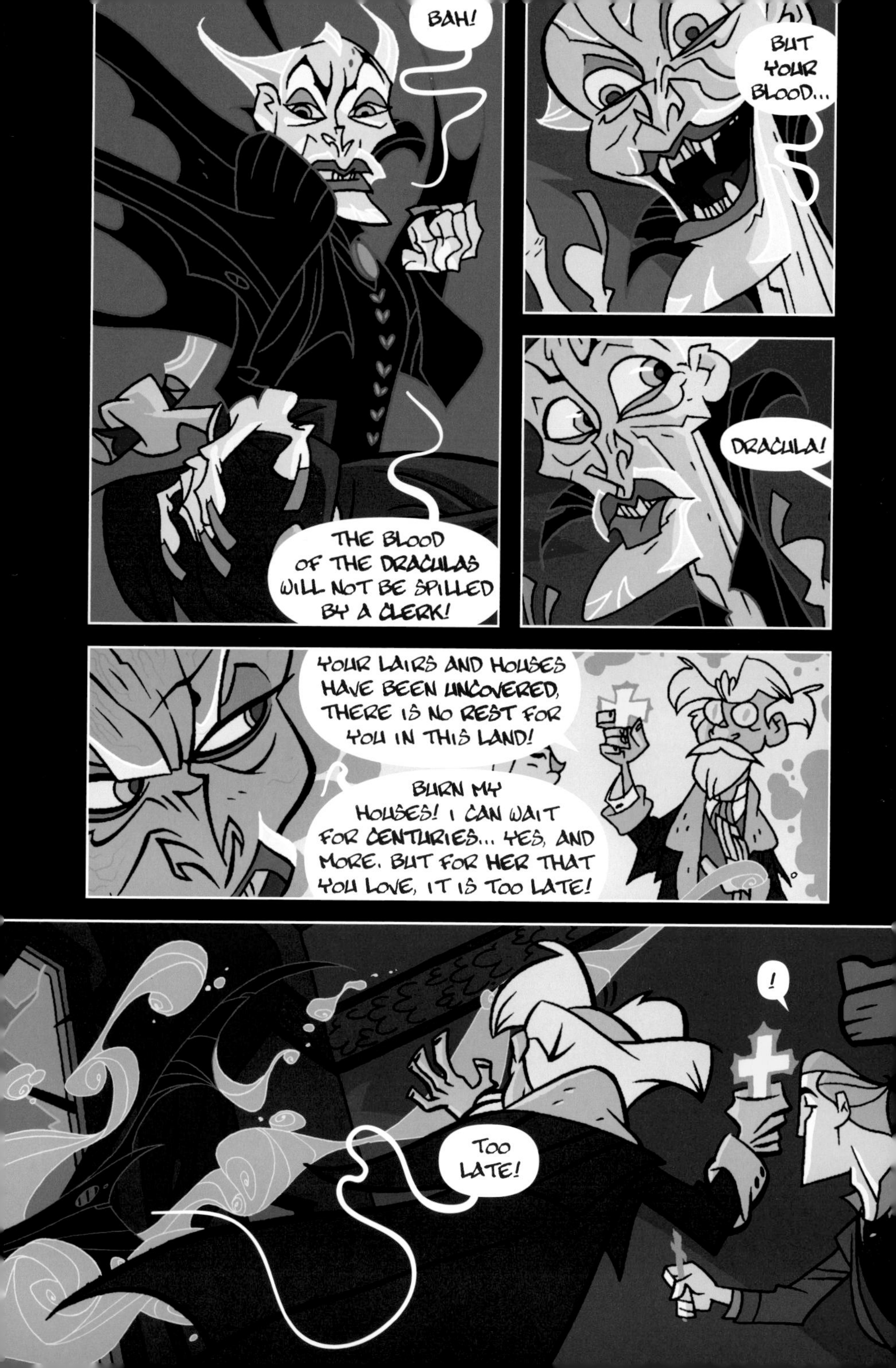
BAH!
BUT YOUR BLOOD...
THE BLOOD OF THE DRACULAS WILL NOT BE SPILLED BY A CLERK!
DRACULA!
YOUR LAIRS AND HOUSES HAVE BEEN UNCOVERED, THERE IS NO REST FOR YOU IN THIS LAND!
BURN MY HOUSES! I CAN WAIT FOR CENTURIES... YES, AND MORE. BUT FOR HER THAT YOU LOVE, IT IS TOO LATE!
!
TOO LATE!

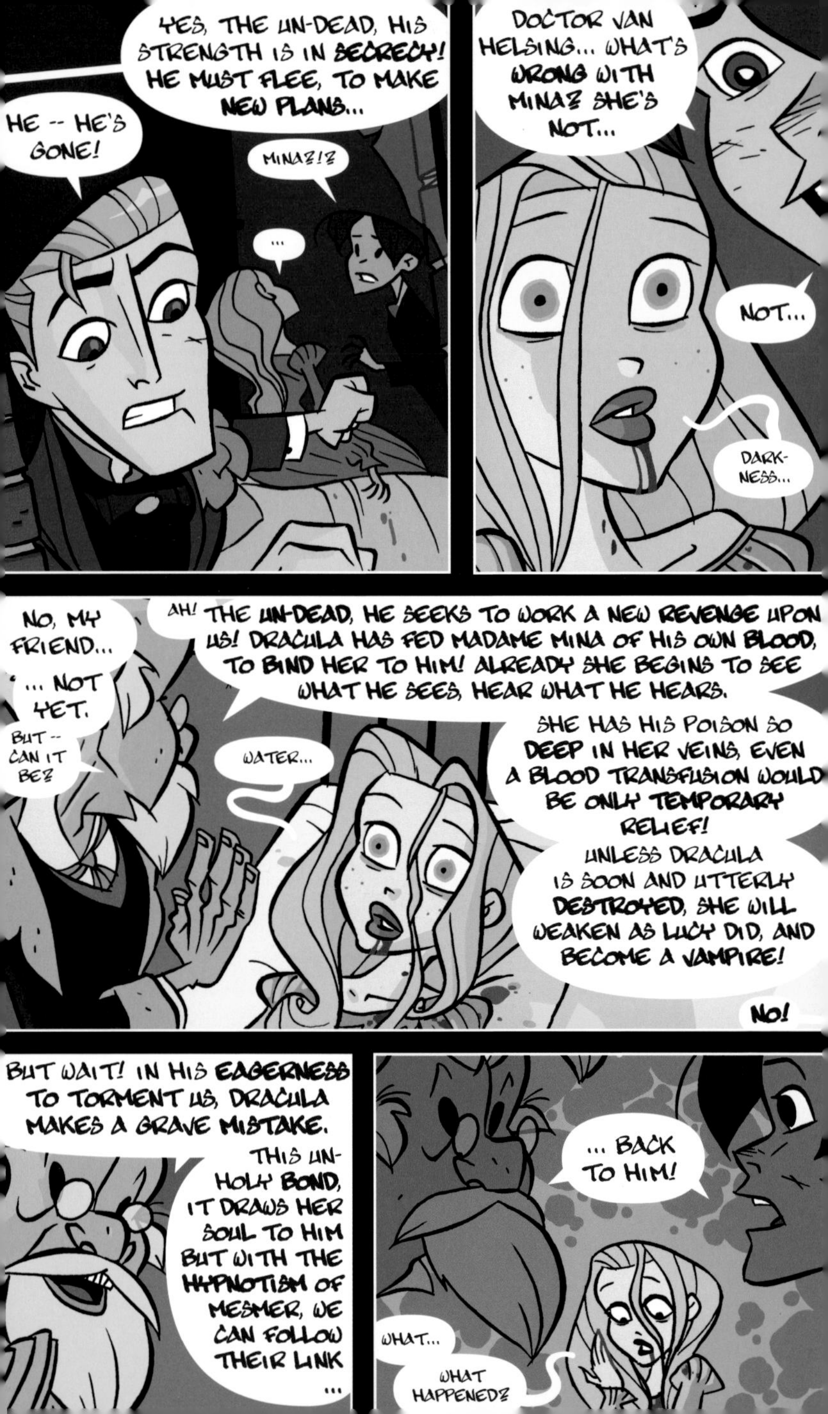
YES, THE UN-DEAD, HIS STRENGTH IS IN SECRECY! HE MUST FLEE, TO MAKE NEW PLANS...
HE -- HE'S GONE!
MINA?!?
...
DOCTOR VAN HELSING... WHAT'S WRONG WITH MINA? SHE'S NOT...
NOT...
DARK-NESS...
NO, MY FRIEND...
... NOT YET.
BUT -- CAN IT BE?
AH! THE UN-DEAD, HE SEEKS TO WORK A NEW REVENGE UPON US! DRACULA HAS FED MADAME MINA OF HIS OWN BLOOD, TO BIND HER TO HIM! ALREADY SHE BEGINS TO SEE WHAT HE SEES, HEAR WHAT HE HEARS.
WATER...
SHE HAS HIS POISON SO DEEP IN HER VEINS, EVEN A BLOOD TRANSFUSION WOULD BE ONLY TEMPORARY RELIEF!
UNLESS DRACULA IS SOON AND UTTERLY DESTROYED, SHE WILL WEAKEN AS LUCY DID, AND BECOME A VAMPIRE!
NO!
BUT WAIT! IN HIS EAGERNESS TO TORMENT US, DRACULA MAKES A GRAVE MISTAKE.
THIS UN-HOLY BOND, IT DRAWS HER SOUL TO HIM BUT WITH THE HYPNOTISM OF MESMER, WE CAN FOLLOW THEIR LINK ...
... BACK TO HIM!
WHAT...
WHAT HAPPENED?

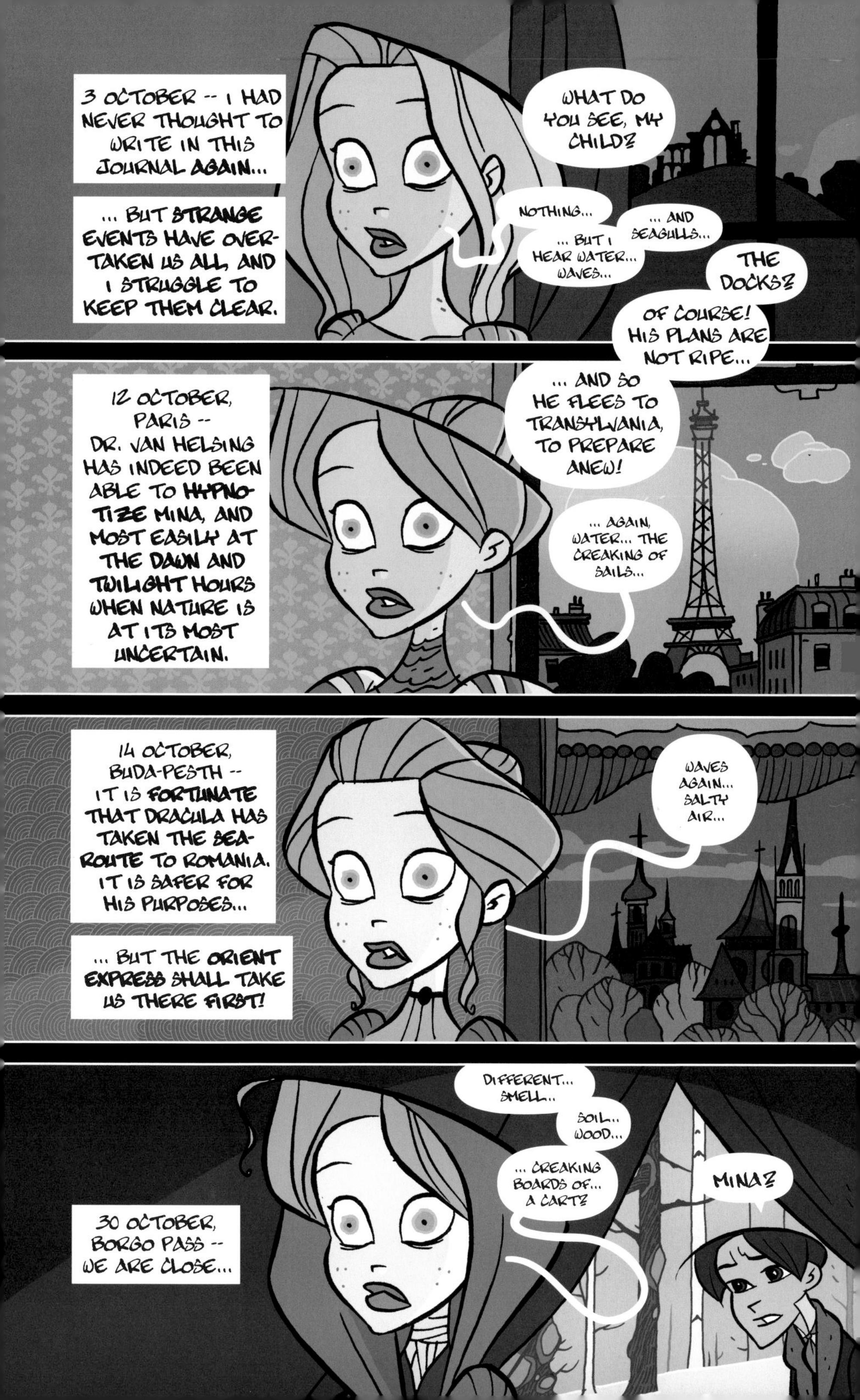
3 OCTOBER -- I HAD NEVER THOUGHT TO WRITE IN THIS JOURNAL AGAIN...
... BUT STRANGE EVENTS HAVE OVERTAKEN US ALL, AND I STRUGGLE TO KEEP THEM CLEAR.
WHAT DO YOU SEE, MY CHILD?
NOTHING...
... BUT I HEAR WATER... WAVES...
... AND SEAGULLS...
THE DOCKS?
OF COURSE! HIS PLANS ARE NOT RIPE...
... AND SO HE FLEES TO TRANSYLVANIA, TO PREPARE ANEW!
12 OCTOBER, PARIS -- DR. VAN HELSING HAS INDEED BEEN ABLE TO HYPNOTIZE MINA, AND MOST EASILY AT THE DAWN AND TWILIGHT HOURS WHEN NATURE IS AT ITS MOST UNCERTAIN.
... AGAIN, WATER... THE CREAKING OF SAILS...
14 OCTOBER, BUDA-PESTH -- IT IS FORTUNATE THAT DRACULA HAS TAKEN THE SEA-ROUTE TO ROMANIA. IT IS SAFER FOR HIS PURPOSES...
... BUT THE ORIENT EXPRESS SHALL TAKE US THERE FIRST!
WAVES AGAIN... SALTY AIR...
30 OCTOBER, BORGO PASS -- WE ARE CLOSE...
DIFFERENT... SMELL...
SOIL... WOOD...
... CREAKING BOARDS OF... A CART?
MINA?

SO! DRACULA HAS COME AGAIN INTO THIS COUNTRY, HE IS BEING CARRIED THROUGH THE MOUNTAINS BY SLEIGH OR HORSE-CART...
... ANOTHER DAY, AT MOST, AND HE WILL BE HERE!
MR. MORRIS HAS MADE OUR PLANS.
EXCELLENT! IT WILL BE YOUR WORK TO STOP THE COUNT ON THE HIGH ROAD. MADAME MINA AND I SHALL STAY BEHIND, TO TAKE OTHER PRECAUTIONS...
BUT MINA --
DO NOT FEAR, FRIEND JONATHAN! I PLACE THIS WAFER OF THE SACRED HOST AGAINST HER FOREHEAD...
TO PROTECT HER FROM THE DAR --
PUF!
AH!
GASP!
QUICKLY! THE POWER OF DRAC-ULA GROWS OVER MISS MINA! BY TOMORROW'S SUNSET, IT WILL BE TOO LATE! YOU MUST GO NOW!
NO!
STAY WITH VAN HELSING, DARLING! AND STAY STRONG...
JACK! MR. HOLMWOOD! MR. MORRIS!
WE WILL DESTROY THE MONSTER BEFORE ANOTHER DAY IS OUT!

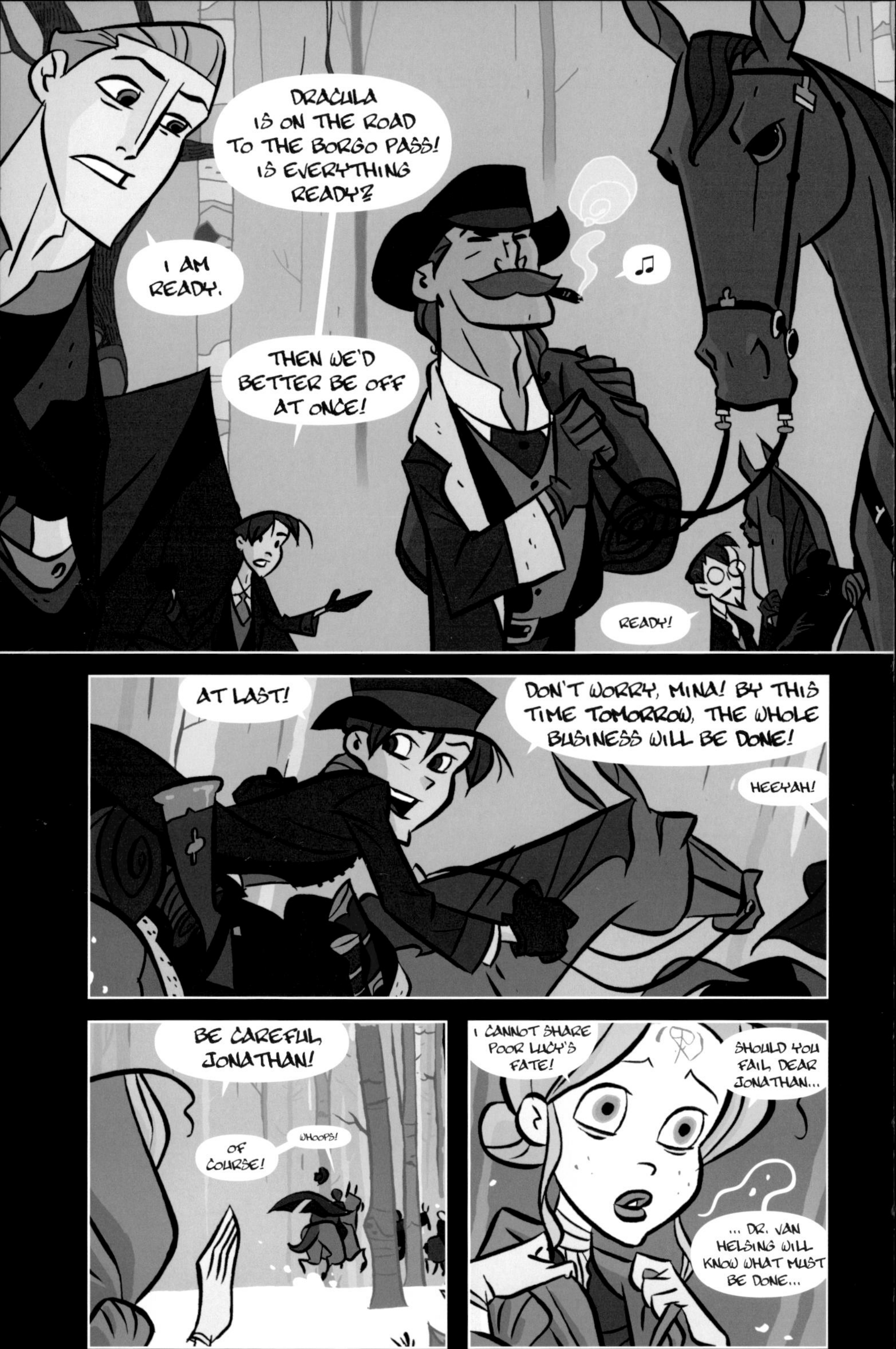
DRACULA IS ON THE ROAD TO THE BORGO PASS! IS EVERYTHING READY?
I AM READY.
♫
THEN WE'D BETTER BE OFF AT ONCE!
READY!
AT LAST!
DON'T WORRY, MINA! BY THIS TIME TOMORROW, THE WHOLE BUSINESS WILL BE DONE!
HEEYAH!
BE CAREFUL, JONATHAN!
OF COURSE!
WHOOPS!
I CANNOT SHARE POOR LUCY'S FATE!
SHOULD YOU FAIL, DEAR JONATHAN...
... DR. VAN HELSING WILL KNOW WHAT MUST BE DONE...

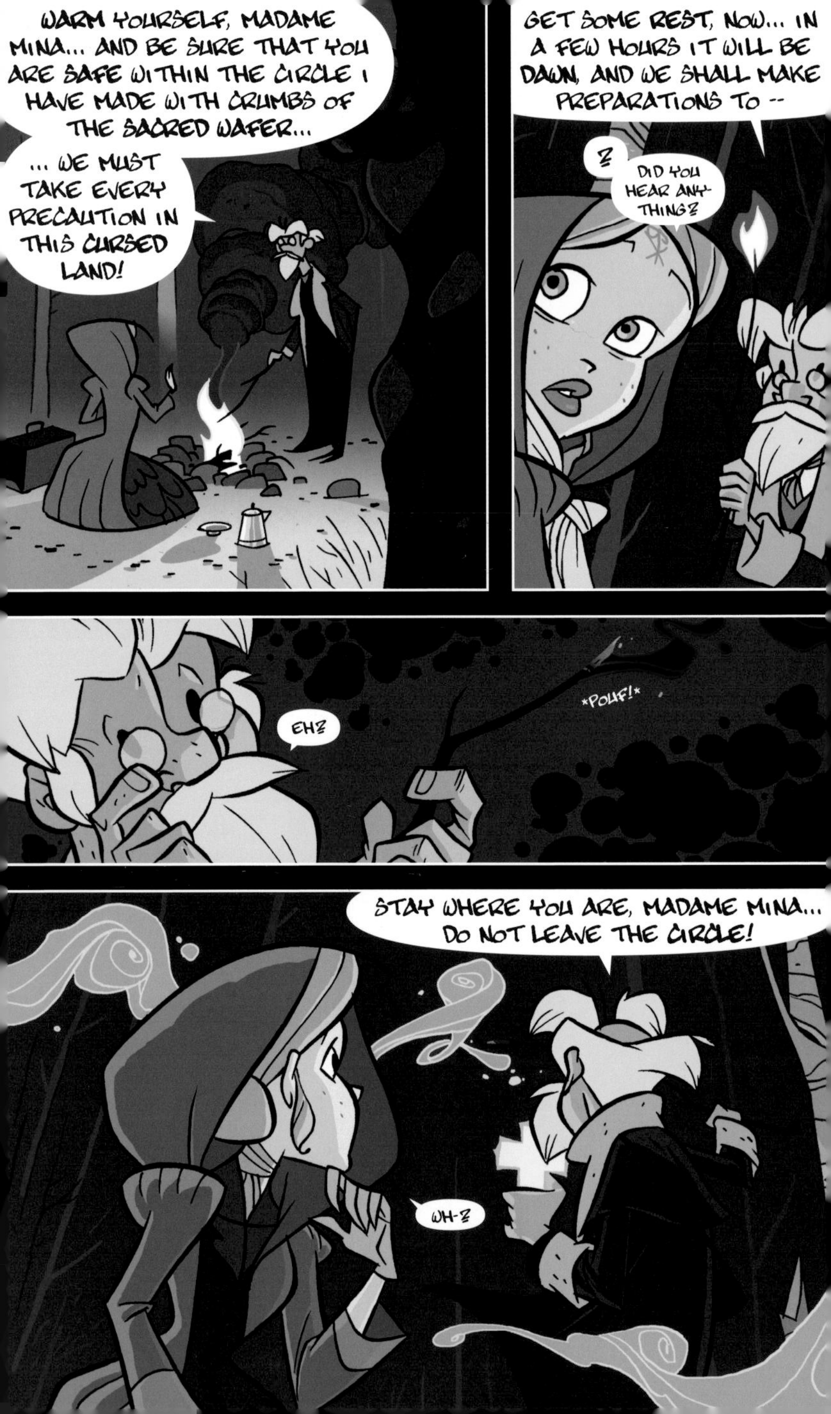
WARM YOURSELF, MADAME MINA... AND BE SURE THAT YOU ARE SAFE WITHIN THE CIRCLE I HAVE MADE WITH CRUMBS OF THE SACRED WAFER...
... WE MUST TAKE EVERY PRECAUTION IN THIS CURSED LAND!
GET SOME REST, NOW... IN A FEW HOURS IT WILL BE DAWN, AND WE SHALL MAKE PREPARATIONS TO --
?
DID YOU HEAR ANYTHING?
EH?
POUF!
STAY WHERE YOU ARE, MADAME MINA... DO NOT LEAVE THE CIRCLE!
WH-?

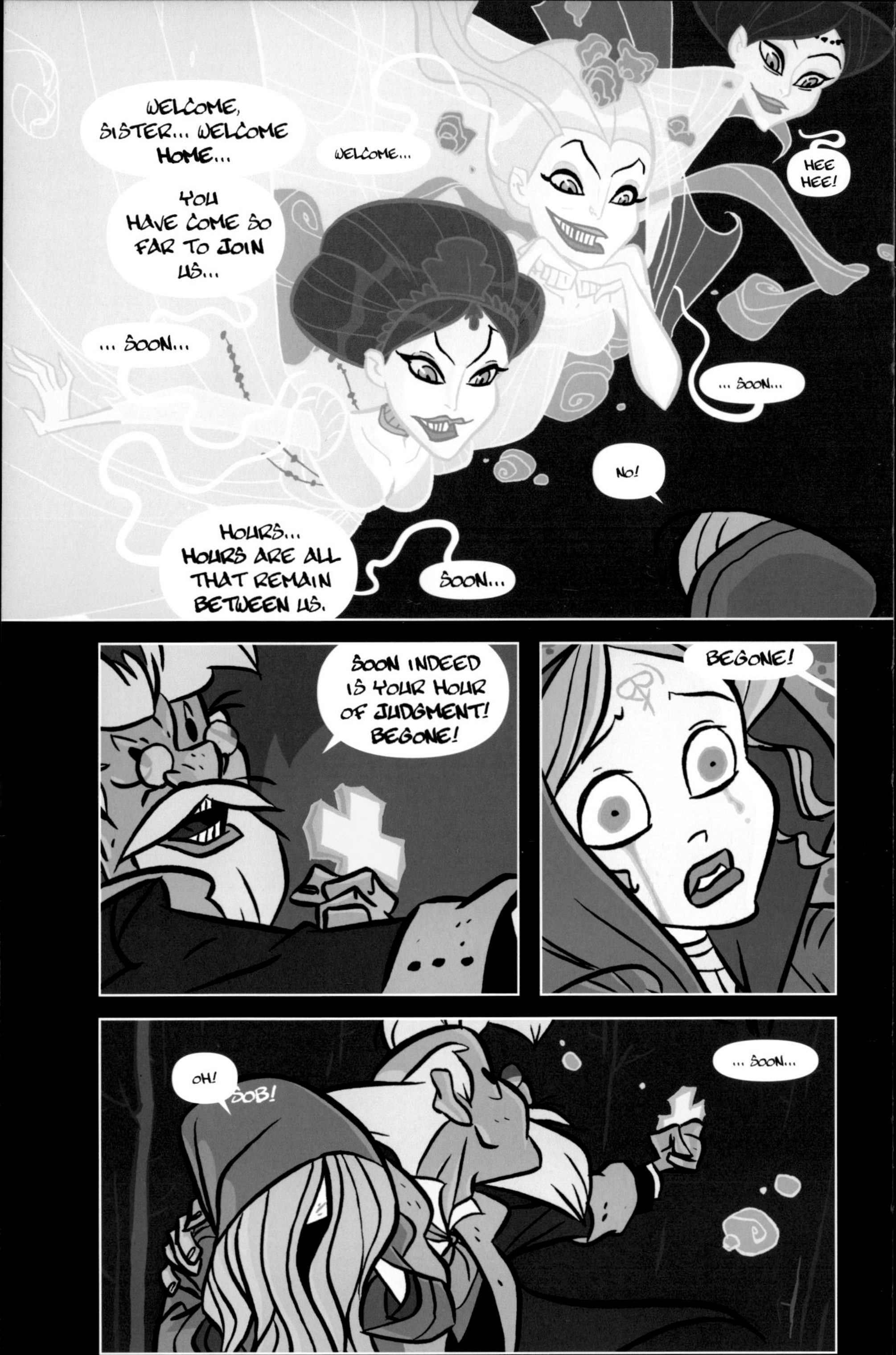
WELCOME, SISTER... WELCOME HOME...
WELCOME...
HEE HEE!
YOU HAVE COME SO FAR TO JOIN US...
... SOON...
... SOON...
NO!
HOURS... HOURS ARE ALL THAT REMAIN BETWEEN US.
SOON...
SOON INDEED IS YOUR HOUR OF JUDGMENT! BEGONE!
BEGONE!
OH!
SOB!
... SOON...

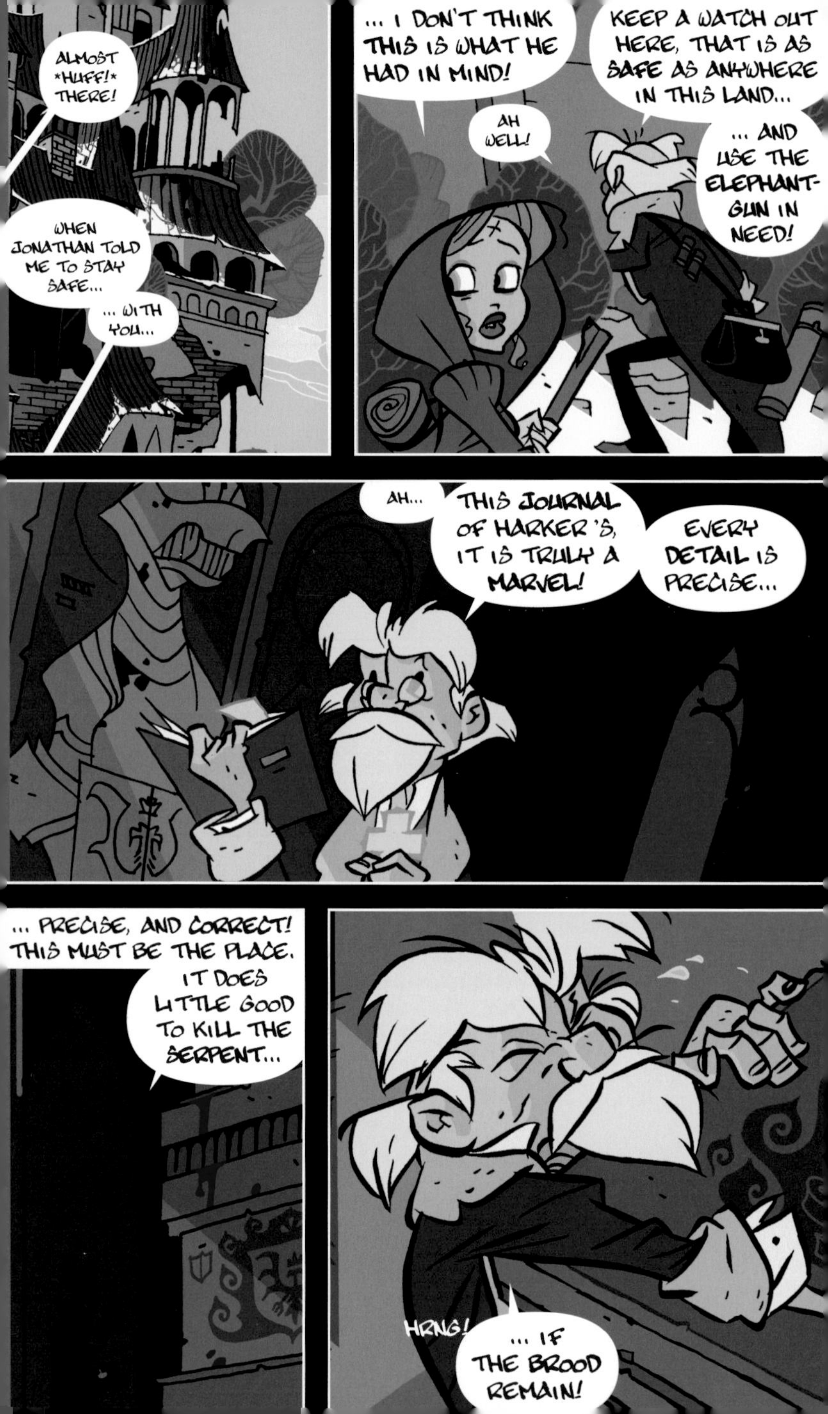
ALMOST *HUFF!* THERE!
WHEN JONATHAN TOLD ME TO STAY SAFE...
... WITH YOU...
... I DON'T THINK THIS IS WHAT HE HAD IN MIND!
AH WELL!
KEEP A WATCH OUT HERE, THAT IS AS SAFE AS ANYWHERE IN THIS LAND...
... AND USE THE ELEPHANT-GUN IN NEED!
AH...
THIS JOURNAL OF HARKER'S, IT IS TRULY A MARVEL!
EVERY DETAIL IS PRECISE...
... PRECISE, AND CORRECT! THIS MUST BE THE PLACE.
IT DOES LITTLE GOOD TO KILL THE SERPENT...
HRNG!
... IF THE BROOD REMAIN!

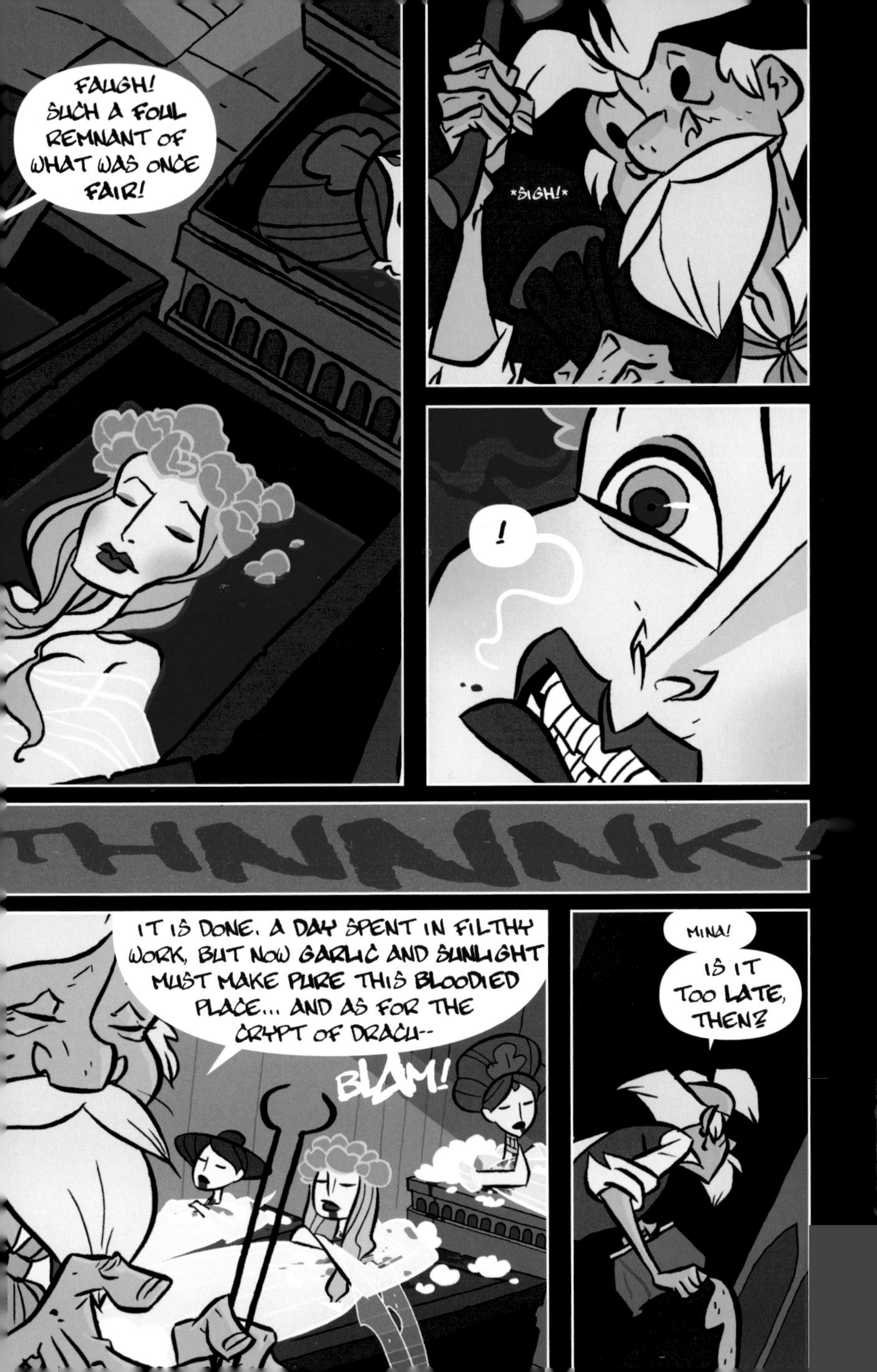

FAUGH! SUCH A FOUL REMNANT OF WHAT WAS ONCE FAIR!
SIGH!
!
THNNNK!
IT IS DONE. A DAY SPENT IN FILTHY WORK, BUT NOW GARLIC AND SUNLIGHT MUST MAKE PURE THIS BLOODIED PLACE... AND AS FOR THE CRYPT OF DRACU--
BLAM!
MINA!
IS IT TOO LATE, THEN?

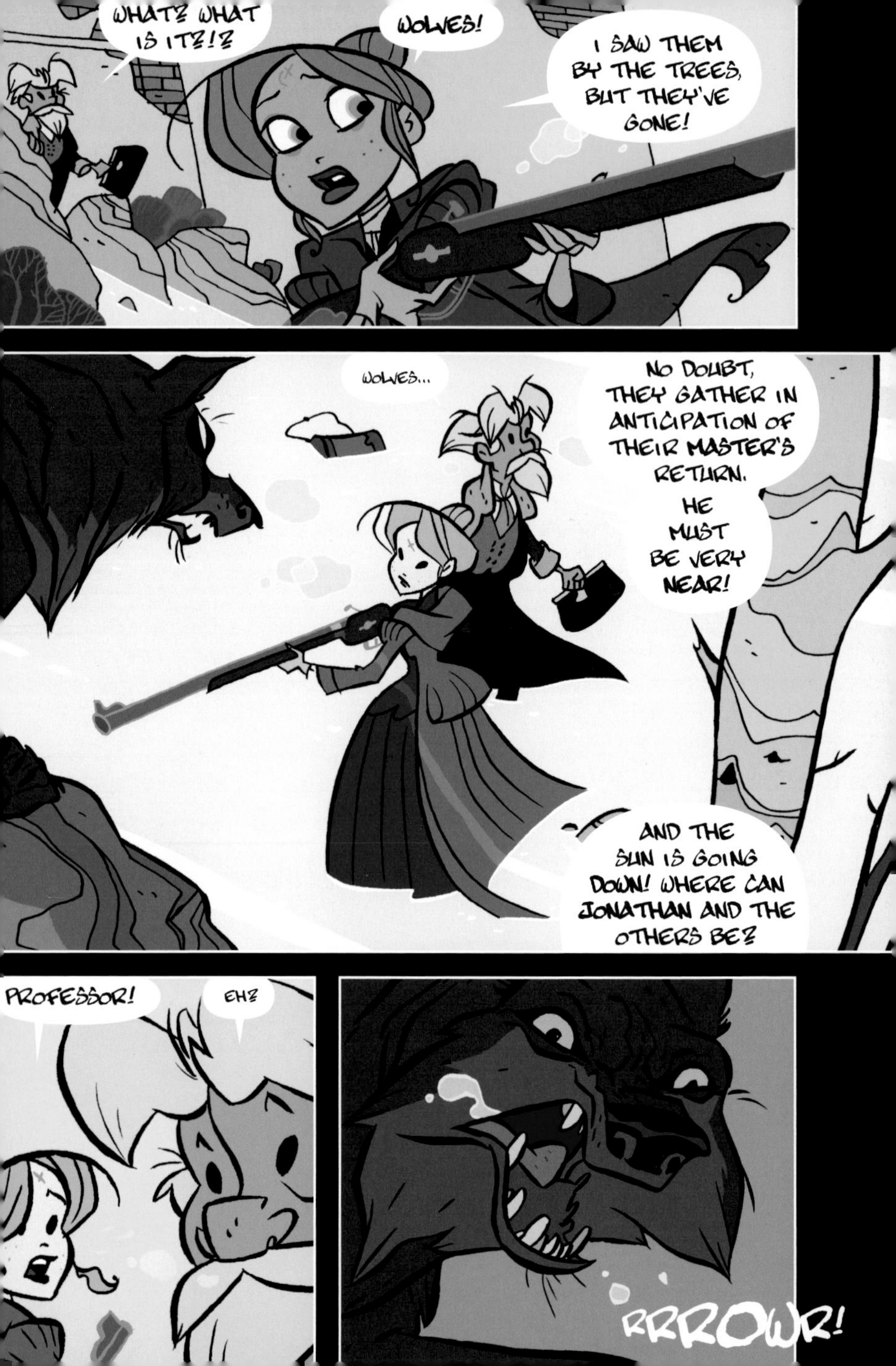
WHAT? WHAT IS IT?!?
WOLVES!
I SAW THEM BY THE TREES, BUT THEY'VE GONE!
WOLVES...
NO DOUBT, THEY GATHER IN ANTICIPATION OF THEIR MASTER'S RETURN.
HE MUST BE VERY NEAR!
AND THE SUN IS GOING DOWN! WHERE CAN JONATHAN AND THE OTHERS BE?
PROFESSOR!
EH?
RRROWR!

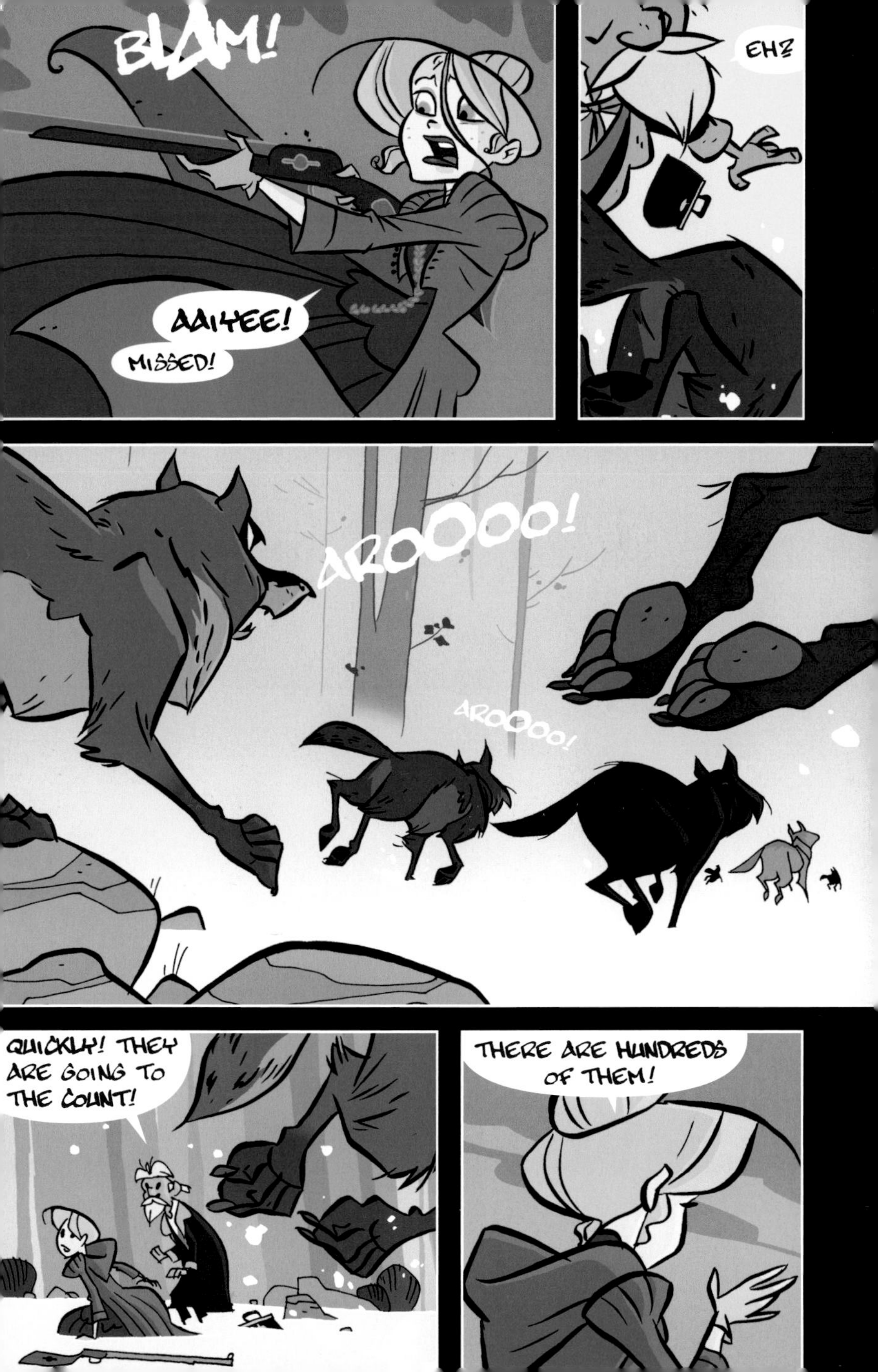
BLAM!
AAIYEE!
MISSED!
EH?
AROOOOO!
AROOOO!
QUICKLY! THEY ARE GOING TO THE COUNT!
THERE ARE HUNDREDS OF THEM!

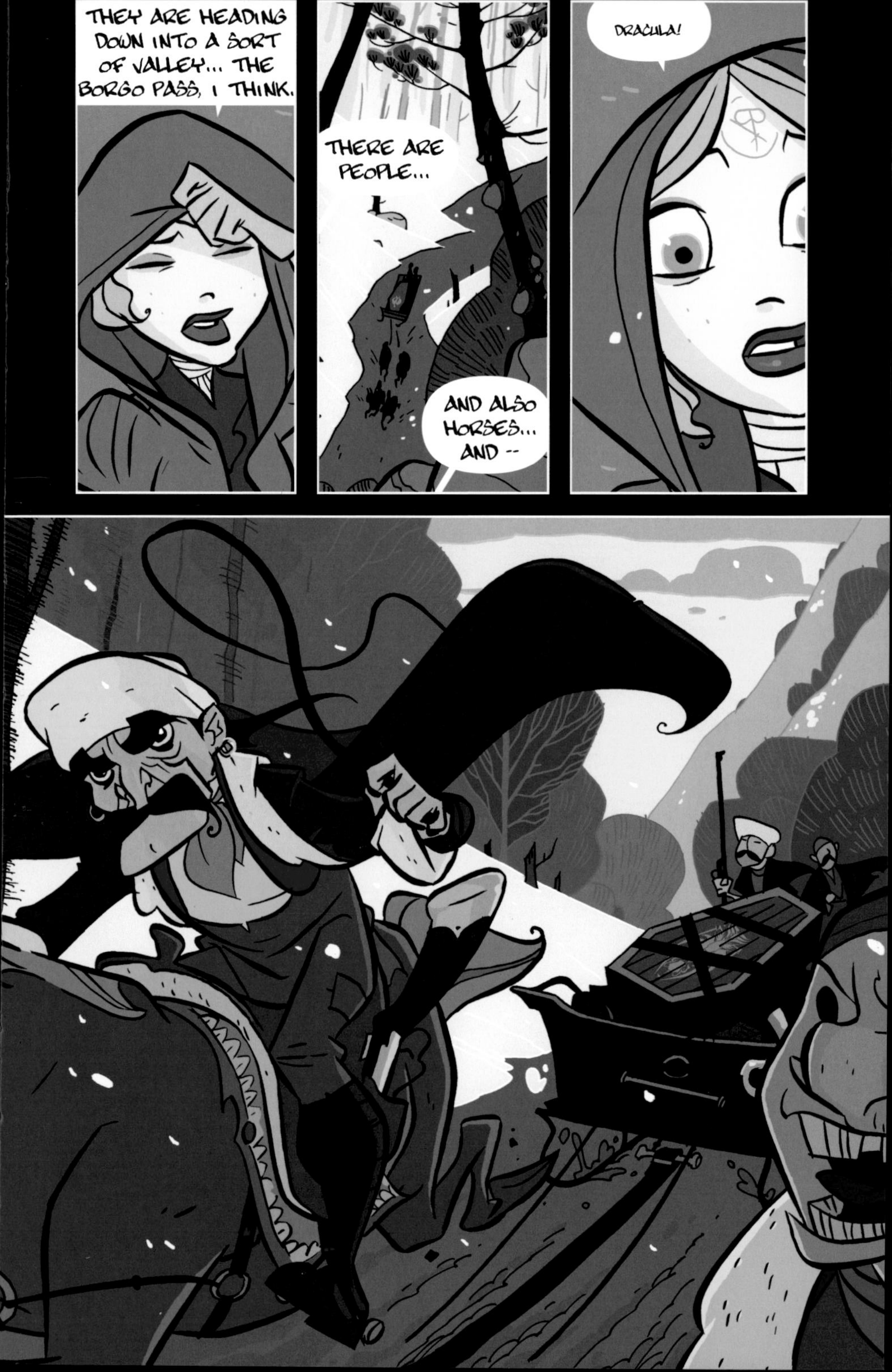
THEY ARE HEADING DOWN INTO A SORT OF VALLEY... THE BORGO PASS, I THINK.
THERE ARE PEOPLE...
AND ALSO HORSES... AND --
DRACULA!

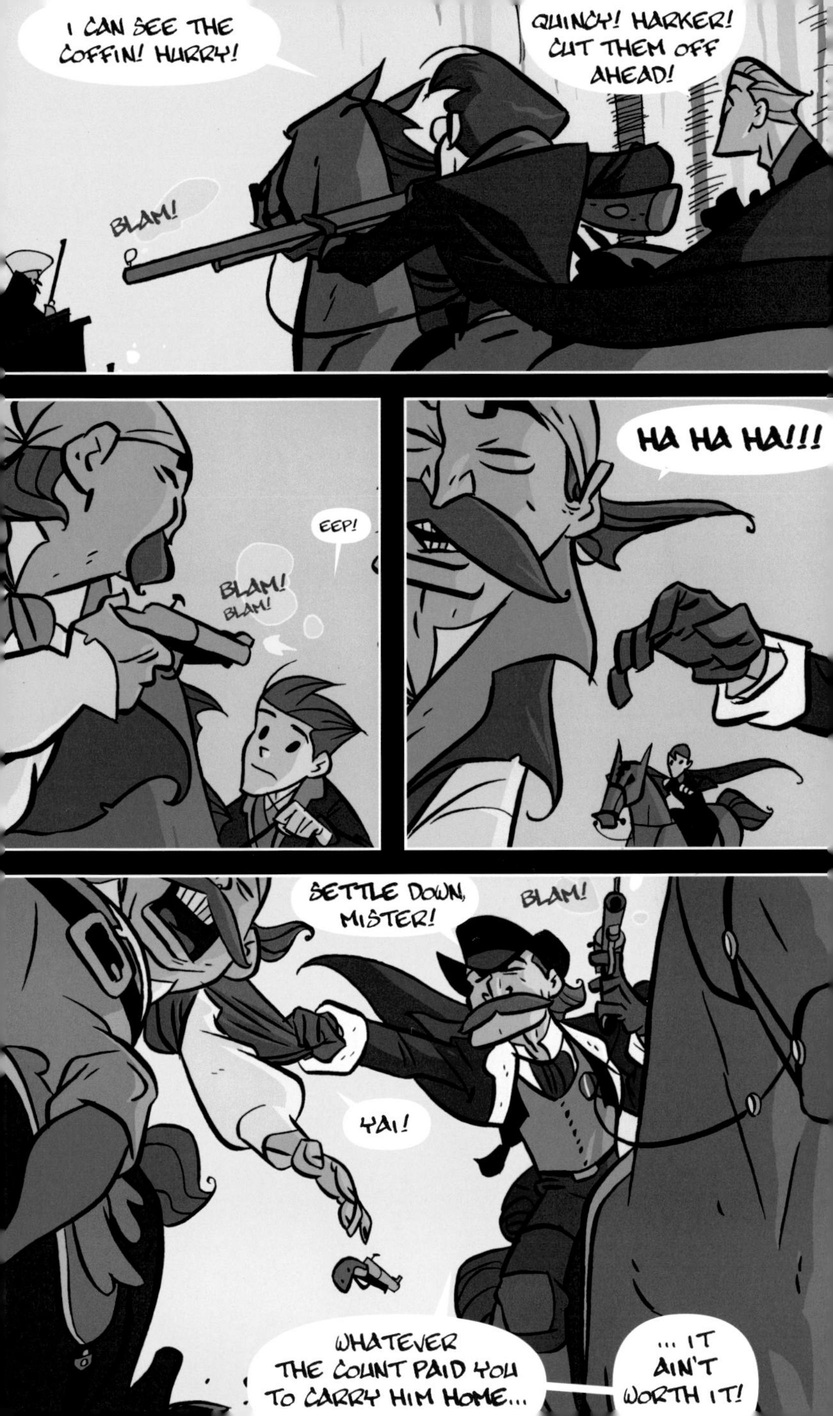
I CAN SEE THE COFFIN! HURRY!
QUINCY! HARKER! CUT THEM OFF AHEAD!
BLAM!
EEP!
BLAM! BLAM!
HA HA HA!!!
SETTLE DOWN, MISTER!
BLAM!
YAI!
WHATEVER THE COUNT PAID YOU TO CARRY HIM HOME...
... IT AIN'T WORTH IT!

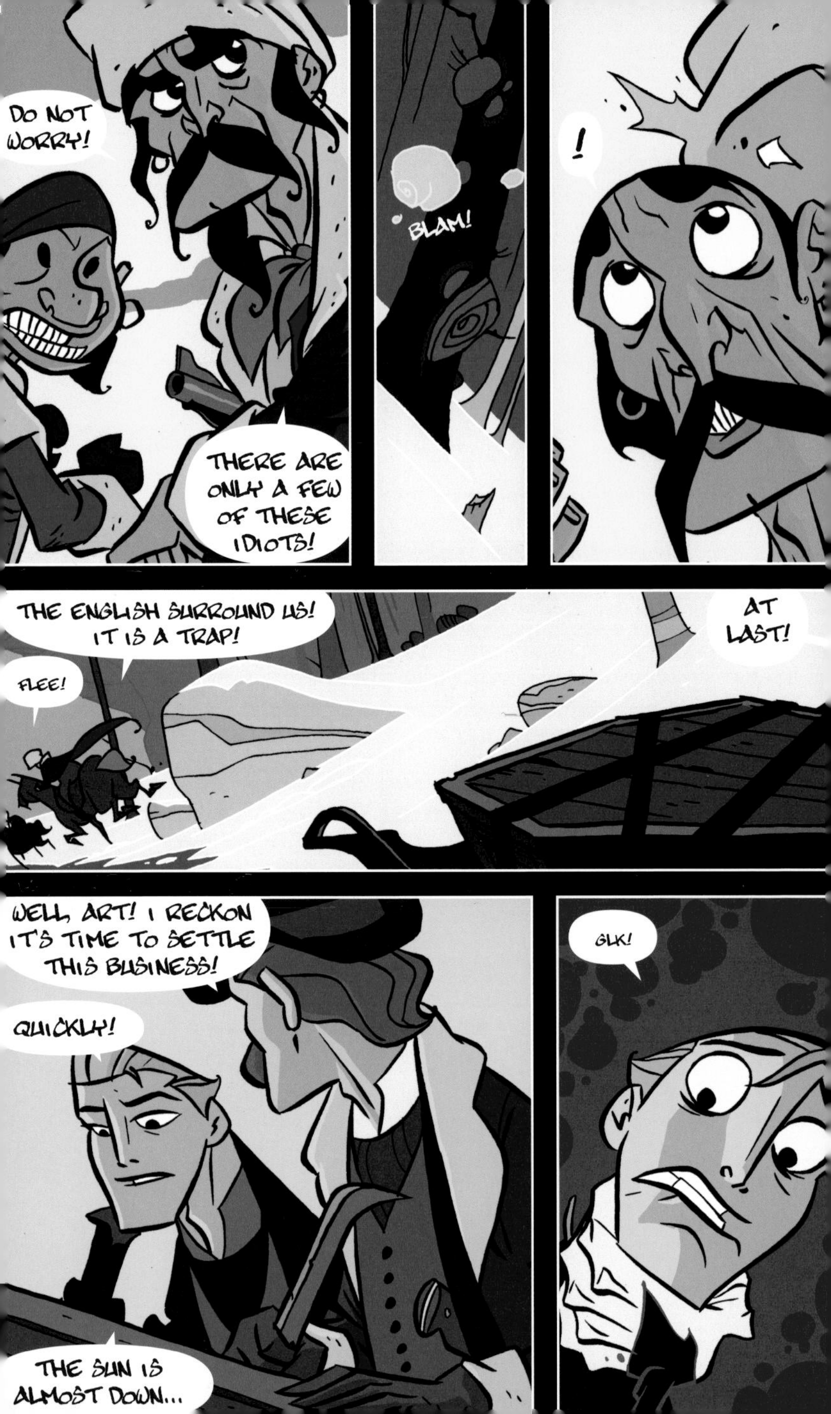
DO NOT WORRY!
THERE ARE ONLY A FEW OF THESE IDIOTS!
BLAM!
!
THE ENGLISH SURROUND US! IT IS A TRAP!
FLEE!
AT LAST!
WELL, ART! I RECKON IT'S TIME TO SETTLE THIS BUSINESS!
QUICKLY!
THE SUN IS ALMOST DOWN...
GLK!

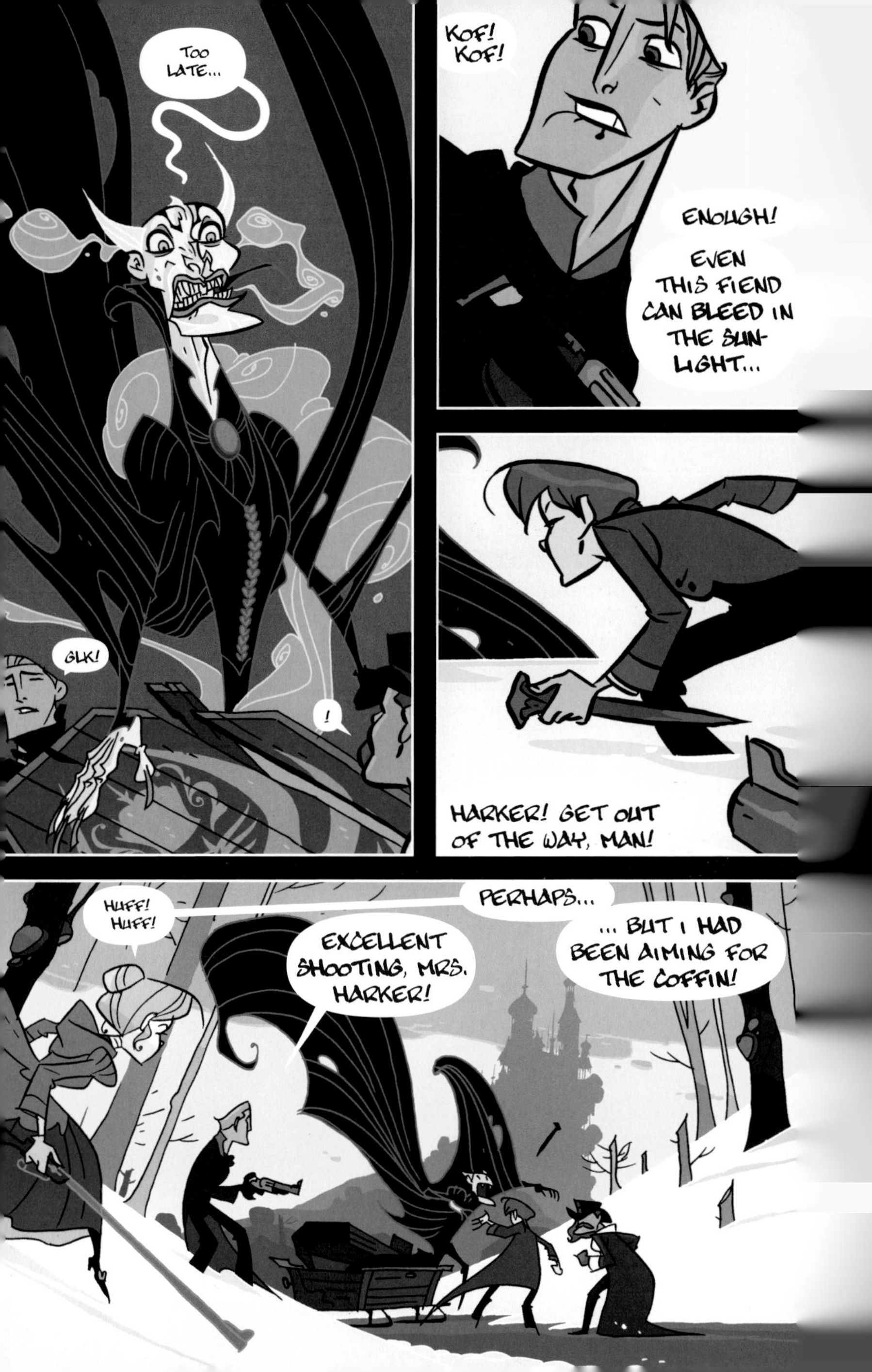
TOO LATE...
KOF! KOF!
ENOUGH!
EVEN THIS FIEND CAN BLEED IN THE SUN-LIGHT...
GLK!
!
HARKER! GET OUT OF THE WAY, MAN!
HUFF! HUFF!
PERHAPS...
EXCELLENT SHOOTING, MRS. HARKER!
... BUT I HAD BEEN AIMING FOR THE COFFIN!

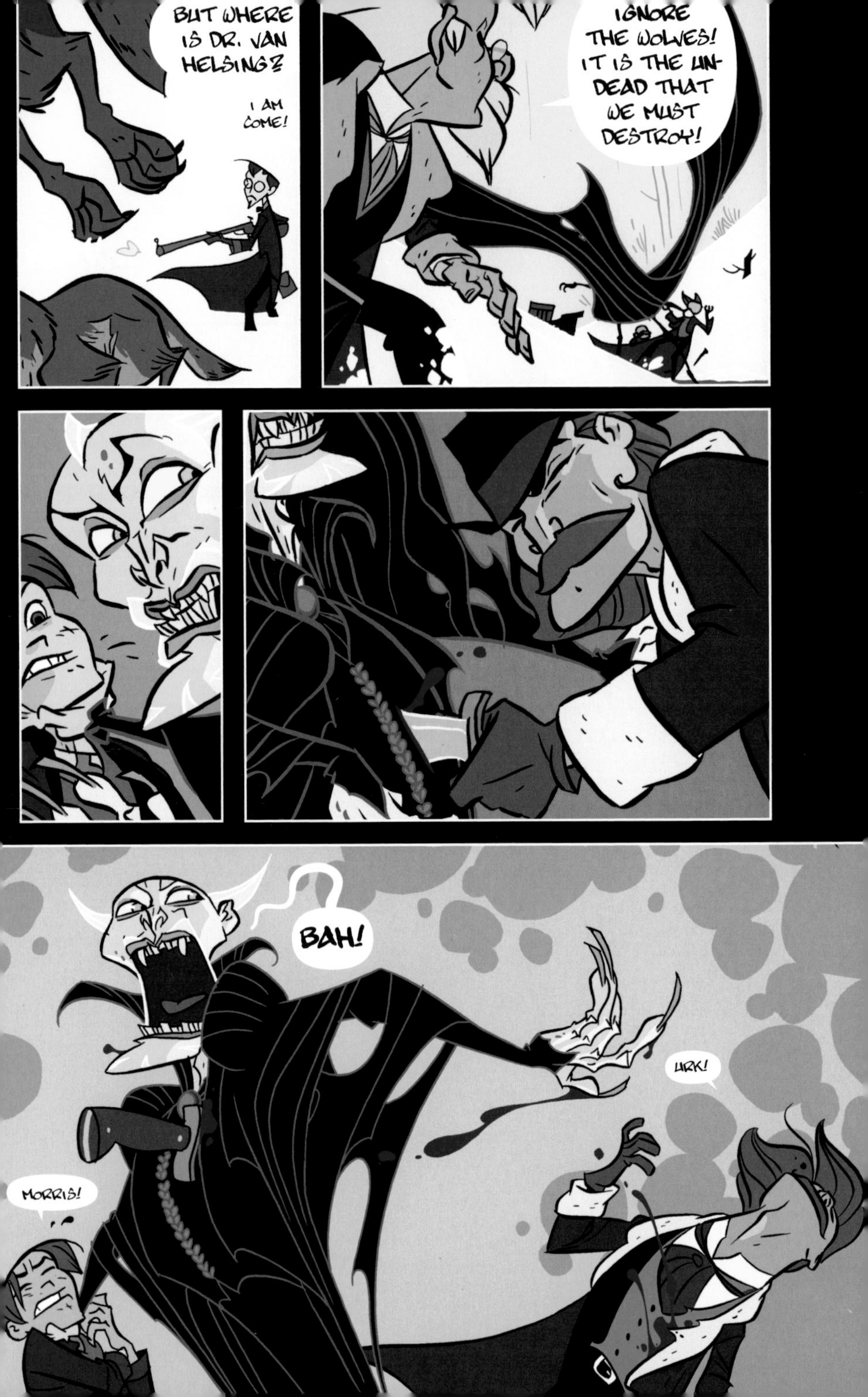
BUT WHERE IS DR. VAN HELSING?
I AM COME!
IGNORE THE WOLVES! IT IS THE UN-DEAD THAT WE MUST DESTROY!
BAH!
URK!
MORRIS!

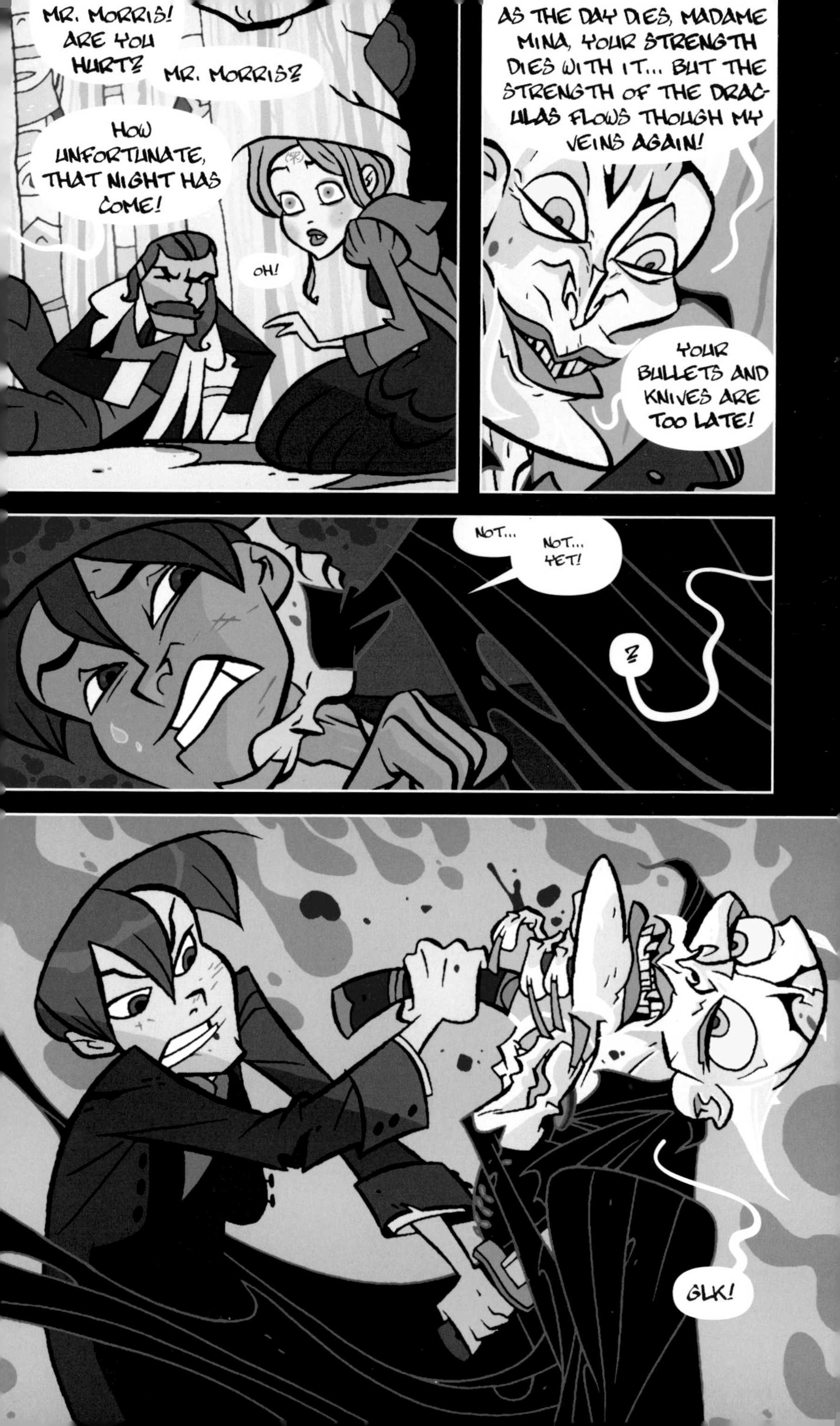
MR. MORRIS! ARE YOU HURT?
MR. MORRIS?
HOW UNFORTUNATE, THAT NIGHT HAS COME!
OH!
AS THE DAY DIES, MADAME MINA, YOUR STRENGTH DIES WITH IT... BUT THE STRENGTH OF THE DRACULAS FLOWS THOUGH MY VEINS AGAIN!
YOUR BULLETS AND KNIVES ARE TOO LATE!
NOT...
NOT... YET!
?
GLK!

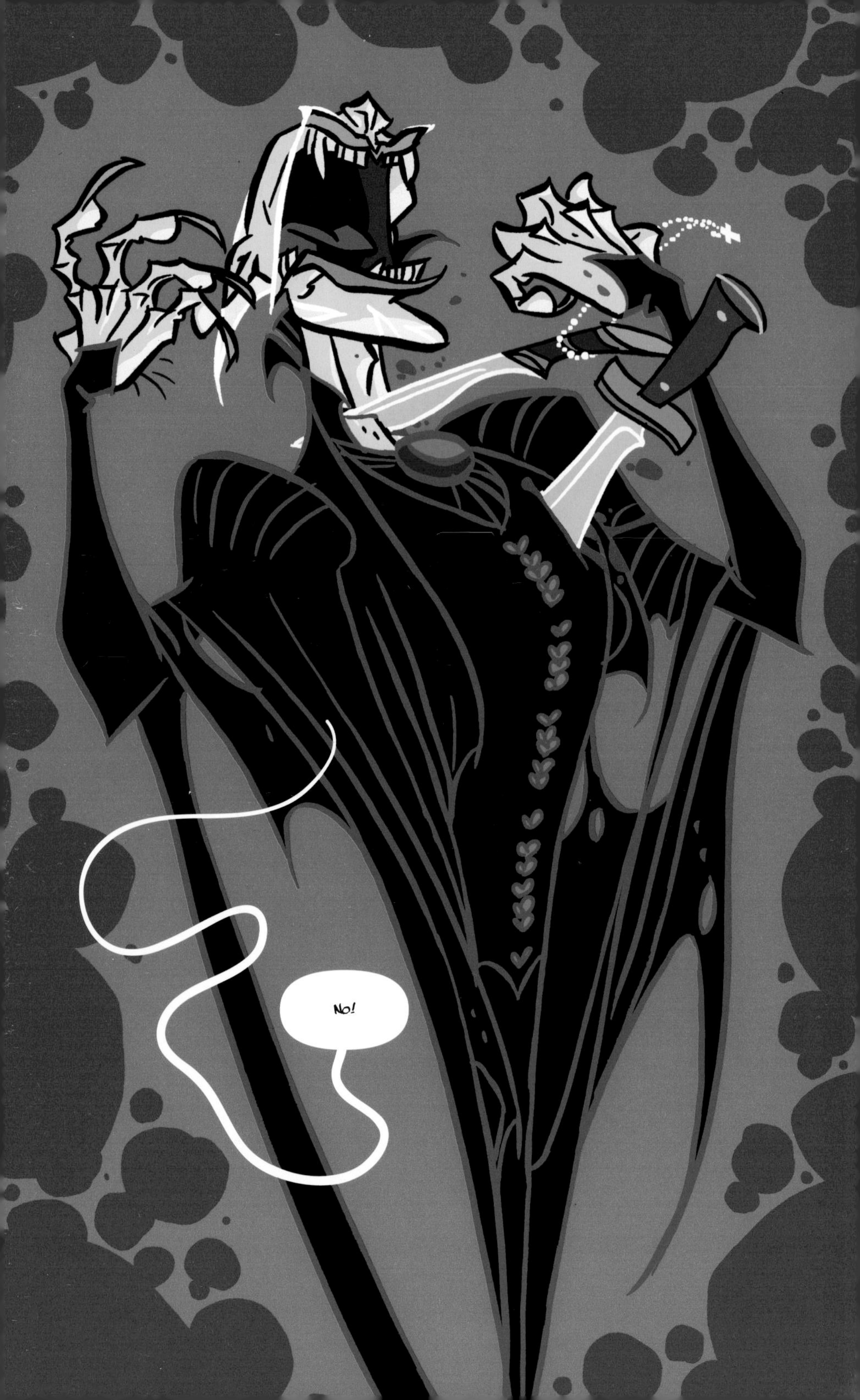
NO!

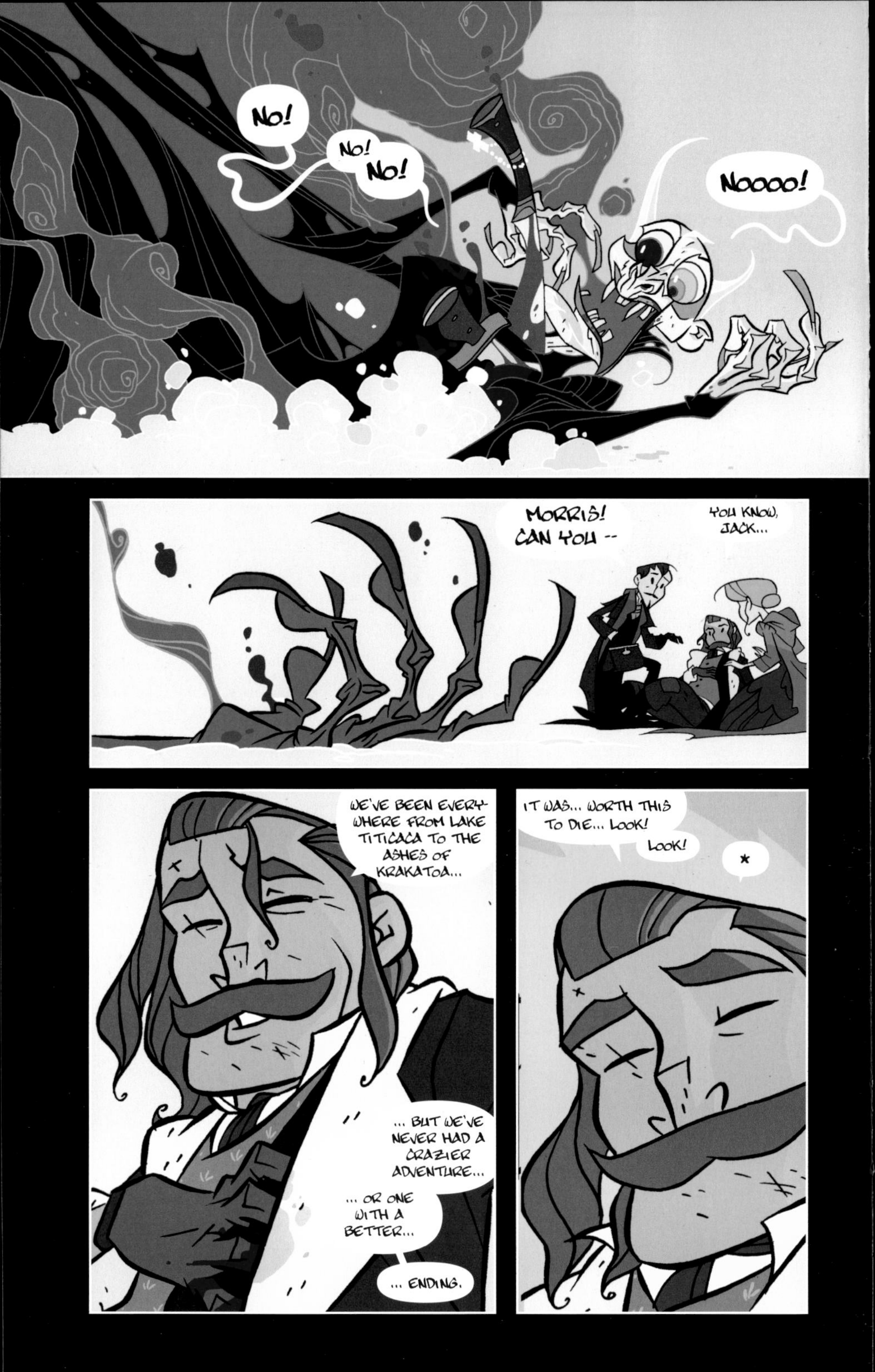

No!
No!
No!
Noooo!
MORRIS! CAN YOU --
YOU KNOW, JACK...
WE'VE BEEN EVERY-WHERE FROM LAKE TITICACA TO THE ASHES OF KRAKATOA...
... BUT WE'VE NEVER HAD A CRAZIER ADVENTURE...
... OR ONE WITH A BETTER...
... ENDING.
IT WAS... WORTH THIS TO DIE... LOOK!
LOOK!
*

STERLING CHILDREN'S BOOKS
New York

An Imprint of Sterling Publishing Co., Inc.
1166 Avenue of the Americas
New York, NY 10036

ISBN 978-1-4549-3500-1

Distributed in Canada by Sterling Publishing Co., Inc.
c/o Canadian Manda Group, 664 Annette Street
Toronto, Ontario M6S 2C8, Canada
Distributed in the United Kingdom by
GMC Distribution ServicesCastle Place, 166 High Street,
Lewes, East Sussex BN7 1XU, England
Distributed in Australia by NewSouth Books,
University of New South Wales, Sydney, NSW 2052, Australia

For information about custom editions, special sales, and premium
and corporate purchases, please contact Sterling Special Sales at
800-805-5489 or specialsales@sterlingpublishing.com.

Manufactured in China
Lot #:
2 4 6 8 10 9 7 5 3 1
05/19

sterlingpublishing.com

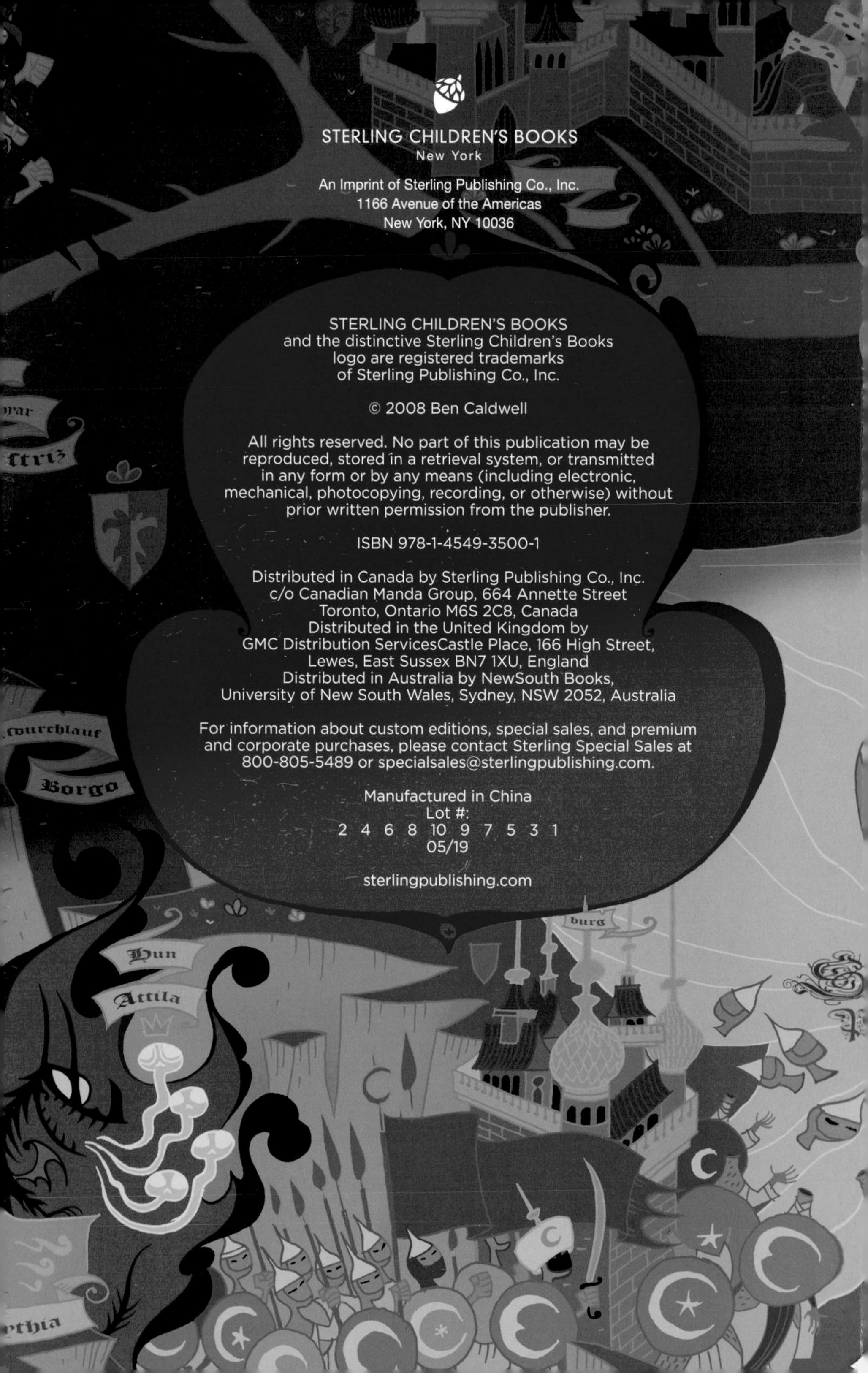
burg
Hun
Attila

BRAM STOKER

DRACULA